Dear Reader,

The poet and writer Robin Morgan once said, "Sisterhood is powerful." The same can be said about the legendary Calhoun sisters. We are pleased to bring you *The Calhouns: Lilah and Suzanna*, the second volume featuring the four Calhoun sisters and their sister by marriage—all united by a decades-old legend and the determination to save their family home.

Sweet sister Lilah saves a mysterious stranger from drowning, a man she discovers can touch her heart with the merest glance. But Professor Max Quartermain is a man with secrets, it seems. What might he reveal...*For the Love of Lilah*?

In *Suzanna's Surrender*, eldest sister Suzanna has her hands full raising two children on her own and searching for the missing Calhoun emeralds. The last thing she needs is Holt Bradford sticking to her like glue. The sexy ex-cop is the perfect man to foil jewel thieves, but would he end up stealing Suzanna's heart, too?

The Calhoun Women: fascinating sisters, fabulous stories!

The Editors

Silhouette Books

NORA ROBERTS

THE CALHOUNS
LILAH
& SUZANNA

Silhouette Books

SILHOUETTE™

The Calhouns: Lilah and Suzanna

ISBN-13: 978-1-335-08076-9

Copyright © 2020 by Harlequin Books S.A.

For the Love of Lilah
First published in 1991. This edition published in 2020.
Copyright © 1991 by Nora Roberts

Suzanna's Surrender
First published in 1991. This edition published in 2020.
Copyright © 1991 by Nora Roberts

This edition published by arrangement with Harlequin Books S.A.

For questions and comments about the quality of this book, please contact us at CustomerService@Harlequin.com.

Silhouette
22 Adelaide St. West, 40th Floor
Toronto, Ontario M5H 4E3, Canada
www.Harlequin.com

Printed in U.S.A.

CONTENTS

FOR THE LOVE OF LILAH

For my great-great-grandmother Selina MacGruder,
who fell in love unwisely and well.

Prologue

Bar Harbor, 1913—

The cliffs call to me. High and fierce and dangerously beautiful, they stand and beckon as seductively as a lover. In the morning, the air was as soft as the clouds that rode the sky to the west. Gulls wheeled and called, a lonely sound, like the distant ring of a buoy that carried up on the wind. It brought an image of a church bell tolling a birth. Or a death.

Like a mirage, other islands glinted and winked through the faint mist the sun had yet to burn from the water. Fishermen piloted their sturdy boats from the bay and out to the rolling sea.

Even knowing he would not be there, I couldn't stay away.

I took the children. It can't be wrong to want to share

with them some of the happiness that I always feel when I walk in the wild grass that leads to the tumbled rocks. I held Ethan's hand on one side, and Colleen's on the other. Nanny gripped little Sean's as he toddled through the grass after a yellow butterfly that fluttered just beyond his questing fingers.

The sound of their laughter—the sweetest sound a mother can hear—lifted through the air. They have such bright and depthless curiosity, such unquestioning trust. As yet, they are untouched by the worries of the world, of uprisings in Mexico, of unrest in Europe. Their world does not include betrayals or guilt or passions that sting the heart. Their needs, so simple, are immediate and have nothing to do with tomorrow. If I could keep them so innocent, so safe and so free, I would. Yet I know that one day they will face all of those churning adult emotions and worries.

But today there were wildflowers to be picked, questions to be answered. And for me, dreams to be dreamed.

There is no doubt that Nanny understands why I walk here. She knows me too well not to see into my heart. She loves me too well to criticize. No one would be more aware than she that there is no love in my marriage. It is, as it has always been, a convenience to Fergus, a duty to me. If not for the children, we would have nothing in common. Even then, I fear he considers them worthwhile possessions, symbols of his success, such as our home in New York, or The Towers, the castlelike house he built for summers on the island. Or myself, the woman he took as wife, one whom he considers attractive enough, well-bred enough to share the Calhoun

*name, to grace his dinner table or adorn his arm when
we walk into the society that is so important to him.*

*It sounds cold when I write it, yet I cannot pretend
there has been warmth in my marriage to Fergus. Certainly there is no passion. I had hoped, when I followed
my parents' wishes and married him, that there would
be affection, which would deepen into love. But I was
very young. There is courtesy, a hollow substitute for
emotion.*

*A year ago perhaps, I could convince myself that I
was content. I have a prosperous husband, children I
adore, an enviable place in society and a circle of elegant friends. My wardrobe is crowded with beautiful clothes and jewelry. The emeralds Fergus gave me
when Ethan was born are fit for a queen. My summer
home is magnificent, again suited to royalty with its
towers and turrets, its lofty walls papered in silk, its
floors gleaming beneath the richest of carpets.*

*What woman would not be content with all of this?
What more could a dutiful wife ask for? Unless she
asked for love.*

*It was love I found along these cliffs, in the artist who
stood there, facing the sea, slicing those rocks and raging water onto canvas. Christian, his dark hair blowing
in the wind, his gray eyes so dark, so intense, as they
studied me. Perhaps if I had not met him I could have
gone on pretending to be content. I could have gone
on convincing myself that I did not yearn for love or
sweet words or a quiet touch in the middle of the night.*

*Yet I did meet him, and my life has changed. I would
not go back to that false contentment for a hundred
emerald necklaces. With Christian I have found something so much more precious than all the gold Fergus*

so cleverly accumulates. It is not something I can hold in my hand or wear around my throat, but something I hold in my heart.

When I meet him on the cliffs, as I will this afternoon, I will not grieve for what we can't have, what we dare not take, but treasure the hours we've been given. When I feel his arms around me, taste his lips against mine, I'll know that Bianca is the luckiest woman in the world to have been loved so well.

Chapter 1

A storm was waiting to happen. From the high curving window of the tower, Lilah could see the silver tongue of lightning licking at the black sky to the east. Thunder bellowed, bursting through the gathering clouds to send its drumbeat along the teeth of rock. An answering shudder coursed through her—not of fear, but of excitement.

Something was coming. She could feel it, not just in the thickening of the air but in the primitive beating of her own blood.

When she pressed her hand to the glass, she almost expected her fingers to sizzle, snapped with the power of the building electricity. But the glass was cool and smooth, and as black as the sky.

She smiled a little at the distant rumble of thunder and thought of her great-grandmother. Had Bianca ever stood here, watching a storm build, waiting for it to crash over the house and fill the tower with eerie light? Had she wished that her lover had stood beside her to share the power and the unleashed passion? Of course she had, Lilah thought. What woman wouldn't?

But Bianca had stood here alone, Lilah knew, just as she herself was standing alone now. Perhaps it had been the loneliness, the sheer ache of it, that had driven Bianca to throw herself out of that very window and onto the unforgiving rocks below.

Shaking her head, Lilah took her hand from the glass. She was letting herself get moody again, and it had to stop. Depression and dark thoughts were out of character for a woman who preferred to take life as it came—and who made it a policy to avoid its more strenuous burdens.

Lilah wasn't ashamed of the fact that she would rather sit than stand, would certainly rather walk than run and saw the value of long naps as opposed to exercise for keeping the body and mind in tune.

Not that she wasn't ambitious. It was simply that her ambitions ran to the notion that physical comfort had priority over physical accomplishments.

She didn't care for brooding and was annoyed with herself for falling into the habit over the past few weeks. If anything, she should be happy. Her life was moving along at a steady if unhurried pace. Her home and her family, equally important as her own comfort, were safe and whole. In fact, both were expanding along very satisfactory lines.

Her youngest sister, C.C., was back from her honeymoon and glowing like a rose. Amanda, the most practical of the Calhoun sisters, was madly in love and planning her own wedding.

The two men in her sisters' lives met with Lilah's complete approval. Trenton St. James, her new brother-in-law, was a crafty businessman with a soft heart under a meticulously tailored suit. Sloan O'Riley, with his cowboy boots and Oklahoma drawl, had her admiration for digging beneath Amanda's prickly exterior.

Of course, having two of her beloved nieces attached to wonderful men made Aunt Coco delirious with happiness. Lilah laughed a little, thinking how her aunt was certain she'd all but arranged the love affairs herself. Now, naturally, the Calhoun sisters' longtime guardian was itching to provide the same service for Lilah and her older sister Suzanna.

Good luck, Lilah wished her aunt. After a traumatic divorce, and with two young children to care for—not to mention a business to run—Suzanna wasn't likely to cooperate. She'd been badly burned once, and a smart woman didn't let herself get pushed into the fire.

For herself, Lilah had been doing her best to fall in love, to hear that vibrant inner click that came when you knew you'd found the one person in the world who was fated for you. So far, that particular chamber of her heart had been stubbornly silent.

There was time for that, she reminded herself. She was twenty-seven, happy enough in her work, surrounded by family. A few months before, they had nearly lost The Towers, the Calhoun's crumbling and eccentric home that stood on the cliffs overlooking the sea. If it hadn't been for Trent, Lilah might not have been able to stand in the tower room she loved so much and look out at the gathering storm.

So she had her home, her family, a job that interested her and, she reminded herself, a mystery to solve. Great-Grandmama Bianca's emeralds, she thought. Though she had never seen them, she was able to visualize them perfectly just by closing her eyes.

Two dramatic tiers of grass-green stones accented with icy diamonds. The glint of gold in the fancy filigree work. And dripping from the bottom strand, that rich and glowing teardrop emerald. More than its financial or even aesthetic value, it represented to Lilah a direct link with an ancestor who fascinated her, and the hope of eternal love.

The legend said that Bianca, determined to end a loveless marriage, had packed a few of her treasured belongings, including the necklace, into a box. Hoping to find a way to join her lover, she had hidden it. Before she had been able to take it out and start a life with Christian, she had despaired and leaped from the tower window to her death.

A tragic end to a romance, Lilah thought, yet she didn't always feel sad when she thought of it. Bianca's spirit remained in The Towers, and in that high room where Bianca had spent so many hours longing for her lover, Lilah felt close to her.

They would find the emeralds, she promised herself. They were meant to.

It was true enough that the necklace had already caused its problems. The press had learned of its existence and had played endlessly on the hidden-treasure angle. So successfully, Lilah thought now, that the annoyance had gone beyond curious tourists and amateur treasure hunters, and had brought a ruthless thief into their home.

When she thought of how Amanda might have been killed protecting the family's papers, the risk she had taken trying to keep any clue to the emeralds out of the wrong hands, Lilah shuddered. Despite Amanda's heroics, the man who had called himself William Livingston had gotten away with a sackful. Lilah sincerely hoped he found nothing but old recipes and unpaid bills.

William Livingston, alias Peter Mitchell, alias a dozen other names wasn't going to get his greedy hands on the emeralds. Not if the Calhoun women had anything to do about it. As far as Lilah was concerned, that included Bianca, who was as much a part of The Towers as the cracked plaster and creaky boards.

Restless, she moved away from the window. She couldn't say why the emeralds and the woman who had owned them preyed so heavily on her mind tonight. But Lilah was a woman who believed in instinct, in premonition, as naturally as she believed the sun rose in the east.

Tonight, something was coming.

She glanced back toward the window. The storm was rolling closer, gathering force. She felt a driving need to be outside to meet it.

Max felt his stomach lurch along with the boat. Yacht, he reminded himself. A twenty-six-foot beauty with all the comforts of home. Certainly more than his own home, which consisted of a cramped apartment, carelessly furnished, near the campus of Cornell University. The trouble was, the twenty-six-foot beauty was sitting on top of a very cranky Atlantic, and the two seasickness pills in Max's system were no match for it.

He brushed the dark lock of hair away from his brow

where, as always, it fell untidily back again. The reeling of the boat sent the brass lamp above his desk dancing. Max did his best to ignore it. He really had to concentrate on his job. American history professors weren't offered fascinating and lucrative summer employment every day. And there was a very good chance he could get a book out of it.

Being hired as researcher for an eccentric millionaire was the fodder of fiction. In this case, it was fact.

As the ship pitched, Max pressed a hand to his queasy stomach and tried three deep breaths. When that didn't work, he tried concentrating on his good fortune.

The letter from Ellis Caufield had come at a perfect time, just before Max had committed himself to a summer assignment. The offer had been both irresistible and flattering.

In the day-to-day scheme of things, Max didn't consider that he had a reputation. Some well-received articles, a few awards—but that was all within the tight world of academia that Max had happily buried himself in. If he was a good teacher, he felt it was because he received such pleasure from giving both information and appreciation of the past to students so mired in the present.

It had come as a surprise that Caufield, a layman, would have heard of him and would respect him enough to offer him such interesting work.

What was even more exciting than the yacht, the salary and the idea of summering in Bar Harbor, to a man with Maxwell Quartermain's mind-set, was the history in every scrap of paper he'd been assigned to catalogue.

A receipt for a lady's hat, dated 1932. The guest list for a party from 1911. A copy of a repair bill on a

1935 Ford. The handwritten instructions for an herbal remedy for the croup. There were letters written before World War I, newspaper clippings with names like Carnegie and Kennedy, shipping receipts for Chippendale armoires, a Waterford chandelier. Old dance cards, faded recipes.

For a man who spent most of his intellectual life in the past, it was a treasure trove. He would have shifted through each scrap happily for nothing, but Ellis Caufield had contacted him, offering Max more than he made teaching two full semesters.

It was a dream come true. Instead of spending the summer struggling to interest bored students in the cultural and political status of America before the Great War, he was living it. With the money, half of which was already deposited, Max could afford to take a year off from teaching to start the book he'd been longing to write.

Max felt he owed Caufield an enormous debt. A year to indulge himself. It was more than he had ever dared to dream of. Brains had gotten him into Cornell on a scholarship. Brains and hard work had earned him a Ph.D. by the time he'd been twenty-five. For the eight years since then, he'd been slaving, teaching classes, preparing lectures, grading papers, taking the time only to write a few articles.

Now, thanks to Caufield, he would be able to take the time he had never dared to take. He would be able to begin the project he kept secret inside his head and heart.

He wanted to write a novel set in the second decade of the twentieth century. Not just a history lesson or an oratory on the cause and effect of war, but a story of people swept along by history. The kind of people he was growing to know and understand by reading through their old papers.

Caufield had given him that time, the research and the opportunity. And it was all gilded by a summer spent luxuriously on a yacht. It was a pity Max hadn't realized how much his system would resent the motion of the sea.

Particularly a stormy one, he thought, rubbing a hand over his clammy face. He struggled to concentrate, but the faded and tiny print on the papers swam then doubled in front of his eyes and added a vicious headache to the grinding nausea. What he needed was some air, he told himself. A good blast of fresh air. Though he knew Caufield preferred him to stay below with his research during the evenings, Max figured his employer would prefer him healthy rather than curled up moaning on his bed.

Rising, he did moan a little, his stomach heaving with the next wave. He could almost feel his skin turn green. Air, definitely. Max stumbled from the cabin, wondering if he would ever find his sea legs. After a week, he'd thought he'd been doing fairly well, but with the first taste of rough weather, he was wobbly.

It was a good thing he hadn't—as he sometimes liked to imagine—sailed on the *Mayflower.* He never would have made it to Plymouth Rock.

Bracing a hand on the mahogany paneling, he hobbled down the pitching corridor toward the stairs that led above deck.

Caufield's cabin door was open. Max, who would never stoop to eavesdropping, paused only to give his stomach a moment to settle. He heard his employer speaking to the captain. As the dizziness cleared from Max's head, he realized they were not speaking about the weather or plotting a course.

"I don't intend to lose the necklace," Caufield said impatiently. "I've gone to a lot of trouble, and expense, already."

The captain's answer was equally taut. "I don't see why you brought Quartermain in. If he realizes why you want those papers, and how you got them, he'll be trouble."

"He won't find out. As far as the good professor is concerned, they belong to my family. And I am rich enough, eccentric enough, to want them preserved."

"If he hears something—"

"Hears something?" Caufield interrupted with a laugh. "He's so buried in the past he doesn't hear his own name. Why do you think I chose him? I do my homework, Hawkins, and I researched Quartermain thoroughly. He's an academic fossil with more brains than wit, and is curious only about what happened in the past. Current events, such as armed robbery and the Calhoun emeralds are beyond him."

In the corridor, Max remained still and silent, the physical illness warring with sick suspicion. *Armed robbery.* The two words reeled in his head.

"We'd be better off in New York," Hawkins complained. "I cased out the Wallingford job while you were kicking your heels last month. We could have the old lady's diamonds inside of a week."

"The diamonds will wait." Caufield's voice hardened. "I want the emeralds, and I intend to have them. I've been twenty years in the business of stealing, Hawkins, and I know that only once in a lifetime does a man have the chance for something this big."

"The diamonds—"

"Are stones." Now the voice was caressing and perhaps a little mad. "The emeralds are a legend. They're going to be mine. Whatever it takes."

Max stood frozen outside the stateroom. The clammy illness roiling inside of his stomach was iced with shock. He hadn't a clue what they were talking about or how to put it together. But one thing was obvious—he was being used by a thief, and there was something other than history in the papers he'd been hired to research.

The fanaticism in Caufield's voice hadn't escaped him, nor had the suppressed violence in Hawkins's. And fanaticism had proved itself throughout history to be a most dangerous weapon. His only defense against it was knowledge.

He had to get the papers, get them and find a way off the boat and to the police. Though whatever he could tell them wouldn't make sense. He stepped back, hoping he could clear his thoughts by the time he got to his stateroom. A wicked wave had the boat lurching and Max pitching through the open doorway.

"Dr. Quartermain." Gripping the sides of his desk, Caufield lifted a brow. "Well, it seems as though you're in the wrong place at the wrong time."

Max grasped the doorjamb as he stumbled back, cursing the unsteady deck beneath his feet. "I—wanted some air."

"He heard every damn word," the captain muttered.

"I'm aware of that, Hawkins. The professor isn't blessed with a poker face. Well then," he began as he slid a drawer open, "we'll simply alter the plans a bit.

I'm afraid you won't be granted any shore leave during our stay in Bar Harbor, Doctor." He pulled out a chrome-plated revolver. "An inconvenience, I know, but I'm sure you'll find your cabin more than adequate for your needs while you work. Hawkins, take him back and lock him in."

A crash of thunder vibrated the boat. It was all Max needed to uproot his legs. As the boat swayed, he rushed back into the corridor. Pulling himself along by the handrail, he fought the motion of the boat. The shouts behind him were lost as he came above deck into the howl of the wind.

A spray of saltwater dashed across his face, blinding him for a moment as he frantically looked for a means of escape. Lightning cracked the black sky, showing him the single stab of light, the pitching seas, the distant, angry rocks and the vague shadow of land. The next roll nearly felled him, but he managed through a combination of luck and sheer will to stay upright. Driven by instinct, he ran, feet sliding on the wet deck. In the next flash of lightning he saw one of the mates glance over from his post. The man called something and gestured, but Max spun around on the slippery deck and ran on.

He tried to think, but his head was too crowded, too jumbled. The storm, the pitching boat, the image of that glinting gun. It was like being caught in someone else's nightmare. He was a history professor, a man who lived in books, rarely surfacing long enough to remember if he'd eaten or picked up his cleaning. He was, he knew, terminally boring, calmly pacing himself on the academic treadmill as he had done all of his life. Surely he couldn't be on a yacht in the Atlantic being chased by armed thieves.

"Doctor."

His erstwhile employer's voice was close enough to cause Max to turn around. The gun being held less than five feet away reminded Max that some nightmares were real. Slowly he backed up until he rammed into the guardrail. There was nowhere left to run.

"I know this is an inconvenience," Caufield said, "but I think it would be wise if you went back to your cabin." A bolt of lightning emphasized the point. "The storm should be short, but quite severe. We wouldn't want you to…fall overboard."

"You're a thief."

"Yes." Legs braced against the rolling deck, Caufield smiled. He was enjoying himself—the wind, the electric air, the white face of the prey he had cornered. "And now that I can be more frank about just what I want you to look for, our work should go much more quickly. Come now, Doctor, use that celebrated brain of yours."

From the corner of his eye, Max saw that Hawkins was closing in from the other side, as steady on the heeling deck as a mountain goat on a beaten path. In a moment, they would have him. Once they did, he was quite certain he would never see the inside of a classroom again.

With an instinct for survival that had never been tested, he swung over the rail. He heard another crack of thunder, felt a burning along his temple, then plunged blindly beneath the dark, swirling water.

Lilah had driven down, following the winding road to the base of the cliff. The wind had picked up, was shrieking now as she stepped out of her car and let it stream through her hair. She didn't know why she'd felt compelled to come here, to stand alone on this narrow and rocky stretch of beach to face the storm.

But she had come, and the exhilaration streamed into her, racing just under her skin, speeding up her heart. When she laughed, the sound hung on the wind then echoed away. Power and passion exploded around her in a war she could delight in.

Water fumed against the rock, spouting up, spraying her. There was an icy feel to it that made her shiver, but she didn't draw back. Instead she closed her eyes for a moment, lifted her face and absorbed it.

The noise was huge, wildly primitive. Above, closer now, the storm threatened. Big and bad and boisterous. The rain, so heavy in the air you could taste it, held up, but the lightning took command, spearing the sky, ripping through the dark while the boom of thunder competed with the crash of water and wind.

She felt as though she were alone in a violent painting, but there was no sense of loneliness and certainly none of fear. It was anticipation that prickled along her skin, just as a passion as dark as the storm's beat in her blood.

Something, she thought again as she lifted her face to the wind, was coming.

If it hadn't been for the lightning, she wouldn't have seen him. At first she watched the dark shape in the darker water and wondered if a dolphin had swum too close to the rocks. Curious, she walked over the shale, dragging her hair away from the greedy fingers of wind.

Not a dolphin, she realized with a clutch of panic. A man. Too stunned to move, she watched him go under. Surely she'd imagined it, she told herself. She was just caught up in the storm, the mystery of it, the sense of immediacy. It was crazy to think she'd seen someone fighting the waves in this lonely and violent span of water.

But when the figure appeared again, floundering, Lilah was kicking off her sandals and racing into the icy black water.

His energy was flagging. Though he'd managed to pry off his shoes, his legs felt abominably heavy. He'd always been a strong swimmer. It was the only sport he had had any talent for. But the sea was a great deal stronger. It carried him along now rather than his own arms and legs. It dragged him under as it chose, then teasingly released him as he struggled to break free for one more gulp of air.

He couldn't even remember why he was fighting. The cold that had long since numbed his body granted the same favor to his brain. His thrashing movements were merely automatic now and growing steadily weaker. It was the sea that guided him, that trapped him, that would, he was coming to accept, kill him.

The next wave battered him, and exhausted, he let it take him under. He only hoped he would drown before he bashed into the rocks.

He felt something wrap around his neck and, with the last of his strength, pushed at it. Some wild thought of sea snakes or grasping weeds had him struggling. Then his face was above the surface again, his burning lungs sucking air. Dimly he saw a face close to his own. Pale, stunningly beautiful. A glory of dark, wet hair floated around him.

"Just hang on," she shouted at him. "We'll be all right."

She was pulling him toward shore, fighting the back-wash of wave. Hallucinating, Max thought. He had to be hallucinating to imagine a beautiful woman coming to his aid a moment before he died. But the possibility of a miracle kicked into his fading sense of survival, and he began to work with her.

The waves slammed into them, dragging them back a foot for every two exhausting feet of progress they made. Overhead the sky opened to pour out a lashing rain. She was shouting something again, but all he could hear was the dull buzzing in his own head.

He decided he must already be dead. There certainly was no more pain. All he could see was her face, the glow of her eyes, the water-slicked lashes. A man could do worse than to die with that image in his mind.

But her eyes were bright with anger, electric with it. She wanted help, he realized. She needed help. Instinctively he put an arm around her waist so that they were towing each other.

He lost track of the times they went under, of the times one would pull the other up again. When he saw the jutting rocks, fangs spearing up through the swirling black, he turned his weary body without thought to shield hers. An angry wave flicked them waist high out of the water, as easily as a finger flicks an ant from a stone.

His shoulder slammed against rock, but he barely felt it. Then there was the grit of sand beneath his knees, biting into flesh. The water fought to suck them back, but they crawled onto the rocky shore.

The initial sickness was hideous, racking through him until he was certain his body would simply break apart. When the worst of it passed, he rolled, coughing, onto his back. The sky wheeled overhead, black, then brilliant. The face was above his again, close. A hand moved gently over his brow.

"You made it, sailor."

He only stared. She was eerily beautiful, like something he might have conjured if he'd had enough imagination. In the flickering lightning he could see her hair was a rich, golden red. She had acres of it. It flowed around her face, down her shoulders, onto his chest. Her eyes were the mystical green of a calm sea. As the water ran from her onto him, he reached up to touch her face, certain they would pass through the image. But he felt her skin, cold, wet and soft as spring rain.

"Real." His voice was a husky croak. "You're real."

"Damn right." She smiled, then cupping his face in her hands, laughed. "You're alive. We're both alive." And kissed him. Deeply, lavishly, until his head spun with it. There was more laughter beneath the kiss. He heard the joy in it, but not the simple relief.

When he looked at her again, she was blurring, that ethereal face fading until all he could see were those incredible, glowing eyes.

"I never believed in mermaids," he murmured before he lost consciousness.

Chapter 2

"Poor man." Coco, splendid in a flowing purple caftan, hovered beside the bed. She kept her voice low and watched, eagle eyed, as Lilah bandaged the shallow crease on their unconscious guest's temple. "What in the world could have happened to him?"

"We'll have to wait and ask." Her fingers gentle, Lilah studied the pale face on the pillow. Early thirties, she guessed. No tan, though it was mid-June. The indoor type, she decided, despite the fact that he had fairly good muscles. His body was well toned, if a bit on the lanky side—the weight of it had given her more than a little trouble when she'd dragged him to the car. His face was lean, a little long, nicely bony. Intellectual, she thought. The mouth was certainly engaging. Rather poetic, like the pallor. Though his eyes were closed now, she knew they were blue. His hair, nearly dry, was full of sand and long and thick. It was dark and straight, like his lashes.

"I called the doctor," Amanda said as she hurried into the bedroom. Her fingers tapped on the footboard as she frowned down at the patient. "He says we should bring him into Emergency."

Lilah looked up as the lightning struck close to the house and the rain slashed against the windows. "I don't want to take him out in this unless we have to."

"I think she's right." Suzanna stood on the other side of the bed. "I also think Lilah should have a hot bath and lie down."

"I'm fine." At the moment she was wrapped in a chenille robe, warmed by that and a healthy dose of brandy. In any case, she was feeling much too proprietary about her charge to turn him over.

"Crazy is what you are." C.C. massaged Lilah's neck as she lectured her. "Diving into the ocean in the middle of a storm."

"I guess I could've let him drown." Lilah patted C.C.'s hand. "Where's Trent?"

C.C. sighed as she thought of her new husband. "He and Sloan are making sure the new construction's protected. The rain's coming down pretty hard and they were worried about water damage."

"I think I should make some chicken soup." Coco, maternal instincts humming, studied the patient again. "That's just what he needs when he wakes up."

He was already waking up, groggily. He heard the distant and lovely sound of women's voices. Low pitched, smooth, soothing. Like music, it lulled him in and out of dreams. When he turned his head, Max felt the gentle feminine touch on his brow. Slowly, he opened eyes still burning from salt water. The dimly lit room blurred, tilted, then slid into soft focus.

There were five of them, he noted dreamily. Five stupendous examples of womanhood. On one side of the bed was a blonde, poetically lovely, eyes filled with concern. At the foot was a tall, trim brunette who seemed both impatient and sympathetic. An older woman with smoky-blond hair and a regal figure beamed at him. A green-eyed, raven-haired Amazon tilted her head and smiled more cautiously.

Then there was his mermaid, sitting beside him in a white robe, her fabulous hair falling in wild curls to her waist. He must have made some gesture, for they all came a little closer, as if to offer comfort. The mermaid's hand covered his.

"I guess this is heaven," he managed through a dry throat. "It's worth dying for."

With a laugh, Lilah squeezed his fingers. "Nice thought, but this is Maine," she corrected. Lifting a cup, she eased brandy-laced tea through his lips. "You're not dead, just tired."

"Chicken soup." Coco stepped forward to tidy the blanket over him. She was vain enough to take an instant liking to him for his waking statement. "Doesn't that sound good, dear?"

"Yes." The thought of something warm sliding down his aching throat sounded glorious. Though it hurt to swallow, he took another greedy gulp of tea. "Who are you?"

"We're the Calhouns," Amanda said from the foot of the bed. "Welcome to The Towers."

Calhouns. There was something familiar about the

name, but it drifted away, like the dream of drowning. "I'm sorry, I don't know how I got here."

"Lilah brought you," C.C. told him. "She—"

"You had an accident," Lilah interrupted her sister, and smiled at him. "Don't worry about it right now. You should rest."

It wasn't a question of should, but must. He could already feel himself drifting away. "You're Lilah," he said groggily. As he drifted to sleep, he repeated the name, finding it lyrical enough to dream on.

"How's the lifeguard this morning?"

Lilah turned from the stove to look at Sloan, Amanda's fiancé. At six-four, he filled the doorway, was so blatantly male—and relaxed with it—she had to smile.

"I guess I earned my first merit badge."

"Next time try making a pot holder." After crossing the room, he kissed the top of her head. "We wouldn't want to lose you."

"I figure jumping into a stormy sea once in my life is enough." With a little sigh, she leaned against him. "I was petrified."

"What the hell were you doing down there with a storm coming?"

"Just one of those things." She shrugged, then went back to fixing tea. For now, she preferred to keep the sensation of being sent to the beach to herself.

"Did you find out who he is?"

"No, not yet. He didn't have a wallet on him, and since he was in pretty rough shape last night, I didn't want to badger him." She glanced up, caught Sloan's expression and shook her head. "Come on, big guy, he's hardly dangerous. If he was looking for a way into the house to have a shot at finding the necklace, he could have taken an easier route than drowning."

He was forced to agree, but after having Amanda shot at, he didn't want to take chances. "Whoever he is, I think you should move him to the hospital."

"Let me worry about it." She began to arrange plates and cups on a tray. "He's all right, Sloan. Trust me?"

Frowning, he put a hand on hers before she could lift the tray. "Vibes?"

"Absolutely." With a laugh, she tossed back her hair. "Now, I'm going to take Mr. X some breakfast. Why don't you get back to knocking down walls in the west wing?"

"We're putting a few up today." And because he did trust her, he relaxed a little. "Aren't you going to be late for work?"

"I took the day off to play Florence Nightingale." She slapped his hand away from the saucer of toast. "Go be an architect."

Balancing the tray, she left Sloan to start down the hallway. The main floor of The Towers was a hodge-podge of rooms with towering ceilings and cracked plaster. In its heyday, it had been a showplace, an elaborate summer home built by Fergus Calhoun in 1904. It had been his symbol of status with gleaming paneling, crystal doorknobs, intricate murals.

Now the roof leaked in too many places to count, the plumbing rattled and the plaster flaked. Like her sisters, Lilah adored every inch of chipped molding. It had been her home, her only home, and held memories of the parents she had lost fifteen years before.

At the top of the curving stairs, she paused. Muffled with distance came the energetic sound of hammering.

The west wing was getting a much needed face-lift. Between Sloan and Trent, The Towers would recapture at least part of its former glory. Lilah liked the idea and, as a woman who considered napping a favored pastime, enjoyed the sound of busy hands.

He was still sleeping when she walked into the room. She knew he had barely stirred through the night because she had stretched out on the foot of the bed, reluctant to leave him, and had slept there, patchily, until morning.

Quietly Lilah set the tray on the bureau and moved over to open the terrace doors. Warm and fragrant air glided in. Unable to resist, she stepped out to let it revitalize her. The sunlight sparkled on the wet grass, glittered on the petals of shell-pink peonies still heavy-headed from rain. Clematis, their saucer-sized blossoms royally blue, spiraled on one of the white trellises in a race with the climbing roses.

From the waist-high terrace wall, she could see the glint of the deep blue water of the bay and the greener, less serene, surface of the Atlantic. It hardly seemed possible that she had been in the water just last night, grasping a stranger and fighting for life. But muscles, unaccustomed to the exercise, ached enough to bring the moment, and the terror, back.

She preferred concentrating on the morning, the generous laziness of it. Made tiny as a toy by the distance, one of the tourist boats streamed by, filled with people clutching cameras and children, hoping to see a whale.

It was June, and the summer people poured into Bar Harbor to sail, to shop, to sun. They would gobble up lobster rolls, haunt the ice cream and T-shirt shops and pack the streets, searching for the perfect souvenir. To them it was a resort. To Lilah, it was home.

She watched a three-masted schooner head out to sea and allowed herself to dream a little before going back inside.

He was dreaming. Part of his mind recognized it as a dream, but his stomach muscles still fisted, and his pulse rate increased. He was alone in an angry black sea, fighting to make his arms and legs swim through the rising waves. They dragged at him, pulling him under into that blind, airless world. His lungs strained. His own heartbeat roared in his head.

His disorientation was complete—black sea below, black sky above. There was a hideous throbbing in his temple, a terrifying numbness in his limbs. He sank, floating down, fathoms deep. Then she was there, her red hair flowing around her, twining around lovely white breasts, down a slender torso. Her eyes were a soft, mystical green. She spoke his name, and there was a laugh in her voice—and an invitation in the laugh. Slowly, gracefully as a dancer, she held out her arms to him, folding him in. He tasted salt and sex on her lips as she closed them over his.

With a groan, he came regretfully awake. There was pain now, ripe and throbbing in his shoulder, sharp and horrible in his head. His thought patterns skidded away from him. Concentrating, he worked his way above the pain, focusing first on a high, coffered ceiling laced with cracks. He shifted a little, acutely aware that every muscle in his body hurt.

The room was enormous—or perhaps it seemed so because it was so scantily furnished. But what furnishings. There was a huge antique armoire with intricately carved doors. The single chair was undoubtedly Louis Quinze, and the dusty nightstand Hepplewhite. The mattress he lay on sagged, but the footboard was Georgian.

Struggling up to brace on his elbows, he saw Lilah standing in the open terrace doors. The breeze was fluttering those long cables of hair. He swallowed. At least he knew she wasn't a mermaid. She had legs. Lord, she had legs—right up to her eyes. She wore flowered shorts, a plain blue T-shirt and a smile.

"So, you're awake." She came to him and, competent as a mother, laid a hand on his brow. His tongue dried up. "No fever. You're lucky."

"Yeah."

Her smile widened. "Hungry?"

There was definitely a hole in the pit of his stomach. "Yeah." He wondered if he'd ever be able to get more than one word out around her. At the moment he was lecturing himself for having imagined her naked when she'd risked her life to save his. "Your name's Lilah."

"That's right." She walked over to fetch the tray. "I wasn't sure you'd remember anything from last night."

Pain capered through him so that he gritted his teeth against it and struggled to keep his voice even. "I remember five beautiful women. I thought I was in heaven."

She laughed and, setting the tray at the foot of the bed, came to rearrange his pillows. "My three sisters and my aunt. Here, can you sit up a little?"

When her hand slid down his back to brace him, he realized he was naked. Completely. "Ah…"

"Don't worry, I won't peek. Yet." She laughed again, leaving him flustered. "Your clothes were drenched— I think the shirt's a lost cause. Relax," she told him as she set the tray on his lap. "My brother-in-law and future brother-in-law got you into bed."

"Oh." It looked as though he was back to single syllables.

"Try the tea," she suggested. "You probably swallowed a gallon of sea water, so I'll bet your throat's raw." She saw the intense concentration in his eyes and the nagging pain behind it. "Headache?"

"Vicious."

"I'll be back." She left him, trailing some potently exotic scent in her wake.

Max used the time alone to build back what little strength he had. He hated being weak—a leftover obsession from childhood when he'd been puny and asthmatic. His father had given up in disgust on building his only and disappointing son into a football star. Though he knew it was illogical, sickness brought back unhappy memories of childhood.

Because he'd always considered his mind stronger than his body, he used it now to block the pain.

Moments later, she was back with an aspirin and witch hazel. "Take a couple of these. After you eat, I can drive you into the hospital."

"Hospital?"

"You might want to have a doctor take a look."

"No." He swallowed the pills. "I don't think so."

"Up to you." She sat on the bed to study him, one leg lazily swinging to some inner tune.

Never in his life had he been so sexually aware of a

woman—of the texture of her skin, the subtle tones of it, the shape of her body, her eyes, her mouth. The assault on his senses left him uneasy and baffled. He'd nearly drowned, he reminded himself. Now all he could think about was getting his hands on the woman who'd saved him. Saved his life, he remembered.

"I haven't even thanked you."

"I figured you'd get around to it. Try those eggs before they get any colder. You need food."

Obediently he scooped some up. "Can you tell me what happened?"

"From the time I came into it." Relaxed, she brushed her hair behind her shoulder and settled more comfortably on the bed. "I drove down to the beach. Impulse," she said with a lazy movement of her shoulders. "I'd been watching the storm build from the tower."

"The tower?"

"Here, in the house," she explained. "I got the urge to go down, watch it roll in from sea. Then I saw you." In a careless gesture, she brushed the hair back from his brow. "You were in trouble, so I went in. We sort of pulled each other to shore."

"I remember. You kissed me."

Her lips curved. "I figured we both deserved it." She touched a gentle hand to the bruise spreading on his shoulder. "You hit the rocks. What were you doing out there?"

"I…" He closed his eyes to try to clear his fuzzy brain. The effort had sweat pearling on his brow. "I'm not sure."

"Okay, why don't we start with your name?"

"My name?" He opened his eyes to give her a blank look. "Don't you know?"

"We didn't have the chance to introduce ourselves formally. Lilah Calhoun," she said, and offered a hand.

"Quartermain." He accepted her hand, relieved that much was clear. "Maxwell Quartermain."

"Drink some more tea, Max. Ginseng's good for you." Taking the witch hazel, she began to rub it gently over the bruise. "What do you do?"

"I'm, ah, a history professor at Cornell." Her fingers eased the ache in his shoulder and cajoled him into relaxing.

"Tell me about Maxwell Quartermain." She wanted to take his mind off the pain, to see him relax into sleep again. "Where are you from?"

"I grew up in Indiana..." Her fingers slid up to his neck to unknot muscles.

"Farm boy?"

"No." He sighed as the tension eased and made her smile. "My parents ran a market. I used to help out after school and over the summer."

"Did you like it?"

His eyes were growing heavy. "It was all right. It gave me plenty of time to study. Annoyed my father— always had my face in a book. He didn't understand. I skipped a couple grades and got into Cornell."

"Scholarship?" she assumed.

"Hmm. Got my doctorate." The words were slurred and weighty. "Do you know how much man accomplished between 1870 and 1970?"

"Amazing."

"Absolutely." He was nearly asleep, coaxed into comfort by her quiet voice and gentle hands. "I'd like to have been alive in 1910."

"Maybe you were." She smiled, amused and charmed. "Take a nap, Max."

When he awakened again, he was alone. But he had a dozen throbbing aches to keep him company. He noted that she had left the aspirin and a carafe of water beside the bed, and gratefully swallowed pills.

When that small chore exhausted him, he leaned back to catch his breath. The sunlight was bright, streaming through the open terrace doors with fresh sea air. He'd lost his sense of time, and though it was tempting just to lie back and shut his eyes again, he needed to take back some sort of control.

Maybe she'd read his mind, he thought as he saw his pants and someone else's shirt neatly folded at the foot of the bed. He rose creakily, like an old man with brittle bones and aching muscles. His body sang a melody of pain as he picked up the clothes and peeked through a side door. He eyed the claw-footed tub and chrome shower works with pleasure.

The pipes thudded when he turned on the spray, and so did his muscles as the water beat against his skin. But ten minutes later, he felt almost alive.

It wasn't easy to dry off—even that simple task had his limbs singing. Not sure the news would be good, he wiped the mist from the mirror to study his face.

Beneath the stubble of beard, his skin was white and drawn. Flowering out from the bandage at his temple was a purpling bruise. He already knew there were plenty more blooming on his body. As a result of salt water, his eyes were a patriotic red, white and blue.

Though he'd never considered himself a vain man—his looks had always struck him as dead average—he turned away from the mirror.

Wincing and groaning and swearing under his breath, he struggled into the clothes.

The shirt fit fairly well. Better, in fact, than many of his own. Shopping intimidated him—rather salesclerks intimidated him with their bright, impatient smiles. Most of the time Max shopped out of catalogues and took what came.

Glancing down at his bare feet, Max admitted that he'd have to go shopping for shoes—and soon.

Moving slowly, he walked out onto the terrace. The sunlight stung his eyes, but the breezy, moist air felt like heaven. And the view... For a moment he could only stop and stare, hardly even breathing. Water and rock and flowers. It was like being on top of the world and looking down at a small and perfect slice of the planet. The colors were vibrant—sapphire, emerald, the ruby red of roses, the pristine white of sails pregnant with wind. There was no sound but the rumble of the sea and then, far off, the musical gong of a buoy. He could smell hot summer flowers and the cool tang of the ocean.

With his hand braced on the wall, he began to walk. He didn't know which direction he should take, so wandered aimlessly and with no little effort. Once, when dizziness overtook him, he was forced to stop, shut his eyes and breathe his way through it.

When he came to a set of stairs leading up, he opted to climb them. His legs were wobbly, and he could already feel fatigue tugging at him. It was pride as much as curiosity that had him continuing.

The house was built of granite, a sober and sturdy

stone that did nothing to take away from the fancy of the architecture. Max felt as though he were exploring the circumference of a castle, some stubborn bulwark of early history that had taken its place upon the cliffs and held it for generations.

Then he heard the anachronistic buzz of a power saw and a man's casual oath. Walking closer, he recognized the busy noises of construction in progress— the slap of hammer on wood, the tinny music from a portable radio, the whirl of drills. When his path was blocked by sawhorses, lumber and tarps, he knew he'd found the source.

A man stepped out of another set of terrace doors. Reddish-blond hair was tousled around a tanned face. He squinted at Max, then hooked his thumbs in his pockets. "Up and around, I see."

"More or less."

The guy looked as if he'd been kicked by a team of mules, Sloan thought. His face was dead white, his eyes bruised, his skin sheened with the sweat of effort. He was holding himself upright through sheer stubbornness. It made it tough to hold on to suspicions.

"Sloan O'Riley," he said, and offered a hand.

"Maxwell Quartermain."

"So I hear. Lilah says you're a history professor. Taking a vacation?"

"No." Max's brow furrowed. "No, I don't think so."

It wasn't evasion Sloan saw in his eyes, but puzzlement, laced with frustration. "Guess you're still a little rattled."

"I guess." Absently he reached up to touch the bandage at his temple. "I was on a boat," he murmured, straining to visualize it. "Working." On what? "The water was pretty rough. I wanted to go on deck, get some air…" Standing at the rail, deck heaving. Panic. "I think I fell—" jumped, was thrown "—I must have fallen overboard."

"Funny nobody reported it."

"Sloan, leave the man alone. Does he look like an international jewel thief?" Lilah strolled lazily up the steps, a short-haired black dog at her heels. The dog jumped at Sloan, tripped, righted himself and managed to get his front paws settled on the knees of Sloan's jeans.

"I wondered where you'd wandered off to," Lilah continued, and cupped a hand under Max's chin to examine his face. "You look a little better," she decided as the dog started to sniff at Max's bare toes. "That's Fred," she told him. "He only bites criminals."

"Oh. Good."

"Since you have his seal of approval, why don't you come down? You can sit in the sun and have some lunch."

He would dearly love to sit, he realized and let Lilah lead him away. "Is this really your house?"

"Hearth and home. My great-grandfather built it just after the turn of the century. Look out for Fred." The dog dashed between them, stepped on his own ear and yelped. Max, who'd gone through a long clumsy stage himself, felt immediate sympathy. "We're thinking of giving him ballet lessons," she said as the dog struggled back to his feet. Noting the blank look on Max's face, she patted his cheek. "I think you could use some of Aunt Coco's chicken soup."

She made him sit and kept an eye on him while he ate. Her protective instincts were usually reserved for family or small, wounded birds. But something about the man tugged at her. He seemed so out of his element, she thought. And helpless with it.

Something was going on behind those big blue eyes, she thought. Something beyond the fatigue. She could almost see him struggle to put one mental foot in front of the other.

He began to think that the soup had saved his life as surely as Lilah had. It slid warm and vital into his system. "I fell out of a boat," he said abruptly.

"That would explain it."

"I don't know what I was doing on a boat, exactly."

In the chair beside him she brought up her limber legs to settle in the lotus position. "Taking a vacation?"

"No." His brow furrowed. "No, I don't take vacations."

"Why not?" She reached over to take one of the crackers from his plate. She wore a trio of glittering rings on her hand.

"Work."

"School's out," she said with a lazy stretch.

"I always teach summer courses. Except…" Something was tapping at the edges of his brain, tauntingly. "I was going to do something else this summer. A research project. And I was going to start a book."

"A book, really?" She savored the cracker as if it were laced with caviar. He had to admire her basic, sensual enjoyment. "What kind?"

Her words jerked him back. He'd never told anyone about his plans to write. No one who knew him would have believed that studious, steady-as-she-goes Quartermain dreamed of being a novelist. "It's just something I've been thinking of for a while, but I had a chance to work on this project…a family history."

"Well, that would suit you. I was a terrible student. Lazy," she said with a smile in her eyes. "I can't imagine anyone wanting to make a career out of a classroom. Do you like it?"

It wasn't a matter of liking it. It was what he did. "I'm good at it." Yes, he realized, he was good at it. His students learned—some more than others. His lectures were well attended and well received.

"That's not the same thing. Can I see your hand?"

"My what?"

"Your hand," she repeated, and took it, turning it palm up. "Hmm."

"What are you doing?" For a heady moment, he thought she would press her lips to it.

"Looking at your palm. More intelligence than intuitiveness. Or maybe you just trust your brains more than your instincts."

Staring at the top of her bent head, he gave a nervous laugh. "You don't really believe in that sort of thing. Palm reading."

"Of course—but it's not just the lines, it's the feeling." She glanced up briefly with a smile that was at once languid and electric. "You have very nice hands. Look here." She skimmed a finger along his palm and had him swallowing. "You've got a long life ahead of you, but see this break? Near-death experience."

"You're making it up."

"They're your lines," she reminded him. "A good imagination. I think you'll write that book—but you'll have to work on that self-confidence."

She looked up again, a trace of sympathy on her face. "Rough childhood?"

"Yes—no." Embarrassed, he cleared his throat. "No more than anyone's, I imagine."

She lifted a brow, but let it pass. "Well, you're a big boy now." In one of her casual moves, she slid her hair back then studied his hand again. "Yes, see, this represents careers, and there's a branch off this way. Things have been very comfortable for you professionally— you've hoed yourself a nice little rut—but this other line spears off. Could be that literary effort. You'll have to make the choice."

"I really don't think—"

"Sure you do. You've been thinking about it for years. Now here's the Mound of Venus. Hmm. You're a very sensual man." Her gaze flicked up to his again. "And a very thorough lover."

He couldn't take his eyes off her mouth. It was full, unpainted and curved teasingly. Kissing her would be like sinking into a dream—the dark and erotic kind. And if a man survived it, he would pray never to wake up.

She felt something creep in over her amusement. Something unexpected and arousing. It was the way he looked at her, she thought. With such complete absorption. As though she were the only woman in the world—certainly the only one who mattered.

There couldn't be a female alive who wouldn't weaken a bit under that look.

For the first time in her life she felt off balance with a man. She was used to having the controls, of setting the tone in her own unstudied way. From the time she'd understood that boys were different from girls, she had used the power she'd been born with to guide members of the opposite sex down a path of her own choosing.

Yet he was throwing her off with a look.

Struggling for a casualness that had always come easily, she started to release his hand. Max surprised them both by turning his over to grip hers.

"You are," he said slowly, "the most beautiful woman I've ever seen."

It was a standard line, even a cliché, and shouldn't have had her heart leaping. She made herself smile as she drew away. "Don't get out much, do you, Professor?"

There was a flicker of annoyance in his eyes before he made himself settle back. It was as much with himself as with her. He'd never been the hand-holding Casanova type. Nor had he ever been put so neatly back in his place.

"No, but that was a simple statement of fact. Now, I guess I'm supposed to cross your palm with silver, but I'm fresh out."

"Palm reading's on the house." Because she was sorry she'd been so glib and abrupt, she smiled again. "When you're feeling better, I'll take you up for a tour of the haunted tower."

"I can't wait."

His dry response had her laughing. "I have a feeling about you, Max. I think you could be a lot of fun when you forget to be intense and thoughtful. Now I'm going downstairs so you can have some quiet. Be a good boy and get some more rest."

He might have been weak, but he wasn't a boy. Max rose as she did. Though the move surprised her, she gave him one of her slow, languid smiles. His color was coming back, she noted. His eyes were clear and, because he was only an inch or so taller than she, nearly on level with hers.

"Is there something else I can get you, Max?"

He felt steadier and took a moment to be grateful. "Just an answer. Are you involved with anyone?"

Her brow lifted as she swept her hair over her shoulder. "In what way?"

"It's a simple question, Lilah, and deserves a simple answer."

The lecturing quality of his tone had her frowning at him. "If you mean am I emotionally or sexually involved with a man, the answer is no. At the moment."

"Good." The vague irritation in her eyes pleased him. He'd wanted a response, and he'd gotten one.

"Look, Professor, I pulled you out of the drink. You strike me as being too intelligent a man to fall for that gratitude transference."

This time he smiled. "Transference to what?"

"Lust seems appropriate."

"You're right. I know the difference—especially when I'm feeling both at the same time." His own words surprised him. Maybe the near-death experience had rattled his brains. For a moment she looked as though she would swipe at him. Then abruptly, and beautifully, she laughed.

"I guess that was another simple statement of fact. You're an interesting man, Max."

And, she told herself as she carried the tray inside, harmless.

She hoped.

Chapter 3

Even after he'd arranged to have funds wired from his account in Ithaca, the Calhouns wouldn't consider Max's suggestion that he move to a hotel. In truth, he didn't put up much of a fight. He'd never been pampered before, or fussed over. More, he'd never been made to feel part of a big, boisterous family. They took him in with a casual kind of hospitality that was both irresistible and gracious.

He was coming to know them and appreciate them for their varied personalities and family unity. It was a house where something always seemed to be happening and where everyone always had something to say. For someone who had grown up an only child, in a home where his bookishness had been considered a flaw, it was a revelation to be among people who celebrated their own, and each other's, interests.

C.C. was an auto mechanic who talked about engine blocks and carried the mysterious glow of a new bride. Amanda, brisk and organized, held the assistant manager's position at a nearby hotel. Suzanna ran a gardening business and devoted herself to her children. No one mentioned their father. Coco ran the house, cooked lavish meals and appreciated male company. She'd only made Max nervous when she'd threatened to read his tea leaves.

Then there was Lilah. He discovered she worked as a naturalist at Acadia National Park. She liked long naps, classical music and her aunt's elaborate desserts. When the mood struck her, she could sit, sprawled in a chair, prodding little details of his life from him. Or she could curl up in a sunbeam like a cat, blocking him and everything else around her out of her thoughts while she drifted into one of her private daydreams. Then she would stretch and smile and let them all in again.

She remained a mystery to him, a combination of smoldering sensuality and untouched innocence—of staggering openness and unreachable solitude.

Within three days, his strength had returned and his stay at the The Towers was open-ended. He knew the sensible thing to do was leave, use his funds to purchase a one-way ticket back to New York and see if he could pick up a few summer tutoring jobs.

But he didn't feel sensible.

It was his first vacation and, however he had been thrust into it, he wanted to enjoy it. He liked waking up in the morning to the sound of the sea and the smell of it. It relieved him that his accident hadn't caused him to fear or dislike the water. There was something incredibly relaxing about standing on the terrace, looking across indigo or emerald water and seeing the distant clumps of islands.

And if his shoulder still troubled him from time to time, he could sit out and let the afternoon sun bake the ache away. There was time for books. An hour, even two, sitting in the shade gobbling up a novel or biography from the Calhoun library.

His life had been full of timetables, never timelessness. Here, in The Towers, with its whispers of the past, momentum of the present and hope for the future, he could indulge in it.

Underneath the simple pleasure of having no schedule to meet, no demands to answer, was his growing fascination with Lilah.

She glided in and out of the house. Leaving in the morning, she was neat and tidy in her park service uniform, her fabulous hair wound in a neat braid. Drifting home later, she would change into one of her flowing skirts or a pair of sexy shorts. She smiled at him, spoke to him, and kept a friendly but tangible distance.

He contented himself with scribbling in a notebook or entertaining Suzanna's two children, Alex and Jenny, who were already showing signs of summer boredom. He could walk in the gardens or along the cliffs, keep Coco company in the kitchen or watch the workmen in the west wing.

The wonder of it was, he could do as he chose.

He sat on the lawn, Alex and Jenny hunched on either side of him like eager frogs. The sun was a hazy silver disk behind a sheet of clouds. Playful and brisk, the breeze carried the scent of lavender and rosemary from a nearby rockery. There were butterflies dancing in the grass, easily eluding Fred's pursuits. Nearby a bird trilled insistently from the branch of a wind-gnarled oak.

Max was spinning a tale of a young boy caught up in the terrors and excitement of the revolutionary war. In weaving fact with fiction, he was keeping the children entertained and indulging in his love of storytelling.

"I bet he killed whole packs of dirty redcoats," Alex said gleefully. At six, he had a vivid and violent imagination.

"Packs of them," Jenny agreed. She was a year younger than her brother and only too glad to keep pace. "Single-handed."

"The Revolution wasn't all guns and bayonets, you know." It amused Max to see the young mouths pout at the lack of mayhem. "A lot of battles were won through intrigue and espionage."

Alex struggled with the words a moment then brightened. "Spies?"

"Spies," Max agreed, and ruffled the boy's dark hair. Because he had experienced the lack himself, he recognized Alex's hunger for a male bond.

Using a teenage boy as the catalyst, he took them through Patrick Henry's stirring speeches, Samuel Adams's courageous Sons of Liberty, through the politics and purpose of a rebellious young country to the Boston Tea Party.

Then as he had the young hero heaving chests of tea into the shallow water of Boston Harbor, Max saw Lilah drifting across the lawn.

She moved with languid ease over the grass, a graceful gypsy with her filmy chiffon skirt teased by the wind. Her hair was loose, tumbling free over the thin straps of a pale green blouse. Her feet were bare, her arms adorned with dozens of slim bracelets.

Fred raced over to greet her, leaped and yipped and made her laugh. As she bent to pet him, one of the straps slid down her arm. Then the dog bounded off, tripping himself up, to continue his fruitless chase of butterflies.

She straightened, lazily pushing the strap back into place as she continued across the grass. He caught her scent—wild and free—before she spoke.

"Is this a private party?"

"Max is telling a story," Jenny told her, and tugged on her aunt's skirt.

"A story?" The array of colored beads in her ears danced as she lowered to the grass. "I like stories."

"Tell Lilah, too." Jenny shifted closer to her aunt and began to play with her bracelets.

"Yes." There was laughter in her voice, an answering humor in her eyes as they met Max's. "Tell Lilah, too."

She knew exactly what effect she had on a man, he thought. Exactly. "Ah…where was I?"

"Jim had black cork all over his face and was tossing the cursed tea into the harbor," Alex reminded him. "Nobody got shot yet."

"Right." As much for his own defense against Lilah as for the children, Max put himself back on the frigate with the fictional Jim. He could feel the chill of the air and the heat of excitement. With a natural skill he considered a basic part of teaching, he drew out the suspense, deftly coloring his characters, describing an historical event in a way that had Lilah studying him with a new interest and respect.

Though it ended with the rebels outwitting the British, without firing a shot, even the bloodthirsty Alex wasn't disappointed.

"They won!" He jumped up and gave a war hoot. "I'm a Son of Liberty and you're a dirty redcoat," he told his sister.

"Uh-uh." She sprang to her feet.

"No taxation without restoration," Alex bellowed, and went flying for the house with Jenny hot on his heels and Fred lumbering after them both.

"Close enough," Max murmured.

"Pretty crafty, Professor." Lilah leaned back on her elbows to watch him through half-closed eyes. "Making history entertaining."

"It is," he told her. "It's not just dates and names, it's people."

"The way you tell it. But when I was in school you were supposed to know what happened in 1066 in the same way you were supposed to memorize the multiplication tables." Lazily she rubbed a bare foot over her calf. "I still can't remember the twelves, or what happened in 1066—unless that was when Hannibal took those elephants across the Alps."

He grinned at her. "Not exactly."

"There, you see?" She stretched, long and limber as a cat. Her head drifted back, her hair spreading over the summer grass. Her shoulders rolled so that the wayward strap slipped down again. The pleasure of the small indulgence showed on her face. "And I think I usually fell asleep by the time we got to the Continental Congress."

When he realized he was holding his breath, he released it slowly. "I've been thinking about doing some tutoring."

Her eyes slitted open. "You can take the boy out of

the classroom," she murmured, then arched a brow. "So, what do you know about flora and fauna?"

"Enough to know a rabbit from a petunia."

Delighted, she sat up again to lean toward him. "That's very good, Professor. If the mood strikes, maybe we can exchange expertise."

"Maybe."

He looked so cute, she thought, sitting on the sunny grass in borrowed jeans and T-shirt, his hair falling over his forehead. He'd been getting some sun, so that the pallor was replaced by the beginnings of a tan. The ease she felt convinced her that she'd been foolish to be unsteady around him before. He was just a nice man, a bit befuddled by circumstances, who'd aroused her sympathies and her curiosity. To prove it, she laid a hand on the side of his face.

Max saw the amusement in her eyes, the little private joke that curved her lips before she touched them to his in a light, friendly kiss. As if satisfied with the result, she smiled, leaned back and started to speak. He circled a hand around her wrist.

"I'm not half-dead this time, Lilah."

Surprise came first. He saw it register then fade into a careless acceptance. Damn it, he thought as he slid a hand behind her neck. She was so certain there would be nothing. With a combination of wounded pride and fluttery panic, he pressed his lips to hers.

She enjoyed kissing—the affection of it, the elemental physical enjoyment. And she liked him. Because of it, she leaned into the kiss, expecting a nice tingle, a comforting warmth. But she hadn't expected the jolt.

The kiss bounced through her system, starting with her lips, zipping to her stomach, vibrating into her fin-

gertips. His mouth was very firm, very serious—and
very smooth. The texture of it had a quiet sound of
pleasure escaping, like a child might make after a first
taste of chocolate. Before the first sensation could be
fully absorbed, others were drifting through to tangle
and mix.

Flowers and hot sun. The scent of soap and sweat.
Smooth, damp lips and the light scrape of teeth. Her
own sigh, a mere shifting of air, and the firm press of
his fingers on the sensitive nape of her neck. There was
something more than simple pleasure here, she realized.
Something sweeter and far less tangible.

Enchanted, she lifted her hand from the carpet of
grass to skim it through his hair.

He was reexperiencing the sensation of drowning,
of being pulled under by something strong and dangerous. This time he had no urge to fight. Fascinated, he
slid his tongue over hers, tasting those secret flavors.
Rich and dark and seductive, they mirrored her scent,
the scent that had already insinuated itself into his system so that he thought he would taste that as well, each
time he took a breath.

He felt something shift inside him, stretch and grow
and heat until it gripped him hard by the throat.

She was outrageously sexual, unabashedly erotic,
and more frightening than any woman he had known.
Again he had the image of a mermaid sitting on a rock,
combing her hair and luring helplessly seduced men to
destruction with the promise of overwhelming pleasures.

The instinct for survival kicked in, so that he drew
back. Lilah stayed as she was, eyes closed, lips parted.
It wasn't until that moment that he realized he still held

her wrist and that her pulse was scrambling under his fingers.

Slowly, holding on to that drugging weightlessness a moment longer, she opened her eyes. She skimmed her tongue over her lips to capture the clinging flavor of his. Then she smiled.

"Well, Dr. Quartermain, it seems history's not the only thing you're good at. How about another lesson?" Wanting more, she leaned forward, but Max scrambled up. The ground, he discovered, was as unsteady as the deck of a ship.

"I think one's enough for today."

Curious, she swung her hair back to look up at him. "Why?"

"Because…" Because if he kissed her again, he'd have to touch her. And if he touched her—and he desperately wanted to touch her—he would have to make love with her, there on the sunny lawn in full sight of the house. "Because I don't want to take advantage of you."

"Advantage of me?" Touched and amused, she smiled. "That's very sweet."

"I'd appreciate it if you wouldn't make me sound like a fool," he said tightly.

"Was I?" The smile turned thoughtful. "Being a sweet man doesn't make you a fool, Max. It's just that most men I know would be more than happy to take advantage. Tell you what, before you take offense at that, why don't we go inside? I'll show you Bianca's tower."

He'd already taken offense and was about to say so when her last words struck a chord. "Bianca's tower?"

"Yes. I'd like to show you." She lifted a hand, waiting.

He was frowning at her, struggling to fit the name

"Bianca" into place. Then with a shake of his head, he helped her to her feet. "Fine. Let's go."

He'd already explored some of the house, the maze of rooms, some empty, some crowded with furniture and boxes. From the outside, the house was part fortress, part manor, with sparkling windows, graceful porches married to jutting turrets and parapets. Inside, it was a rambling labyrinth of shadowed hallways, sun-washed rooms, scarred floors and gleaming banisters. It had already captivated him.

She took him up a set of circular stairs to a door at the top of the east wing.

"Give it a shove, will you, Max?" she asked, and he was forced to thud the wood hard with his good shoulder. "I keep meaning to ask Sloan to fix this." Taking his hand, she walked inside.

It was a large, circular room, ringed with curving windows. A light layer of dust lay softly on the floor, but someone had tossed a few colorful pillows onto the window seat. An old floor lamp with a stained and tassled shade stood nearby.

"I imagine she had lovely things up here once," Lilah began. "To keep her company. She used to come up here to be alone, to think."

"Who?"

"Bianca. My great-grandmother. Come look at the view." Feeling a need to share it with him, she drew him to the window. From there it was all water and rock. It should have seemed lonely, Max thought. Instead it was exhilarating and heartbreaking all at once. When he put a hand to the glass, Lilah glanced over in surprise. She had done the same countless times, as if wishing for something just out of reach.

"It's…sad." He'd meant to say beautiful or breathtaking, and frowned.

"Yes. But sometimes it's comforting, too. I always feel close to Bianca in here."

Bianca. The name was like an insistent buzz in his head.

"Has Aunt Coco told you the story yet?"

"No. Is there a story?"

"Of course." She gave him a curious look. "I just wondered if she'd given you the Calhoun version rather than what's in the press."

A faint throbbing began in his temple where the wound was healing. "I don't know either version."

After a moment, she continued. "Bianca threw herself through this window on one of the last nights of summer in 1913. But her spirit stayed behind."

"Why did she kill herself?"

"Well, it's a long story." Lilah settled on the window seat, her chin comfortably propped on her knees, and told him.

Max listened to the tale of an unhappy wife, trapped in a loveless marriage during the heady years before the Great War. Bianca had married Fergus Calhoun, a wealthy financier, and had borne him three children. While summering on Mount Desert Island, she had met a young artist. From an old date book the Calhouns had unearthed, they knew his name had been Christian, but nothing more. The rest was legend, that had been passed down to the children from their nanny who had been Bianca's confidante.

The young artist and the unhappy wife had fallen

in love, deeply. Torn between duty and her heart, Bianca had agonized over her choice and had ultimately decided to leave her husband. She had taken a few personal items, known now as Bianca's treasure, and had hidden them away in preparation. Among them had been an emerald necklace, given to her on the birth of her first son and second child, Lilah's grandfather. But rather than going to her lover, Bianca had thrown herself through the tower window. The emeralds have never been found.

"We didn't know the story until a few months ago," Lilah added. "Though I'd seen the emeralds."

His mind was whirling. Nagged by the pain, he pressed his fingers to his temple. "You've seen them?"

She smiled. "I dreamed about them. Then during a séance—"

"A séance," he said weakly, and sat.

"That's right." She laughed and patted his hand. "We were having a séance, and C.C. had a vision." He made a strangled sound in his throat that had her laughing again. "You had to be there, Max. Anyway, C.C. saw the necklace, and that's when Aunt Coco decided it was time to pass on the Calhoun legend. To get where we are today, Trent fell in love with C.C. and decided not to buy The Towers. We were in pretty bad shape and were on the point of being forced to sell. He came up with the idea of turning the west wing into a hotel, with the St. James's name. You know the St. James hotels?"

Trenton St. James, Max thought. Lilah's brother-in-law owned one of the biggest hotel corporations in the country. "By reputation."

"Well, Trent hired Sloan to handle the renovations—and Sloan fell for Amanda. All in all, it couldn't have worked out better. We were able to keep the house, combine it with business, and culled two romances out of the bargain."

Annoyance flickered into her eyes, darkening them. "The downside has been that the story about the necklace leaked, and we've been plagued with hopeful treasure hunters and out-and-out thieves. Just a few weeks ago, some creep nearly killed Amanda and stole stacks of the papers we'd been sorting through to try to find a clue to the necklace."

"Papers," he repeated as a sickness welled in his stomach. It was coming back now and with such force he felt as though he were being battered on the rocks again. Calhoun, emeralds, Bianca.

"What's wrong, Max?" Concerned, Lilah leaned over to lay a hand on his brow. "You're white as a sheet. You've been up too long," she decided. "Let me take you down so you can rest."

"No, I'm fine. It's nothing." He jerked away to rise and pace the room. How was he going to tell her? How could he tell her, after she had saved his life, taken care of him? After he'd kissed her? The Calhouns had opened their home to him, without hesitation, without question. They had trusted him. How could he tell Lilah that he had, however inadvertently, been working with men who were planning to steal from her?

Yet he had to. Marrow-deep honesty wouldn't permit anything else.

"Lilah…" He turned back to see her watching him, a combination of concern and wariness in her eyes. "The boat. I remember the boat."

Relief had her smiling. "That's good. I thought it

would come back to you if you stopped worrying. Why don't you sit down, Max? It's easier on the brain."

"No." The refusal was sharp as he concentrated on her face. "The boat—the man who hired me. His name was Caufield. Ellis Caufield."

She spread her hands. "And?"

"The name doesn't mean anything?"

"No, should it?"

Maybe he was wrong, Max thought. Maybe he was letting her family story meld in his mind with his own experience. "He's about six foot, very trim. About forty. Dark-blond hair graying at the temples."

"Okay."

Max let out a frustrated breath. "He contacted me at Cornell about a month ago and offered me a job. He wanted me to sort through, catalogue and research some family papers. I'd get a generous salary, and several weeks on a yacht—plus all my expenses and time to work on my book."

"So, seeing as you're not brain damaged, you took the job."

"Yes, but damn it, Lilah, the papers—the receipts, the letters, the ledgers. They had your name on them."

"Mine?"

"Calhoun." He jammed his useless hands into his pockets. "Don't you understand? I was hired, and worked on that boat for a week, researching your family history from the papers that were stolen from you."

She only stared. It seemed a long time to Max before she unfolded herself from the window seat and stood. "You're telling me that you've been working for the man who tried to kill my sister?"

"Yes."

She never took her eyes from his. He could almost feel her trying to get into his thoughts, but when she spoke, her voice was very cool. "Why are you telling me this now?"

Frazzled, he dragged a hand through his hair. "I didn't remember it all until now, until you told me about the emeralds."

"That's odd, isn't it?"

He watched the shutter come down over her eyes and nodded. "I don't expect you to believe me, but I didn't remember. And when I took the job, I didn't know."

She continued to watch him carefully, measuring every word, every gesture, every expression. "You know, it seemed strange to me that you hadn't heard about the necklace, or the robbery. It's been in the press for weeks. You'd have to be living in a cave not to have heard."

"Or a classroom," he murmured. Caufield's mocking words about having more intelligence than wit came back to him and made him wince. "Look, I'll tell you whatever I can before I leave."

"Leave?"

"I can't imagine any of you will want me to stay after this."

She considered him, instinct warring against common sense. With a long sigh, she lifted a hand. "I think you'd better tell the whole story to the whole family, all at once. Then we'll decide what to do about it."

It was Max's first family meeting. He hadn't grown up in a democracy, but under his father's uncompromising dictatorship. The Calhouns did things differently. They gathered around the big mahogany dining room table, so completely united that Max felt like an intruder for the first time since he'd awakened upstairs. They listened, occasionally asking questions as he repeated what he had told Lilah in the tower.

"You didn't check his references?" Trent asked. "You just contracted to do a job with a man you'd never met, and knew nothing about?"

"There didn't seem to be any reason to. I'm not a businessman," he said wearily. "I'm a teacher."

"Then you won't object if we check yours." This from Sloan.

Max met the suspicious eyes levelly. "No."

"I already have," Amanda put in. Her fingers were tapping against the wood of the table as all eyes turned to her. "It seemed the logical step, so I made a couple of calls."

"Leave it to Mandy," Lilah muttered. "I guess it never occurred to you to discuss it with the rest of us."

"No."

"Girls," Coco said from the head of the table. "Don't start."

"I think Amanda should have talked about this." The Calhoun temper edged Lilah's voice. "It concerns all of us. Besides, what business does she have poking into Max's life?"

They began to argue heatedly, all four sisters tossing in opinions and objections. Sloan kicked back to let it run its course. Trent closed his eyes. Max merely stared. They were discussing him. Didn't they realize they were arguing about him, tossing him back and forth across the table like a Ping-Pong ball?

"Excuse me," he began, and was totally ignored. He tried again and earned his first smile from Sloan.

"Damn it, knock it off!" It was his annoyed professor's voice and did the trick. All of the women stopped to turn on him with irritated eyes.

"Look, buster," C.C. began, but he cut her off.

"You look. In the first place, why would I be telling you everything if I had some ulterior motive? And since you want to corroborate who I am and what I do, why don't you stop pecking at each other long enough to find out?"

"Because we like to peck at each other," Lilah told him grandly. "And we don't like anyone getting in the way while we're at it."

"That'll do." Coco took advantage of the lull. "Since Amanda's already checked on Max—though it was a bit impolite—"

"Sensible," Amanda objected.

"Rude," Lilah corrected.

They might have been off and running again, but Suzanna held up a hand. "Whatever it was, it's done. I think we should hear what Amanda found out."

"As I was saying." Amanda flicked a glance over at Lilah. "I made a couple of calls. The dean of Cornell speaks very highly of Max. As I recall the terms were 'brilliant' and 'dedicated.' He's considered one of the foremost experts on American history in the country. He graduated magna cum laude at twenty, and had his doctorate by twenty-five."

"Egghead," Lilah said with a comforting smile when Max shifted in his seat.

"Our Dr. Quartermain," Amanda continued, "comes from Indiana, is single and has no criminal record. He's been on the staff at Cornell for over eight years, and has published several well-received articles. His most recent was an overview of the social-political atmosphere in America prior to World War I. In academic circles, he's considered a wunderkind, serious minded, unflaggingly responsible, with unlimited potential." Sensing his embarrassment, Amanda softened her tone. "I'm sorry for intruding, Max, but I didn't want to take any chances, not with my family."

"We're all sorry." Suzanna smiled at him. "We've had an unsettling couple of months."

"I understand that." And they certainly couldn't know how much he detested the term *wunderkind.* "If my academic profile eases your minds, that's fine."

"There's one more thing," Suzanna continued. "None of this explains what you were doing in the water the night Lilah found you."

Max gathered his thoughts while they waited. It was easy to take himself back now, as easy as it was for him to put himself into the Battle of Bull Run or Woodrow Wilson's White House.

"I'd been working on the papers. A storm was coming in so the sea was rough. I guess I'm not much of a sailor. I was trying to crawl out on deck, for some air, when I heard Caufield talking to Captain Hawkins."

As concisely as he could, he told them what he had heard, how he had realized what he'd gotten into.

"I don't know what I was going to do. I had some wild idea about getting the papers and getting off the boat so I could take them to the police. Not very brilliant considering the circumstances. In any case, they caught me. Caufield had a gun, but this time the storm was on my side. I got up on deck, and took my chances in the water."

"You jumped overboard, in the middle of a storm?" Lilah asked.

"It wasn't very smart."

"It was very brave," she corrected.

"Not when you consider he was shooting at me." Frowning, Max rubbed a hand over the bandage on his temple.

"The way you describe this Ellis Caufield doesn't fit." Amanda tapped her fingers again as she thought it through. "Livingston, the man who stole the papers was dark haired, only about thirty."

"So, he dyed his hair." Lilah lifted her hands. "He couldn't come back using the same name and the same appearance. The police have his description."

"I hope you're right." A slow, humorless smile spread over Sloan's face. "I hope the sonofabitch is back so I can have another go at him."

"So we all can have another go at him," C.C. corrected. "The question is, what do we do now?"

They began to argue about that, with Trent telling his wife she wasn't going to do anything—Amanda reminding him it was a Calhoun problem—Sloan suggesting hotly that she keep out of it. Coco decided it was time for brandy and was ignored.

"He thinks I'm dead," Max murmured, almost to himself. "So he feels safe. He's probably still close by, on the same boat. The *Windrider*."

"You remember the boat?" Lilah held up a hand, signaling for silence. "You can describe it?"

"In detail," Max told her with a small smile. "It was my first yacht."

"So we take that information to the police." Trent glanced around the table, then nodded. "And we do a little checking ourselves. The ladies know the island as well as they know this house. If he's on it, or around it, we'll find him."

"I'm looking forward to it." Sloan glanced over at Max and went with his instincts. "You in, Quartermain?"

Surprised, Max blinked, then found himself smiling. "Yeah, I'm in."

I went to Christian's cottage. Perhaps it was risky as I might have been seen by some acquaintance, but I wanted so badly to see where he lived, how he lived, what small things he kept around him.

It's a small place near the water, a square wooden cottage with its rooms crowded with his paintings and smelling of turpentine. Above the kitchen is a sun-drenched loft for his studio. It seemed to me like a doll's house with its pretty windows and low ceilings—old leafy trees shading the front and a narrow porch dancing along the back where we could sit and watch the water.

Christian says that at low tide the water level drops so that you can walk across the smooth rocks to the little glade of trees beyond. And at night, the air is full of sound. Musical crickets, the hoot of owls, the lap of temperate water.

I felt at home there, as quietly content as I have been in my life. It seemed to me that we had lived there together for years. When I told Christian, he gathered me close, just to hold me.

"I love you, Bianca," he said. "I wanted you to come here. I needed to see you in my house, watch you stand among my things." When he drew me away, he was

smiling. "Now, I'll always see you here, and I'll never be without you."

I wanted to swear to him I would stay. God, the words leaped into my throat only to be blocked there by duty. Wretched duty. He must have sensed it for he kissed me then, as if to seal the words inside.

I had only an hour with him. We both knew I would have to go back to my husband, to my children, to the life I had chosen before I met him. I felt his arms around me, tasted his lips, sensed the straining need inside him that was such a vibrant echo of my own.

"I want you." I heard my own whisper and felt no shame. "Touch me, Christian. Let me belong to you." My heart was racing as I pressed wantonly against him. "Make love to me. Take me to your bed."

How tightly his arms gripped me, so tightly I couldn't get my breath. Then his hands were on my face, and I felt the tremor in his fingertips. His eyes were nearly black. So much could be read there. Passion, love, desperation, regret.

"Do you know how often I've dreamed of it? How many nights I've lain awake aching for you?" Then he released me to stride across the room to where my portrait hung on his wall. "I want you, Bianca, every time I take a breath. And I love you too much to take what can't be mine."

"Christian—"

"Do you think I could let you go if I'd ever touched you?" There was anger now, ripe and violent as he whirled back. "I hate knowing that we sneak like sinners just to spend an hour together, as innocent as children. If I don't have the strength to turn away from you completely, then I will have enough to keep you from taking a step you'd only regret."

"How could I regret belonging to you?"

"Because you already belong to someone else. And every time you go back to him, I dream of killing him with my bare hands if only because he can look at you when I can't. If we took this last step, I'd leave you no choice. There would be no going back to him, Bianca. No going back to your home, or your life."

And I knew it was true, as he stood between me and the image of me he'd created.

So I left him to come home, to tie a ribbon in Colleen's hair, to chase a ball with Ethan, to dry Sean's tears when he scraped his knee. To dine in miserable politeness with a husband who is more and more of a stranger to me.

Christian's words were true, and it is a truth I must face. The time is coming when I will no longer be able to live in both worlds, but must choose one, only one.

Chapter 4

"I have the most marvelous idea," Coco announced. Like a ship in full sail, she streamed into the kitchen where Lilah, Max, Suzanna and her family were having breakfast.

"Good for you," Lilah said over a bowl of chocolate-chip ice cream. "Anyone who can think at this hour deserves a medal, or should be committed."

Like a mother hen, Coco checked the herbs she had potted on the window. She clucked over the basil before she turned back. "I have no idea why I didn't think of it before. It's really so—"

"Alex is kicking me under the table."

"Alex, don't kick your sister," Suzanna said mildly. "Jenny, don't interrupt."

"I wasn't kicking her." Milk dribbled down Alex's chin. "She got her knee in the way of my foot."

"Did not."

"Did too."

"Turkey face."

"Booger head."

"Alex." Suzanna bit down on the inside of her lip to maintain the properly severe maternal disapproval. "Do you want to eat that cereal or wear it?"

"She started it," he muttered.

"Did not," Jenny said under her breath.

"Did too."

Another glance at their mother had them subsiding to eye each other with grim dislike over their cereal bowls.

"Now that that's settled." Amused, Lilah licked her spoon. "What's your marvelous idea, Aunt Coco?"

"Well." She fluffed her hair, absently checking her reflection in the toaster, approving it, then beaming. "It all has to do with Max. Really it's so obvious. But, of course, we were worried about his health, then it's so difficult to think clearly with this construction going on. Do you know one of those young men was out on the terrace this morning in nothing but a pair of jeans and a tool belt? Very distracting." She peeked out of the kitchen window, just in case.

"I'm sorry I missed it." Lilah winked at Max. "Was it the guy with the long blond hair tied back with a leather thong?"

"No, the one with dark curly hair and a mustache. I must say, he's extremely well built. I suppose one would keep fit swinging hammers or whatever all day. The noise is a bother, though. I hope it doesn't disturb you, Max."

"No." He'd learned to flow with Coco's rambling thought patterns. "Would you like some coffee?"

"Oh, that's sweet of you. I believe I will." She sat while he got up to pour her a cup. "They've literally transformed the billiard room already. Of course, we've a long way to go—thank you, dear," she added when Max set a cup of coffee in front of her. "And all those tarps and tools and lumber make things unsightly. But it will all be worth it in the end." As she spoke, she doctored her coffee with cream and heaps of sugar. "Now, where was I?"

"A marvelous idea," Suzanna reminded her, putting a restraining hand on Alex's shoulder before he could fling any soggy cereal at his sister.

"Oh, yes." Coco set her cup down without taking a sip. "It came to me last night when I was doing the tarot cards. There were some personal matters I'd wanted to resolve, and I'd wanted to get a feel for this other business."

"What other business?" Alex wanted to know.

"Grown-up business." Lilah dug a knuckle into his ribs to make him laugh. "Boring."

"You guys better go find Fred." Suzanna checked her watch. "If you want to go with me today, you've got five minutes."

They were up and shooting out of the room like little bullets. Surreptitiously Max rubbed his shin where Alex's foot had connected.

"The cards, Aunt Coco?" Lilah said when the explosion was over.

"Yes. I learned that there was danger, past and future. Disconcerting." She cast a worried look over both her nieces. "But we're to have help dealing with it. There seemed to be two different sources of aid. One was cerebral, the other physical—potentially violent." Uneasy, she frowned a little. "I couldn't place the physical source, though it seemed I should because it was from someone familiar. I thought it might be from Sloan. He's so, well, Western. But it wasn't. I'm quite sure it wasn't." Brushing that aside, she smiled again. "But naturally the cerebral source is Max."

"Naturally." Lilah patted his hand as he shifted uncomfortably in his chair. "Our resident genius."

"Don't tease him." Suzanna rose to take bowls to the sink.

"Oh, he knows I don't just like him for his brain. Don't you, Max?"

He was mortally afraid he would blush in a minute. "If you keep interrupting your aunt, you'll be late for work."

"And so will I," Suzanna pointed out. "What's the idea, Aunt Coco?"

She'd started to drink again, and again set the coffee down untouched. "That Max should do what he came here to do." Smiling, she spread her manicured hands. "Research the Calhouns. Find out as much as possible about Bianca, Fergus, everyone involved. Not for that awful Mr. Caufield or whatever his name is, but for us."

Intrigued, Lilah thought the idea over. "We've already been through the papers."

"Not with Max's objective, and scholarly eye," Coco pointed out. Already fond of him, she patted his shoulder. Her interpretation of the cards also had indicated that he and Lilah would suit very well. "I'm sure if he put his mind to it, he could come up with all kinds of wonderful theories."

"It's a good idea." Suzanna came back to the table. "How do you feel about it?"

Max considered. Though he didn't put any stock in tarot cards, he didn't want to hurt Coco's feelings. Besides, however she had come up with the idea, it was sound. It would be a way of paying them back and a way to justify staying on in Bar Harbor a few more weeks.

"I'd like to do something. There's a good chance that even with the information I gave them the police won't find Caufield. While everyone's looking for him, I could be concentrating on Bianca and the necklace."

"There." Coco sat back. "I knew it."

"I'd wanted to check out the library, the newspaper, interview some of the older residents, but Caufield shut down the idea." The more he thought about it, the more Max liked the notion of working on his own. "Claimed he wanted everything to come out of the family papers, or his own sources." He moved his cup aside. "Obviously he couldn't give me a free hand or I'd find out the truth."

"Now you have a free hand," Lilah put in. It amused her that she could already see the wheels turning. "But I don't think you'll find the necklace in a library."

"But I may find a photograph of it, or a description."

Lilah simply smiled. "I've already given you that."

He didn't put much stock in dreams and visions, either, and shrugged. "All the same, I might find something tangible. And I'll certainly find something on Fergus and Bianca Calhoun."

"I suppose it'll keep you busy." Unoffended by his lack of faith in her mystical beliefs, Lilah rose. "You'll need a car to get around. Why don't you drop me off at work and use mine?"

Irked by her lack of faith in his research abilities, Max spent hours in the library. As always, he felt at home there, among stacks of books, in the center of the murmuring quiet, with a notebook at his elbow. To him, research was a quest—perhaps not as exciting as riding a white charger. It was a mystery to be solved, though the clues were less adventurous than a smoking gun or a trail of blood.

But with patience, cleverness and skill, he was a knight, or a detective, carefully working his way to an answer.

The fact that he had always been drawn to such places had disappointed his father bitterly, Max knew. Even as a boy he had preferred mental exercise over the physical. He had not picked up the torch to follow his father's blaze of glory on the high school football field. Nor had he added trophies to the shelf.

Lack of interest and a long klutzy adolescence had made him a failure in sports. He had detested hunting, and on the last outing his father had pressured him into had come up with a vicious asthma attack rather than a buck.

Even now, years later, he could remember his father's disgusted voice creeping into his hospital room.

"Damn boy's a pansy. Can't understand it. He'd rather read than eat. Every time I try to make a man out of him, he ends up wheezing like an old woman."

He'd gotten over the asthma, Max reminded himself. He'd even made something out of himself, though his father wouldn't consider it a man. And if he never felt completely adequate, at least he could feel competent.

Shrugging off the mood, he went back to his quest.

He did indeed find Fergus and Bianca. There were little gems of information peppered through the research books. In the familiar comfort of a library, Max took reams of notes and felt the excitement build.

He learned that Fergus Calhoun had been self-made, an Irish immigrant who through grit and shrewdness had become a man of wealth and influence. He'd landed in New York in 1888, young, poor and, like so many who had poured into Ellis Island, looking for his fortune. Within fifteen years, he had built an empire. And he had enjoyed flaunting it.

Perhaps to bury the impoverished youth he had been, he had surrounded himself with the opulent, muscling his way into society with wealth and will. It was in polite, exclusive society that he had met Bianca Muldoon, a young debutante of an old, established family with more gentility than money. He had built The Towers, determined to outdo the other vacationing rich, and had married Bianca the following year.

His golden touch had continued. His empire had grown, and so had his family with the birth of three children. Even the scandal of his wife's suicide in the summer of 1913 hadn't affected his monetary fortune.

Though he had become somewhat of a recluse after her death, he had continued to wield his power from The Towers. His daughter had never married and, estranged from her father, had gone to live in Paris. His youngest son had fled, after a peccadillo with a married woman, to the West Indies. Ethan, his eldest child, had married and had two children of his own, Judson, Lilah's father, and Cordelia Calhoun, now Coco McPike.

Ethan had died in a sailing accident, and Fergus had lived out the last years of his long life in an asylum, committed there by his family after several outbursts of violent and erratic behavior.

An interesting story, Max mused, but most of the details could have been gleaned from the Calhouns themselves. He wanted something else, some small tidbit that would lead him in another direction.

He found it in a tattered and dusty volume titled *Summering in Bar Harbor.*

It was such a flighty and poorly written work that he nearly set it aside. The teacher in him had him reading on, as he would read a student's ill-prepared term paper. It deserved a C- at best, Max thought. Never in his life had he seen so many superlatives and cluttered adjectives on one page. Glamorously to gloriously, magnificent to miraculous. The author had been a wide-eyed admirer of the rich and famous, someone who saw them as royalty. Sumptuous, spectacular and splendiferous. The syntax made Max wince, but he plodded on.

There were two entire pages devoted to a ball given at The Towers in 1912. Max's weary brain perked up. The author had certainly attended, for the descriptions were in painstaking detail, from fashion to cuisine. Bianca Calhoun had worn gold silk, a flowing sheath with a beaded skirt. The color had set off the highlights in her titian hair. The scooped bodice had framed…the emeralds.

They were described in glowing and exacting detail. Once the adjectives and the romantic imagery were edited, Max could see them. Scribbling notes, he turned the page. And stared.

It was an old photograph, perhaps culled from a newspaper print. It was fuzzy and blurred, but he had no trouble recognizing Fergus. The man was as rigid and stern-faced as the portrait the Calhouns kept over the mantel in the parlor. But it was the woman sitting in front of him that stopped Max's breath.

Despite the flaws of the photo, she was exquisite, ethereally beautiful, timelessly lovely. And she was the image of Lilah. The porcelain skin, the slender neck left bare with a mass of hair swept up in the Gibson style. Oversize eyes he was certain would have been green. There was no smile in them, though her lips were curved.

Was it just the romance of the face, he wondered, or did he really see some sadness there?

She sat in an elegant lady's chair, her husband behind her, his hand on the back of the chair rather than on her shoulder. Still, it seemed to Max that there was a certain possessiveness in the stance. They were in formal wear—Fergus starched and pressed, Bianca draped and fragile. The stilted pose was captioned, Mr. and Mrs. Fergus Calhoun, 1912.

Around Bianca's neck, defying time, were the Calhoun emeralds.

The necklace was exactly as Lilah had described to him, the two glittering tiers, the lush single teardrop that dripped like emerald water. Bianca wore it with a coolness that turned its opulence into elegance and only intensified the power.

Max trailed a fingertip along each tier, almost certain he would feel the smoothness of the gems. He understood why such stones become legends, to haunt men's imaginations and fire their greed.

But it eluded him, a picture only. Hardly realizing what he was doing, he traced Bianca's face and thought of the woman who had inherited it.

There were women who haunt and inflame.

* * *

Lilah paused in her stroll down the nature path to give her latest group time to photograph and rest. They had had an excellent crowd in the park that day, with a hefty percentage of them interested enough to hike the trails and be guided by a naturalist. Lilah had been on her feet for the best part of eight hours, and had covered the same ground eight times—sixteen if she counted the return trip.

But she wasn't tired, yet. Nor did her lecture come strictly out of a guidebook.

"Many of the plants found on the island are typically northern," she began. "A few are subarctic, remaining since the retreat of the glaciers ten thousand years ago. More recent specimens were brought by Europeans within the last two hundred and fifty years."

With a patience that was a primary part of her, Lilah answered questions, distracted some of the younger crowd from trampling the wildflowers and fed information on the local flora to those who were interested. She identified the beach pea, the seaside goldenrod, the late-blooming harebell. It was her last group of the day, but she gave them as much time and attention as the first.

In any case she always enjoyed this seaside stroll, listening to the murmur of pebbles drifting in the surf or the echoing call of gulls, discovering for herself and the tourists what treasures lurked in the tide pools.

The breeze was light and balmy, carrying that ancient and mysterious scent that was the sea. Here the rocks were smooth and flat, worn to elegance by the patient ebb and flow of water. She could see the glitter of quartz running in long white rivers down the black stone. Overhead, the sky was a hard summer blue, nearly cloudless. Under it, boats glided, buoys clanged, orange markers bobbed.

She thought of the yacht, the *Windrider*, and though she searched as she had on each tour, she saw nothing but sleek tourist boats or the sturdy crafts of lobstermen.

When she saw Max hiking the nature trail down to join the group, she smiled. He was on time, of course. She'd expected no less. She felt a slow tingle of warmth when his gaze lifted from his feet to her face. He really had wonderful eyes, she thought. Intent and serious, and just a little shy.

As always when she saw him, she had an urge to tease him and an underlying longing to touch. An interesting combination, she thought now, and one she couldn't remember experiencing with anyone else.

She looked so cool, he thought, the mannish uniform over the willowy feminine form. The military khaki and the dangle of gold and crystal at her ears. He wondered if she knew how suited she was to stand before the sea while it bubbled and swayed at her back.

"At the intertidal zone," she began, "life has acclimated to tidal change. In spring, we have the highest and lowest tides, with a rise and fall of 14.5 feet."

She went on in that easy, soothing voice, talking of intertidal creatures, survival and food chains. Even as she spoke, a gull glided to perch on a nearby rock to study the tourists with a beady, expectant eye. Cameras clicked. Lilah crouched down beside a tide pool. Fascinated by her description of life there, Max moved to see for himself.

There were long purple fans she called dulse, and she had the children in the group groaning when she told them it could be eaten raw or boiled. In the dark little pool of water, she found a wealth of living things, all waiting, she said, for the tide to come in again before they went back to business.

With a graceful fingertip she pointed out the sea anemones that looked more like flowers than animals, and the tiny slugs that preyed on them. The pretty shells that were mollusks and snails and whelks. She sounded like a marine biologist one moment and a stand-up comedian the next.

Her appreciative audience bombarded her with questions. Max caught one teenage boy staring at her with a moony kind of lust and felt instant sympathy.

Tossing her braid behind her back, she wound up the tour, explaining about the information available at the visitors' center, and the other naturalist tours. Some of the group started to meander their way back along the path, while others lingered behind to take more pictures. The teenager loitered behind his parents, asking any question his dazzled brain could form on the tide pools, the wildflowers and, though he wouldn't have looked twice at a robin, the birds. When he'd exhausted all angles, and his mother called impatiently for the second time, he trudged reluctantly off.

"This is one nature walk he won't forget anytime soon," Max commented.

She only smiled. "I like to think they'll all remember some pieces of it. Glad you could make it, Professor." She did what her instincts demanded and kissed him fully, softly on the mouth.

Looking back, the teenager experienced a flash of miserable envy. Max was simply knocked flat. Lilah's lips were still curved as she eased away.

"So," she asked him, "how was your day?"

Could a woman kiss like that then expect him to continue a normal conversation? Obviously this one could, he decided and took a long breath. "Interesting."

"Those are the best kind." She began to walk up the path that would lead back to the visitors' center. Arching a brow, she glanced over her shoulder. "Coming?"

"Yeah." With his hands in his pockets, he started after her. "You're very good."

Her laugh was light and warm. "Why, thank you."

"I meant—I was talking about your job."

"Of course you were." Companionably she tucked an arm through his. "It's too bad you missed the first twenty minutes of the last tour. We saw two slate-colored juncos, a double-crested cormorant and an osprey."

"It's always been one of my ambitions to see a slate-colored junco," he said, and made her laugh again. "Do you always do the same trail?"

"No, I move around. One of my favorites is Jordan Pond, or I might take a shift at the Nature Center, or hike up in the mountains."

"I guess that keeps it from getting boring."

"It's never boring, or I wouldn't last a day. Even on the same trail you see different things all the time. Look." She pointed to a thatch of plants with narrow leaves and faded pink blooms. "Rhodora," she told him. "A common azalea. A few weeks ago it was at peak. Stunning. Now the blooms will die off, and wait until spring." She brushed her fingertips over the leaves. "I like cycles. They're reassuring."

Though she claimed to be an unenergetic woman, she walked effortlessly along the trail, keeping an eye out for anything of interest. It might be lichen clinging to a rock, a sparrow in flight or a spray of hawkweed. She liked the scent here, the sea they were leaving behind, the green smell of trees that began to crowd in to block the view.

"I didn't realize that your job kept you on your feet most of the day."

"Which is why I prefer to stay off them at all other times." She tilted her head to look at him. "Tell you what though, the next time I have an afternoon, I'll give you a more in-depth tour. We can kill two birds with one stone, so to speak. Take in the scenery, and poke around for your friend, Caufield."

"I want you to stay out of it."

The statement took her so off guard that she walked another five feet before it registered. "You what?"

"I want you to stay out of it," he repeated. "I've been giving it a lot of thought."

"Have you?" If he had known her better, he might have recognized the hint of temper in the lazy tone. "And just how did you come to that particular conclusion?"

"He's dangerous." The voice, laced with hints of fanaticism came back clearly. "I think he might even be unbalanced. It's certain that he's violent. He's already shot at your sister, and at me. I don't want you getting in his way."

"It's not a matter of what you want. It's family business."

"It's been mine since I took a swim in a storm." Caught between sunlight and shade on the path, he stopped to put his hands on her shoulders. "You didn't hear him that night, Lilah. I did. He said nothing would stop him from getting the necklace, and he meant it.

This is a job for the police, not for a bunch of women who—"

"A bunch of women who what?" she interrupted with a gleam in her eyes.

"Who are too emotionally involved to react cautiously."

"I see." She nodded slowly. "So it's up to you and Sloan and Trent, the big, brave men to protect us poor, defenseless women and save the day?"

It occurred, a bit too late, that he was on very shaky ground. "I didn't say you were defenseless."

"You implied it. Let me tell you something, Professor, there isn't one of the Calhoun women who can't handle herself and any man who comes swaggering down the road. That includes geniuses and unbalanced jewel thieves."

"There, you see?" His hands lifted from her shoulders, then settled again. "Your reaction is pure emotion without any logic or thought."

The heated eyes narrowed. "Do you want to see emotion?"

Besides brains, he prided himself on a certain amount of street smarts. Cautious, he eased back. "I don't think so."

"Fine. Then I suggest you take care with your phrasing, and think twice before you tell me to keep out of something that is wholly my concern." She brushed by him to continue toward the voices around the visitors' center.

"Damn it, I don't want you hurt."

"I don't intend to get hurt. I have a very low threshold for pain. But I'm not going to sit around with my hands folded while someone plots to steal what's mine."

"The police—"

"Haven't been a hell of a lot of help," she snapped. "Did you know that Interpol has been looking for Livingston, and his many aliases, for fifteen years? No one was able to trace him after he shot at Amanda and stole our papers. If Caufield and Livingston are one and the same, then it's up to us to protect what's ours."

"Even if it means getting your brains bashed in?"

She tossed a look over her shoulder. "I'll worry about my brains, Professor. You worry about yours."

"I'm not a genius," he muttered, and surprised a smile out of her.

The exasperation on his face took the edge off her temper. She stepped off the path. "I appreciate the concern, Max, but it's misplaced. Why don't you wait out here, sit on the wall? I've got to go in and get my things."

She left him muttering to himself. He only wanted to protect her. Was that so wrong? He cared about her. After all, she had saved his life. Scowling, he sat on the stone wall. People were milling in and out of the building. Children were whining as parents tugged, dragged or carried them to cars. Couples were strolling along hand in hand while others pored eagerly through guide books. He saw a lot of skin broiled Maine-lobster-red by the sun.

He glanced at his own forearms and was surprised to see that they were tanned. Things were changing, he realized. He was getting a tan. He had no schedule to keep, no itinerary to follow. He was involved in a mystery, and with an incredibly sexy woman.

"Well…" Lilah adjusted the strap of her purse on her arm. "You're looking very smug."

He looked up at her and smiled. "Am I?"

"As a cat with feathers in his mouth. Want to let me in on it?"

"Okay. Come here." He rose, gave her one firm yank and closed his mouth over hers. All of his new and amazed feelings poured into the kiss. If he took the kiss deeper than expected, it only added to the dawning pleasure of discovery. If kissing her made the people walking around them disappear, it only accented the newness. Starting fresh.

It was happiness rather than lust she felt from him. It confused her. Or perhaps it was the way his lips slid over hers that dimmed coherent thought. She didn't resist. The reason for her earlier irritation was already forgotten. All she knew now was that it felt wonderful, somehow perfect, to be standing with him on the sunny patio, feeling his heart thud against hers.

As his mouth slipped from hers, she let out a long, pleased sigh, opening her eyes slowly. He was grinning at her, and the delighted expression on his face had her smiling back. Because she wasn't sure what to do with the tender feelings he tugged from her, she patted his cheek.

"Not that I'm complaining," she began, "but what was that for?"

"I just felt like it."

"An excellent first step."

Laughing, he swung an arm around her shoulder as they started toward the parking lot. "You've got the sexiest mouth I've ever tasted."

He didn't see the cloud come into her eyes. If he had, she couldn't have explained it. It always came down to sex, she supposed and made an effort to shrug the vague disappointment away. Men usually saw her just that way, and there was no reason to let it start bothering her now, particularly when she'd enjoyed the moment as much as he.

"Glad I could oblige," she said lightly. "Why don't you drive?"

"All right, but first I've got something to show you." After settling into the driver's seat, he picked up a manilla envelope. "I went through a lot of books in the library. There are several mentions of your family in histories and biographies. There was one in particular I thought would interest you."

"Hmm." She was already stretched out and thinking of a nap.

"I made a copy of it. It's a picture of Bianca."

"A picture?" She straightened again. "Really? Fergus destroyed all her pictures after she died, so I've never seen her."

"Yes, you have." He drew the copy out and handed it to her. "Every time you look in the mirror."

She said nothing, but with her eyes focused on the grainy copy she lifted a hand to her own face. The same jaw, the same mouth, nose, eyes. Was this why she felt the bond so strongly? she wondered, and felt tears burn her throat.

"She was beautiful," Max said quietly.

"So young." The words came out as a sigh. "Younger than I when she died. She'd already fallen in love when this was taken. You can see it, in her eyes."

"She's wearing the emeralds."

"Yes, I know." As he had, she traced a fingertip over them. "How difficult it must have been for her, tied to one man, loving another. And the necklace—a symbol of one man's hold on her, and a reminder of her children."

"Is that how you see it, a symbol?"

"Yes. I think her feelings for it, about it, were terribly strong. Otherwise, she wouldn't have hidden it." She slipped the paper back into the envelope. "A good day's work, Professor."

"It's just a beginning."

As she looked at him, she linked her fingers with his. "I like beginnings. Everything that follows has such possibilities. We'll go home and show this to everyone, after we make a couple of stops."

"Stops?"

"It's time for another beginning. You need some new clothes."

He hated shopping. He told her, repeatedly and firmly, but she blithely ignored him and strolled from shop to shop. He held his ground on a fluorescent T-shirt, but lost it again over one depicting a lobster dressed like a maître d'.

She wasn't intimidated by clerks, but sailed through the process of selection and purchase with a languid air of pure relaxation. Most of the merchants called her by name, and during the chats that accompanied the buying and selling, she would casually ask about a man fitting Caufield's description.

"Are we finished yet?" There was a plea in his voice that made her chuckle as they stepped out onto the sidewalk again. It was teeming with people in bright summer clothes.

"Not quite." She turned to study him. Harassed, definitely. Adorable, absolutely. His arms were full of bags and his hair was falling into his eyes. Lilah brushed it back. "How are you fixed for underwear?"

"Well, I…"

"Come on, there's a shop right down here that has great stuff. Tiger prints, obscene sayings, little red hearts."

"No." He stopped dead. "Not on your life."

It was a struggle, but she kept her composure. "You're right. Completely unsuitable. We'll just stick with those nice white briefs that come three to a package."

"For a woman with no brothers, you sure know a lot about men's underwear." He shifted the bags, and as an afterthought, shoved half of them into her arms. "But I think I can handle this one on my own."

"Okay. I'll window-shop."

She was easily diverted by a window filled with crystals of different sizes and shapes. They dangled from wire, shooting colored light behind the glass. Beneath them was a display of handmade jewelry. She was on the point of stepping inside to wrangle over a pair of earrings when someone bumped her from behind.

"Sorry." The apology was terse. Lilah glanced up at a burly man with a weathered face and graying hair. He looked a great deal more irritated than the slight bump warranted, and something about the pale eyes had her taking a step back. Still, she shrugged and smiled.

"It's all right."

Frowning after him a moment, she started to turn back into the shop. She spotted Max a few feet away, staring in shock. Then he was moving fast, and the expression on his face had her catching her breath.

"Max—"

With one hard shove, he had her in the shop. "What

did he say to you?" he demanded with an edge to his voice that had her eyes widening. "Did he touch you? If the bastard put his hands on you—"

"Hold on." Since they had most of the people in the shop staring, Lilah kept her voice low. "Calm down, Max. I don't know what you're talking about."

There was a violence trembling through his blood he'd never experienced before. The echo of it in his eyes had several tourists edging back out the door. "I saw him standing next to you."

"That man?" Baffled, she glanced out the window, but he had long since moved on. "He just bumped into me. The sidewalks are crowded in the summer."

"He didn't say anything to you?" He didn't even realize that his hands had firmed into fists and that the fists were ready to do damage. "He didn't hurt you?"

"No, of course not. Come on, let's go sit down." Her tone was soothing now as she nudged him out. But instead of taking one of the benches that lined the street, Max kept Lilah behind him and searched the crowd. "If I'd known buying underwear would put you in such a state, Max, I wouldn't have brought it up."

There was fury in his eyes when he whirled around. "It was Hawkins," he said grimly. "They're still here."

Chapter 5

She didn't know what to make of him. Alone, with the lamplight glowing gold, Lilah sat in the tower room, watching night fall gently over water and rock. And thought of Max. He wasn't nearly as simple a man as she had believed at first—and as she was certain he believed of himself.

One moment he was shy and sweet and easily intimidated. The next he was as fierce as a Viking, the mild blue eyes electric, the poet's mouth grim. The metamorphosis was as fascinating as it was baffling, and left Lilah off balance. It wasn't a sensation she cared for.

After he had seen the man he called Hawkins, Max had all but dragged her to the car—muttering under his breath all the way—bundled her inside, then had driven off. Her idea about following Hawkins had been briskly and violently vetoed. Back at The Towers, he'd called the police, relating the information as calmly as he would list assigned reading for a student. Then, in a typical male move had powwowed with Sloan and Trent.

The authorities had not yet located Caufield's boat, nor, from Max's descriptions, had they identified either Caufield or Hawkins.

It was much too complicated, Lilah decided. Thieves and aliases and international police. She preferred the simple. Not the humdrum, she thought, but the simple. Life had been anything but since the press had begun their love affair with the Calhoun emeralds, and things had become only more convoluted since Max had washed up on the beach.

But she was glad he had. She wasn't sure why. Certainly she'd never considered the shy and brainy sort her type. It was true that she enjoyed men in general, simply for being men. An offshoot, she supposed, from living in a female household most of her life. But when she dated, she most often looked for fun and easy companionship. Someone to dance with or to laugh with over a meal. She'd always hoped she would fall in love with one of those carefree, uncomplicated men and start a carefree, uncomplicated life.

Sober college professors with outdated notions of chivalry and serious minds hardly met the qualifications.

Yet he was so sweet, she thought with a little smile. And when he kissed her, there was nothing sober or cerebral about it.

With a little sigh, she wondered just what she should do about Dr. Maxwell Quartermain.

"Hey." C.C. poked her head through the doorway. "I thought I'd find you in here."

"Then I must be becoming too predictable." Happy to have company, Lilah curled up her legs to make room on the window seat. "What's going on with you, Mrs. St. James?"

"Nearly finished the reconditioning on that Mustang." She sighed as she sat. "Lord, what a honey. I had an electrical system that gave me fits today, and two tune-ups." An unaccustomed fatigue was dragging at her, making her close her eyes and think about an early night. "Then all this excitement at home. Imagine, you bumping into one of the characters the cops are after."

"The curse and blessing of small towns."

"I cruised around a little before I came home." C.C. rolled her tired shoulders. "Down to Hulls Cove and back."

"You shouldn't be poking around alone."

"Just looking." C.C. shrugged. "Anyway, I didn't see anything. Our fearless men are out right now on search and destroy."

A quick bolt of alarm shot into Lilah. "Max went with them?"

On a yawn, C.C. opened her eyes. "Sure. Suddenly, they're the Three Musketeers. Is there anything more annoying than machismo?"

"Tooth decay," Lilah said absently, but there were nerves bumping along in her system she didn't care for. "I thought Max was going to stick to the research books."

"Well, he's one of the boys now." She patted Lilah's ankle. "Don't worry, honey. They can handle themselves."

"For heaven's sake, he's a history professor. What if they actually run into trouble?"

"He already has," C.C. reminded her. "He's tougher than he looks."

"What makes you think so?" Unreasonably distressed, Lilah got up to pace. The unaccustomed show of energy had C.C. lifting a brow.

"The man jumped out of a boat in the middle of a storm and almost made it to shore, despite the fact he'd been grazed by a bullet. The next day, he was on his feet again—looking like hell, but on his feet. There's a stubborn streak behind those quiet eyes. I like him."

Restless, Lilah moved her shoulders. "Who doesn't? He's a likable man."

"Well, with everything that Amanda found out—the wonder boy stuff—you'd expect him to be conceited, or stiff-necked. But he's not. He's sweet. Aunt Coco's ready to adopt him."

"He is sweet," Lilah agreed as she sat again. "And I don't want him to get hurt because of some misguided sense of gratitude."

C.C. leaned forward to look into her sister's eyes. There was more than casual concern in them, she thought, and smiled to herself. "Lilah, I know you're the mystic in the family, but I'm getting definite vibes. Are you getting serious about Max?"

"Serious?" The word had Lilah's nerves stretching. "Of course not. I'm fond of him, and I feel a certain responsibility toward him." *And when he kisses me, I go directly to meltdown.* She frowned a little. "I enjoy him," she slowly added.

"He's very attractive."

"You're a married woman now, kiddo."

"But not blind. There's something appealing about all that intelligence, those romantic and scholarly looks." She waited a beat. "Don't you think?"

Lilah sat back. Her lips were curved again to match the amusement in her eyes. "Are you apprenticing with Aunt Coco as matchmaker?"

"Just checking. I guess I'm so happy I want everyone I love to feel the same way."

"I am happy." She took a long, limbering stretch. "I'm too lazy not to be."

"Speaking of lazy, I feel like I could sleep for a week. Since Trent's out playing Hardy Boys, I think I'll go to bed." C.C. started to rise when a wave of dizziness had her plopping down again. Lilah was up like a shot and bending over her.

"Hey. Hey, honey. Are you all right?"

"Got up too fast, that's all." As the light grayed, she lifted a hand to her spinning head. "I feel a little…"

Moving fast, Lilah shoved C.C.'s head between her knees. "Just breathe slow. Take it easy."

"This is stupid." But she did as she was told until the faintness passed. "I'm just overtired. Maybe I'm coming down with something, damn it."

"Mmm." Because she suspected just what C.C. had come down with, Lilah's lips curved. "Tired? Have you been feeling sick?"

"Not really." Steadier, C.C. straightened. "Out of sorts, I guess. A little queasy the past couple of mornings, that's all."

"Honey." With a laugh, Lilah tapped her knuckles on her sister's head. "Wake up and smell the baby powder."

"Huh?"

"Hasn't it occurred to you that you could be pregnant?"

"Pregnant?" The dark green eyes widened like saucers. "Pregnant? Me? But we've only been married a little over a month."

Lilah laughed again and cupped C.C.'s face in her hands. "You haven't spent all that time playing pinochle, have you?"

C.C.'s mouth opened and closed before she managed to form a word. "It just never crossed my mind.... A baby." Her eyes changed, misting, softening. "Oh, Lilah."

"Could be Trenton St. James IV."

"A baby," C.C. repeated, and laid a hand over her stomach in a gesture that was filled with awe and protectiveness. "Do you really think?"

"I really think." She slid back on the seat to hug C.C. tight. "I don't have to ask you how you feel about it. It's all over your face."

"Don't say anything to anyone yet. I want to be sure." Laughing, she squeezed Lilah against her. "Suddenly I don't feel tired at all. I'll call the doctor first thing in the morning. Or maybe I should pick up one of those tests from the drugstore. I could do both."

Lilah let her ramble. Long after C.C. had gone, the echoes of her joy remained in the room.

It was what the tower needed, Lilah thought. That jolt of pure happiness. She stayed where she was, content now, watching the moon rise. Half-full, bone white, it hung in the sky and had her dreaming.

What would it be like, being with someone, smugly married, having a child growing inside you? Making a life with someone who would know you so well. Know every part of you and love you despite the flaws. Maybe because of them.

Lovely, she thought. It would be simply lovely. And if she had yet to find that for herself, she had only to look at C.C. and Amanda to know it could happen.

With some regret she switched off the light and started downstairs to her room. The house was quiet now. She imagined it must be at least midnight, and everyone had gone to bed. A wise choice, she mused, but she couldn't seem to shake the restlessness.

To comfort herself, she indulged in a long, fragrant bath before slipping into her favorite robe. Those were the little things that always pleased her—hot, scented water, cool, thin silk. Still unsettled, she walked out onto the terrace to see if the night air would lull her.

It was much too romantic, she thought. The glitter of moonlight silvering the trees, the quiet whoosh of water on rock, the scents from the garden. As she stood, a bird, as restless as she, began a lonely night song. It made her long for something. For someone. A touch, a whisper in the dark. An arm around her shoulders.

A mate.

Not just the physical, but the emotional, the spiritual partner. She had had men desire her and knew that could never be enough. There had to be someone who could look beyond the color of her hair or the shape of her face and into her heart.

Perhaps she was asking for too much, Lilah thought with a sigh. But wasn't that better than asking for too little? In the meantime she would have to concentrate on other things and leave her heart in fate's capricious hands.

She had started to turn back into her room when a

movement caught her eye. In the swaying moonlight she saw two shadows bent low, moving with silent swiftness across the lawn. Before she could do more than register the shapes, they had melted into the garden.

She didn't even think about it. A home was meant to be defended. Her bare feet were noiseless on the stone steps as she walked down them. Whoever was trespassing on Calhoun territory was about to get the scare of their lives.

Like a ghost, she slipped into the garden, the robe floating around her. There were voices, muffled and excited, a faint yellow beam of a flashlight. There was a laugh, quickly smothered, then the sound of a shovel striking earth.

That more than anything brought the Calhoun temper bubbling to the surface. With the courage of the righteous, she strode forward.

"What the hell do you think you're doing?"

The shovel clanged on stone as it was dropped. The flashlight went spiraling into the azaleas. Two teenagers, wound up with the treasure hunt, looked around wildly for the source of the voice. They saw the pale figure of a woman draped in white. Summing up her quarry, Lilah lifted her arms for effect, knowing the full sleeves would billow nicely.

"I am guardian of the emeralds." She nearly chuckled, pleased with the way her voice floated. "Do you dare to face the curse of the Calhouns? Hideous death is certain for any who defile this ground. Run, if you value your lives."

They didn't have to be told twice. The treasure map they had paid ten bucks for fluttered to the ground as they raced back down the path, shoving each other and tripping over their own scrambling feet. Chuckling to herself, Lilah picked up the map.

She'd seen its like before. Some enterprising soul was making them up and selling them to gullible tourists. After shoving it into her pocket, she decided to give her two uninvited guests a little extra boost. She dashed after them. Ready to send up a ghostly wail, she burst out of the garden.

The wail turned into a grunt as she rammed into another shadow. Stopped in a dead run, Max overbalanced, swore, then went tumbling to the ground on top of her.

"What the hell are you doing?"

"It's me," she managed, then sucked in a breath. "What the hell are you doing?"

"I saw someone. Stay here."

"No." She grabbed his arms and held on. "It was just a couple of kids with a treasure map. I scared them off."

"You—" Furious, he braced on an elbow. Despite the dark, the anger shone clearly in his eyes. "Are you out of your mind?" he demanded. "You came out here, alone, to face down two intruders?"

"Two terrified teenagers with a treasure map," she corrected. Her chin lifted. "It's my house."

"I don't give a damn whose house it is. It might have been Caufield and Hawkins. It might have been anyone. No one with an ounce of sense follows potential robbers into a dark garden alone, in the middle of the night."

She had her breath back and studied him blandly. "What were you doing?"

"I was going after them," he began, then caught her expression. "That's different."

"Why? Because I'm a woman?"

"No. Well, yes."

"That's stupid, untrue and sexist."

"That's sensible, factual and sexist." They'd been arguing in furious whispers. Now he sighed. "Lilah, you might have been hurt."

"The only one who hurt me was you, with that flying tackle."

"I didn't tackle you," he muttered. "I was watching them and didn't see you. And I certainly didn't expect to find you out here sneaking around in the dark."

"I wasn't sneaking." She blew hair out of her eyes. "I was playing ghost, and very effectively."

"Playing ghost." He shut his eyes. "Now I know you're out of your mind."

"It worked," she reminded him.

"That's beside the point."

"It's precisely the point, the other being that you knocked me down before I could finish the job."

"I've already apologized."

"No, you haven't."

"All right. I'm sorry if I…" He started to push himself off her and made the mistake of glancing down. Her robe had come loose during the fall and lay open to the waist. Like alabaster, her breasts glowed in the moonlight. "Oh, Lord," he managed to say through suddenly dry lips.

She'd lost her breath again. Lying still, she watched his eyes change. Irritation to shock, shock to wonder, wonder to a deep and dark desire. As his gaze skimmed up, came back to hers, every muscle in her body melted like hot wax.

No one had ever looked at her just that way. There was such intensity in his eyes, the same focused con-

centration they had held when he'd struggled to block
out pain. They roamed to her mouth, lingering there
until her lips trembled apart on his name.

It was like moving into a dream, he thought as he
lowered himself onto her again. Everything was just
one click out of focus, soft and fuzzy. His hands were
in her hair, lost in it. Beneath his, her lips were warm,
beautifully warm. Her arms came around him as if they
had been waiting. He heard her sigh, long and deep.

His mouth was so gentle on hers, as if he were afraid
she might vanish if he dared too much too soon. Yet
she could feel the tension in the way he held himself,
the way his hands fisted in her hair, the way his breath
shuddered out as he brushed his lips over hers.

Her limbs grew heavy, her head light. Though she
wanted to keep her eyes open, as his were, they drifted
closed. The most pleasant of aches coursed through her
as he nibbled delicately at her parted lips. Her murmur
mixed with his, indecipherable.

The grass whispered as she shifted beneath him. Its
cool, fresh fragrance seemed perfectly suited to him.
As his fingers slid softly over her breast, she heard her
own quiet moan of acceptance.

She was unbelievably perfect, he thought dizzily.
Like some fantasy conjured on a lonely night. Long
slender limbs, silky skin, an avid and generous mouth.
The sheer physical pleasure of her was like a drug, and
he was already addicted.

Murmuring her name, he skimmed his lips to her
throat. There her pulse beat like thunder, heating her
skin so that her scent tangled with each breath he took.
Tasting her was like dining on sin. Touching her was

paradise. He brought his lips back to hers to lose himself on that glorious edge between heaven and hell.

She could almost feel herself floating an inch above the cool grass. Her body felt free as air, soft as water. When his mouth met hers again, she let herself drift into the new kiss. Then it happened.

It was not the sweet click of a door opening that she had been hoping for. It was a rushing roar, like a gust of wind sweeping through her body. Behind it, speeding in its wake, was a pain, sharp, sweet and stunning. She stiffened against it, her cry of protest muffled against his lips.

If she had slapped him, his passion wouldn't have cooled more quickly. He jerked back to see her staring at him, her eyes wide and filled with fear and confusion. Appalled by his behavior, he scrambled to his knees. He was trembling, he realized. So was she. Small wonder. He had acted like a maniac, knocking her down, pawing her.

Lord help him, he wanted to do it again.

"Lilah…" His voice was a husky rasp, and he struggled to clear it. She didn't move a muscle. Her eyes never left his. He wanted to stroke her cheek, to gather her close and hold her, but was afraid to touch her again. "I'm sorry. Very sorry. You looked so beautiful. I guess I lost my head."

She waited for a moment, for the balance and ease that was so much a part of her. But it didn't come. "Is that it?"

"I…" What did she want him to say? he wondered. He felt like a monster already. "You're an incredibly desirable woman," he said carefully. "But that's no excuse for what happened just now."

What had happened? She was afraid she had fallen in love with him, and if she had, love hurt. She didn't like it one damn bit. "You want me, physically."

He cleared his throat. *Want* wasn't the word. *Craved* was closer, but still fell pitifully short of the mark. As gently as he would for a child, he brought her robe together again. "Any man would," he said, nerves straining.

Any man, she thought and closed her eyes on the slash of disappointment. She hadn't been waiting for any man, but for one man. "It's all right, Max." Her voice was a shade overbright as she sat up. "No harm done. It's just a matter of us finding the other physically attractive. Happens all the time."

"Yes, but—" Not to him, he thought. Not like this. He frowned down at a blade of grass. It was easier for her, he supposed. She was so open, so uninhibited. There had probably been dozens of men in her life. Dozens, he thought on a jolt of fury that had him tearing the blade in two. "What do you suggest we do about it?"

"Do about it?" Her smile was strained, but he wasn't even looking at her. "Why don't we just see if it passes. Like the flu."

He looked at her then, with something dangerous edging his eyes. "It won't. Not for me. I want you. A woman like you would know just how badly I want you."

The words brought both a thrill and an ache. "A woman like me," she repeated softly. "Yes, that's the crux of it, isn't it, Professor?"

"The crux of what?" he began, but she was already on her feet.

"A woman who enjoys men, and who's very generous with them."

"I didn't mean—"

"One who'll wrestle half-naked on the grass. A little bohemian for you, Dr. Quartermain, but you're not above experimenting a little bit here and there—with a woman like me."

"Lilah, for God's sake—" He, too, was on his feet, baffled.

"I wouldn't apologize again if I were you. There's certainly no need." Hurt beyond measure, she tossed back her hair. "Not when it concerns a woman like me. After all, you've got me pegged, don't you?"

Good Lord, were those tears in her eyes? He gestured helplessly. "I haven't got a clue."

"Right again. All you understand about this is your own wants." She swallowed the tears. "Well, Professor, I'll take them under consideration and let you know."

Completely lost, he watched her gather the skirts of her robe and dart up the stairs. Moments later her terrace doors closed with an audible click.

She didn't cry. Lilah reminded herself it was an exhausting experience that usually left her with a miserable headache. She couldn't think of a single man who was worth the trouble. Instead, she dragged open the drawer of her nightstand and pulled out her emergency bar of chocolate.

After plopping down onto the bed, she took a healthy bite and stared at the ceiling.

Sexy. Beautiful. Desirable. Big damn deal, she thought and bit off another hunk. For all his celebrated brains, Maxwell Quartermain was as big a jerk as any other man. All he saw was a pretty package, and once he'd unwrapped it, that would be that. He wouldn't see any substance, any of the softer needs.

Oh, he was more polite than most. A gentleman to the last, she thought in disgust. She hadn't had to untangle herself. God knew he'd been in a hurry to do that for himself.

Lost his head. At least he was honest, she thought, and brushed impatiently at a tear that sneaked past her guard.

She knew the kind of image she projected. It rarely bothered her what people thought of her. She understood herself, was comfortable with Lilah Maeve Calhoun. There certainly was no shame in the fact that she enjoyed men. Though she hadn't enjoyed them to the extent that others, including, she supposed, her family might think.

Uninhibited? Perhaps, but that wasn't synonymous with promiscuity. Did she flirt? Yes, it came naturally to her, but it wasn't done with malice or guile.

If a man flirted with women he was suave. If a woman flirted, she was a tease. Well, as far as she was concerned the game between the sexes was a two-way street, and she enjoyed playing. And as for the good professor...

She curled up into a tight, defensive ball. Oh, God, he'd hurt her. All that stuttering, apologizing, explaining. And all the time he looked so appalled.

A woman like you. The phrase played back in her head.

Couldn't he see what he'd done to her with that careful tenderness? Hadn't he been able to feel how deeply he'd affected her? All she had wanted was for him to touch her again, to smile in that sweet, shy way of his and tell her that he cared. About who she was, what she was, how she felt inside. She'd wanted comfort and reassurance, and he'd given her excuses. She had looked up at him, with the stab of love still streaking through her, the terror of it still trembling, and he'd jerked back as if she'd clipped him on the jaw.

She wished she had. If this was love, she didn't want her share after all.

Because it was quiet, or perhaps because her ears were tuned for him, she heard Max come up the steps, sensed him hesitate near her doors. She stopped breathing, though her heart picked up a quick beat. Would he come in now, push those doors open and come to her, tell her what she wanted so badly to hear? She could almost see his hand reach for the knob. Then she heard his footsteps again as he moved on down the terrace to his own room.

Her breath came out in a sigh. It wouldn't fit his principles to enter her bedroom uninvited. Outside, on the grass, he'd been following his instincts rather than his intellect, she admitted. No one was more in favor of that than Lilah. For him, it had been the moment, the moon, the mood. It was difficult to blame him, certainly impossible to expect him to feel as she felt. Want as she wanted.

She sincerely hoped he didn't sleep a wink.

She sniffled, swallowed chocolate, then began to think. Only two months before, C.C. had come to her, hurt and infuriated because Trent had kissed her, then apologized for it.

Pursing her lips, Lilah rolled onto her back again. Maybe it was typical male stupidity. It was difficult to fault the breed for something they were born with. If

Trent had apologized because he'd cared about her sister, then it could follow that Max had played the same cards.

It was an interesting theory, and one that shouldn't be too difficult to prove. Or disprove, she thought with a sigh. Either way, it was probably best to know before she got in any deeper. All she needed was a plan.

Lilah decided to do what she did best, and slept on it.

Chapter 6

It wasn't difficult in a house the size of The Towers to avoid someone for a day or two. Max noted that Lilah had effortlessly stayed out of his way for that amount of time. He couldn't blame her, not after how badly he had botched things.

Still, it irked him that she wouldn't accept a simple and sincere apology. Instead she'd turned it into... damned if he knew what she'd turned it into. The only thing he was sure of was that she'd twisted his words, and their meaning, then had stalked off in a snit.

And he missed her like crazy.

He kept busy enough, buried in his research books, poring over the old family papers that Amanda had meticulously filed according to date and content. He found what he considered the last public sighting of the necklace in a newspaper feature covering a dinner

dance in Bar Harbor, August 10, 1913. Two weeks before Bianca's death.

Though he considered it a long shot, he began a list
of every servant's name he came across who had worked
at The Towers the summer of 1913. Some of them could
conceivably be alive. Tracking them or their families
down would be difficult but not impossible. He had
interviewed the elderly before on their memories of
their youth. Quite often, those memories were as clear
as crystal.

The idea of talking to someone who had known Bianca, who had seen her—and the necklace—excited
him. A servant would remember The Towers as it had
been, would have knowledge of their employers' habits. And, he had no doubt, would know their secrets.

Confident in the notion, Max bent over his lists.

"Hard at work, I see."

He glanced up, blinking, to see Lilah in the doorway of the storeroom. She didn't have to be told she'd
dragged him out of the past. The blank, owlish look he
gave her made her want to hug him. Instead she leaned
lazily against the jamb.

"Am I interrupting?"

"Yes—no." Damn it, his mouth was watering. "I was
just, ah, making a list."

"I have a sister with the same problem." She was
wearing a full-skirted sundress in sheer white cotton,
her gypsy hair like cables of flames against it. Long
chunks of malachite swung at her ears when she crossed
the room.

"Amanda." Because the pencil had gone damp in his
hand, he set it aside. "She did a terrific job of catalog-
ing all this information."

"She's a fiend for organization." Casually she rested a hip on the card table he was using. "I like your shirt."

It was the one she'd chosen for him, with the cartoon lobster. "Thanks. I thought you'd be at work."

"It's my day off." She slid off the table to round it and lean over his shoulder. "Do you ever take one?"

Though he knew it was ridiculous, he felt his muscles bunch up. "Take what?"

"A day off." Brushing her hair aside, she turned her face toward his. "To play."

She was doing it deliberately, there could be no doubt. Maybe she enjoyed watching him make a fool out of himself. "I'm busy." He managed to tear his gaze away from her mouth and stared down at the list he was making. He couldn't read a word. "Really busy," he said almost desperately. "I'm trying to note down all the names of the people who worked here the summer Bianca died."

"That's quite an undertaking." She leaned closer, delighted with his reaction to her. It had to be more than lust. A man didn't fight so hard against basic lust. "Do you want some help?"

"No, no, it's a one-man job." And he wanted her to go away before he started to whimper.

"It must have been a terrible time here, after she died. Even worse for Christian, hearing about it, reading about it, and not being able to do anything. I think he loved her very much. Have you ever been in love?"

Once again, she drew his eyes back to hers. She wasn't smiling now. There was no teasing light in her eyes. For some reason he thought it was the most serious question she had ever asked him.

"No."

"Neither have I. What do you think it's like?"

"I don't know."

"But you must have an opinion." She leaned a little closer. "A theory. A thought."

He was all but hypnotized. "It must be like having your own private world. Like a dream, where everything's intensified, a bit off balance and completely yours."

"I like that." He watched her lips curve, could almost taste them. "Would you like to take a walk, Max?"

"A walk?"

"Yes, with me. Along the cliffs."

He wasn't even sure he could stand. "A walk would be good."

Saying nothing, she offered him her hand. When he rose, she led him through the terrace doors.

The wind was up, pushing the clouds across a blue sky. It tore at Lilah's skirts and sent her hair flying. Unconcerned, she strolled into it, her hand lightly clasped in his. They crossed the lawn and left the busy sounds of building behind.

"I'm not much on hiking," she told him, "since I spend most days doing just that, but I like to go to the cliffs. There are very strong, very beautiful memories there."

He thought again of all the men who must have loved her. "Yours?"

"No, Bianca's, I think. And if you don't choose to believe in such things, the view's worth the trip."

He started down the slope beside her. It felt easy, simple, even friendly. "You're not angry with me anymore."

"Angry?" Deliberately she lifted a brow. She had no intention of making things too simple. "About what?"

"The other night. I know I upset you."

"Oh, that."

When she added nothing else, he tried again. "I've been thinking about it."

"Have you?" Her eyes, mysterious with secrets, lifted to his.

"Yes. I realize I probably didn't handle it very well."

"Would you like another chance?"

He stopped dead in his tracks and made her laugh.

"Relax, Max." She gave him a friendly kiss on the cheek. "Just give it some thought. Look, the mountain cranberry's blooming." She bent to touch a spray of pink bell-shaped flowers that clung to the rocks. Touch, but not pick, he noted. "It's a wonderful time for wildflowers up here." Straightening, she tossed her hair back. "See those?"

"The weeds?"

"Oh, and I thought you were a poet." With a shake of her head, she had her hand tucked back in his. "Lesson number one," she began.

As they walked, she pointed out tiny clumps of flowers that pushed out of crevices or thrived in the thin, rocky soil. She showed him how to recognize the wild blueberry that would be ripe and ready the following month. There was the flutter of butterfly wings and the drone of bees deep in the grass. With her, the common became exotic.

She snipped off a thin leaf, crushing it to release a pungent fragrance that reminded him of her skin.

He stood with her on a precipice thrown out over the water. Far below, spray fumed on the rock, beating them smooth in a timeless war. She helped him spot the nests, worked cleverly onto narrow ridges and clinging tenaciously to faults in the rocks.

It was what she did every day for groups of strangers, and for herself. There was a new kind of pleasure in sharing it all with him, showing him something as simple and special as the tiny white sandwort or the wild roses that grew as tall as a man. The air was like wine, freshened by the wind, so that she sat on a huddle of rock to drink it with each breath.

"It's incredible here." He couldn't sit. There was too much to see, too much to feel.

"I know." She was enjoying his pleasure as much as the sun on her face and the wind in her hair. It was in his as well, streaming through the shaggy locks. There was fascination in his eyes, darkening them to indigo as the faint smile curved his lips. The wound on his temple was healing, but she thought it would leave a slight scar that would add something rakish to the intelligent face.

As a thrush began to trill, she circled her knee with her arms. "You look good, Max."

Distracted, he glanced over his shoulder. She was sitting easily on the rocks, as relaxed as she would have been on a cushy sofa. "What?"

"I said you look good. Very good." She laughed as his jaw dropped. "Hasn't anyone ever told you you're attractive?"

What game was she playing now? he wondered, and shrugged uncomfortably. "Not that I remember."

"No star-struck undergraduate, no clever English Lit professor? That's very remiss. I imagine more than one of them tried to catch your eye—and a bit more than that—but you were too buried in books to notice."

His brows drew together. "I haven't been a monk."

"No." She smiled. "I'm already aware of that."

Her words reminded him vividly of what had happened between them two nights before. He had touched her, tasted her, had managed, barely, to pull himself back before taking her right there on the grass. And she had rushed off, he remembered, furious and hurt. Now she was taunting him, all but daring him to repeat the mistake.

"I never know what to expect from you."

"Thank you."

"That wasn't a compliment."

"Even better." Her eyes slanted, half-closed now against the sun. When she spoke, her voice was almost a purr. "But you like predictability, don't you, Professor? Knowing what happens next."

"Probably as much as you like irritating me."

Laughing, she held out a hand. "Sorry, Max, sometimes it's irresistible. Come on, sit down. I promise to behave."

Wary, he sat on the rock beside her. Her skirts fluttered teasingly around her legs. In a gesture he felt was almost maternal, she patted his thigh.

"Want to be pals?" she asked him.

"Pals?"

"Sure." Her eyes danced with amusement. "I like you. The serious mind, the honest soul." He shifted, making her laugh. "The way you shuffle around when you're embarrassed."

"I do not shuffle."

"The authoritative tone when you're annoyed. Now you're supposed to tell me what you like about me."

"I'm thinking."

"I should have added your dry wit."

He had to smile. "You're the most self-possessed person I've ever met." He glanced at her. "And you're kind, without making a fuss about it. You're smart, but you don't make a fuss about that, either. I guess you don't make a fuss about anything."

"Too tiring." But his words had a glow spreading around her heart. "It's safe to say we're friends then?"

"Safe enough."

"That's good." She gave his hand a gentle squeeze. "I think it's important for us to be friends before we're lovers."

He nearly fell off the rock. "Excuse me?"

"We both know we want to make love." When he began to stammer she gave him a patient smile. She'd thought it through very carefully and was sure—well, nearly sure—this was right for both of them. "Relax, it isn't a crime in this state."

"Lilah, I realize I've been...that is, I know I've made advances."

"Advances." Desperately in love, she laid a hand on his cheek. "Oh, Max."

"I'm not proud of my behavior," he said stiffly, and had her hand sliding away. "I don't want..." His tongue tied itself into knots.

The hurt was back, a combination of rejection and defeat she detested. "You don't want to go to bed with me?"

Now his stomach was in knots, as well. "Of course I do. Any man—"

"I'm not talking about any man." They were the poorest two words he could have chosen. It was him, only him she cared about. She needed to hear him say he wanted her, if nothing else. "Damn it, I'm talking about you and me, right here, right now." Temper pushed her off the rock. "I want to know about your feelings. If I wanted to know how any man felt, I'd pick up the phone or drive into the village and ask any man."

Keeping his seat, he considered her. "For someone who does most things slowly, you have a very quick temper."

"Don't use that professorial tone on me."

It was his turn to smile. "I thought you liked it."

"I changed my mind." Because her own attitude confused her, she turned away to look out over the water. It was important to remain calm, she reminded herself. She was always able to remain calm effortlessly. "I know what you think of me," she began.

"I don't see how you can, when I'm far from sure myself." He took a moment to gather his thoughts. "Lilah, you're a beautiful woman—"

She whirled back, eyes electric. "If you tell me that again, I swear, I'll hit you."

"What?" Completely baffled, he threw his hands up and rose. "Why? Good God, you're frustrating."

"That's much better. I don't want to hear that my hair's the color of sunset, or that my eyes are like sea foam. I've heard all that. I don't care about that."

He began to think that being a monk, completely divorced from the mysterious female, had its advantages. "What do you want to hear?"

"I'm not going to tell you what I want to hear. If I do, then what's the point?"

At wit's end, he raked both hands through his hair. "The point is, I don't know what the point is. One minute you're telling me about sandwarts—"

"Sandwort," she said between her teeth.

"Fine. We're talking about flowers and friendship, and the next you're asking me if I want to take you to bed. How am I supposed to react to that?"

Her eyes narrowed. "You tell me."

He went on a mental search for safe ground and found none. "Look, I realize you're used to having men…"

Her narrowed eyes glinted. "Having them what?"

If he was going to sink, Max decided, he might as well go down with a flourish. "Just shut up." He grabbed her arms, dragged her hard against him and crushed his mouth to hers.

She could taste the frustration, the temper, the edgy passion. It seemed that what he was feeling was a reflection of her own emotions. For the first time, she struggled against him, fighting to hold back her response. And for the first time, he ignored the protest and demanded one.

His hand was in her billowing hair, pulling her head back so that he could plunder mindlessly. Her body was arched, straining away from him, but he locked her closer, so close even the wind couldn't slip between them.

This was different, she thought. No man had ever forced her to…feel. She didn't want this ache, these needs, this desperation. Since the last time they had been together she had convinced herself that love could be painless, and simple and comfortable, if only she were clever enough.

But there was pain. No amount of passion or desire could completely coat it.

Furious with both of them, he tore his mouth from hers, but his hands dug into her shoulders. "Is that what you want?" he demanded. "Do you want me to forget every rule, every code of decency? You want to know how I feel? Every time I'm around you I itch to get my hands on you. And when I do I want to drag you off somewhere and make love to you until you forget that there was ever anyone else."

"Then why don't you?"

"Because I care about you, damn it. Enough to want to show you some respect. And too much to want to be just the next man in your bed."

The temper faded from her eyes to be replaced by a vulnerability more poignant than tears. "You wouldn't be." She lifted a hand to his face. "You're a first for me, Max. There's never been anyone else like you." He said nothing, and the doubt in his eyes had her hand slipping to her side again. "You don't believe me."

"I've found it difficult to think clearly since I met you." Abruptly he realized he was still gripping her shoulders, and gentled his hold. "You could say you dazzle me."

She looked down. How close she had come, she realized, to telling him everything that was in her heart. And humiliating herself, embarrassing him. If it was just to be physical between them, then she would be strong enough to accept it. "Then we'll leave it at that for now." She managed a smile. "We've been taking ourselves too seriously anyway." To comfort herself, she gave him a soft, lingering kiss. "Friends?"

He let out a long breath. "Sure."

"Walk back with me, Max." She slipped a hand into his. "I feel like a nap."

An hour later, he sat on the sunny terrace outside of his room, the notebook on his lap forgotten and his mind crowded with thoughts of her.

He didn't come close to understanding her—was certain he couldn't come closer if he had several decades to consider the problem. But he did care, enough to add a good jolt of fear to the rest of the emotions she pulled out of him. What did he, a painfully middle-class college professor, have to offer a gorgeous, exotic and free-spirited woman who exuded sex like other women exuded perfume?

He was so pitifully inept that he was stuttering around her one minute and grabbing her like a Neanderthal the next.

Maybe the best thing for him was to remember that he was more comfortable and certainly more competent with his books than with women.

How could he tell her that he wanted her so badly he could hardly breathe? That he was terrified to act on his needs because, once done, he knew he'd never be free of her? An easy summer romance for her, a life-altering event for him.

He was falling in love with her, which was ridiculous. He couldn't have a place in her life, and hoped he was smart enough to get a grip on his emotions before they carried him too far. In a few weeks, he would go back to his nicely ordered routine. It was what he wanted. It had to be.

And he couldn't survive it if she haunted him.

"Max?" Trent, taking the circular route to the west wing, stopped. "Interrupting?"

"No." Max glanced down at the blank sheet on his lap. "Nothing to interrupt."

"You looked like you were trying to puzzle out a particularly difficult problem. Anything to do with the necklace?"

"No." Max looked up, squinted against the sun. "Women."

"Oh. Good luck." He lifted a brow. "Particularly if it's a Calhoun woman."

"Lilah." Weary, Max rubbed his hands over his face. "The more I think about her, the less I understand."

"A perfect start in a relationship." Because he was feeling smug about his own, Trent took a moment and sat down. "She's a fascinating woman."

"I've decided the word's *unstable.*"

"Beautiful."

"You can't tell her that. She bites your head off." Intrigued, he studied Trent. "Does C.C. threaten to hit you if you tell her she's beautiful?"

"Not so far."

"I thought it might be a family trait." He began to tap his pencil against the pad. "I don't know very much about women."

"Well then, I should tell you all I know." Steepling his fingers, Trent sat back. "They're frustrating, exciting, baffling, wonderful and infuriating."

Max waited a moment. "That's it?"

"Yeah." He glanced up, lifting a hand in salute as Sloan approached.

"Coffee break?" Sloan asked, and finding the idea appealing, took out a cigar.

"A discussion on women," Trent informed him. "You might like to add something to my brief dissertation."

Sloan took his time lighting the cigar. "Stubborn as mules, mean as alley cats and the best damn game in town." He blew out smoke and grinned at Max. "You've got a thing for Lilah, don't you?"

"Well, I—"

"Don't be bashful." Sloan's grin widened as he poked out with the cigar. "You're among friends."

Max wasn't accustomed to discussing women, and certainly not his feelings toward a particular woman. "It would be difficult not to be interested."

Sloan gave a hoot of laughter and winked at Trent. "Son, you'd be dead if you weren't interested. So what's the problem?"

"I don't know what to do about her."

Trent's lips curved. "Sounds familiar. What do you want to do?"

Max slanted Trent a long, slow look that had him chuckling.

"Yeah, there is that." Sloan puffed contentedly on his cigar. "Is she, ah, interested?"

Max cleared his throat. "Well, she's indicated that she—that is, earlier we took a walk up on the cliffs, and she…yeah."

"But?" Trent prompted.

"I'm already in over my head."

"Then you might as well go under for the third time," Sloan told him, and eyed the tip of his cigar. "'Course, if you make the lady unhappy, I'd have to pound your face in." He stuck the cigar back into his mouth. "I'm right fond of her."

Max studied him a moment, then laid his head back and laughed. "There's no way to win here. I think I finally figured that out."

"That's the first step." Trent shifted. "Since we've got a minute here without the ladies I thought you both should know that I finally got a report on this Hawkins character. Jasper Hawkins, smuggler, out of Miami. He's a known associate of our old friend Livingston."

"Well, well," Sloan murmured, crushing out the cigar.

"It begins to look like Livingston and Caufield are one and the same. No sign of the boat yet."

"I've been thinking about that," Max put in. "It might be that they covered their tracks there. Even if they figured I was dead, they'd have to consider that the body would wash up eventually, be identified. Questions would be asked."

"So they ditched the boat," Trent mused.

"Or switched it." Max spread his hands. "They won't back off. I'm sure of that. Caufield, or whoever he is, is obsessed with the necklace. He'd change tactics, but he wouldn't give up."

"Neither will we," Trent murmured. The three men exchanged quiet looks. "If the necklace is in this house, we'll find it. And if that bastard—" He cut himself off as he spotted his wife racing through the doors at the far end of the terrace. "C.C." He was up quickly, starting toward her. "What's wrong? What are you doing home?"

"Nothing. Nothing's wrong." With a laugh, she threw her arms around him. "I love you."

"I love you, too." But he drew away to study her face. Her cheeks were flushed, her eyes brilliant and wet. "Well, it must be good news." He brushed her hair back, checking her brow as he did so. He knew she hadn't been feeling quite herself for the past week.

"The best." She glanced over at Sloan and Max. "Excuse us." Gripping Trent's hand, she pulled him down the terrace toward their room where she could tell him in private. Halfway there, she exploded. "Oh, I can't wait. I know I broke the sound barrier getting home after the test came in."

"What test? You're sick?"

"I'm pregnant." She held her breath, watching his face. Concern to shock, shock to wonder.

"You—pregnant?" He gaped down at her flat stomach, then back into her face. "A baby? We're having a baby?"

Even as she nodded, he was scooping her up, to swing her around and around as she clung to him.

"What the hell's with them?" Sloan wondered.

"Men." Behind Max, Lilah glided from another room. "You're all so dense." With a sigh, she laid a hand on Max's shoulder, watching her sister and Trent through misty eyes. "We're having a baby, you dummies."

"I'll be damned." After a whoop, Sloan headed down to slap Trent on the back and kiss C.C. Hearing the sniffle behind him, Max rose.

"You okay?"

"Sure." She brushed a tear from her lashes, but another fell. "She's my baby sister." She sniffed again, then gave a watery laugh when Max offered her a handkerchief. "Trust you." She dabbed her eyes, blew her nose then sighed. "I'm going to keep it awhile, okay? We're all going to cry buckets when we go down and make the announcement to the rest of the family."

"That's all right." Unsure of himself, he stuck his hands into his pockets.

"Let's go down and see if there's any champagne in the fridge."

"Well, I think I should stay up here. Out of the way."

With a shake of her head, she took his hand firmly in

hers. "Don't be a jerk. Like it or not, Professor, you're part of the family."

He let her lead him away and discovered he did like it. He liked it a lot.

It was the stray puppy that started it. Such a poor, bedraggled little thing. Homeless and helpless. I have no idea how he found his way to the cliffs. Perhaps someone had disposed of an unwanted litter, or the pup had become separated from its mother. But we found him, Christian and I, on one of our golden afternoons. He was hiding in a huddle of rocks, half-starved and whimpering, a tiny black bundle of bones and scruffy black fur.

How patiently Christian lured him out, with a gentle voice and bits of bread and cheese. It touched me to see this sweetness in the man I love. With me, he is always tender, but I have seen the fierce impatience in him, for his art. I have felt the near-violent passion fighting for freedom when he holds me in his arms.

Yet with the puppy, the poor little orphan, he was instinctively kind. Perhaps sensing this, the pup licked his hand and allowed himself to be petted even after the meager meal had been gobbled down.

"A scrapper." Christian laughed as he took his beautiful artist's hands over the dirty fur. "Tough little fellow, aren't you?"

"He needs a bath," I said, but laughed as well when the dusty paws streaked my dress. "And a real meal." Delighted with the attention, the pup licked my face, his whole body trembling with delight.

Of course, I fell in love. He was such a homely little bundle, so trusting, so needy. We played with him, as charmed as children, and had a laughing argument over what to call him.

We named him Fred. He seemed to approve as he yipped and danced and tumbled in the dirt. I will never forget the sweetness of it, the simplicity. My love and I sitting on the ground with a little lost pup, pretending that we would take him home together, care for him together.

In the end, I took Fred with me. Ethan had been asking for a pet, and I felt he was old enough now to be both appreciative and responsible. What a clamor there was when I brought the puppy to the nursery. The children were wide-eyed and excited, each taking turns holding and hugging until I'm sure young Fred felt like a king.

He was bathed and fed with a great deal of ceremony. Stroked and cuddled and tickled until he fell asleep in exhausted euphoria.

Fergus returned. The excitement over Fred had caused me to forget our plans for the evening. I'm sure my husband was right to be annoyed that I was far from ready to go out and dine. The children, unable to contain their delight, raced about, adding to his impatience. Little Ethan, proud as a new father, carried Fred into the parlor.

"What the devil have you got?" Fergus demanded.

"A puppy." Ethan held the wriggling bundle up for his father's inspection. "His name is Fred."

Noting my husband's expression, I took the puppy from my son and began to explain how it had come about. I suppose I'd hoped to appeal to Fergus's softer side, to the love, or at least the pride he felt for Ethan. But he was adamant.

"I'll not have a mongrel in my house. Do you think I have worked all my life to own such things only to have some flea-ridden mutt relieving himself on the carpets, chewing on the draperies?"

"He'll be good." Lip quivering, Colleen hugged my skirts. *"Please, Papa. We'll keep him in the nursery and watch him."*

"You'll do no such thing, young lady." Fergus dismissed Colleen's tears with a glance and turned to Ethan, whose eyes were also brimming. There was a fractional softening in his expression. After all this was his first son, his heir, his immortality. *"A mongrel's no pet for you, my lad. Why any fisherman's son might own a mongrel. If it's a dog you want, we'll look into it when we get back to New York. A fine dog, with a pedigree."*

"I want Fred." With his sweet face crumbling, Ethan looked up at his father. Even little Sean was crying now, though I doubt he understood.

"Out of the question." With his temper obviously straining, Fergus walked to the whiskey decanter and poured. *"It's completely unsuitable. Bianca, have one of the servants dispose of it."*

I know I paled as quickly as the children. Even Fred whimpered, pressing his face to my breast. *"Fergus, you can't be so cruel."*

There was surprise in his eyes, I have no doubt of it. It had never occurred to him that I would speak to him so, and in front of the children. *"Madam, do as I bid."*

"Mama said we could keep him," Colleen began, her youthful temper lifting her voice. *"Mama promised. You can't take him away. Mama won't let you."*

"I run this home. If you don't wish a strapping, mind your tone."

I found myself clutching Colleen's shoulders, as much to suppress her as to protect. He would not lift a hand to my children. Fury at the thought of it blinded me to all else. I know I trembled as I bent to her, to shift Fred back into her arms.

"Go upstairs to Nanny now," I said quietly. "Take your brothers."

"He won't kill Fred." Is there a rage more poignant than that of a child? "I hate him, and I won't let him kill Fred."

"Shh. It will be all right, I promise you. It will be all right. Go up to Nanny."

"A poor job you've done, Bianca," Fergus began when the children had left us. "The girl is old enough to know her place."

"Her place?" The fury had my heart roaring in my head. "What is her place, Fergus? To sit quietly in some corner, her hands folded, her thoughts and feelings unspoken until you have bartered her off into a suitable marriage? They are children. Our children. How could you hurt them so?"

Never in our marriage had I used such a tone with him. Never had I thought to. For a moment I was certain that he would strike me. It was in his eyes. But he seemed to pull himself back, though his fingers were white as marble against the glass he held.

"You question me, Bianca?" His face was very pale with his rage, his eyes very dark. "Do you forget whose house you stand in, whose food you eat, whose clothes you wear?"

"No." Now I felt a new kind of grief, that our marriage should be brought down to only that. "No, I don't forget. I can't forget. I would sooner wear rags

and starve than see you hurt my children so. I will not allow you to take that dog from them and have him destroyed."

"Allow?" He was no longer pale, but crimson with fury. "Now it is you who forget your place, Bianca. Is it any wonder the children openly defy me with such a mother?"

"They want your love, your attention." I was shouting now, beyond restraint. "As I have wanted it. But you love nothing but your money, your position."

How bitterly we argued then. The names he called me I can't repeat. He dashed the glass against the wall, shattering the crystal and his own control. There was a wildness in his eyes when his hands came around my throat. I was afraid for my life, terrified for my children. He shoved me aside so that I fell into a chair. He was breathing quickly as he stared down at me.

Very slowly, with great effort, he composed himself. The violent color faded from his cheeks. "I can see now that I've been too generous with you," he said. "From this point, it will change. Don't think you will continue to go your own way as you choose. We will cancel our plans for this evening. I have business in Boston. While I'm there, I will interview governesses. It's time the children learned respect, and how to appreciate their position. Between you and their nanny, they have become spoiled and willful." He took his watch from his pocket and studied the time. "I will leave tonight and be gone two days. When I return I expect you to have remembered your duties. If the mongrel is still in my house when I return, both you and the children will be punished. Am I clear, Bianca?"

"Yes." My voice shook. "Quite clear."

"*Excellent. In two days then.*"

He walked out of the parlor. I did not move for an hour. I heard the carriage come for him. Heard him instruct the servants. In that time my head had cleared and I knew what I had to do.

Chapter 7

"What the hell good is messing with all these papers?" Hawkins paced the sun-washed room in the rented house. He had never been a patient man and preferred to use his fists or a weapon rather than his brain. His associate, now going by the name of Robert Marshall, sat at an oak desk, carefully leafing through the papers he had stolen from The Towers a month before. He had dyed his hair a nondescript brown and had grown a credible beard and mustache that he tinted the same shade.

If Max Quartermain had seen him, he would have called him Ellis Caufield. Whatever name he chose, whatever disguise he employed, he was a thief whose unscrupulous mind had centered on the Calhoun emeralds.

"I went through a great deal of trouble to get these

papers," Caufield said mildly. "Now that we've lost the professor, I'll have to decipher them myself. It will simply take a little longer."

"This whole job stinks." Hawkins stared out the window at the thick trees that sheltered the house. It was tucked behind a grove of quaking aspen, and the cool leaves quivered continually in the breeze. With the windows of the study thrown open, the scents of pine and sweet peas wafted into the room. He could only smell his own frustration. The bright glint of blue that was the bay didn't lift his mood. He'd spent enough time in prison to feel shut in, however lovely the surroundings.

Cracking his knuckles, he turned away from the view. "We could be stuck in this place for weeks."

"You should learn to appreciate the scenery. And the room." His partner's nervous habit was an annoyance, but he tolerated it. For the time being, he needed Hawkins. After the emeralds had been found…well, that was another matter. "I certainly prefer the house to the boat for the long term. And finding the right accommodations across the bay on this island was difficult and expensive."

"That's another thing." Hawkins pulled out a cigarette. "We're spending a bundle, and all we've got to show for it is a bunch of old papers."

"I assure you, the emeralds will be more than worth any overhead."

"If the bloody things exist."

"They exist." Caufield waved the smoke away in a fussy gesture, but his eyes were intense. "They exist. Before the summer ends, I'm going to hold them in my hands." He lifted them. They were smooth and white and clever. He could all but see the glittery green stones dripping from his palms. "They're going to be mine."

"Ours," Hawkins corrected.

Caufield looked up and smiled. "Ours, of course."

After dinner, Max went back to his lists. He told himself he was being responsible, doing what needed to be done. In truth he'd needed to put some distance between himself and Lilah. He couldn't delude himself into thinking it was only desire he felt for her. That was a basic biological reaction and could be triggered by a face on a television screen, a voice on the radio.

There was nothing so simple or so easily dismissed about his reaction to Lilah.

Every day he was around her his emotions became more tangled, more unsteady and more ungovernable. It had been difficult enough when he had looked at her and wanted her. Now he looked at her and felt his needs meld with dreams that were unrealistic, foolish and impossible.

He'd never given much thought to falling in love, and none at all to marriage and family. His work had always been enough, filling the gaps nicely. He enjoyed women, and if he fell far short of being the Don Juan of Cornell, he had managed a few comfortable and satisfying relationships. Still, he'd never felt a burning need to race to the altar or to start building picket fences.

Bachelorhood had suited him, and when he had thought about the future, he had imagined himself getting crusty, perhaps taking up the pipe and buying a nice dog for companionship.

He was an uncomplicated man who lived a quiet life. At least until recently. Once he had helped the Calhouns locate the emeralds, he would go back to that quiet life. And he would go back alone. While things might never be exactly the same for him, he knew that she would forget the awkward college professor before the winter winds blew across the bay.

And he figured the sooner he finished what he had agreed to do and went away, the easier it would be to go. Gathering his lists, he decided it was time to take the next step toward ending the most incredible summer of his life.

He found Amanda in her room, going over her own lists. These were for her wedding, which would take place in three weeks.

"I'm sorry to interrupt."

"That's okay." Amanda pushed her glasses back up her nose and smiled. "I've got everything under control here except my nerves." She tapped her papers together and set them aside on the slant-top desk. "I was all for eloping, but Aunt Coco would have murdered me."

"I guess weddings take a lot of work."

"Even planning a small family ceremony is like plotting a major offensive. Or being in the circus," she decided, and laughed. "You end up juggling photographers with color schemes and fittings and floral arrangements. But I'm getting good at it. I took care of C.C.'s, I ought to be able to do the same for myself. Except…" Pulling her glasses off, she began to fold and unfold the earpieces. "The whole thing scares the good sense right out of me. So, take my mind off it, Max, and tell me what's on yours."

"I've been working on this. I don't know how complete it is." He set his list in front of her. "The names of all the servants I could find, the ones who worked here the summer Bianca died."

Lips pursed, Amanda slid her glasses back on. She appreciated the precise handwriting and neat columns. "All of these?"

"According to the ledger I went through. I thought we could contact the families, maybe even luck out and find a few still alive."

"Anyone who worked here back then would have to be over the century mark."

"Not necessarily. A lot of the help could have been young. Some of the maids, the garden and kitchen help." When she began to tap her pencil on the desk, he shrugged. "It's a long shot, I know, but—"

"No." Her gaze still on the list, she nodded. "I like it. Even if we can't reach anyone who actually worked here then, they might have told stories to their children. It's a safe bet some of them were local—maybe still are." She looked up at him. "Good thinking, Max."

"I'd like to help you try to pin some of the names down."

"I can use all the help I can get. It's not going to be easy."

"Research is what I'm best at."

"You've got yourself a deal." She held out a hand to shake. "Why don't we split the list in half and start tomorrow? I imagine the cook, the butler, the house-keeper, Bianca's personal maid and the nanny all traveled with them from New York."

"But the day help, and the lower positions were hired locally."

"Exactly. We could divide the list in that way, then cross-reference…" She trailed off as Sloan came in through the terrace doors carrying a bottle of champagne and two glasses.

"Leave you alone for five minutes and you start entertaining other men in your room." He set the wine aside. "And talking about cross-referencing, too. Must be serious."

"We hadn't even gotten to alphabetizing," Amanda told Sloan.

"Looks like I got here just in time." He took the pencil out of her hand before drawing her to her feet. "In another minute you might have been hip deep in correlations."

They certainly didn't need him, Max decided. By the way they were kissing each other, it was apparent they'd forgotten all about him. On his way out, he cast one envious look over his shoulder. They were just smiling at each other, saying nothing. It was obvious that they were two people who knew what they wanted. Each other.

Back in his room, Max decided he would spend the rest of the evening working on notes for his book. Or, if he could gather up the courage, he could sit in front of the old manual typewriter Coco had unearthed for him. He could take that step, that big one, and begin writing the story instead of preparing to write it.

He took one look at the battered Remington and felt his stomach clutch. He wanted to sit down, to lay his fingers on those keys, just as desperately as a man wants to hold a loved and desired woman in his arms. He was as terrified of facing the single blank sheet of paper as he would have been of a firing squad. Maybe more so.

He just needed to prepare, Max told himself. His reference books needed to be positioned better. His notes had to be more easily accessible. The light had to be adjusted.

He thought of dozens of minute details to be perfected before he could begin. Once he had accomplished that, had tried and failed to think of more, he sat.

Here he was, he realized, about to begin something he'd dreamed of doing his entire life. All he had to do was write the first sentence, and he would be committed.

His fingers curled into fists on the keys.

Why did he think he could write a book? A thesis, a lecture, yes. That's what he was trained to do. But a book, God, a novel wasn't something anyone could be taught to do. It took imagination and wit and a sense of drama. Daydreaming a story and articulating it on paper were two entirely different things.

Wasn't it foolish to begin something that was bound to lead to failure? As long as he was preparing to write the book, there was no risk and no disappointment. He could go on preparing for years without any sense of shame. If he started it, really started it, there would be no more hiding behind notes and research books. When he failed, he wouldn't even have the dream.

Wound tight, he ran his fingers over the keys while his mind jumped with dozens of excuses to postpone the moment. When the first sentence streaked from his brain to his fingers and appeared on the blank sheet of paper, he let out a long, unsteady breath.

Three hours later, he had ten full sheets. The story that had swum through his head for so long was taking shape with words. His words. He knew it was probably dreadful, but it didn't seem to matter. He was writing, actually writing. The process of it fascinated and exhilarated. The sound of it, the clatter and thud of the keys, delighted him.

He'd stripped off his shirt and shoes and sat bent over, his brows together, his eyes slightly unfocused. His fingers would race over the keys then stop while he strained to find the way to take what was in his head and put it on paper.

That was how Lilah found him. He'd left his terrace doors open for the breeze, though he'd long since stopped noticing it. The room was dark but for the slant of light from the lamp on the desk. She stood watching him, aroused by his total concentration, charmed by the way his hair fell into his eyes.

Was it any wonder she had come to him? she thought. She was so completely in love with him, how could she stay away? It couldn't be wrong to want to have a night with him, to show him that love in a way he might understand and accept. She needed to belong to him, to forge a bond that would matter to both of them.

Not sex, but intimacy. It had begun the moment he had lain half-drowned on the shingle and lifted a hand to her face. There was a connection she couldn't escape. And as she had risen from her own bed to come to his, one that she no longer wanted to escape.

Her instinct had led her to his room tonight as surely as it had led her to the beach during the storm.

The decision was hers, she knew. However badly he wanted her, he wouldn't take what wasn't offered. And he would hesitate to take even that because of his rules and his codes. Perhaps if he'd loved her... But she couldn't let herself think of that. In time, he would love her. Her own feelings were too deep and too strong not to find their match.

So she would take the first step. Seduction.

His concentration was so intense that a shout wouldn't have broken it. But her scent, whispering across the room on the night breeze, shattered it. Desire pumped into his blood before he glanced up and saw her in the doorway. The white robe fluttered around her. Caught in the fanning air, her hair danced over her shoulders. Behind her the sky was a black canvas, and she had— illusion to reality—stepped out of it. She smiled and his fingers went limp on the keys.

"Lilah."

"I had a dream." It was true, and speaking the truth helped calm her nerves. "About you and me. There was moonlight. I could almost feel the light on my skin until you touched me." She stepped inside, the movement causing the silk to make a faint shushing sound, like water rippling over water. "Then I didn't feel anything but you. There were flowers, the fragrance very light, very sweet. And a nightingale, that long liquid call for a mate. It was a lovely dream, Max." She stopped beside his desk. "Then I woke up, alone."

He was certain the ball of tension in his stomach would rip free any moment and leave him helpless. She was more beautiful than any fantasy, her hair like wildfire across her shoulders, her graceful body silhouetted enticingly beneath the thin, shifting silk.

"It's late." He tried to clear the huskiness from his throat. "You shouldn't be here."

"Why?"

"Because…it's—"

"Improper?" she suggested. "Reckless?" She brushed the hair from his brow. "Dangerous?"

Max lurched to his feet to grasp the back of the chair. "Yes, all of that."

There were age-old women's secrets in her eyes. "But I feel reckless, Max. Don't you?"

Desperate was the word. Desperate for just one touch. His fingers whitened on the chair back. "There's a matter of respect."

Her smile was suddenly very warm and very sweet. "I respect you, Max."

"No, I mean..." She looked so lovely when she smiled that way, so young, so fragile. "We decided to be friends."

"We are." With her eyes on his, she lifted her hand to smooth back her hair. Her rings glittered in the lamplight.

"And this is—"

"Something we both want," she finished. When she stepped toward him, he jerked back. The chair tumbled over. Her laughter wasn't mocking, but warm and delighted. "Do I make you nervous, Max?"

"That's a mild word for it." He could barely drag air through his dry throat. At his sides his hands were fisted, twins of the fists in the pit of his stomach. "Lilah, I don't want to ruin what we have together. Lord knows I don't want you to break my heart."

She smiled, feeling a surge of hope through her own nerves. "Could I?"

"You know you could. You've probably lost track of the hearts you've broken."

There it was again, she thought as disappointment shuddered through her. He still saw her, would likely always see her, as the careless siren who lured men, then discarded them. He didn't understand that it was her heart on the line, had been her heart on the line all along. She wouldn't let it stop her—couldn't. Tonight, being with him tonight, was meant. She felt it too strongly to be wrong.

"Tell me, Professor, do you ever dream of me?" She stepped toward him; he backed up. Now they stood in the shadows beyond the lamplight. "Do you ever lie in the dark and wonder what it would be like?"

He was losing ground fast. His mind was so full of her there wasn't room for anything but need. "You know I do."

Another step and they were caught in a slash of moonlight as white as her robe, and as seductive. "And when you dream of it, where are we?"

"It doesn't seem to matter where." He had to touch her, couldn't resist, even if it was only to brush his fingertips over her hair. "We're alone."

"We're alone now." She slid her hands over his shoulders to link them behind his neck. "Kiss me, Max. The way you did the first time, when we were sitting on the grass in the sunlight."

His fingers were in her hair, taut as wires. "It won't end there, Lilah. Not this time."

Her lips curved as they lifted to his. "Just kiss me."

He fought to gentle his grip, to keep his mouth easy as it cruised over hers. Surely he was strong enough to hold back this clawing need to ravage. He wouldn't hurt her. He swore it. And clung to the dim hope that he could have this one night with her and emerge unscathed.

So sweet, she thought. So lovely. The tenderness of the kiss was all the more poignant as she could feel the tremble of repressed passion in both of them. Her heart, already brimming with love, overflowed. When their lips parted, there were tears glittering in her eyes.

"I don't want it to end there." She touched her lips to his again. "Neither of us do."

"No."

"Make love with me, Max," she murmured. She kept her eyes on his as she stepped back, unbelting her robe. "I need you tonight." The robe slithered to the floor.

Beneath it her skin was as white and smooth as marble. Her long slender limbs might have been carved and polished by an artist's hands. She stood, cloaked only in moonlight, and waited.

He'd never seen anything more perfect, more elegant or fragile. Suddenly his hands felt big and clumsy, his fingers rough. His breath tore raggedly through his lips as he touched her. Though his fingers barely floated over her skin, he was terrified he would leave bruises behind. Fascinated, he watched his hand skim over her, tracing the slope of her shoulders, sliding down the graceful arms and back again. Carefully, very carefully, brushing over the water-soft skin of her breasts.

First her legs went weak. No one had ever touched her like this, with such drugging gentleness. It was as though she were the first woman he had ever seen and he was memorizing her face and form through his fingertips. She had come to seduce, yet her arms lay weighted at her sides. And she was seduced. Her head fell back in an involuntary gesture of surrender. He had no way of knowing that this surrender was her first.

That vulnerable column of her throat was impossible to resist. He pressed his mouth against it even as his palm brushed lightly over the point of her breast.

The combination had a bolt of sensation shooting through her. Stunned by it, she jolted and gasped out his name.

He retreated instantly, cursing himself. "I'm sorry." He was half-blind with needs and shook his head to clear it. "I've always been clumsy."

"Clumsy?" In a haze of longing, she swayed toward him, running her lips over his shoulder, his throat, down his chest. "Can't you feel what you're doing to me? Don't stop." Her mouth found his and lingered. "I think I'd die if you did."

The barrage on his system nearly felled him. Her hands streaked over him, impatient and greedy. Her mouth, Lord her mouth was hot and quick, searing his skin with every breathy kiss. He couldn't think, could barely breathe. There was nothing to do but feel.

Straining for control, he lifted her face to his, calming her lips, drugging them and her as he centered all of his needs into that one endless kiss. Yes, he could feel what he was doing to her, and it amazed him. On a low, throaty groan, she went limp in a surrender more erotic than any seduction. Her body seemed to melt into his in total pliancy, total trust. When he lifted her into his arms she made a small, lazy sound of pleasure.

Her eyes were nearly closed. He could see the glint of green under the cover of her lashes. As he carried her to the bed he felt as strong as Hercules. Gently, watching her face, he laid her on the covers.

There was moonlight here, streaming through the windows like liquid silver. He could hear the wind sighing through the trees and the distant drum of water on rock. Her scent, as mysterious as Eve, reached for him as easily as her arms.

He took her hands. Struck by the romance of the night, he brought them to his lips, skimming his mouth over her knuckles, down her fingertips, over her palms. All the time, he watched her as he scraped lightly with his teeth, soothed and aroused with his tongue. He heard her breath quicken, watched her eyes cloud with dazed pleasure and confusion as he made love to her hands. He felt the thunder of her pulse when he pressed his lips to her wrist.

He was bringing her something she hadn't prepared for. Total helplessness. Did he know how completely she was in his power? she wondered hazily. The drunk and weighty pleasure was flowing from her fingertips into every part of her. When his lips slid down her arm to nuzzle the inside of her elbow, a moan was wrenched from her.

She wasn't even aware that she was moving under him, inviting him to take anything, everything he wanted. When his mouth came to hers at last, his name was the only word she could form.

He fought back greed. It was impossible not to feel it, with her body so hot, so soft, so agile beneath his. But he refused to give in to it. Tonight, for there might only be tonight, would last. He wanted more than that fast and frantic union his body ached for. He wanted the dazzling pleasure of learning every inch of her, of discovering her secrets, her weaknesses. With patience he could brand in his brain what it was like to touch her and feel her tremble, what it was like to taste and hear her sigh. When her hands moved over him, he knew she was as lost in the night as he.

He slid down her slowly, searing her flesh with openmouthed kisses, whispering fingertips. With torturous patience he lingered at her breasts until they were achingly full with pleasure. Down, gradually down, while her fingers clenched and unclenched in his hair. He could hear her now, soft, incoherent pleas, gasping sighs as he trailed his mouth down her torso, nipped teasing teeth across her hip. She felt his breath flutter against her thigh and cried out, rearing up as the first hot wave slammed into her. She flew over the edge then cartwheeled down as he roamed relentlessly to her knee.

He couldn't get enough. Every taste of her was more potent than the last. He sated himself on it as the tension began to roar in his temples, burn in his blood. Grasping her flailing hands, he drove himself mad by pushing her to peak again. When her body went lax, when her breath was sobbing, he brought his mouth back to hers.

She was willing to beg, but she couldn't speak. Sensation after sensation tore through her, leaving her weak and giddy and aching for more. Desperate for him, she fumbled with the catch of his jeans. She would have screamed with frustration if his mouth hadn't seduced hers into a groan.

Tugging, gasping, she dragged the denim over his hips, too delirious to know that her urgent fingers were making him shudder. Damp flesh slid over damp flesh as they pulled the jeans aside.

"Wait." The word came harshly through his lips as he fought to hold on to the last of his control. "Look at me." His fingers tightened in her hair as she opened her eyes. "Look at me," he repeated. "I want you to remember."

Muscles trembling with the effort to go slowly, he slipped into her. Her eyes went cloudy but remained on his as they set an easy rhythm. She knew as he filled her, with himself, with such perfect beauty, that she would always remember.

It was so sweet, so natural, the way his head rested between her breasts. Lilah smiled at the sensation as she stroked his hair. One hand was still linked with his as it had been when they'd slid over the crest together. Half-dreaming now, she imagined what it would be like to fall asleep together, just like this, night after night.

He could feel her relax beneath him, her body warm and pliant, her skin still sheened with the dew of passion. Her heartbeat was slowing gradually. For a moment he could pretend that this was one night among many. That she could belong to him in that complex and intimate way a woman belonged to a man.

He knew he'd given her pleasure, and that for a time they had been as bound together as two people could be. But now, he hadn't an idea what he should say—because all he wanted to say was that he loved her.

"What are you thinking?" she murmured.

He steadied himself. "My brain's not working yet."

Her laugh was low and warm. She shifted, wriggling down until they were face-to-face. "Then I'll tell you what I'm thinking." She brought her mouth to his in a languid, lingering kiss. "I like your lips." Teasingly she nipped the lower one. "And your hands. Your shoulders, your eyes." As she spoke, she trailed a fingertip up and down his spine. "In fact, at the moment I can't think of anything I don't like about you."

"I'll remind you of that the next time I irritate you." He combed her hair back because he enjoyed seeing it spread over his sheets. "I can't believe I'm here with you, like this."

"Didn't you feel it, Max, almost from the beginning?"

"Yes." He traced her mouth with a fingertip. "I figured it was wishful thinking."

"You don't give yourself enough credit, Professor." She traced light, lazy kisses over his face. "You're an attractive man with an admirable mind and a sense of compassion that's irresistible." Her eyes didn't light with amusement when he shifted. Instead she lay a hand on his cheek. "When you made love with me tonight, it was beautiful. The most beautiful night of my life."

She saw it in his eyes. Not embarrassment now, but plain disbelief. Because she was defenseless, stripped to the soul, nothing could have hurt her more. "Sorry," she said tightly and moved away. "I'm sure that sounds trite coming from me."

"Lilah…"

"No, it's fine." She pressed her lips together until she was certain her voice would be light and breezy again. "No use complicating things." As she sat up, she tossed her hair back. "There aren't any strings here, Professor. No trapdoors, no fine print. We're two consenting adults who enjoy each other. Agreed?"

"I'm not sure."

"Let's just say we'll take it a day at a time. Or a night at a time." She leaned over to kiss him. "Now that we've got that settled, I'd better go."

"Don't." He took her hand before she could slip off the bed. "Don't go. No strings," he said carefully as he studied her. "No complications. Just stay with me to-night."

She smiled a little. "I'll just seduce you again."

"I was hoping you'd say that." He pulled her against him. "I want you with me when the sun comes up."

Chapter 8

When the sun came up to pour golden light through the windows and chase away the last dusky shadows, she was in his arms. It seemed incredible to him that her head would be resting on his shoulder, her hand fisted lightly over his heart. She slept like a child, deeply, curled toward him for warmth and comfort.

Though the night was over, he lay still, loath to wake her. The birds had begun their morning chorus. It was so quiet, he could hear the wind breathing through the trees. He knew that soon the sound of saws and hammers would disrupt the peace and bring reality back. So he clung to this short interlude between the mystery of the night and the bustle of day.

She sighed and settled closer as he stroked her hair. He remembered how generous she had been in those dark sleepy hours. It seemed he had only to think, to wish, and she would turn toward him. Again and again they had loved, in silence and with perfect understanding.

He wanted to believe in miracles, to believe that it had been as special and monumental a night for her as it had been for him. He was afraid to take her words at face value.

No one's ever made me feel the way you do.

Yet they had played over and over in his head, giving him hope. If he was careful and patient and weighed each step before it was taken, maybe he could make a miracle.

Though he didn't feel suited to the role of prince, he tilted her face to his to wake her with a kiss.

"Mmm." She smiled but didn't open her eyes. "Can I have another?"

Her voice, husky with sleep, sent desire shivering along his skin. He forgot to be careful. He forgot to be patient. His mouth took hers the second time with an edgy desperation that had her system churning before she was fully awake.

"Max." Throbbing, she locked herself around him. "I want you. Now. Right now."

He was already inside her, already dragging her with him where they both wanted to go. The ride was fast and furious, shooting them both to the top where they clung, breathless and giddy.

When her hands slid off his damp back, she still hadn't opened her eyes. "Good morning," she managed. "I just had the most incredible dream."

Though he was still light-headed, he braced on his forearms to look down at her. "Tell me about it."

"I was in bed with this very sexy man. He had big

blue eyes, dark hair that was always falling in his face."
Smiling, she opened her eyes and brushed it back for
him. "This long, streamlined body." Still watching him,
she moved her hands deliberately over him. "I didn't
want to wake up, but when I did, it was even better
than the dream."

Afraid he was crushing her, he rolled to reverse their
positions. "What are the chances of spending the rest
of our lives in this bed?"

She dropped a kiss on his shoulder. "I'm game." Then
she groaned when the drone of power tools cut through
the morning quiet. "It can't be seven-thirty."

As reluctant as she, he glanced at the clock beside
the bed. "I'm afraid it can."

"Tell me it's my day off."

"I wish I could."

"Lie," she suggested, laying her cheek on his chest.

"Will you let me take you to work?"

She winced. "Don't say that word."

"Go for a drive with me after?"

She lifted her head again. "Where?"

"Anywhere."

Tilting her head, she smiled. "My favorite place."

Max kept his mind off Lilah—or tried to—by focusing on the multilayered task of locating people to go
with the names on his list. He checked court records,
police records, church records and death certificates.
His meticulous legwork was rewarded with a handful
of addresses.

When he felt he'd exhausted all the leads for that
day, he drove by C.C.'s garage. He found her buried to
the waist under the hood of a black sedan.

"I'm sorry to interrupt," he shouted over the din jingling out of a portable radio.

"Then don't." There was a streak of grease over her brow, but her scowl disappeared when she looked up and saw Max. "Hi."

"I could come back."

"Why, just because I snapped your head off?" She grinned, taking a rag out of her coveralls to wipe her hands. "Buy you a drink?" She jerked her head toward a soft drink machine.

"No, thanks. I just stopped by to ask you about a car."

"You're driving Lilah's, aren't you? Is it acting up?"

"No. The thing is I might be doing a lot of driving in the next few days, and I don't feel right using her car. I thought you might know if there's anything for sale in the area."

C.C. pursed her lips. "You want to buy a car?"

"Nothing extravagant. Just some convenient transportation. Then when I get back to New York..." He trailed off. He didn't want to think about going back to New York. "I can always sell it later."

"It so happens I do know somebody with a car for sale. Me."

"You?"

Nodding, she stuffed the rag back into her pocket. "With a baby coming, I've decided to turn in my Spitfire for a family car."

"Spitfire?" He wasn't sure what that was, but it didn't sound like the kind of car a dignified college professor would drive.

"I've had her for years, and I sure would feel better selling her to someone I know." She already had his hand and was pulling him outside.

There it sat, a fire-engine-red toy with a white rag top and bucket seats. "Well, I…"

"I rebuilt the engine a couple of years ago." C.C. was busy opening the hood. "She drives like a dream. There's less than ten thousand miles on the tires. I'm the original owner, so I can guarantee she's been treated like a lady. And there's…" She glanced up and grinned. "I sound like a guy in a plaid sports jacket."

He could see his face in the shiny red paint. "I've never owned a sports car."

The wistfulness in his voice made C.C. smile. "Tell you what, leave me Lilah's car, drive her around. See how she suits you."

Max found himself behind the wheel, trying not to grin like a fool as the wind streamed through his hair. What would his students think, he wondered, if they could see sturdy old Dr. Quartermain tooling around in a flashy convertible? They'd probably think he'd gone around the bend. Maybe he had, but he was having the time of his life.

It was a car that would suit Lilah, he thought. He could already see her sitting beside him, her hair dancing as she laughed and lifted her arms to the wind. Or kicked back in the seat, her eyes closed, letting the sun warm her face.

It was a nice dream, and it could come true. At least for a while. And maybe he wouldn't sell the car when he got back to New York. There was no law that said he had to drive a practical sedan. He could keep it to remind him of a few incredible weeks that had changed his life.

Maybe he'd never be sturdy old Dr. Quartermain again.

He cruised up the winding mountain roads, then back

down again to try out the little car in traffic. Delighted with the world in general, he sat at a light, tapping his fingers against the wheel to the beat of the music on the radio.

There were people jamming the sidewalks, crowding the shops. If he'd seen a parking place, he might have whipped in, strolled into a shop himself just to test his endurance. Instead, he entertained himself by watching people scout for that perfect T-shirt.

He noticed the man with dark hair and a trim dark beard standing on the curb, staring at him. Full of himself and the spiffy car, Max grinned and waved. He was halfway down the block before it hit him. He braked, causing a bellow of bad-tempered honking. Thinking fast, he turned a sharp left, streaked down a side street and fought his way through traffic back to the intersection. The man was gone. Max searched the street but couldn't find a sign of him. He cursed low and bitterly over the lack of a parking space, over his own slow-wittedness.

The hair had been dyed, and the beard had hid part of the face. But the eyes… Max couldn't forget the eyes. It had been Caufield standing on the crowded sidewalk, looking at Max not with admiration or absent interest, but with barely controlled rage.

He had himself under control by the time he picked Lilah up at the visitors' center. He had made what he considered the logical decision not to tell her. The less she knew, the less she was involved. The less she was involved, the better chance there was that she wouldn't be hurt.

She was too impulsive, he reflected. If she knew

Caufield had been in the village, she would try to hunt him down herself. And she was too clever. If she managed to find him… The idea made Max's blood run cold. No one knew better than he how ruthless the man could be.

When he saw Lilah coming across the lot toward the car, he knew he'd risk anything, even his life, to keep her safe.

"Well, well, what's this?" Brows lifted, she tapped a finger on the fender. "My old heap wasn't good enough, so you borrowed my sister's?"

"What?" Foolishly he'd forgotten the car and everything else since he'd recognized Caufield. "Oh, the car."

"Yes, the car." She leaned over to kiss him, and was puzzled by his absent response and the pat on her shoulder.

"Actually, I'm thinking of buying it. C.C.'s in the market for a family car, so…"

"So you're going to buy yourself a snappy little toy."

"I know it's not my usual style," he began.

"I wasn't going to say that." Her brows drew together as she studied his face. Something was going on in that complicated mind of his. "I was going to say good for you. I'm glad you're giving yourself a break." She hopped in and stretched. Her lifted hand reached for his, but he only gave it a light squeeze, then released it. Telling herself she was being oversensitive, she fixed a smile in place. "So, how about that drive? I was thinking we could cruise down the coast."

"I'm a little tired." He hated lying, but he needed to get back to talk to Trent and Sloan, to feed the new description to the police. "Can I have a rain check?"

"Sure." She managed to keep her smile in place. He

was so polite, so distant. Wanting some echo of their previous intimacy, she put a hand over his when he slipped into the car beside her. "I'm always up for a nap. Your room or mine?"

"I'm not... I don't think that's a good idea."

His hand was tense over the gearshift, and his fingers made no move to link with hers. He wouldn't even look at her, hadn't really looked at her, she realized, since she'd crossed the lot.

"I see." She lifted her hand from his and let it fall in her lap. "Under the circumstances, I'm sure you're right."

"Lilah—"

"What?"

No, he decided. He needed to do this his way. "Nothing." Reaching for the keys, he switched on the ignition.

They didn't speak on the way home. Max continued to convince himself that lying to her was the best way. Maybe she was miffed because he'd put off the drive, but he'd make it up to her. He just had to keep out of her way until he'd handled a few details. In any case his mind was crowded with possibilities that he needed time and space to work through. If Caufield and Hawkins were both still on the island, both of them bold enough to stroll through the village, did that mean they had found something useful in the papers? Were they still looking? Had they, as he had, dipped into the resources at the library to find out more?

They knew he was alive now. Would they manage to connect him with the Calhouns? If they considered him a liability, would his relationship with Lilah put her in danger?

That was a risk he couldn't afford to take.

He turned up the winding road that brought the peak of The Towers into view.

"I may have to go back to New York sooner than I expected," he said, thinking out loud.

To keep from protesting, she pressed her lips tight. "Really?"

He glanced over, cleared his throat. "Yes...ah, business. I could continue to do my research from there."

"That's very considerate of you, Professor. I'm sure you'd hate to leave a job half-done. And you wouldn't have any awkward relationships to interfere."

His mind was already focused on what needed to be done, and he made an absent sound of agreement.

By the time they pulled up at The Towers, Lilah had managed to turn the hurt into anger. He didn't want to be with her, and by his attitude it was plain he regretted that they'd ever been together. Fine. She wasn't about to sit around and sulk because some highbrow college professor wasn't interested in her.

She resisted slamming the car door, barely resisted biting his hand off at the wrist when he set it on her shoulder. "Maybe we can drive down the coast tomorrow."

She glanced at his hand, then at his face. "Don't hold your breath."

He jammed his hands into his pockets as she strolled up the steps. Definitely miffed, he thought.

By the time he had relayed his information to the other men and had fought his way through the pecking order at the police station, he really was tired. It might have been tension or the fact that he'd only had a couple hours' sleep the night before, but he gave in, stretched across his bed and tuned out until dinner.

Feeling better, he wandered downstairs. He thought about finding Lilah, asking her to walk in the gardens after the meal. Or maybe they'd take a drive after all, in the moonlight. It hadn't been a very big lie, and now that he'd unburdened himself to the police, he wouldn't have to dwell on it. In any case, if he decided it was best to leave, he might not have another evening with her.

Yes, a drive. Maybe he could ask her if she'd consider visiting him in New York—or just going away for a weekend somewhere. It didn't have to end, not if he started taking those careful steps.

He strolled into the parlor, found it empty and strolled out again. Just the two of them, watching the moon on the water, maybe pulling over to walk along the beach. He could begin to court her properly. He imagined she'd be amused by the term, but it was what he wanted to do.

He followed the sound of a piano into the music room. Suzanna was alone, playing for herself. The music seemed to match the expression in her eyes. There was a sadness in them, too deep for anyone else to feel. But when she saw him, she stopped and smiled.

"I didn't mean to interrupt."

"That's all right. It's time to get back to the real world anyway. Amanda took the kids into town so I was taking advantage of the lull."

"I was just looking for Lilah."

"Oh, she's gone."

"Gone?"

Suzanna was pushing back from the piano when Max barked the word and had her rising slowly. "Yes, she went out."

"Where? When?"

"Just a little while ago." Suzanna studied him as she crossed the room. "I think she had a date."

"A—a date?" He felt as though someone had just swung a sledgehammer into his solar plexus.

"I'm sorry, Max." Concerned, she laid a comforting hand on his. She didn't think she'd ever seen a man more miserably in love. "I didn't realize. She may have just gone out to meet friends, or to be by herself."

No, he thought, shaking his head. That would be worse. If she was alone, and Caufield was anywhere close… He shook off the panic. It wasn't Lilah the man was after, but the emeralds.

"It's all right, I only wanted to talk to her about something."

"Does she know how you feel?"

"No—yes. I don't know," he said lamely. He saw his romantic dreams about moonlight and courtship go up in smoke. "It doesn't matter."

"It would to her. Lilah doesn't take people or their feelings lightly, Max."

No strings, he thought. No trapdoors. Well, he'd already fallen through the trapdoor, and his feelings were the noose around his neck. But that wasn't the point. "I'm just concerned about her going out alone. The police haven't caught Hawkins or Caufield yet."

"She went out to dinner. I can't see anyone popping up in a restaurant and demanding emeralds she doesn't have." Suzanna gave his hand a friendly squeeze. "Come on, you'll feel better when you've eaten. Aunt Coco's lemon chicken should be about ready."

He sat through dinner, struggling to pretend that he had an appetite, that the empty place at the table didn't bother him. He discussed the progress of the servants list with Amanda, dodged Coco's request to read his cards and felt generally miserable. Fred, sitting on his left foot, benefited from his mood by gobbling up the morsels of chicken Max slipped to him.

He considered driving into town, casually cruising, stopping at a few clubs and restaurants. But decided that would make him look like as big a jerk as he felt. In the end he retreated to his room and lost himself in his book.

The story didn't come as easily as it had the night before. Now it was mostly fits and starts with a lot of long pauses. Still he found even the pauses constructive as an hour passed into two, and two into three. It wasn't until he glanced at his watch and saw it was after midnight that he realized he hadn't heard Lilah come home. He'd deliberately left his door ajar so that he would know when she passed down the hall.

There was a good chance he'd been engrossed in his work and hadn't noticed when she'd walked by to her room. If she'd gone out to dinner, surely she'd be home by now. No one could eat for five hours. But he had to know.

He went quietly. There was a light in Suzanna's room, but the others were dark. At Lilah's door, he hesitated, then knocked softly. Feeling awkward, he put his hand on the knob. He'd spent the night with her, he reminded himself. She could hardly be offended if he looked in to see if she was asleep.

She wasn't. She wasn't even there. The bed was made; the old iron head-and footboards that had probably belonged to a servant had been painted a gleaming white. The rest was color, so much it dazzled the eyes.

The spread was a patchwork quilt, expertly made from scraps of fabrics. Polka dots, checks, stripes, faded reds and blues. It was piled high with pillows of varied shapes and sizes. The kind of bed, Max thought, a person could sink into and sleep the day away. It suited her.

The room was huge, as most were in The Towers, but she'd cluttered it and made it cozy. On the walls that were painted a dramatic teal were sketches of wildflowers. The bold signature in the corners told him she'd done them herself. He hadn't even known she could draw. It made him realize there was quite a bit he didn't know about the woman he was in love with.

After closing the door behind him, he wandered the room, looking for pieces of her.

A baker's rack was packed with books. Keats and Byron jumbled with grisly murder mysteries and contemporary romances. A little sitting area was grouped in front of one of her windows, a blouse tossed carelessly over the back of a Queen Anne chair, earrings and glittering bracelets scattered over a Hepplewhite table. There was a bowl of smooth gemstones beside a china penguin. When he picked the bird up, it played a jazzy rendition of "That's Entertainment."

She had candles everywhere, in everything from elegant Meissen to a tacky reproduction of a unicorn. Dozens of pictures of her family were scattered throughout. He picked up one framed snapshot of a couple, arms around each other's waists as they laughed into the camera. Her parents, he thought. Lilah's resemblance to the man, Suzanna's to the woman were strong enough to make him certain of it.

When the cuckoo in the clock on the wall jumped

out, he jolted and realized it was twelve-thirty. Where the hell was she?

Now he paced, from the window where she'd hung faceted crystals to the brass urn filled with dried flowers, from bookcase to bureau. Nerves humming, he picked up an ornate cobalt bottle to sniff. And smelled her. He set it down hastily when the door opened.

She looked…incredible. Her hair windblown, her face flushed. She wore some sheer drapey dress that swirled around her legs in bleeding colors. Long multicolored columns of beads danced at her ears. She lifted a brow and closed the door.

"Well," she said. "Make yourself at home."

"Where the hell have you been?" The demand shot out, edged with frustration and worry.

"Did I miss curfew, Daddy?" She tossed a beaded bag onto the bureau. She'd lifted a hand to remove an earring when he whirled her around.

"Don't get cute with me. I've been worried sick. You've been out for hours. No one knew where you were." Or who you were with, he thought, but managed to bite that one back.

She jerked her arm free. He saw the temper flash hot into her eyes, but her voice was cool and slow and unmoved. "It may surprise you, Professor, but I've been going out on my own for a long time."

"It's different now."

"Oh?" Deliberately she turned back to the bureau. Taking her time, she unfastened an earring. "Why?"

"Because we…" Because we're lovers. "Because we don't know where Caufield is," he said with more control. "Or how dangerous he might be."

"I've also been looking out for myself for a long

time." Deceptively sleepy, her eyes met his in the mirror. "Is the lecture over?"

"It's not a lecture, Lilah, I was worried. I have a right to know your plans."

Still watching him, she slid bracelets from her arms. "Just how do you figure that?"

"We're—friends."

The smile didn't reach her eyes. "Are we?"

He jammed impotent hands into his pockets. "I care about you. And after what happened last night, I thought we... I thought we meant something to each other. Now, twenty-four hours later you're out with someone else. Looking like that."

She stepped out of her shoes. "We went to bed last night, and enjoyed it." She nearly choked over the bitterness lodged in her throat. "As I recall we agreed there'd be no complications." Tilting her head, she studied him. Her easy shrug masked the fact that her hands were balled tight. "Since you're here, I suppose we could arrange a repeat performance." Her voice a purr, she stepped closer to run a finger down the front of his shirt. "That's what you want from me, isn't it, Max?"

Furious, he pushed her hand aside. "I don't care to be the second act of the evening."

The flush vanished, leaving her cheeks pale before she turned away. "Congratulations," she whispered. "Direct hit."

"What do you want me to say? That you can come and go as you please, with whomever you please, and I'll sit up and beg for the scraps from the table?"

"I don't want you to say anything. I just want you to leave me alone."

"I'm not going anywhere until we've straightened this out."

"Fine." The cuckoo chirped out again as she unzipped her dress. "Stay as long as you like. I'm getting ready for bed."

She stepped out of the dress, tossed it aside, then walked over to her vanity in a lacy, beribboned chemise. Sitting, she picked up her brush to drag it through her hair.

"What are you so angry about?"

"Angry." She set her teeth as she slapped the bristles against her scalp. "What makes you think I'm angry? Just because you're waiting for me in my room, incensed that I had the nerve to make plans of my own when you didn't have the time or inclination to spend an hour with me. Unless it was in the sack."

"What are you talking about?" He took her arm, then yelped when she rapped the brush hard on his knuckles.

"I'll let you know when I want to be touched."

He swore, grabbed the brush and tossed it across the room. Too enraged to see the surprise in her eyes, he hauled her to her feet. "I asked you a question."

She cocked her chin. "If you've finished your temper tantrum—" He nearly lifted her off her feet.

"Don't push," he said between his teeth.

"You hurt me." The words exploded out of her. "Last night, even this morning, I was worth a little of your time and attention. As long as there was sex. Then this afternoon, you couldn't even look at me. You couldn't wait to dump me off here and get away from me."

"That's crazy."

"That's just what happened. Damn you, you made up lame excuses and practically patted me on the head.

And tonight, you've got an itch and you're annoyed that I wasn't here to scratch it."

He was as pale as she now. "Is that what you think of me?"

She sighed then, and the anger dropped out of her voice. "It's what you think of me, Max. Now let me go."

His grip loosened so that she slipped away. "I had something on my mind this afternoon. It wasn't that I didn't want to spend time with you."

"I don't want excuses." She went to the terrace doors to fling them open. Maybe the wind would blow the tears away. "You've made it clear how you feel."

"Obviously I haven't. The last thing I wanted to do was hurt you, Lilah." But he'd lied to her, he thought. That had been his first mistake. "Just before I came to pick you up, I saw Caufield in the village."

She spun around. "What? You saw him? Where?"

"I was waiting at a light, and I saw him on the sidewalk. He's dyed his hair and grown a beard. By the time I'd realized, I was caught up in traffic and had to double back. He was gone."

"Why didn't you tell me you'd seen him?"

"I didn't want to worry you, and I wasn't going to have you getting some lamebrained idea about hunting him up yourself. You have a habit of acting on impulse, and I—"

"You jerk." The flush was back in her cheeks when she stepped forward to give him a shove. "That man is determined to take something from my family, and you don't have the sense to tell me you've seen him a few miles from here. If I'd known I might have been able to find him."

"Exactly my point. I'm not having you involved any

more than necessary. That's why I thought it might be best if I went back to New York. They know I'm here now, and I'm not having you caught in the middle."

"You're not having?" She would have shoved him again, but he caught both her hands.

"That's right. You're going to stay out of it."

"Don't tell me—"

"I am telling you," he interrupted, pleased when she gaped at him. "What's more, you're not going to go wandering off at night until he's in custody. After I thought it over, I decided it was best if I stayed close and watched out for you. I'm going to take care of you whether you like it or not."

"I don't like it, and I don't need to be taken care of."

"Nonetheless." And he considered the argument closed.

It was her turn to stutter. "Why, you arrogant, self-important—"

"That's enough," he said in his best professor's voice and had her blinking. "There's no use arguing when the most intelligent decision's been made. Now, I think it's best if I take you to work every day. Whenever you make other plans, you'll let me know."

Her anger turned to simple shock. "I will not."

"Yes," he said mildly, "you will." He moved her hands behind her back to bring her closer. "About to-night," he began when their bodies brushed. "Clearly, you're laboring under a misconception concerning my motives, and my feelings."

She arched back, more surprised than annoyed when he didn't release her. "I don't want to talk about it."

"No, you prefer yelling about it, but that's unconstructive, and not my style." Both his hands and his voice were very firm. "To be precise, I didn't come here because I had an itch, though I certainly have every intention of making love with you."

Baffled, she stared at him. "What the devil's gotten into you?"

"I've suddenly realized that the best way to handle you is the way I handle difficult students. It takes more than patience. It requires a firm hand and a clear-cut outline of intentions and goals."

"A difficult—" She took a deep breath to hold on to her temper. "Max, I think you'd better go take some aspirin and lie down."

"As I was saying." He whispered a kiss over her cheek. "It isn't just a matter of sex, despite the fact that that aspect is incredibly satisfying. It's more of a matter of my being completely bewitched by you."

"Don't," she said weakly when he leaned close to nip at her ear.

"Maybe I've made the mistake of indicating that it's only the way you look, the way you feel under my hands, the way you taste that attracts me." He drew her bottom lip into his mouth, sucking gently until her eyes unfocused. "But it's more than that. I just don't know how to tell you." Her pulse beat fast and hard against his hands as he walked her backward. "There's never been anyone like you in my life. I intend to keep you there, Lilah."

"What are you doing?"

"I'm taking you to bed."

She struggled to clear her head as his lips skimmed down her throat. "No, you're not." She was angry with him about something. But the reason floated just out of reach as his mouth seduced her.

"I need to show you how I feel about you." Still toying with her lips, he lowered her to the mattress.

Her hands were free now and slipped under his shirt to run along the warm flesh beneath. She didn't want to think. There were so many feelings to be absorbed, and she drew him closer, eager.

"I was jealous," he murmured as he slid one lacy strap from her shoulder and replaced it with his mouth. "I don't want another man touching you."

"No." He was touching her now, long, lingering strokes up and down her trembling body. "Just you."

He sank into a kiss, spinning it out, wallowing in the flavor, the texture, until he was drunk on it. Then, like an addict, he went back for more.

This was comfort and care and romance, she thought hazily. To float together like this, with a sweet breeze blowing over heated bodies, soft murmurs muffled against clinging lips. Desire so perfectly balanced with affection. Nothing mattered so much as this—holding on to the hope of love.

She lifted his shirt over his head and let her hands roam. He was strong. It was more than the subtle ridge of muscles over his back and shoulders. It was the strength inside that aroused her. The integrity, the dedication to do what was right. He would be strong enough to be loyal and honest and gentle with those he loved.

He shifted her so that she was cocooned by pillows. Kneeling beside her, he began to untie each tiny ribbon down the center of the ivory silk. The contrast of patient fingers and hungry eyes left her breathless. He parted the material, caressing the newly exposed flesh with his lips. It amazed and humbled him that her skin should be as soft as the silk.

As patiently as he, she undressed him. Though the need to hurry was clawing at both of them, they held back, the understanding spoken.

She rose, wrapping her arms around his neck until they were torso to torso, thigh to thigh. With the bright light showering around them, they explored each other. A shudder then a sigh, a request and an answer. Questing lips sought out new secrets. Eager hands discovered new pleasures.

When she locked herself around him, he filled her. Glorying in the sensation, she arched back, taking him deeper, gasping out his name as the first shock waves struck. He could see her, her willowy body bowed, her skin glowing in the light while her bright hair rained down her back. As she shuddered, the stunned pleasure rushed into her face.

Then his vision grayed, his own body trembled. His hands slid down to grip her hips. She was wrapped tight around him when they shot over the peak together.

Chapter 9

Max was whistling as he poured his coffee. It was the penguin's natty little tune and suited his mood. He had plans. Big ones. A drive along the coast, dinner at some out-of-the-way spot, then a nice long walk on the beach.

He sipped, scalded his tongue and grinned.

He was having a romance.

"Well, it's nice to see someone in such a bright mood so early in the morning." Coco sailed into the kitchen. She'd dyed her hair a raven black the night before, and the result had put her in a cheerful state of mind. "How about some blueberry pancakes?"

"You look terrific."

She beamed and reached for a frilly apron. "Why, thank you, dear. A woman needs a change now and again, I always say. Keeps men on their toes." After taking a large mixing bowl from the cupboard, she glanced back at him. "I must say, Max, you're looking rather well yourself this morning. The sea air or…something must agree with you."

"It's wonderful here. I'll never be able to thank you enough for letting me stay."

"Nonsense." In her haphazard way she began dumping ingredients into the bowl. It never failed to amaze Max how anyone could cook so carelessly with such exquisite results. "It was meant, you know. I knew it the moment Lilah brought you home. She was always one for bringing things home. Wounded birds, baby rabbits. Even a snake once." The memory of that made her pat her breast. "This was the first time she brought in an unconscious man. But that's Lilah," she continued, gaily mixing as she talked. "Always the unexpected. Quite talented, too. She knows all those Latin terms for weeds and the migratory habits of birds and things. When she's in the mood, she can draw beautifully."

"I know. I saw the sketches in her room."

She slanted him a look. "Did you?"

"I…" He took a quick gulp of coffee. "Yes. Do you want a cup?"

"No, I'll have my coffee when this is done." Oh, my, my, she thought, things were moving along just beautifully. The cards didn't lie. "Yes, our Lilah's quite a fascinating girl. Headstrong like the others, but in such a casual, deceptively amiable sort of way. I've always said that the right sort of man would recognize how special she is." Keeping an eye on Max, she rinsed and drained blueberries. "He'd need to be patient, but not malleable. Strong enough to keep her from veering off course too far, and wise enough not to try to change her." Gently folding the berries into the batter she smiled. "But then, if you love someone why would you want to change her?"

"Aunt Coco, are you pumping poor Max?" Lilah strolled in, yawning.

"What a thing to say." Coco heated the griddle and clucked her tongue. "Max and I were having a nice conversation. Weren't we, Max?"

"It certainly was a fascinating one."

"Really?" Lilah took the cup from him, and since he didn't make the move, leaned over to kiss him good morning. Watching, Coco all but rubbed her hands together. "I'll take that as a compliment, and since I see blueberry pancakes on the horizon, I won't complain."

Because the kiss had delighted her, Coco hummed as she got out dishes. "You're up early."

"It's becoming a habit of mine." Sipping Max's coffee, Lilah sent him a lazy smile. "I'll have to break it soon."

"The rest of the brood will be trooping down any minute." And Coco liked nothing better than to have all of her chicks in one place. "Lilah, why don't you set the table?"

"I'll definitely have to break it." With a sigh, she handed Max back his coffee. But she kissed Coco's cheek. "I like your hair. Very French."

With what sounded almost like a giggle, Coco began to spoon up batter. "Use the good china, dear. I feel like celebrating."

Caufield hung up the phone and went into a small, nasty rage. He pounded the desk with his fists, tore a few pamphlets to bits and ended by smashing a crystal bud vase against the wall. Because he'd seen the mood before, Hawkins hung back until it passed.

After three calming breaths, Caufield sat back. The glaze of blank violence faded from his eyes as he steepled his fingers. "We seem to be victims of fate, Hawkins. The car our good professor was driving is registered to Catherine Calhoun St. James."

On an oath, Hawkins heaved his bulk away from the wall. "I told you this job stinks. By rights he should be dead. Instead he plops right down in their laps. He'll have told them everything by now."

Caufield tapped the tips of his fingers together. "Oh, assuredly."

"And if he recognized you—"

"He didn't." Exercising control, Caufield laced his fingers then laid them on the desk. "He never would have waved in my direction. He doesn't have the wit for it." Feeling his fingers tighten, he deliberately relaxed them. "The man's a fool. I learned more in one year on the streets than he in all of his years in higher institutions. After all, we're here, not on the boat."

"But he knows," Hawkins insisted, viciously cracking his knuckles. "Now they all know. They'll take precautions."

"Which only adds spice to the game and it's time to begin playing. Since Dr. Quartermain has joined the Calhouns, I believe I'll pay one of the ladies a call."

"You're out of your mind."

"Have a care, old friend," Caufield said mildly. "If you don't like my rules, there's nothing holding you here."

"I'm the one who paid for the damn boat." Hawkins

dragged a hand through his short wiry hair. "I've put over a month in this job already. I've got an investment."

"Then leave it to me to make it pay off." Thinking, Caufield rose to go to the window. There were pretty summer flowers in neat borders just outside. It reminded him that he'd come a long way from the tenements of south Chicago. With the emeralds, he'd go even further.

Perhaps a nice villa in the South Seas where he could relax and refresh himself while Interpol ran in circles looking for him. He already had a new passport, a new background, a new name in reserve—and a tidy sum gathering interest in a discreet Swiss account.

He'd been in the business most of his life, quite successfully. He didn't need the emeralds for the percentage of their value he'd cull by fencing them. But he wanted them. He intended to have them.

As Hawkins paced and abused his knuckles, Caufield continued to gaze out of the window. "Now, as I recall, during my brief friendship with the lovely Amanda, she mentioned that her sister Lilah knew the most about Bianca. Perhaps she knows the most about the emeralds, as well."

This, at least, made some sense to Hawkins. "Are you going to grab her?"

Caufield winced. "That's your style, Hawkins. Credit me with a little more finesse. I believe I'll pay a visit to Acadia. They say the naturalist tours are very informative."

Lilah had always preferred the long, sunny days of summer. Though she felt there was something to be said for the long stormy nights of winter, as well. In truth, it was time she preferred. She didn't wear a watch. Time was something to be appreciated just for its existence, not as something to keep track of. But for the first time in her memory, she wished time would hurry.

She missed him.

It didn't matter how foolish it made her feel. She was in love and giddy with it. When the feeling was so strong, she resented every hour they weren't together.

It was stronger. She had fallen in love with his sweetness, his basic goodness. She had recognized his insecurity and, as she had with broken wings and damaged paws, had wanted to fix it.

She still loved all of those things, but now she had seen a different side of him. He'd been—masterful. She cringed at the term that entered her head and would have sworn she found it offensive. But it hadn't been offensive, not in Max. It had been illuminating.

He had taken charge. He had taken her, she thought with a quick flash of excitement. Though she still resented being compared to a difficult student, she had to admire his technique. He'd simply stated his intentions and moved on them.

She'd be the first to admit that she'd have frozen another man in his tracks with a few well-chosen words if he'd attempted the same thing. But Max wasn't any other man.

She hoped he was beginning to believe it.

While her mind wandered, she kept an eye on her group. Jordan Pond was a favored spot and she had a full load.

"Please, don't disturb the plant life. I know the flowers are tempting, but we have thousands of visitors who'll want to enjoy them, in their natural setting.

The bottle-shaped flower you see in the pond is yellow cow lily, or spatterdock. The leaves floating on the surface are bladderwort, and common to most Acadia ponds. It is their tiny bladders that help the plant float, and that trap small insects."

In his ripped jeans and tattered backpack, Caufield listened to her lecture. Behind his dark glasses, his eyes were watchful. He paid attention, though the talk of bog and pond plants meant nothing to him. He held back a sneer when the group gasped as a heron glided overhead to wade in the shallows several yards away.

As if fascinated, he lifted the camera strapped around his neck and snapped pictures of the bird, the wild orchards, even of a bullfrog who had come out to bask on a floating leaf.

Most of all, he bided his time.

She continued to lecture, tirelessly answering questions as they moved along the trail beside the glassy water. She spelled a weary mother by hitching a toddler on her hip and pointing out a family of black ducks.

When the lecture was over, the group was free to follow the circular trail around the pond or retreat to their cars.

"Miss Calhoun?"

Lilah glanced around. She'd noticed the bearded hiker in the group, though he hadn't asked any questions during the lecture. There was a hint of the South in his voice.

"Yes?"

"I wanted to tell you how terrific your talk was. I teach high school geography and reward myself every summer with a trip through a national park. You're really one of the best guides I've come across."

"Thank you." She smiled, and though it was a natural gesture for her, felt reluctant to offer her hand. She didn't recognize the sweaty, bearded hiker, but she picked up something disturbing. "You'll have to visit the Nature Center while you're here. Enjoy your stay."

He put a hand on her arm. It was a casual move, far from demanding, but she disliked it intensely.

"I was hoping you could give me a little one-on-one, if you've got a minute. I like to give the kids a full-scale report when school starts in the fall. A lot of them never see the inside of a park."

She forced herself to shake off the mood. It was her job, she reminded herself, and she appreciated talking to someone with a genuine interest. "I'd be happy to answer any questions."

"Great." He pulled out a notebook he'd been careful to scribble in.

She relaxed a little, giving him a more in-depth talk than the average group required.

"This is so kind of you. I wonder, could I buy you some coffee, or a sandwich?"

"That isn't necessary."

"But it would be a pleasure."

"I have plans, but thanks."

He kept his smile in place. "Well, I'll be around for a few more weeks. Maybe some other time. I know this is going to sound strange, but I'd swear I'd seen you before. Have you ever been to Raleigh?"

Her instincts were humming, and she wanted to get away from him. "No, I haven't."

"It's the darnedest thing." As if puzzled, he shook his head. "You seem so familiar. Well, thanks again. I'd better start back to camp." He turned, then stopped.

"I know. The papers. I've seen your picture. You're the woman with the emeralds."

"No. I'm afraid I'm the woman without them."

"What a story. I read about it down in Raleigh a month or two ago, and then…well, I have to confess, I'm just addicted to those supermarket tabloids. Comes from living alone and reading too many essays." He gave her a sheepish smile that would have charmed her if her senses hadn't been working overtime.

"I guess the Calhouns have been lining a lot of bird cages lately."

He rocked back on his heels and laughed. "Pays to keep a sense of humor. I guess it's a hassle, but it gives people like me a lot of vicarious excitement. Missing emeralds, jewel thieves."

"Treasure maps."

"There's a map?" His voice sharpened and he worked hard at easing it again. "I hadn't heard."

"Sure, you can pick them up in the village." She reached in her pocket and drew the latest one out. "I've been collecting them. A lot of people are spending hard-earned money only to find out too late that *x* doesn't mark the spot."

"Ah." He had to fight against clenching his jaw. "Capitalism."

"You bet. Here, a souvenir." She handed it to him, careful for reasons she couldn't quite place not to brush his fingers. "Your students might get a kick out of it."

"I'm sure they will." To give himself time, he folded it and slipped it into his pocket. "I really am fascinated by the whole thing. Maybe we can have that sandwich soon and you can give me a firsthand account of what it's like to look for buried treasure."

"Mostly, it's tedious. Enjoy your stay in the park."

Knowing there was no safe way to detain her, he watched her go. She had a long, graceful body, he noted. He certainly hoped he wouldn't have to damage it.

"You're late." Max met her on the trail when she was still twenty yards from the parking area.

"It seems to be my day for teachers." She leaned into the kiss, pleased with how warm and solid it was. "I was detained by a Southern gentleman who wanted information on flora for his geography class."

"I hope he was bald and fat."

She didn't quite manage the laugh and rubbed the chill from her arms instead. "No, actually, he was quite trim and had an abundance of hair. But I turned down his request that I become the mother of his children."

"Did he make a pass at you?"

"No." She held a hand up before he could rush by her. And did laugh. "Max, I'm kidding—and if I wasn't, I can dodge passes all by myself."

He didn't feel as foolish as he might have even a day before. "You haven't been dodging mine."

"I can intercept them, too. Now what's behind your back?"

"My hands."

She laughed again and gave him a delighted kiss. "What else?"

He held out a clutch of painted daisies. "I didn't pick them," he said, knowing her feelings. "I bought them from Suzanna. She said you had a weakness for them."

"They're so cheerful," she murmured, absurdly touched. She buried her face in them, then lifted it to his. "Thanks."

As they began to walk, he draped an arm around her shoulders. "I bought the car from C.C. this afternoon."

"Professor, you're full of surprises."

"I thought you might like to hear about the progress Amanda and I are making on those lists. We could drive down the coast, have some dinner. Be alone."

"It sounds wonderful, but my flowers'll wilt."

He grinned down at her. "I bought a vase. It's in the car."

When the sun was setting behind the hills to the west, they walked along a cobble beach that formed a natural seawall on the southern point of the island. The water was calm, barely murmuring over the mounds of smooth stones. With the approach of dusk, the line between the sky and sea blurred until all was a soft, deep blue. A single gull, heading home, soared overhead with one long, defiant cry.

"This is a special place," Lilah told him. With her hand in his, she walked down the slope of cobbles to stand close to the verge of water. "A magic one. Even the air's different here." She closed her eyes to take a deep breath of it. "Full of stored energy."

"It's beautiful." Idly he bent to pick up a rock, just to feel the texture. In the near distance an island melted into the twilight.

"I often drive down here, just to stand and feel. I think I must have been here before."

"You just said you'd been here before."

Her eyes were soft and dreamy as she smiled. "I mean a hundred years ago, or five hundred. Don't you believe in reincarnation, Professor?"

"Actually, I do. I did a paper on it in college and after

completing the research, I found it was a very viable theory. When you apply it to history—"

"Max." She framed his face with her hands. "I'm crazy about you." Her lips were curved when they met his, curved still when she drew away.

"What was that for?"

"Because I can see you, waist deep in thick books and cramped notes, your hair falling into your face and your eyebrows all drawn together the way they get when you're concentrating, doggedly pursuing truth."

Frowning, he tossed the cobble from hand to hand. "That's a pretty boring image."

"No, it's not." She tilted her head, studying him. "It's a true one, an admirable one. Even courageous."

He gave a short laugh. "Boxing yourself into a library doesn't take courage. When I was a kid, it was a handy escape. I never had an asthma attack reading a book. I used to hide there, in books," he continued. "It was fun imagining myself sailing with Magellan, or exploring with Lewis and Clark, dying at the Alamo or marching across a field at Antietam. Then my father would…"

"Would what?"

Uncomfortable, he shrugged. "He'd hoped for something different. He was a high school football star. Wide receiver. Played semipro for a while. The kind of man who's never been sick a day in his life. Likes to toss back a few beers on Saturday night and hunt on weekends during the season. I'd start wheezing as soon as he put a thirty-thirty in my hands." He tossed the cobble aside. "He wanted to make a man out of me, and never quite managed it."

"You made yourself." She took his hands, feeling a

trembling anger for the man who hadn't appreciated or understood the gift he'd been given. "If he isn't proud of you, the lack is in him, not in you."

"That's a nice thought." He was more than a little embarrassed that he'd pulled those old, raw feelings out. "In any case, I went my own way. I was a lot more comfortable in a classroom than I was on a football field. And the way I figure it, if I hadn't hidden in the library all those years, I wouldn't be standing here with you right now. This is exactly where I want to be."

"Now that's a nice thought."

"If I tell you you're beautiful, are you going to hit me?"

"Not this time."

He pulled her against him, just to hold her as night fell. "I need to go to Bangor for a couple of days."

"What for?"

"I located a woman who worked as a maid at The Towers the year Bianca died. She's living in a nursing home in Bangor, and I made arrangements to interview her." He tilted Lilah's face to his. "Come with me."

"Just give me time to rearrange my schedule."

When the children were asleep, I told Nanny of my plans. I knew she was shocked that I would speak of leaving my husband. She tried to soothe. How could I explain that it wasn't poor Fred who had caused my decision. The incident had made me realize how futile it was to remain in an unhappy and stifling marriage. Had I convinced myself that it was for the children? Their father didn't see them as children who needed to be loved and coddled, but as pawns. Ethan and Sean he would strive to mold in his image, erasing every part of them he considered weak. Colleen, my sweet little girl, he would ignore until such time as he could marry her for profit or status.

I would not have it. Fergus, I knew, would soon wrench control from me. His pride would demand it. A governess of his choosing would follow his instructions and ignore mine. The children would be trapped in the middle of the mistake I had made.

For myself, he would see that I became no more than an ornament at his table. If I defied him, I would pay the price. I have no doubt that he meant to punish me for questioning his authority in front of our children. Whether it would be physical or emotional, I didn't know, but I was sure the damage would be severe. Discontent I might hide from the children, open animosity I could not.

I would take them and go, find somewhere we could disappear. But first I went to Christian.

The night was moon-washed and breezy. I kept my cloak pulled tight, the hood over my hair. The puppy was snuggled at my breast. I had the carriage take me to the village, then walked to his cottage through the quiet streets with the smell of water and flowers all around. My heart was pounding in my ears as I knocked. This was the first step, and once taken, I could never go back.

But it wasn't fear, no, it wasn't fear that trembled through me when he opened the door. It was relief. The moment I saw him I knew the choice had already been made.

"Bianca," he said. "What are you thinking of?"

"I must talk to you." He was already pulling me inside. I saw that he'd been reading in the lamplight.

Its warm glow and the scent of his paints soothed me more than words. I set the pup down and he immediately began to explore, sniffing into corners and making himself at home.

Christian made me sit, and no doubt sensing my nerves, brought me a brandy. As I sipped, I told him of the scene with Fergus. Though I struggled to remain calm, I could see his face, the violence in it, as his hands had closed over my throat.

"My God!" With this, Christian was crouching beside my chair, his fingers skimming up my throat. I hadn't known there were bruises there where Fergus's thumbs had pressed.

Christian's eyes went black. His hands gripped the arms of the chair before he lunged to his feet. "I'll kill him for this."

I jumped up to stop him from storming out of the cottage. My fear was such I'm not sure what I said, though I know I told him that Fergus had left for Boston, that I couldn't bear more violence. In the end it was my tears that stopped him. He held me as though I was a child, rocking and comforting while I poured out my heart and my desperation.

Perhaps I should have been ashamed to have begged him to take me and the children away, to have thrust that kind of burden and responsibility on him. If he had refused, I know I would have gone on alone, taken my three babies to some quiet village in Ireland or England. But Christian wiped away my tears.

"Of course we'll go. I'll not see you or the children spend another night under the same roof with him. He'll never lay a hand on any of you again. It will be diffi-

cult, Bianca. You and the children won't have the kind of life you're used to. And the scandal—"

"I don't care about the scandal. The children need to feel loved and safe." I rose then, to pace. "I can't be sure what's right. Night after night I've lain in bed asking myself if I have the right to love you, to want you. I took vows, made promises, and was given three children." I covered my face with my hands. "A part of me will always suffer for breaking those vows, but I must do something. I think I'll go mad if I don't. God may never forgive me, but I can't face a lifetime of unhappiness."

He took my hands to pull them away from my face. "We were meant to be together. We knew it, both of us, the first time we saw each other. I was content with those few hours as long as I knew you were safe. But I'll not stand by and see you give your life to a man who'll abuse you. From tonight, you're mine, and will be mine forever. Nothing and no one will change that."

I believed him. With his face close to mine, his fine gray eyes so clear and sure, I believed. And I needed.

"Then tonight, make me yours."

I felt like a bride. The moment he touched me, I knew I had never been touched before. His eyes were on mine as he took the pins from my hair. His fingers trembled. Nothing, nothing has ever moved me more than knowing I had the power to weaken him. His lips were gentle against mine even as I felt the tension vibrating through his body. There in the lamplight he unfastened my dress, and I his shirt. And a bird began to sing in the brush.

I could see by the way he looked at me that I pleased him. Slowly, almost torturously he drew off my petticoats, my corset. Then he touched my hair, running his hands through it, and looking his fill.

"I'll paint you like this one day," he murmured. "For myself."

He lifted me into his arms, and I could feel his heart pounding in his chest as he carried me to the bedroom.

The light was silver, the air like wine. This was no hurried coupling in the dark, but a dance as graceful as a waltz, and as exhilarating. No matter how impossible it seems, it was as though we had loved countless times before, as though I had felt that hard, firm body against mine night after night.

This was a world I had never experienced, yet it was achingly, beautifully familiar. Each movement, each sigh, each need was as natural as breath. Even when the urgency stunned me, the beauty didn't lessen. As he made me his, I knew I had found something every soul searches for. Simple love.

Leaving him was the most difficult thing I have ever done. Though we told each other it would be the last time we were separated, we lingered and loved again. It was nearly dawn before I returned to The Towers. When I looked at the house, walked through it, I knew I would miss it desperately. This, more than any place in my life, had been home. Christian and I, with the children, would make our own, but I would always hold The Towers in my heart.

There was little I would take with me. In the quiet before sunrise, I packed a small case. Nanny would help me put together what the children would need, but this I wanted to do alone. Perhaps it was a symbol of independence. And perhaps that is why I thought of the emeralds. They were the only things Fergus had given me that I considered mine. There were times I had de-

tested them, knowing they had been given to me as a prize for producing a proper heir.

Yet they were mine, as my children were mine.

I didn't think of their monetary value as I took them out, held them in my hands and watched them gleam in the light of the lamp. They would be a legacy for my children, and their children, a symbol of freedom, and of hope. And with Christian, of love.

As dawn broke, I decided to put them, together with this journal, in a safe place until I joined Christian again.

Chapter 10

The woman seemed ancient. She sat, looking as frail and brittle as old glass, in the shade of a gnarled elm. Close by, pert young pansies basked in a square of sunlight and flirted with droning bees. Residents made use of the winding stone paths through the lawns of the Madison House. Some were wheeled by family or attendants; others walked, in pairs or alone, with the careful hesitance of age.

There were birds trilling. The woman listened, nodding to herself as she plied a crochet hook and thread with fingers that refused to surrender to arthritis. She wore bright pink slacks and a cotton blouse that had been a gift from one of her great-grandchildren. She had always loved vivid colors. Some things don't fade with age.

Her skin was nut-brown, as creased and lined as an

old map. Until two years before, she had lived on her own, tending her own garden, cooking her own meals. But a fall, a bad one that had left her helpless with pain on her kitchen floor for nearly twelve hours, had convinced her it was time to change.

Stubborn and set in her ways, she had refused offers by several members of her large family to live with them. If she couldn't have her own place, she'd be damned if she would be a burden. She'd been comfortably off, well able to afford a good home and good medical care. At the Madison House, she had her own room. And if the days of puttering in her garden were past, at least she could enjoy the flowers here.

She had company if she wanted it, privacy if she didn't. Millie Tobias figured that at ninety-eight and counting, she'd earned the right to choose.

She was pleased that she was having visitors. Yes, she thought as she worked her needle, she was right pleased. The day had already started off well. She'd awakened that morning with no more than the usual sundry aches. Her hip was twitching a bit, which meant rain on the way. No matter, she mused. It was good for the flowers.

Her hands worked, but she rarely glanced at them. They knew what to do with needle and thread. Instead, she watched the path, her eyes aided by thick, tinted lenses. She saw the young couple, the lanky young man with shaggy dark hair; the willowy girl in a thin summer dress, her hair the color of October leaves. They walked close, hand in hand. Millie had a soft spot for young lovers and decided they looked pretty as a picture.

Her fingers kept moving as they walked off the path to join her in the shade.

"Mrs. Tobias?"

She studied Max, saw earnest blue eyes and a shy smile. "Ayah," she said. "And you'd be Dr. Quartermain." Her voice was a crackle, heavy with down-east. "Making doctors young these days."

"Yes, ma'am. This is Lilah Calhoun."

Not a shy bone in this one, Millie decided, and wasn't displeased when Lilah sat on the grass at her feet to admire the crocheting.

"This is beautiful." Lilah touched a fingertip to the gossamer blue thread. "What will it be?"

"What it wants to. You're from the island."

"Yes, I was born there."

Millie let out a little sigh. "Haven't been back in thirty years. Couldn't bear to live there after I lost my Tom, but I still miss the sound of the sea."

"You were married a long time?"

"Fifty years. We had a good life. We made eight children, and saw all of them grown. Now I've got twenty-three grandchildren, fifteen great-grandchildren and seven great-great-grandchildren." She let out a wheezy laugh. "Sometimes I feel like I've propagated this old world all on my own. Take your hands out of your pockets, boy," she said to Max. "And come on down here so's I don't have to crane my neck." She waited until he was settled. "This here your sweetheart?" she asked him.

"Ah...well..."

"Well, is she or isn't she?" Millie demanded, and flashed her dentures in a grin.

"Yes, Max." Lilah sent him an amused and lazy smile. "Is she or isn't she?"

Cornered, Max let out a little huff of breath. "I suppose you could say so."

"Slow to make up his mind, is he?" she said to Lilah and winked. "Nothing wrong with that. You've got the look of her," she said abruptly.

"Of whom?"

"Bianca Calhoun. Isn't that what you came to talk to me about?"

Lilah laid a hand on Millie's arm. The flesh was thin as paper. "You remember her."

"Ayah. She was a great lady. Beautiful with a good and kind heart. Doted on her children. A lot of the wealthy ladies who came summering on the island were happy to leave their children to nursemaids and nannies, but Mrs. Calhoun liked to see to them herself. She was always taking them for walks, or spending time in the nursery. Saw them off to bed herself, every night, unless her husband made plans that would take her out before their bedtime. A good mother she was, and nothing better can be said of a woman than that."

She gave a decisive nod and perked up when she saw that Max was taking notes. "I worked there three summers, 1912, '13 and '14." And with the odd trick of old age, she could remember them with perfect clarity.

"Do you mind?" Max took out a small tape recorder. "It would help us remember everything you tell us."

"Don't mind a bit." In fact, it pleased her enormously. She thought it was just like being on a TV talk show. Her fingers worked away as she settled more comfortably in the chair. "You live in The Towers still?" she asked Lilah.

"Yes, my family and I."

"How many times I climbed up and down those stairs. The master, he didn't like us using the main staircase, but when he wasn't about, I used to come down that way and fancy myself a lady. A-swishing my skirts and holding my nose in the air. Oh, I was a pistol in those days, and not hard to look at either. Used to flirt with one of the gardeners. Joseph was his name. But that was just to make my Tom jealous, and hurry him along a bit."

She sighed, looking back. "Never seen a house like it, before or since. The furniture, the paintings, the crystal. Once a week we'd wash every window with vinegar so they'd sparkle like diamonds. And the mistress, she'd like fresh flowers everywhere. She'd cut roses and peonies out of the garden, or pick the wild orchids and lady's slippers."

"What can you tell us about the summer she died?" Max prompted.

"She spent a lot of time in her tower room that summer, looking out the window at the cliffs, or writing in her book."

"Book?" Lilah interrupted. "Do you mean a journal, a diary?"

"I suppose that's what it was. I saw her writing in it sometimes when I brought her up some tea. She'd always thank me, too. Call me by name. 'Thank you, Millie,' she would say, 'it's a pretty day.' Or, 'You didn't have to trouble, Millie. How is your young man?' Gracious, she was." Millie's mouth thinned. "Now the master, he wouldn't say a word to you. Might as well have been a stick of wood for all he noticed."

"You didn't like him," Max put in.

"Wasn't my place to like or dislike, but a harder, colder man I've never met in all my years. We'd talk about it sometimes, me and one of the other girls. Why did such a sweet and lovely woman marry a man like that? Money, I would have said. Oh, the clothes she had, and the parties, the jewelry. But it didn't make her happy. Her eyes were sad. She and the master would go out in the evenings, or they'd entertain at home. He'd go his own way most other times, business and politics and the like, hardly paying any mind to his wife, and less to his children. Though he was partial to the boy, the oldest boy."

"Ethan," Lilah supplied. "My grandfather."

"A fine little boy, he was, and a handful. He liked to slide down the banisters and play in the dirt. The mistress didn't mind him getting dirty, but she made certain he was all polished up when the master got home. A tight ship he ran, Fergus Calhoun. Was it any wonder the poor woman looked elsewhere for a little softness?"

Lilah closed a hand over Max's. "You knew she was seeing someone?"

"It was my job to clean the tower room. More than once I looked out that window and saw her running out to the cliffs. She met a man there. I know she was a married woman, but it wasn't for me to judge then, or now. Whenever she came back from seeing him, she looked happy. At least for a little while."

"Do you know who he was?" Max asked her.

"No. A painter, I think, because there were times he had an easel set up. But I never asked anyone, and never told what I saw. It was the mistress's secret. She deserved one."

Because her hands were tiring, she let them still in her lap. "The day before she died, she brought a little puppy home for the children. A stray she said she'd found out on the cliffs. Lord, what a commotion. The children were wild about that dog. The mistress had one of the gardeners fill up a tub on the patio, and she and the children washed the pup themselves. They were laughing, the dog was howling. The mistress ruined one of her pretty day frocks. After, I helped the nanny clean up the children. It was the last time I saw them happy."

She paused a moment to gather her thoughts while two butterflies danced toward the pansies. "There was a dreadful fight when the master came home. I'd never heard the mistress raise her voice before. They were in the parlor and I was in the hall. I could hear them plain. The master wouldn't have the dog in the house. Of course, the children were crying, but he said, just as cold, that the mistress was to give it to one of the servants and have it destroyed."

Lilah felt her own eyes fill. "But why?"

"It wasn't good enough, you see, being a mutt. The little girl, she stood right up to him, but she was only a wee thing, and it made no difference to him. I thought he might strike her—his voice had that meanness in it—but the mistress told the children to take the dog and go up to their nanny. It got worse after that. The mistress was fit to be tied. I wouldn't have said she had a temper, but she cut loose. The master said terrible things to her, vicious things. He said he was going to Boston for a few days, and that she was to get rid of the dog, and to remember her place. When he came out of the parlor, his face—I'll never forget it. He looked mad, I said to myself, then I peeked into the parlor and there was the mistress, white as a ghost, just sitting in a chair with her hand pressed to her throat. The next night, she was dead."

Max said nothing for a moment. Lilah was looking away, her eyes blind with tears. "Mrs. Tobias, had you heard anything about Bianca planning to leave her husband?"

"Later I did. The master, he dismissed the nanny, even though those poor babies were wild with grief. She—Mary Beals was her name—she loved the children and the mistress like they were her own. I saw her in the village the day they were to take the mistress back to New York for burying. She told me that her lady would never have killed herself, that she would never have done that to the children. She insisted that it had been an accident. And then she told me that the mistress had decided to leave, that she'd come to see she couldn't stay with the master. She was going to take the children away. Mary Beals said she was going to New York herself and that she was going to stay with the children no matter what Mr. Calhoun said. I heard later that she'd gotten her position back."

"Did you ever see the Calhoun emeralds, Mrs. Tobias?" Max asked.

"Oh, ayah. Once seen, you'd never forget them. She would wear them and look like a queen. They disappeared the night she died." A faint smile moved her mouth. "I know the legend, boy. You could say I lived it."

Composed again, Lilah looked back. "Do you have any idea what happened to them?"

"I know Fergus Calhoun never threw them into the sea. He wouldn't so much as flip a penny into a wishing well, so close with his money he was. If she meant to leave him, then she meant to take them with her. But he came back, you see."

Max's brows drew together. "Came back?"

"The master came back the afternoon of the day

she died. That's why she hid them. And the poor thing never had a chance to take them, and her children, and get away."

"Where?" Lilah murmured. "Where could she have put them?"

"In that house, who could say?" Millie picked up her work again. "I went back to help pack up her things. A sad day. Wasn't one of us dry-eyed. We put all her lovely dresses in tissue paper and locked them in a trunk. We were told to clear the room out, even her hair combs and perfume. He wanted nothing left of her in there. I never saw the emeralds again."

"Or her journal?" Max waited while Millie pursed her lips. "Did you find the journal in her room?"

"No." Slowly she shook her head. "There was no diary."

"How about stationery, or cards, letters?"

"Her writing paper was in the desk, and the little book she kept her appointments in, but I didn't see a diary. We put everything away, didn't even leave a hairpin. The next summer, he came back. He kept her room locked up, and there wasn't a sign of the mistress in the house. There had been photographs, and a painting, but they were gone. The children hardly laughed. Once I came across the little boy standing outside his mother's room, just staring at the door. I gave my notice in the middle of the season. I couldn't bear to work in that house, not with the master. He'd grown even colder, harder. And he took to going up to the tower room and sitting for hours. I married Tom that summer, and never went back to The Towers."

Later, Lilah stood on the narrow balcony of their hotel room. Below she could see the long blue rectangle of the pool, hear the laughter and splashing of families and couples enjoying their vacation.

But her mind wasn't on the bright summer sun or the shouts and rippling water. It was on the days eighty years past, when women wore long, graceful dresses and wrote their dreams in private journals.

When Max came up quietly behind her to slip his arms around her waist, she leaned back into him, comforted.

"I always knew she was unhappy," Lilah said. "I could feel that. Just as I could feel she was hopelessly in love. But I never knew she was afraid. I never picked up on that."

"It was a long time ago, Lilah." Max pressed a kiss to her hair. "Mrs. Tobias might have exaggerated. Remember, she was a young, impressionable woman when it all happened."

Lilah turned to look quietly, deeply into his eyes. "You don't believe that."

"No." He stroked his knuckles over her cheek. "But we can't change what happened. We can't help her now."

"But we can, don't you see? By finding the necklace, and the journal. She must have written everything she felt in that book. Everything she wanted, and feared. She wouldn't have left it where Fergus would find it. If she hid the emeralds, she hid the book, too."

"Then we'll find them. If we follow Mrs. Tobias's account, Fergus came back before Bianca expected him. She didn't have the opportunity to get the emeralds out of the house. They're still there, so it's only a matter of time before we find them."

"But—"

He shook his head, cupping his hands around her

face. "Aren't you the one who says to trust your feelings? Think about it. Trent comes to The Towers and falls in love with C.C. Because of his idea to renovate and turn part of the house into a retreat, the old legend comes out. Once it's made public, Livingston or Caufield or whatever we choose to call him develops an obsession. He makes a play for Amanda, but she's already hooked on Sloan—who's also there because of the house. Caufield's impatient, so he steals some of the papers. That brings me into it. You fish me out of the water, take me into your home. Since then we've been able to piece more together. We've found a photograph of the emeralds. We've located a woman who actually knew Bianca, and who's corroborated the fact that she hid the necklace in the house. It's all connected, every step. Do you think we'd have gotten this far if we weren't meant to find them?"

Her eyes softened as she linked her hands over his wrists. "You're awfully good for me, Professor. A little optimistic logic's just what I need right now."

"Then I'll give you some more. I think the next step is to start tracking down the artist."

"Christian? But how?"

"You leave it to me."

"All right." Wanting his arms around her, she laid her head on his shoulder. "There's another connection. You might think it's out of left field, but I can't help thinking about it."

"Tell me."

"A couple of months ago, Trent was walking the cliffs. He found Fred. We've never been able to figure out what the puppy was doing out there all alone. It made me think of the little dog Bianca brought to her

children, the one she and Fergus argued about so bitterly only a day before she died. I wonder what happened to that dog, Max." She let out a long sigh. "Then
I think about those children. It's difficult to imagine
one's grandfather as a little boy. I never even knew him
because he died before I was born. But I can see him,
standing outside of his mother's door, grieving. And it
breaks my heart."

"Shh." He tightened his arms around her. "It's better to think that Bianca had some happiness with her
artist. Can't you see her running to him on the cliffs,
stealing a few hours in the sun, or finding some quiet
place where they could be alone?"

"Yes." Her lips curved against his throat. "Yes, I can.
Maybe that's why I love sitting in the tower. She wasn't
always unhappy there, not when she thought of him."

"And if there's any justice, they're together now."

Lilah tilted her head back to look at him. "Yes, you
are awfully good for me. Tell you what, why don't we
take advantage of that pool down there? I'd like to swim
with you when it wasn't a matter of life or death."

He kissed her forehead. "You've got a deal."

She did more floating than swimming. Max had
never seen anyone who could actually sleep on the
water. But Lilah could—her eyes comfortably closed
behind tinted glasses, her body totally relaxed. She wore
two tiny scraps of leopard-print cloth that raised Max's
blood pressure—and that of every other male within a
hundred yards. But she drifted, hands moving gently
in the water. Occasionally she would kick into a lazy
sidestroke, her hair flowing out around her. Now and
again, she would reach out to link her hand with his, or

twine her arms around his neck, trusting him to keep her buoyant.

Then she kissed him, her lips wet and cool, her body as fluid as the water around them.

"Time for a nap," she said, and left him in the pool to stretch out on a chaise under an umbrella.

When she awoke, the shadows were long and only a few diehards were left in the water. She looked around for Max, vaguely disappointed that he hadn't stayed with her. Gathering up her wrap, she went back inside to find him.

The room was empty, but there was a note on the bed in his careful handwriting.

Had a couple of things to see to. Be back soon.

With a shrug, she tuned the radio to a classical station and went in to take a long, steamy shower.

Revived and relaxed, she toweled off, then began to cream her skin in long, lazy strokes. Maybe they could find some cozy little restaurant for dinner, she mused. Someplace where there were dim corners and music. They could linger over the meal while the candles burned down, and drink cool, sparkling wine.

Then they would come back, draw the drapes on the balcony, close themselves in. He would kiss her in that thorough, drugging way until they couldn't keep their hands off each other. She picked up her bottle of scent, spritzing it onto her softened skin. They would make love slowly or frantically, gently or desperately, until, tangled together, they slept.

They wouldn't think about Bianca or tragedies, about emeralds or thieves. Tonight they would only think about each other.

Dreaming of him, she stepped out into the bedroom.

He was waiting for her. It seemed he'd been waiting for her all of his life. She paused, her eyes darkened by the candles he'd lit, her damp hair gleaming with the delicate light. Her scent wafted into the room, mysterious, seductive, to tangle with the fragrance of the clutch of freesias he'd bought her.

Like her, he had imagined a perfect night and had tried to bring it to her.

The radio still played, low romantic strings. On the table in front of the open balcony doors two slender white tapers glowed. Champagne, just poured, frothed in tall tulip glasses. Behind the table, the sun was sinking in the sky, a scarlet ball, bleeding into the deepening blue.

"I thought we'd eat in," he said, and held out a hand for hers.

"Max." Emotion tightened her throat. "I was right all along." Her fingers linked with his. "You are a poet."

"I want to be alone with you." Taking one of the fragile blooms, he slipped it into her hair. "I'd hoped you wouldn't mind."

"No." She let out a shaky breath when he pressed his lips to her palm. "I don't mind."

He picked up the glasses, handed her one. "Restaurants are so crowded."

"And noisy," she agreed, touching her glass to his.

"And someone might object if I nibbled on you rather than the appetizers."

Watching him, she took a sip. "I wouldn't."

He slid a finger up her throat, then tilted her chin so that their lips met. "We'd better give dinner a try," he said after a long moment.

They sat, close together to watch the sun set, to feed

each other little bites of lobster drenched with sweet, melted butter. She let champagne explode on her tongue, then turned her mouth to his where the flavor was just as intoxicating.

As a Chopin prelude drifted from the radio, he pressed a light kiss to her shoulder, then skimmed more up her throat.

"The first time I saw you," he said as he slipped a bite of lobster between her lips, "I thought you were a mermaid. And I dreamed about you that first night." Gently he rubbed his lips over hers. "I've dreamed about you every night since."

"When I sit up in the tower, I think about you—the way I imagine Bianca once thought about Christian. Do you think they ever made love?"

"He couldn't have resisted her."

Her breath shuddered out between her lips. "She wouldn't have wanted him to." With her eyes on his, she began to unbutton his shirt. "She would have ached needing him, wanting to touch him." On a sigh, she ran her hands over his chest. "When they were together, alone together, nothing else could have mattered."

"He would have been half-mad for her." Taking her hands, he brought her to her feet. He left her for a moment, to draw the shades so that they were closed in with music and candlelight. "Thoughts of her would have haunted him, day and night. Her face…" He skimmed his fingers over Lilah's cheeks, over her jaw, down her throat. "Every time he closed his eyes, he would have seen it. Her taste…" He pressed his lips to hers. "Every time he took a breath it would be there to remind him what it was like to kiss her."

"And she would have lain in bed, night after night,

wanting his touch." Heart racing, she pushed the shirt from his shoulders, then shivered when he reached for the belt of her robe. "Remembering how he looked at her when he undressed her."

"He couldn't have wanted her more than I want you." The robe slithered to the floor. His arms drew her closer. "Let me show you."

The candles burned low. A single thread of moonlight slashed through the chink in the drapes. There was music, swelling with passion, and the scent of fragile flowers.

Murmured promises. Desperate answers. A low husky laugh, a sobbing gasp. From patience to urgency, from tenderness to madness, they drove each other. Through the dark, endless night they were tireless and greedy. A gentle touch could cause a tremor; a rough caress a soft sigh. They came together with generous affection, then again like warriors.

Each time they thought they were sated, they would turn to each other once more to arouse or to soothe, to cling or to stroke, until the candles gutted out and the gray light of dawn crept into the room.

Chapter 11

Hawkins was sick and tired of waiting around. As far as he was concerned every day on the island was a day wasted. Worse, he'd given up a tidy little job in New York that would have earned him at least ten grand. Instead, he'd invested half that much in a heist that looked more and more like a bust.

He knew Caufield was good. The fact was, there were few better at lifting locks and dancing around the police. In the ten years of their association, they had pulled off some very smooth operations. Which was why he was worried.

There was nothing smooth about this job. Damn college boy had messed things up good and proper. Hawkins resented the fact that Caufield wouldn't let him take care of Quartermain. He knew Caufield didn't think he had any finesse, but he could have arranged a nice, quiet accident.

The real problem was that Caufield was obsessed with the emeralds. He talked about them day and night—and he talked as though they were living things rather than some pretty sparklers that would bring in some good, crisp cash.

Hawkins was beginning to believe that Caufield didn't intend to fence the emeralds after all. He smelled the double cross and had been watching his partner like a hawk. Every time Caufield went out, Hawkins would pace the empty house, looking for some clue to his partner's true intentions.

Then there were the rages. Caufield was well-known for his unstable temper, but those ugly tantrums were becoming more frequent. The day before, he had stormed into the house, white-faced and wild-eyed, his body trembling with fury because the Calhoun woman hadn't been at her station in the park. He'd trashed one of the rooms, hacking away at furniture with a kitchen knife until he'd come to himself again.

Hawkins was afraid of him. Though he was a stocky man with ready fists, he had no desire to match Caufield physically. Not when the man got that gleam in his eyes.

His only hope now, if he wanted his rightful share and a clean escape, was to outwit his partner.

With Caufield out of the house again, haunting the park, Hawkins began a slow, methodical search. Though he was a big man, often considered dull-witted by his associates, he could toss a room and hardly raise the dust. He sifted through the stolen papers, then turned away in disgust. There was nothing of use there. If Caufield had found anything, he would never have left it in plain view. He decided to start with the obvious, his partner's bedroom.

He shook out the books first. He knew Caufield liked to pretend he was educated, even erudite, though he'd had no more schooling than Hawkins himself. There was nothing in the volumes of Shakespeare and Steinbeck but words.

Hawkins searched under the mattress, through the drawers in the bureau. Since Caufield's pistol wasn't around, he decided the man had tucked it into his knapsack before setting off to find Lilah. Patient, Hawkins looked behind the mirrors, behind drawers, beneath the rug. He was beginning to think he had misjudged his partner when he turned to the closet.

There, in the pocket of a pair of jeans, he found the map.

It was crudely drawn on yellowed paper. For Hawkins, there was no mistaking its meaning. The Towers was clearly depicted, along with direction and distance and a few out-of-proportion landmarks.

The map to the emeralds, Hawkins thought as he smoothed out the creases. A bitter fury filled him while he studied each line and marker. The double-dealing Caufield had found it among the stolen papers and hidden it away for himself. Well, two could play that game, he thought. He slipped out of the room as he tucked the paper into his own pocket. Wouldn't Caufield have a fine rage when he discovered his partner had snatched the emeralds out from under his nose. Hawkins thought it was almost a pity that he wouldn't be around to see it.

He found Christian. It was so much easier than Max had supposed that he could only sit and stare at the book in his hand. In less than a half day in the library, he'd stumbled across the name in a dusty volume titled *Artists and Their Art: 1900-1950*. He had patiently dug away through the As, was meticulously slogging through the Bs, when there it was. Christian Bradford, 1884-1976. Though the given name had caused Max to perk up, he hadn't expected it to be so easy. But it all fell into place.

> *Though Bradford did not come to enjoy any real success until his last years, his early work has become valuable since his death.*

Max skimmed over the treatise on the artist's style.

> *Considered a gypsy in his day, due to his habit of moving from one location to another, Bradford often sold his work for room and board. A prolific artist, he would often complete a painting in a matter of days. It is said he would work for twenty hours straight when the mood was on him. It remains a mystery why he produced nothing during the years between 1914 and 1916.*

Oh God, Max thought, and rubbed his damp palms on his slacks.

> *Married in 1925 to Margaret Doogan, Bradford had one child, a son. Little more is known about his personal life, as he remained an obsessively private man until his death. He suffered a debilitating heart attack in the late sixties, but continued to paint. He died in Bar Harbor, Maine, where he had kept a cottage for more than a half century. He was survived by his son and a grandson.*

"I've found you," Max murmured. Turning the page, he studied the reproduction of one of Bradford's works. It was a storm, fighting its way in from the sea. Passionate, violent, frenzied. It was a view Max knew—the view from the cliffs beneath The Towers.

An hour later, a half-dozen books under his arm, he arrived home. There was still an hour before he could pick up Lilah at the park, an hour before he could tell her they had jumped the next hurdle. Giddy with success, he greeted Fred so exuberantly that the dog raced up and down the hall, running into walls and tripping on his tail.

"Goodness." Coco trotted down the stairs. "What a commotion."

"Sorry."

"No need to apologize, I wouldn't know what to do if a day went by without a commotion. Why, Max, you look positively delighted with yourself."

"Well, as it happens, I—"

He broke off when Alex and Jenny came bounding down, firing invisible laser pistols. "Dead meat!" Alex shouted. "Dead meat!"

"If you must kill something," Coco said, "please do it outside. Fred needs an airing anyway."

"Death to the invaders," Alex announced. "We'll fry them like bacon."

In total agreement, Jenny aimed her laser at Fred and sent the dog scampering down the hall again. Deciding he made a handy invader, they raced after him. Even with the distance, the sound of the back door slamming boomed through the house.

"I don't know where they get those violent imaginations," Coco commented with a relieved sigh. "Suzanna's so mild-tempered, and their father…" Something dark came into her eyes when she trailed off. "Well, that's another story. So tell me, what has you so happy?"

"I was just in the library, and I—"

This time it was the phone that interrupted. Coco slipped off an earring as she picked up the receiver. "Hello. Yes. Oh, yes, he's right here." She cupped a hand over the mouthpiece. "It's your dean, dear. He'd like to speak to you."

Max set the books on the telephone stand as Coco began to straighten pictures a few discreet feet away. "Dean Hodgins? Yes, I am, thank you. It's a beautiful spot. Well, I haven't really decided when I'm coming back… Professor Blake?"

Coco glanced back at the alarm in his voice.

"When? Is it serious? I'm sorry he's ill. I hope… I beg your pardon?" Letting out a long breath, Max leaned back against the banister. "I'm very flattered, but—" He lapsed into silence again, dragging a hand through his hair. "Thank you. Yes, I understand that. If I could have a day or two to consider. I appreciate it. Yes, sir. Goodbye."

When he simply stood, staring into space, Coco cleared her throat. "I hope it wasn't bad news, dear."

"What?" He focused on her, then shook his head. "No, well, yes. That is, the head of the history department had a heart attack last week."

"Oh." Immediately sympathetic, Coco came forward. "How dreadful."

"It was mild—if you can term anything like that mild. The doctors consider it a warning. They're recommending that he cut back on his workload, and he's taken them seriously, because he's decided to retire." He gave Coco a baffled look. "It seems he's recommended me to take over his position."

"Well now." She smiled and patted his cheek, but she was watching him carefully. "That's quite an honor, isn't it?"

"I'd have to go back next week," he said to himself. "To take over as acting head of the department until a final decision's made."

"Sometimes it's difficult to know what to do, which fork in the road to take. Why don't we have a nice cup of tea?" she suggested. "Then I'll read the leaves and we'll see."

"I really don't think—" The next interruption relieved him, and Coco clucked her tongue as she went to answer the banging on the door.

"Oh, my" was all she said. With her hand pressed to her breast, she said it again. "Oh, my!"

"Don't just stand there with your mouth hanging open, Cordelia," a crisp, authoritative voice demanded. "Have someone deal with my bags."

"Aunt Colleen." Coco's hand fluttered to her side. "What a…lovely surprise."

"Ha! You'd as soon see Satan himself on the doorstep." Leaning on a glossy, gold-tipped cane, she marched across the threshold.

Max saw a tall, rail-thin woman with a mass of luxurious white hair. She wore an elegant white suit and gleaming pearls. Her skin, generously lined, was as pale as linen. She might have been a ghost but for the deep blue eyes that scanned him.

"Who the hell is this?"

"Um. Um."

"Speak up, girl. Don't stutter." Colleen tapped the

cane impatiently. "You never kept a lick of the sense God gave you."

Coco began to wring her hands. "Aunt Colleen, this is Dr. Quartermain. Max, Colleen Calhoun."

"Doctor," Colleen barked. "Who's sick? Damned if I'm going to stay in a contagious house."

"That's a Ph.D., Miss Calhoun." Max offered a cautious smile. "It's nice to meet you."

"Ha." She sniffed and glanced around the hall. "Still letting the place fall down around your ears. Best if it was struck by lightning. Burned to the ground. See to those bags, Cordelia, and have someone bring me some tea. I've had a long trip." So saying, she clumped off toward the parlor.

"Yes, ma'am." Hands still fluttering, Coco sent Max a helpless look. "I hate to ask…"

"Don't worry about it. Where should I take her luggage?"

"Oh, God." Coco pressed her hands to her cheeks. "The first room on the right on the second floor. We'll have to stall her so that I can prepare it. Oh, and she won't have paid the driver. Tightfisted old… I'll call Amanda. She can warn the others. Max—" she clutched his hands "—if you believe in prayer, use it now and pray that this is a very short visit."

"Where's the damn tea?" Colleen demanded in a bellow and thumped her cane.

"Just coming." Coco turned and raced down the hall.

Pulling all her rabbits out of her hat, Coco plied her aunt with tea and petits fours, dragged Trent and Sloan away from their work and begged Max to fall in. Arrangements were made for Amanda to pick up Lilah and for Suzanna to close early and pitch in to prepare the guest room.

It was like preparing for an invasion, Max thought as he joined the group in the parlor. Colleen sat, erect as a general, while she measured her opponents with the same steely eye.

"So, you're the one who married Catherine. Hotels, isn't it?"

"Yes, ma'am," Trent answered politely while Coco fluttered around the room.

"Never stay in 'em," Colleen said dismissively. "Got married quick, wouldn't you say?"

"I didn't want to give her a chance to change her mind."

She almost smiled, then sniffed and aimed at Sloan. "And you're the one who's after Amanda."

"That's right."

"What's that accent?" she demanded, eyes sharpening. "Where are you from?"

"Oklahoma."

"O'Riley," she mused for a moment, then pointed a long white finger. "Oil."

"There you go."

"Humph." She lifted her tea to sip. "So you've got some harebrained notion about turning the west wing into a hotel. Better off burning it down and claiming the insurance."

"Aunt Colleen." Scandalized, Coco gaped at her. "You don't mean that."

"I say what I mean. Hated this place most of my life." She shifted to brood up at the portrait of her father. "He'd have hated seeing paying guests in The Towers. It would have mortified him."

"I'm sorry, Aunt Colleen," Coco began. "But we have to make the best of things."

"Did I ask for an apology?" Colleen snapped. "Where the hell are my grandnieces? Don't they have the courtesy to pay their respects?"

"They'll be along soon." Desperate, Coco poured more tea. "This was so unexpected, and we've—"

"A home should always be prepared for guests," Colleen retaliated with relish, then frowned at the doorway when Suzanna came in. "Which one is this?"

"I'm Suzanna." Dutifully she came forward to kiss her great-aunt's cheek.

"You favor your mother," Colleen decided with a grudging nod. "I was fond of Deliah." She shot a look at Max. "You after her?"

He blinked as Sloan struggled to turn a laugh into a cough. "Ah, no. No, ma'am."

"Why not? Something wrong with your eyes?"

"No." He shifted in his chair as Suzanna grinned and settled on a hassock.

"Max is visiting for a few weeks," said Coco, coming to the rescue. "He's helping us out with a little— historical research."

"The emeralds." Eyes gleaming, Colleen sat back. "Don't take me for a fool, Cordelia. We get newspapers aboard ship. Cruise ships," she said to Trent. "Much more civilized than hotels. Now, tell me what the hell is going on around here."

"Nothing, really." Coco cleared her throat again. "You know how the press blows things out of proportion."

"Was there a thief in this house, shooting off a gun?"

"Well, yes. It was disturbing, but—"

"You." Colleen hefted her cane and poked it at Max. "You with the Ph.D. I assume you can articulate clearly. Explain the situation, briefly."

At the pleading glance from Coco, Max set his unwanted tea aside. "The family decided, after a series of events, to investigate the veracity of the legend of the Calhoun emeralds. Unfortunately, news of the necklace leaked, causing interest and speculation among various people, some of them unsavory. The first step was to catalogue old family papers, to verify the existence of the emeralds."

"Of course they existed," Colleen said impatiently. "Haven't I seen them with my own eyes?"

"You were difficult to reach," Coco began, and was silenced with a look.

"In any case," Max continued. "The house was broken into, and a number of the papers stolen." Max skimmed over his involvement to bring her up to date.

"Hmm." Colleen frowned at him. "What do you do, write?"

Max's brow lifted in surprise. "I teach. History. At, ah, Cornell University."

Colleen sniffed again. "Well, you've made a mess of it. The lot of you. Bringing thieves under the roof, splashing our name all over the press, nearly getting yourselves killed. For all we know the old man sold the emeralds."

"He'd have kept a record," Max put in, and had Colleen studying him again.

"You're right there, Mr. Ph.D. He kept account of every penny he made, and every penny he spent." She closed her eyes a moment. "Nanny always told us she hid them away. For us." Fierce, her eyes opened again. "Fairy tales."

"I love fairy tales," Lilah said from the doorway. She stood, flanked by C.C. and Amanda.

"Come in here where I can see you."

"You first," Lilah muttered to C.C.

"Why me?"

"You're the youngest." She gave her sister a gentle shove.

"Throwing a pregnant woman to the wolves," Amanda muttered.

"You're next."

"What's that on your face?" Colleen demanded of C.C.

C.C. wiped a hand over her cheek. "Motor oil, I guess."

"What's the world coming to? You've got good bones," she decided. "You'll age well. You pregnant yet?"

Dipping her hands in her pockets, C.C. grinned. "As a matter of fact, yes. Trent and I are expecting in February."

"Good." Colleen waved her away. Steeling herself, Amanda stepped forward.

"Hello, Aunt Colleen. I'm glad you decided to come for the wedding."

"Might, might not." Lips pursed, she studied Amanda. "You know how to write a proper letter, in any case. It reached me last week, with the invitation." She was a lovely thing, Colleen thought, like her sisters. She felt a sense of pride in that, but would have bitten off her tongue before admitting it. "Any reason you couldn't marry a man from a nice Eastern family?"

"Yes. None of them annoyed me as much as Sloan."

With what might have been a laugh, Colleen waved her away.

When she focused on Lilah, her eyes burned and she had to press her lips tight to keep them from quivering. It was like looking at her mother, with all the years, and all the hurt wiped away.

"So, you're Lilah." When her voice cracked, she lowered her brows, looking so formidable that Coco trembled.

"Yes." Lilah kissed both her cheeks. "The last time I saw you I was eight, I think. And you scolded me for going barefoot."

"And just what are you doing with your life?"

"Oh, as little as possible," Lilah said blithely. "How about you?"

Colleen's lips twitched, but she rounded on Coco. "Haven't you taught these girls manners?"

"Don't blame her." Lilah sat on the floor at Max's feet. "We're incorrigible." She glanced over her shoulder, smiled at Max, then set a companionable hand on his knee.

Colleen didn't miss a trick. "So, you've got your eye on this one."

Tossing back her hair, Lilah smiled. "I certainly do. Cute, isn't he?"

"Lilah," Max muttered. "Give me a break."

"You didn't kiss me hello," she said quite clearly.

"Leave the boy alone." More amused than she would have admitted, Colleen thumped her cane. "At least he has manners." She waved a hand at the tea things. "Take this business away, Cordelia, and bring me a brandy."

"I'll get it." Lilah unfolded herself and strolled over

to the liquor cabinet. She winked at Suzanna as her sister wheeled over the tea cart. "How long do you think she plans to make our lives a living hell?"

"I heard that."

Undaunted, Lilah turned with the brandy snifter. "Of course you did, Auntie. Papa always told us you had ears like a cat."

"Don't call me 'Auntie.'" She snatched the brandy. Colleen was used to deference—her personality and her money had always demanded it. Or to fear—the kind she easily instilled in Coco. But she enjoyed, tremendously, irreverence. "The trouble is your father never lifted a hand to any of you."

"No," Lilah murmured. "He didn't have to."

"No one loved him more than I," Colleen said briskly. "Now, it's time to decide what to do about this mess you've gotten yourselves into. The sooner mended, the sooner I can rejoin my cruise."

"You don't mean—" Coco caught herself and hastily rephrased. "Do you plan to stay with us until the emeralds are found?"

"I plan to stay until I'm ready to leave." Colleen aimed a look, daring disagreement.

"How lovely," Coco said between unsteady lips. "I believe I'll go in and see about dinner."

"I dine at seven-thirty. Precisely."

"Of course." Even as Coco rose, the familiar chaos could be heard racing down the hall. "Oh, dear."

Suzanna sprang to her feet. "I'll head them off." But she was a bit late as both children came barreling into the room.

"Cheat, cheat, cheat," Jenny accused, eyes brimming.

"Crybaby." But Alex was near tears himself as he gave her a brotherly shove.

"Who are these hooligans?" Colleen asked, interest perking.

"These hooligans are my children." Suzanna studied them both and saw that though she had tidied them herself less than twenty minutes before, they were both grimy and grim faced. Obviously her idea that they spend a quiet hour playing a board game had been a disaster.

Colleen swirled her brandy. "Bring them here. I'll have a look at them."

"Alex, Jenny." The warning tone worked very well. "Come meet Aunt Colleen."

"She isn't going to kiss us, is she?" Alex muttered as he dragged his feet across the room.

"I certainly will not. I don't kiss grubby little boys." She had to swallow. He looked so like her baby brother, Sean. Formally she offered a hand. "How do you do?"

"Okay." Flushing a bit, he touched the thin-boned hand.

"You're awfully old," Jenny observed.

"Quite right," Colleen agreed before Suzanna could speak. "If you're lucky, the same problem will be yours one day." She would have liked to have stroked the girl's shiny blond hair, but it would have shattered her image. "I'll expect you to refrain from shouting and clattering about while I'm in the house. Furthermore…" She trailed off when something brushed her leg. Glancing down, she saw Fred sniffing the carpet for crumbs. "What is that?"

"That's our dog." Seized with inspiration, Alex

reached down to heft the fat puppy in his arms. "If you're mean to us, he'll bite you."

"He'll do no such thing." Suzanna put a hand on Alex's shoulder.

"He might." Alex pouted. "He doesn't like bad people. Do you, Fred?"

Colleen's skin went even whiter. "What is his name?"

"His name is Fred," Jenny said gaily. "Trent found him on the cliffs and brought him home for us." She struggled the dog away from her brother to hold him out. "And he doesn't bite. He's a good dog."

"Jenny, put him down before he—"

"No." Colleen waved Suzanna's warning aside. "Let me see him." Fred wriggled, smearing dirt on Colleen's pristine white suit as she sat him in her lap. Her hands shook as they stroked his fur. "I had a dog named Fred once." A single tear spilled over and down her pale cheek. "I only had him for a little while, but I loved him very much."

Saying nothing, Lilah groped for Max's hand and held tight.

"You can play with him, if you want," Alex told her, appalled that someone so old would cry. "He doesn't really bite."

"Of course he won't bite." Recovering, Colleen set the dog on the floor, then straightened painfully. "He knows I'd just bite him back. Isn't someone going to show me to my room, or do I have to sit here all day and half the damn night?"

"We'll take you up." Lilah tugged on Max's hand so that he rose to help her to her feet.

"Bring the brandy," Colleen said imperiously, and started out stumping with her cane.

"Delightful relatives you have, Calhoun," Sloan murmured.

"Too late to back out now, O'Riley." Amanda heaved a relieved breath. "Come on, Aunt Coco, I'll help you in the kitchen."

"Which room have you stuck me in?" Only slightly breathless, Colleen paused on the second-floor landing.

"The first one, here." Max opened the door, then stepped back.

The terrace doors had been opened to let in the breeze. The furniture had been hastily polished, a few extra pieces dragged in from storage. Fresh flowers sat atop the rosewood bureau. The wallpaper was peeling, but paintings had been culled from other rooms to hide the worst of it. A delicate lace spread had been unfolded from a cedar chest and adorned the heavy four-poster.

"It'll do," Colleen muttered, determined to fight the nostalgia. "Make sure there are fresh towels, girl. And you, Quartermain, is it? Pour me another dose of that brandy and don't be stingy."

Lilah peeked into the adjoining bath and saw all was as it should be. "Is there anything else, Auntie?"

"Mind your tone, and don't call me 'Auntie.' You can send a maid up when it's time for dinner."

Lilah stuck her tongue in her cheek. "I'm afraid it's the staff's year off."

"Unconscionable." Colleen leaned heavily on her cane. "Are you telling me you haven't even day help?"

"You know very well we've been under the financial gun for some time."

"And you'll still not get a penny from me to put into this cursed place." She walked stiffly to the open doors and looked out. God, the view, she thought. It never changed. How many times over how many years had she envisioned it? "Who has my mother's room?"

"I do," Lilah said, lifting her chin.

Very slowly, Colleen turned. "Of course, you would." Her voice had softened. "Do you know how much you favor her?"

"Yes. Max found a picture in a book."

"A picture in a book." Now the bitterness. "That's all that's left of her."

"No. No, there's much more. A part of her is still here, will always be here."

"Don't talk nonsense. Ghosts, spirits—that's Cordelia's influence, and it's a load of hogwash. Dead's dead, girl. When you're as close to it as I am, you'll know that."

"If you'd felt her as I've felt her, you'd know differently."

Colleen closed herself in. "Shut the door behind you. I like my privacy."

Lilah waited until they were out in the hall to swear. "Rude, bad-tempered old bat." Then with a lazy shrug, she tucked her arm through Max's. "Let's go get some air. To think I'd actually felt something for her downstairs when she held Fred."

"She's not so bad, Lilah." They passed through his room and onto the terrace. "You may be just as crotchety when you're eighty-something."

"I'll never be crotchety." She closed her eyes, tossed back her hair and smiled. "I'll have a nice rocking chair set in the sun and sleep old age away." She ran a hand up his arm. "Are you ever going to kiss me hello?"

"Yes." He cupped her face and did so thoroughly. "Hello. How was your day?"

"Hot and busy." But now she felt delightfully cool and relaxed. "That teacher I told you about was back. He seems overly earnest to me. Gives me the willies."

Max's smile disappeared. "You should report him to one of the rangers."

"What, for sending off bad vibrations?" She laughed and hugged him. "No, there's just something about him that hits me wrong. He's always wearing dark glasses, as if I might see something he didn't want seen if he took them off."

"You're letting your…" His grip tightened. "What does he look like?"

"Nothing special. Why don't we take a nap before dinner? Aunt Colleen exhausted me."

"What," Max said very precisely, "does he look like?"

"He's about your height, trim. Somewhere around thirty, I'd guess. Wears the hiker's uniform of T-shirt and ripped jeans. He doesn't have a tan," she said, frowning suddenly. "Which is odd seeing as he said he'd been camping for a couple of weeks. Average sort of brown hair, well over the collar. A very neat beard and mustache."

"It could be him." His fingers dug in as the possibility iced through him. "My God, he's been with you."

"You think—you think it's Caufield." The idea left her shaken so that she leaned back against the wall. "What an idiot I've been. I had the same feeling, the same feeling with this man as I did when Livingston came to take Amanda out for dinner." She ran both hands through her hair. "I must be losing my touch."

Max's eyes were dark as he stared out at the cliffs. "If he comes back, I'll be ready for him."

"Don't start playing hero." Alarmed, she grabbed his arms. "He's dangerous."

"He's not getting near you again." The complete and focused intensity was back on his face. "I'll be taking your shift with you tomorrow."

Chapter 12

He never let her out of his sight. Though they had given the authorities the description, Max took no chances. By the time the day was over, he knew more about the intertidal zone than anyone could want to know. He could recognize Irish moss from rockweed—though he still grimaced at Lilah's claim that the moss made excellent ice cream.

But there hadn't been a sign of Caufield.

On the off chance that he had been speaking the truth about camping in the park, the rangers had made a quiet and thorough search but had found no trace of him.

No one had seen the bearded man watching the fruitless search through field glasses. No one had seen the rage come into his eyes when he realized his cover had been blown.

As they drove home, Lilah unwound her braid. "Feel better?" she asked Max.

"No."

She pushed her hands under her hair to let the wind catch it. "Well, you should. It was sweet of you to worry about me, though."

"It has nothing to do with sweetness."

"I think you're disappointed that you didn't get to go into hand-to-hand combat."

"Maybe I am."

"Okay." She leaned over to nip at his ear. "Want to rumble?"

"It's not a joke," he muttered. "I'm not going to feel right until he's taken care of."

Lilah snuggled back in the seat. "If he had any sense he'd give up and go away. We live in the house and we've hardly made any progress."

"That's not true. We verified the existence of the emeralds. We found a photograph of them. We located Mrs. Tobias, and have her eyewitness account of what happened the day before Bianca died. And we've identified Christian."

"We've what?" She sprang up straight. "When did we identify Christian?"

Max grimaced as he glanced over at her. "I forgot to tell you. Don't look like that. First your great-aunt invades the house and sets everyone on their ears. Then you tell me about the man in the park. I thought I had told you."

She inhaled, then exhaled deeply to keep her patience. "Why don't you tell me now?"

"It was in the library yesterday," he began, and filled her in on what he'd found.

"Christian Bradford," Lilah said, trying out the name to see how it fit. "There's something familiar about it.

I wonder if I've seen some of his paintings. It wouldn't be surprising if there were some in this area, since he lived here on and off. Died here."

"Didn't you study art in college?"

"I didn't study at all unless I was boxed in. Mostly I drifted through, and art was always more a hobby than anything else. I didn't want to work at it because I liked playing at it better. And I wanted to be a naturalist all along."

"An ambition?" He grinned. "Lilah, you'll ruin your image."

"Well, it was my only one. Everybody's entitled. Bradford, Bradford," she repeated, gnawing at the word. "I'd swear it rings a bell." She closed her eyes on it, opening them again when they pulled up at The Towers. "Got it. We knew a Bradford. He grew up on the island. Holt, Holt Bradford. The dark, broody, surly sort. He was a few years older—probably in his early thirties now. He left ten or twelve years ago, but it seems to me I heard he was back. He owns a cottage in the village. My God, Max, if he's Christian's grandson, it would be the same cottage."

"Don't get ahead of yourself. We'll look into it, one step at a time."

"If you have to be logical, I'll talk to Suzanna. She knew him a little better. I remember that she knocked him off his motorcycle the first week she had her license."

"I did not knock him off his motorcycle," Suzanna denied, and sank her aching body into a hot, frothy tub. "He fell off his motorcycle when he failed to yield. I had the right-of-way."

"Whatever." Lilah sat on the edge of the tub. "What do we know about him?"

"He has a nasty temper. I thought he was going to murder me that day. He wouldn't have scraped himself all up if he'd been wearing protective gear."

"I mean his background, not his personality."

Weary, Suzanna opened her eyes. Ordinarily the bathroom was the only place she could find true peace and privacy. Now even that had been invaded. "Why?"

"I'll tell you after. Come on, Suze."

"All right, let me think. He was ahead of me in school. Three or four years, I think. Most of the girls were crazy about him because he looked dangerous. His mother was very nice."

"I remember," Lilah murmured. "She came to the house after..."

"Yes, after Mom and Dad were killed. She used to do handwork. She'd done some lovely pieces for Mom. We still have some of them, I think. And her husband was a lobsterman. He was lost at sea when we were teenagers. I really don't remember that much."

"Did you ever talk to him?"

"Who, Holt? Not really. He'd sort of swagger around and glare. When we had that little accident he mostly swore at me. Then he went off somewhere—Portland. I remember because Mrs. Marsley was talking about him just the other day when I was selling her some climbing roses. He was a cop for a while, but there was some kind of incident, and he gave it up."

"What kind of incident?"

"I don't know. Whenever she starts I just let it flow in one ear and on out. I think he's repairing boats or something."

"He never talked about his family with you?"

"Why in the world should he? And why would you care?"

"Because Christian's last name was Bradford, and he had a cottage on the island."

"Oh." Suzanna let out a long breath as she absorbed the information. "Isn't that just our luck?"

Lilah left her sister to soak, and set off to find Max. Before she could go into his room, Coco waylaid her.

"Oh, there you are."

"Darling, you look frazzled." Lilah kissed her cheek.

"And who wouldn't be? That woman…" Coco took a deep calming breath. "I'm doing twenty minutes of yoga every morning just to cope. Be a dear and take this in to her."

"What is it?"

"Tonight's menu." Coco set her teeth. "She insists on treating this as though it's one of her cruises."

"As long as we don't have to play shuffleboard."

"Thank you, dear. Oh, did Max tell you his news?"

"Hmm? Oh, yes, belatedly."

"Has he decided? I know it's a wonderful opportunity, but I hate to think he'll be leaving so soon."

"Leaving?"

"If he takes the position, he'll have to go back to Cornell next week. I was going to read the cards last night, but with Aunt Colleen, I just couldn't concentrate."

"What position, Aunt Coco?"

"Head of the history department." She gave Lilah a baffled look. "I thought he'd told you."

"I was thinking of something else." She struggled to keep her voice even. "He's going to leave in a few days?"

"He'll have to decide." Coco cupped a hand under Lilah's chin. "You'll both have to decide."

"He hasn't chosen to bring me in on this one." She stared down at the menu until the words blurred. "It's a terrific opportunity, one I'm sure he's hoped for."

"There are a lot of opportunities in life, Lilah."

She only shook her head. "I couldn't do anything to discourage him from doing something he wants. Not if I loved him. It has to be his decision."

"Who the hell is jabbering out there?" Colleen thumped her cane on the floor.

"I'd like to take that cane and—"

"More yoga," Lilah suggested, forcing a smile. "I'll deal with her."

"Good luck."

"You bellowed, Auntie," Lilah said as she breezed through the door.

"You didn't knock."

"No, I didn't. Tonight's menu, Miss Calhoun. We hope it meets with your approval."

"Little snip." Colleen snatched the paper away, then frowned up at her grandniece. "What's wrong with you, girl? You're white as a sheet."

"Pale skin runs in the family. It's the Irish."

"It's temper that runs in the family." She'd seen eyes that had looked like that before, she thought. Hurt, confused. But then she had been only a child, unable to understand. "Trouble with your young man."

"What makes you say so?"

"Just because I never tied myself down with a man doesn't mean I don't know them. I dallied in my day."

"Dallied." This time the smile came more easily. "A nice word. I suppose some of us are meant to dally through life." She ran a finger down the bedpost. "Just as there are some women men love but don't fall in love with."

"You're jabbering."

"No, I'm trying to be realistic. I'm not usually."

"Realism is cold comfort."

Lilah's brow lifted. "Oh, Lord, I'm afraid I'm more like you than I realized. What a scary thought."

Colleen disguised a chuckle. "Get out of here. You give me a headache. Girl," she said, and Lilah paused at the door, "any man who puts that look into your eyes is worth everything or nothing at all."

Lilah gave a short laugh. "Why, Auntie, you're absolutely right."

She went to his room, but he wasn't there. She'd yet to decide whether to confront Max about his plans or to wait until he told her himself. For better or worse, she thought she would follow her instincts. Idly she picked up a shirt he'd left at the foot of his bed. It was the silly screenprint she'd talked him into on that first shopping trip. The shirt, and the memory, still made her smile. Setting it aside, she crossed to his desk.

He had it piled with books—thick volumes on World War I, a history of Maine, a treatment on the Industrial Revolution. She lifted a brow over a book on fashion in the 1900s. He'd picked up one of the pamphlets from the park that gave a detailed map of the island.

In another pile were the art books. Lilah picked up the top one and opened it to where Max had marked it. As he had, she felt the quick thrill of discovery on reading Christian Bradford's name. Lowering into the chair in front of the typewriter, she read the brief biography twice.

Fascinated, excited, she set the book down to reach for another. It was then she noticed the typed pages, neatly stacked. More reports, she thought with a faint smile. She remembered how tidily he had typed up their interview with Millie Tobias.

From the top of the high tower of rock, she faced the sea.

Curious, Lilah settled more comfortably and read on. She was midway through the second chapter when Max came in. Her emotions were so ragged she had to brace before she could speak.

"Your book. You started your book."

"Yeah." He shoved his hands into his pockets. "I was looking for you."

"It's Bianca, isn't it?" Lilah set down the page she was holding. "Laura—she's Bianca."

"Parts of her." He couldn't have explained how it felt to know that she had read his words—words that had come not so much from his head as from his heart.

"You've set it here, on the island."

"It seemed right." He didn't move toward her, he didn't smile, but only stood looking uncomfortable.

"I'm sorry." The apology was stiff and overly polite. "I shouldn't have read it without asking, but it caught my eye."

"It's all right." With his hands still balled in his pockets, he shrugged. She hated it, he thought. "It doesn't matter."

"Why didn't you tell me?"

"There wasn't really anything to tell. I only have about fifty pages, and it's rough. I thought—"

"It's beautiful." She fought back the hurt as she rose. "What?"

"It's beautiful," she repeated, and found that hurt turned quickly to anger. "You've got enough sense to know that. You've read thousands of books in your life, and know good work from bad. If you didn't want to share it with me, that's your business."

Still stunned, he shook his head. "It wasn't that I—"

"What was it then? I'm important enough to share your bed, but not to be in on any of the major decisions in your life."

"You're being ridiculous."

"Fine." Rolling easily with her temper, she tossed back her hair. "I'm being ridiculous. Apparently I've been ridiculous for some time now."

The tears crowding her voice confused as much as unnerved him. "Why don't we sit down and talk this through?"

She went with her instincts and shoved the chair at him. "Go ahead. Have a seat. But there's no need to talk anything through. You've started your book, but didn't think it was necessary to mention it. You've been offered a promotion, but didn't consider it worth bringing up. Not to me. You've got your life, Professor, and I've got mine. That's what we said right from the beginning. It's just my bad luck that I fell in love with you."

"If you'd just—" Her last words sank in, dazzling him, dazing him, delighting him. "Oh, God, Lilah." He started to rush forward, but she threw up both hands.

"Don't touch me," she said so fiercely, he stopped, baffled.

"What do you expect me to do?"

"I don't expect anything. If I had stuck to that from the beginning, you wouldn't have been able to hurt me like this. As it is, it's my problem. Now, if you'll excuse me."

He grabbed her arm before she reached the door. "You can't say things like this, you can't tell me you're in love with me then just walk away."

"I'll do exactly as I please." Eyes cold, she jerked her arm free. "I don't have anything more to say to you, and there's nothing you can say I want to hear right now."

She walked out of his room into her own and locked the door behind her.

Hours later, she sat in her room, cursing herself for losing her pride and her temper so completely. All she had succeeded in accomplishing was embarrassing herself and Max, and giving herself a vicious headache.

She'd slashed at him, and that had been wrong. She'd pushed him, and that had been stupid. Any hope she'd had of steering him gently into love had been smashed because she'd demanded things he hadn't wanted to give. Now, more than likely, she had ruined a friendship that had been vitally important to her.

There could be no apologizing. No matter how miserable she felt, she couldn't apologize for speaking the truth. And she could never claim to be sorry to have fallen in love.

Restless, she walked out on the terrace. There were clouds over the moon. The wind shoved them across the sky so that the light glimmered for a moment then was smothered. The heat of the day was trapped; the night almost sultry. Fireflies danced over the black carpet of lawn like sparks from a dying fire.

In the distance thunder rumbled, but there was no freshening scent of rain. The storm was out at sea, and even if the capricious wind blew it to land, it might be hours before it hit and relieved the hazy heat. She could smell the flowers, hot and heady, and glanced toward the garden. Her thoughts were so involved that she stared at the glimmer of light for a full minute before it registered.

Not again, she thought, and was almost depressed enough to let the amateur treasure hunters have their thrill. But Suzanna worked too hard on the gardens to have some idiot with a map dig up her perennials. In any case, at least chasing off a trespasser was constructive.

She moved quietly down the steps and into the deeper gloom of the garden. It was simple enough to follow the beam of light. As she walked toward it, Lilah debated whether to use the Calhoun curse or the old The Police Are On Their Way. Both were reliable ways of sending trespassers scurrying. Any other time the prospect might have amused her.

When the light blinked out, she stopped, frowning, to listen. There was only the sound of her own breathing. Not a leaf stirred, and no bird sang in the brush. With a shrug, she moved on. Perhaps they had heard her and had already retreated, but she wanted to be certain.

In the dark, she nearly fell over the pile of dirt. All amusement vanished when her eyes adjusted and she saw the destruction of Suzanna's lovely bed of dahlias.

"Jerks," she muttered, and kicked at the dirt with a sandaled foot. "What the hell is wrong with them?" On a little moan, she bent down to pick up a trampled bloom. Her fingers clenched over it when a hand slapped against her mouth.

"Not a sound." The voice hissed at her ear. Reacting to it, she started to struggle, then froze when she felt the point of the knife at her throat. "Do exactly what I say, and I won't cut you. Try to yell, and I'll slice this across your throat. Understand?"

She nodded and let out a long careful breath when his hand slid away from her mouth. It would have been foolish to ask what he wanted. She knew the answer. But this wasn't some adventure-seeking tourist out for a late-night lark.

"You're wasting your time. The emeralds aren't here."

"Don't play games with me. I've got a map."

Lilah closed her eyes and bit back a hysterical and dangerous laugh.

Max paced his room, scowled at the floor and wished he had something handy to kick. He'd messed things up beautifully. He wasn't exactly sure how he'd managed it, but he'd hurt Lilah, infuriated her and alienated her all in one swoop. He'd never seen a woman go through so many emotions in such a short time. From unhappiness to fury, from fury to frost—hardly letting him get in a single word.

He could have defended himself—if he'd been totally certain of the offense. How could he have known that she'd be offended he hadn't mentioned the book? He hadn't wanted to bore her. No, that was a lie, he admitted. He hadn't told her because he'd been afraid. Plain and simple.

As far as the promotion went, he'd meant to tell her, but it had slipped his mind. How could she believe that he'd have accepted the position and left without telling her?

"What the hell was she supposed to think, you jerk?" he muttered, and plopped down into a chair.

So much for all his careful plans, his step-by-step

courtship. His tidy little itinerary for making her fall in love with him had blown up in his face. She'd been in love with him all along.

She loved him. He dragged a hand through his hair. Lilah Calhoun was in love with him, and he hadn't had to wave a magic wand or implement any complicated plan. All he'd had to do was be himself.

She'd been in love with him all along, but he'd been too stupid to believe it even when she'd tried to tell him. Now she'd locked herself in her room and wouldn't listen to him.

As far as he could see, he had two choices. He could sit here and wait until she cooled off, then he could beg. Or he could get up right now, beat down her door and demand that she hear him out.

He liked the second idea. In fact, he thought it was inspired.

Without taking the time to debate with himself, he went through the terrace doors. Since it was two in the morning, it made more sense to rattle the glass than beat on the inside door and wake up the household. And it was more romantic. He'd shove open those doors, stride across the room and drag her into his arms until she...

His erotic dream veered off as he caught a glimpse of her just before she disappeared into the garden.

Fine, he thought. Maybe better. A sultry garden in the middle of the night. Perfumed air and passion. She wasn't going to know what hit her.

"You know where they are." Hawkins dragged her head back by the hair and she nearly cried out.

"If I knew where they were, I'd have them."

"It's a publicity stunt." He whirled her around, laying the edge of the knife against her cheek. "I figured it out. You've just been playing games to get your names in the paper. I've put time and money into this deal, and it's going to pay off tonight."

She was too terrified to move. Even a tremor might have the blade slicing over her skin. She recognized rage in his eyes, just as she recognized him. This was the man Max had called Hawkins. "The map," she began, then heard Max call her name. Before she could take a breath, the knife was at her throat again.

"Make a sound and I kill you, then him."

He'd kill them both anyway, she thought frantically. It had been in his eyes. "The map," she said in a whisper. "It's a fake." She gasped when the blade pricked her skin. "I'll show you. I can show you where they are."

She had to get him away, away from Max. He was calling her again, and the frustration in his voice had tears welling in her eyes.

"Down that way." She gestured on impulse and let Hawkins drag her down the path until Max's voice faded. At the side edge, the garden gave way to the rocks where the smell and sound of the sea grew stronger. "Over there." She stumbled as he pulled her over the uneven ground. Beside her, the slope ran almost gently to a ridge. Below that, dizzying feet below, were the jagged teeth of rocks and the temperamental sea.

When the first flash of lightning struck, she jolted, then looked desperately over her shoulder. The wind had come up, but she hadn't noticed. The clouds still hid the moon and smothered the light.

Was she far enough away? she wondered. Had Max given up looking for her and gone back inside? Where it was safe.

"If you're trying to pull something on me—"

"No. They're here." She tripped on a jumble of rocks and went down hard. "Under here. In a box under the rocks."

She would inch away slowly, she told herself as every instinct screamed for her to run. While he was involved, she would inch away, then spring up and race to the house. He grabbed the hem of her skirt, ripping it.

"One wrong move, and you're dead." She saw the gleam of his eyes as he bent close. "If I don't find the box, you're dead."

Then his head went up, like a wolf scenting. Out of the dark with a vicious oath, Max leaped.

She screamed then as she saw the wicked edge of the knife glint in the flash of lightning. They hit the ground beside her, rolling over dirt and rock. She was still screaming when she jumped on Hawkins's back to grope for his knife hand. The blade sliced into the ground an inch from Max's face before she was bucked off.

"Damn it, run!" Max shouted at her, gripping Hawkins's beefy wrist with both hands. Then he grunted as a fist grazed his temple.

They were rolling again, the impetus taking them down the slope and onto the ridge. She did run, but toward them, sliding along the loose dirt and sending a shower of pebbles to rain over the struggling bodies. Panting for breath, she grabbed a rock. Her next scream sliced the air as Max's leg dangled over the edge into space.

All he could see was the contorted face above his. All he could hear was Lilah shouting his name. Then he saw stars when Hawkins rammed his head against the rock. For an instant, Max teetered on the edge, the brink between sky and sea. His hand slipped down the sweaty forearm. When the knife came down, he smelled the blood and heard Hawkins's grunt of triumph.

There was something else in the air—something passionate and pleading—as insubstantial as the wind but as strong as bedrock. It slammed into him like a fist. The understanding went through him that he wasn't only fighting for his life, but for Lilah's and the life they would make together.

He wouldn't lose it. With every ounce of strength, he smashed his fist into the face grinning over his. Blood spouted out of Hawkins's nose, then they were grappling again with the knife wedged between them.

Lilah lifted the rock in both hands, started to bring it down when the men at her feet reversed positions. Sobbing, she scrambled back. There were shouts behind her and wild barking. She held tight to the only weapon she had and prayed that she would have the chance to use it.

Then the struggling stopped, and both men went still. With a grunt, Max pushed Hawkins aside and managed to gain his knees. His face was streaked with dirt and blood, his clothes splattered with it. Weakly he shook his head to clear it and looked up at Lilah. She stood like an avenging angel, hair flying, the rock gripped in her hands.

"He rolled on the knife," Max said in a distant voice. "I think he's dead." Dazed, he stared down at his hand, at the dark smear that was the blood of the man he'd killed. Then he looked up at her again. "Are you hurt?"

"Oh, Max. Oh, God." The rock slipped from her fingers as she tumbled to her knees beside him.

"It's okay." He patted her shoulder, stroked her hair.

"It's okay," he repeated though he was deathly afraid he would faint.

The dog got there first, then the others came thundering down the slope in nightgowns or robes and hastily pulled-on jeans.

"Lilah." Amanda was there, desperate hands running over her sister's body in a search for wounds. "Are you all right? Are you hurt?"

"No." But her teeth were starting to chatter in the sultry night. "No, he was—Max came." She looked over to see Trent crouched beside him, examining a long gash down his arm. "You're bleeding."

"Not much."

"It's shallow," Trent said between his teeth. "I imagine it hurts like hell."

"Not yet," Max murmured.

Trent looked over as Sloan walked back from the man sprawled on the ridge. Tight-lipped, Sloan shook his head. "It's done," he said briefly.

"It was Hawkins." Max struggled to his feet and stood, swaying. "He had Lilah."

"We'll discuss this later." Her voice uncharacteristically crisp, Coco took Max's good arm. "They're both in shock. Let's get them inside."

"Come on, baby." Sloan reached down to gather Lilah into his arms. "I'll give you a ride home."

"I'm not hurt." From the cradle of his arms she swiveled her head around to look for Max. "He's bleeding. He needs help."

"We'll fix him up," Sloan promised her as they started across the lawn. "Don't you worry, sweetie, the teacher's tougher than you think."

Up ahead, The Towers was ablaze with lights. Another roll of thunder walked the sky above its peaks, then echoed into silence. Abruptly, a tall, thin figure appeared on the second-floor terrace, a cane in one hand, a glinty chrome revolver in the other.

"What the hell is going on around here?" Colleen shouted. "How is a body supposed to get a decent night's sleep with all this hoopla?"

Coco sent one weary glance upward. "Oh, be quiet and go back to bed."

For some reason, Lilah laid her head on Sloan's shoulder and began to laugh.

It was nearly dawn when things settled. The police had come and gone, taking away their grisly package. Questions had been asked and answered—asked and answered again. Lilah had been plied with brandy, fussed over and ordered into a hot bath.

They hadn't let her tend Max's wound. Which might have been for the best, she thought now. Her hands hadn't been steady.

He'd bounced back from the incident remarkably well, she mused as she curled on the window seat in the tower room. While she had still been numb and shaky, he had stood in the parlor, his arm freshly bandaged, and given the investigating officer a clear and concise report of the whole event.

He might have been lecturing one of his classes on the cause and effect of the German economy on World War I, she thought with the ghost of a smile. It had been obvious that Lieutenant Koogar had appreciated the precision and clarity.

Lilah liked to think that her own account had been calm enough, though she hadn't been able to control the trembling very well even when her sisters had joined ranks around her.

Suzanna had finally told the lieutenant enough was enough and had bundled Lilah upstairs.

But despite the bath and brandy, she hadn't been able to sleep. She was afraid if she closed her eyes that she would see it unfolding again, see Max teetering on the edge of the ridge. They'd hardly spoken since the whole horrible business had happened. They would have to, of course, she reflected. She wanted to clear her thoughts and find just the right words.

But then he walked in, while the sky behind her was being gilded with sunrise, and she was afraid she would never find them.

He stood awkwardly, favoring his left arm, his face shadowed by fatigue. "I couldn't sleep," he began. "I thought you might be up here."

"I guess I needed to think. It's always easier for me to think up here." Feeling as awkward as he, she smoothed back her hair. It fell untamed, the color of the young sun, against the white shoulders of her robe. "Would you like to sit?"

"Yeah." He crossed the room and eased his aching muscles down onto the seat beside her. The silence dragged on, one minute, then two. "Some night," he said at length.

"Yes."

"Don't," he murmured when her eyes filled.

"No." She swallowed them back and stared out at the quiet dawn. "I thought he would kill you. It was like a nightmare—the dark, the heat, the blood."

"It's done now." He took her hand, curled strong fingers around hers. "You led him away from the garden. You were trying to protect me, Lilah. I can't thank you for it."

Off guard, she looked back at him. "What was I supposed to do, let him jump out of the petunias and stab you in the dark?"

"You were supposed to let me take care of you."

She tried to jerk her hand free, but he held firm. "You did, didn't you? Whether I wanted you to or not. You came rushing out like a crazy man, jumping on a maniac with a knife and nearly—" She broke off, struggling for composure while he only sat watching her with those patient eyes. "You saved my life," she said more calmly.

"Then we're even, aren't we?" She shrugged and went back to watching the sky. "The oddest thing happened during those last few minutes I was fighting with Hawkins. I felt myself slipping, losing ground. Then I felt something else, something incredibly strong. I'd say it was simple adrenaline, but it didn't come from me. It was something—other," he said, studying her profile. "I suppose you could call it a force. And I knew that I wasn't meant to lose, that there were reasons I couldn't. I guess I'll always wonder if that force, if that feeling came from you, or from Bianca."

Her lips curved as she looked back at him. "Why, Professor, how illogical."

He didn't smile. "I was coming to your room, to make you listen to me, when I saw you go into the garden. Normally I would consider it only right—or logical—to back off and give you time to recover after what's happened. But things change, Lilah. You're going to listen now."

For a moment she leaned her brow on the cool glass.

Then she nodded. "All right, you're entitled. But first I'd like to say that I know I was angry earlier—about the book. It was the wrong reaction—"

"No, it wasn't. You trusted me with a great deal, and I didn't trust you. I was afraid you'd be kind."

"I don't understand."

"Writing's something I've wanted to do most of my life, but I...well, I'm not used to taking risks."

She had to laugh and, going with instinct, leaned over to kiss the bandage on his arm. "Max, what a thing to say now of all times."

"I haven't been used to taking risks," he corrected. "I thought if I told you about the book and got up the courage to show you a few pages, you'd see it as a pipe dream and be kind."

"It's stupid to be so insecure about something you have such talent for." Then she sighed. "And it was stupid for me to take it so personally. Take it from someone who isn't particularly kind. It's going to be a wonderful book, Max. Something you can be very proud of."

He cupped a hand behind her neck. "Let's see if you say that after I make you read several hundred more pages." He leaned toward her, touched his lips gently to hers. But when he started to deepen the kiss, she jumped up.

"I'll give you the first critique when it's published." Nerves humming, she began to pace.

"What is it, Lilah?"

"Nothing. So much has happened." She took a deep breath before she turned, smile firmly in place. "The promotion. I was so involved with myself before that I didn't even congratulate you."

"I wasn't keeping it from you."

"Max, let's not go over all of that again. The important thing is it's a wonderful honor. I think we should have a party to celebrate before you go."

A smile ghosted around his mouth. "Do you?"

"Of course. It isn't every day you get made head of your department. The next thing you know, you'll be dean. It's only a matter of time. And then—"

"Lilah, sit down. Please."

"All right." She clung to the desperate gaiety. "We'll have Aunt Coco bake a cake, and—"

"You're happy about the offer then?" he interrupted.

"I'm very proud of you," she said, and brushed the hair from his brow. "I like knowing that the powers that be appreciate how valuable you are."

"And you want me to accept?"

Her brows drew together. "Of course. How could you refuse? This is a wonderful opportunity for you, something you've worked for and earned."

"That's a pity." He shook his head and leaned back, still watching her. "I've already declined."

"You did what?"

"I declined, with appreciation. It's one of the reasons I never mentioned the whole business to you. I didn't see it as an issue."

"I don't understand. A career opportunity like this isn't something you casually turn aside."

"It depends on your career. I also tendered my resignation."

"You—you quit? But that's crazy."

"Yes, probably." And because it was, he had to grin. "But if I went back to Cornell to teach, the book would end up in a file somewhere gathering dust." He held out his hand, palm up. "You looked at this once and told me I'd have to make a choice. I've made it."

"I see," she said slowly.

"You only see part of it." He glanced around the tower. The light was pearly now, slowly going gold. There couldn't be a better time or a better place. He took both of her hands.

"I've loved you from the first moment I saw you. I couldn't believe that you could ever feel the same way, no matter how much I wanted it. Because I didn't, I made things more difficult than they might have been. No, don't say anything, not yet. Just listen." He pressed their joined hands to his lips. "You've changed me. Opened me. I know that I was meant to be with you, and if it took deceit and a necklace that's been lost the best part of a century, then that's what it had to take. Whether or not we'll ever find the emeralds, they brought you to me, and you're all the treasure I'll ever need."

He brought her close to kiss her mouth as morning rose and washed the last shadows from the room.

"I don't want this to be a dream," she murmured. "I've sat here before thinking of you, wishing for this."

"This is real." He framed her face then kissed her again to prove it.

"You're all I want, Max. I've been looking for you for such a long time." Gently she combed her fingers through the hair on his brow. "I was so afraid you wouldn't love me back, that you'd go away. That I'd have to let you go away."

"This has been home since the first night. I can't explain it."

"You don't have to."

"No." He turned his lips into her palm. "Not to you. One last thing." Again he took her hands. "I love you, Lilah, and I have to ask if you're willing to take the risk of marrying an unemployed former teacher who thinks he can write a book."

"No." She smiled and linked her arms around his neck. "But I'm going to marry a very talented and brilliant man who is writing a wonderful book."

With a laugh, he rested his brow on hers. "I like your way better."

"Max." She snuggled into the crook of his arm. "Let's go tell Aunt Coco. She'll be so thrilled she'll fix us blueberry pancakes for an engagement breakfast."

He eased her back against the pillows. "How about an engagement brunch?"

She laughed and flowed into the kiss. "This time I like your way better."

* * * * *

SUZANNA'S SURRENDER

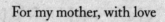
For my mother, with love

Prologue

The moment I saw her, my life was changed. More than fifty years have passed since that moment, and I'm an old man whose hair has turned white, whose body has grown frail. Yet my memories are full of color and strength.

Since my heart attack, I am to rest every day. So I have come back here to the island—her island—where it all began for me. It has changed, as I have. The great fire in '47 destroyed much. New buildings, new people have come. Cars crowd the streets without the charm of the jingling carriages. But I am lucky to be able to see it as it was, and as it is.

My son is a man now, a good one who chose to make his living from the sea. We have never understood each other, but have dealt together well enough. He has a quiet, lovely wife and a son of his own. The boy, young Holt, brings me a special kind of joy. Perhaps it is because I can see myself in him so clearly. The impatience, the fire, the passions that were once mine. Perhaps he, too, will feel too much, want too much. Yet I can't be sorry for it. If I could tell him one thing, it would be to grab hold of life and take.

My life has been full, and I'm grateful for the years I had with Margaret. I was no longer young when she became my wife. What we shared was not a blaze, but the quiet warmth of a banked fire. She brought me comfort, and I hope I gave her happiness. She's been gone for nearly ten years, and my memories of her are sweet.

Yet it is the memory of another woman that haunts me. This memory is so painfully clear, so complete. No amount of time could dull it. The years have not faded my image of her, nor have they altered by a single degree the desperate love I felt. Yes, feel still—will always feel though she is lost to me.

Perhaps now that I have brushed so close to death, I can open myself to it again, let myself remember what I have never been able to forget. Once it was too painful, and I lost the pain in a bottle. Finding no comfort there, I at last buried my misery in my work. Painting again, I traveled. But always, always, was pulled back here where I had once begun to live. Where I know I will one day die.

A man loves that way only once, and only if he is fortunate. For me, it was Bianca. It has always been Bianca.

It was June, the summer of 1912, before the Great War ripped the world apart. The summer of peace and beauty, of art and poetry, when the village of Bar Harbor opened itself to the wealthy and gave refuge to artists.

She came to the cliffs where I worked, her hand holding that of a child. I turned from my canvas, the brush still in my hand, the mood of the sea and the painting still on me. There she was, slender and lovely, the sunset hair swept up off her neck. The wind tugged at it, and at the skirts of the pale blue frock she wore. Her eyes were the color of the sea I was so frantically trying to recreate on canvas. They watched me, curious, wary. She had the pale and luminous skin of the Irish.

The moment I saw her, I knew I had to paint her. And I think I knew, as we stood in the wind, that I would have to love her.

She apologized for interrupting my work. The faint and musical lilt of Ireland was in the soft, polite voice. The child now in her arms was her son. She was Bianca Calhoun, another man's wife. Her summer home was on the ridge above. The Towers, the elaborate castle Fergus Calhoun had built. Even though I had only been on Mount Desert Island a short time, I had heard of Calhoun, and his home. Indeed I had admired the arrogant and fanciful lines of it, the turrets and peaks, the towers and parapets.

Such a place suited the woman who stood before me. She had a timeless beauty, a quiet steadiness, a graciousness that could never be taught, and banked passions simmering in her large green eyes. Yes, I was already in love, but then it was only with her beauty. As an artist, I wanted to interpret that beauty in my own way, with paint or pencils. Perhaps I frightened her by staring so intently. But the child, his name was Ethan, was fearless and friendly. She looked so young, so untouched, that it was difficult to believe the child was hers, and that she had two more besides.

She didn't stay long that day, but took her son and went home to her husband. I watched her walk through the wild roses, the sun in her hair.

I couldn't paint the sea anymore that day. Her face had already begun to haunt me.

Chapter 1

She wasn't looking forward to this. It had to be done, of course. Suzanna dragged a fifty-pound bag of mulch over to her pickup, then muscled it into the bed. That small physical task wasn't the problem. In fact, she was pleased to be able to make the delivery her second stop on her way home.

It was the first stop she wished she could avoid. But for Suzanna Calhoun Dumont, duty could never be avoided.

She'd promised her family that she would speak to Holt Bradford, and Suzanna kept her promises. Or tried to, she thought, and wiped a forearm over her sweaty brow.

But damn it, she was tired. She'd put in a full day in Southwest Harbor, landscaping a new house, and she had a full schedule the next day. That wasn't taking into account that her sister Amanda was getting married in little more than a week, or that The Towers was mass confusion in preparation for the wedding and with the remodeling of the west wing. It didn't even begin to deal with the fact that she had two energetic children at home who would want, and deserved, their mother's time and attention that evening. Or the paperwork that was piling up on her desk—or the fact that one of her part-time employees had quit just that morning.

Well, she'd wanted to start a business, Suzanna reminded herself. And she'd done it. She glanced back at her shop, locked for the night with the display of summer blooms in the window, at the greenhouse just behind the main building. It belonged to her—and the bank, she thought with a little smile—every pansy, petunia and peony. She'd proven she wasn't the incompetent failure her ex-husband had told her she was. Over and over again.

She had two beautiful children, a family who loved her and a landscaping-and-gardening business that was holding its own. She didn't even suppose Bax's claim that she was dull could apply now. Not when she was in the middle of an adventure that had started eighty years before.

There certainly wasn't anything mundane about searching for a priceless emerald necklace, or being dogged by international jewel thieves who would stop at nothing to get their hands on her great-grandmother Bianca's legacy.

Not that she'd been much more than a supporting player so far, Suzanna mused as she climbed into the truck. It had been her sister C.C. who had started it by falling in love with Trenton St. James III, of the St.

James Hotels. It had been his idea to turn part of the financially plagued family home into a luxury retreat. In doing so, the old legend of the Calhoun emeralds had leaked to the ever-eager press and had set off a chain reaction that had run a course from the absurd to the dangerous.

It had been Amanda who had nearly been killed when the desperate and obsessed thief going by the name of William Livingston had stolen family papers he'd hoped would lead him to the lost emeralds. And it had been her sister Lilah who had had her life threatened during the latest attempt.

In the week that had passed since that night, the police hadn't turned up a trace of Livingston, or his latest known alias, Ellis Caufield.

It was odd, she thought as she joined the stream of traffic, how The Towers and the lost emeralds had affected the entire family. The Towers had brought C.C. and Trent together. Then Sloan O'Riley had come to design the retreat and had fallen in love with Amanda. The shy history professor, Max Quartermain, had lost his heart to Suzanna's free-spirited sister, Lilah, and both of them had nearly been killed. Again, because of the emeralds.

There were times Suzanna wished they could forget about the necklace that had belonged to her great-grandmother. But she knew, as they all knew, that the necklace Bianca had hidden away before her death was meant to be found.

So they continued, following up every lead, exploring every dusty path. Now it was her turn. During his research, Max had uncovered the name of the artist Bianca had loved.

It was a story that never failed to make Suzanna wistful, but it was just her bad luck that the connection with the artist led to his grandson.

Holt Bradford. She sighed a little as she drove through the traffic-jammed streets of the village. She couldn't claim to know him well—wasn't sure anyone could. But she remembered him as a teenager. Surly, bad tempered and aloof. Of course, girls had been attracted by his go-to-hell attitude. The attraction helped along, no doubt, by the dark, brooding looks and angry gray eyes.

Odd she should remember the color of his eyes, she mused. But then again, the one time she had seen them up close and personal he'd all but burned her alive with them.

He'd probably forgotten the altercation, she assured herself. She hoped so. Altercations made her shaky and sweaty, and she'd had enough of them in her marriage to last a lifetime. Certainly Holt wouldn't still hold a grudge—it had been more than ten years. After all, he hadn't been hurt very much when he'd taken a header off his motorcycle. And it had been his fault, she thought, setting her chin. She'd had the right of way.

In any case, she had promised Lilah she would talk to him. Any connection with Bianca's lost emeralds had to be followed up. As Christian Bradford's grandson, Holt might have heard stories.

Since he'd come back to Bar Harbor a few months before, he had taken up residence in the same cottage his grandfather had lived in during his romance with Bianca. Suzanna was Irish enough to believe in fate. There was a Bradford in the cottage and Calhouns in The Towers. Surely between them, they could find the answers to the mystery that had haunted both families for generations.

The cottage was on the water, sheltered by two lovely old willows. The simple wooden structure made her think of a doll's house, and she thought it a shame that no one had cared enough to plant flowers. The grass was freshly mowed, but her professional eye noted that there were patches that needed reseeding, and the whole business could use a good dose of fertilizer.

She started toward the door when the barking of a dog and the rumble of a man's voice had her skirting around to the side.

There was a rickety pier jutting out above the calm, dark water. Tied to it was a neat little cabin cruiser in gleaming white. He sat in the stern, patiently polishing the brass. He was shirtless, his tanned skin taut over bone and muscle, and gleaming with sweat. His black hair was curled past where his collar would be if he'd worn one. Apparently he didn't find it necessary to cover himself with anything more than a pair of ripped and faded cutoffs. She noticed his hands, limber, long fingered, and wondered if he had inherited them from his artist grandfather.

Water lapped quietly at the boat. Behind it, she saw a fish hawk soar then plummet. It gave a cry of triumph as it rose up again, a silver fish caught wriggling in its claws. The man in the boat continued to work, untouched by or oblivious to the drama of life and death around him.

Suzanna fixed what she hoped was a polite smile on her face and walked toward the pier. "Excuse me."

When his head shot up, she stopped dead. She had the quick but vivid impression that if he'd had a weapon,

it would have been aimed at her. In an instant, he had
gone from relaxed to full alert, with an edgy kind of
violence in the set of his body that had her mouth going
dry.

As she struggled to steady her heartbeat, she noted
that he had changed. The surly boy was now a dangerous man. There was no other word that came to mind.
His face had matured so that it was all planes and angles, sharply defined. The stubble of a two-day beard
added to the rough-and-ready look.

But it was his eyes once again, that dried up her
throat. A man with eyes that sharp, that potent, needed
no weapon.

He squinted at her but didn't rise or speak. He had to
give himself a moment to level. If he'd been wearing his
weapon, it would have been out and in his hand. That
was one of the reasons he was here, and a civilian again.

He might have forced himself to relax—he knew
how—but he remembered her face. A man didn't forget
that face. God knows, he hadn't. Timeless. In one of his
youthful fantasies, he'd imagined her as a princess, lost
and lovely in flowing silks. And himself as the knight
who would have slain a hundred dragons to have her.

The memory made him scowl.

She'd hardly changed, he thought. Her skin was still
pale Irish roses and cream, the shape of her face still
classically oval. Her mouth had remained full and ro-
mantically soft, her eyes that deep, deep, dreamy blue,
luxuriously lashed. They were watching him now with
a kind of baffled alarm as he took his time looking her
over.

She'd pulled her hair back in a smooth ponytail, but

he remembered how it had flowed, long and loose and gleaming blond over her shoulders.

She was tall—all the Calhoun women were—but she was too thin. His scowl deepened at that. He'd heard she'd been married and divorced, and that both had been difficult experiences. She had two children, a boy and girl. It was difficult to believe that the slender wand of a woman in grubby jeans and a sweaty T-shirt had ever given birth.

It was harder to believe, harder to accept, that she could jangle his nerves just by standing ten feet away.

With his eyes still on hers, he went back to his polishing. "Do you want something?"

She let out the breath she hadn't been aware she was holding. "I'm sorry to just drop in this way. I'm Suzanna Dumont. Suzanna Calhoun."

"I know who you are."

"Oh, well…" She cleared her throat. "I realize you're busy, but I'd like to talk with you for a few minutes. If this isn't a good time—"

"What about?"

Since he was being so gracious, she thought, annoyed, she'd get right to the point. "About your grandfather. He was Christian Bradford, wasn't he? The artist?"

"That's right. So?"

"It's kind of a long story. Can I sit down?"

When he only shrugged, she walked to the pier. It groaned and swayed under her feet, and she lowered herself carefully.

"Actually, it started back in 1912 or '13, with my great-grandmother, Bianca."

"I've heard the fairy tale." He could smell her now, flowers and sweat, and it made his stomach tighten.

"She was an unhappy wife with a rich and difficult husband. She compensated by taking a lover. Somewhere along the line, she supposedly hid her emerald necklace. Insurance if she got up the guts to leave. Instead of taking off into the sunset with her lover, she jumped out of the tower window, and the emeralds were never found."

"It wasn't precisely—"

"Now your family's decided to start a treasure hunt," he went on as if she hadn't spoken. "Got a lot of press out of it, and more trouble than I imagine you bargained for. I heard you had some excitement a couple of weeks ago."

"If you can call my sister being held at knifepoint excitement, yes." The fire had come into her eyes. She wasn't always good at defending herself, but when it came to her family, she was a scrapper. "The man who was working with Livingston, or whatever the bastard's calling himself now, nearly killed Lilah and her fiancé."

"When you've got priceless emeralds with a legend attached, the rats gnaw through the woodwork." He knew about Livingston. Holt had been a cop for ten years, and though he'd spent most of that time in Vice, he'd read reports on the slick and often violent jewel thief.

"The legend and the emeralds are my family's business."

"So why come to me? I turned in my shield. I'm retired."

"I didn't come to you for professional help. It's personal." She took another breath, wanting to be clear and concise. "Lilah's fiancé used to be a history professor at Cornell. A couple of months ago, Livingston, going under the name of Ellis Caufield, hired him to go through the family's papers he'd stolen from us."

Holt continued to polish the brightwork. "Doesn't sound like Lilah developed any taste."

"Max didn't know the papers were stolen," Suzanna said between her teeth. "When he found out, Caufield nearly killed him. In any case, Max came to The Towers and continued his research for us. We've documented the emeralds' existence, and we've even interviewed a servant who worked at The Towers the year Bianca died."

Holt shifted and continued to work. "You've been busy."

"Yes. She corroborates the story that the necklace was hidden, and that Bianca was in love, and planning to leave her husband. The man she was in love with was an artist." She waited a beat. "His name was Christian Bradford."

Something flickered in his eyes then was gone. Very deliberately he set down his rag. He pulled a cigarette from a pack, flicked on a lighter then slowly blew out a haze of smoke.

"Do you really expect me to believe that little fantasy?"

She'd hoped for surprise, even amazement. She'd gotten boredom. "It's true. She used to meet him on the cliffs near The Towers."

He gave her a thin smile that was very close to a sneer. "Saw them, did you? Oh, I've heard about the ghost, too." He drew in more smoke, lazily released it. "The melancholy spirit of Bianca Calhoun, drifting through her summer home. You Calhouns are just full of—stories."

Her eyes darkened, but her voice remained very controlled. "Bianca Calhoun and Christian Bradford were in love. The summer she died, they met often on the cliffs just below The Towers."

That touched a chord, but he only shrugged. "So what?"

"So there's a connection. My family can't afford to overlook any connection, particularly one so vital as this one. It's very possible she told him where she put the emeralds."

"I don't see what a flirtation—an unsubstantiated flirtation—between two people some eighty years ago has to do with emeralds."

"If you could get past this prejudice you seem to have toward my family, we might be able to figure it out."

"Not interested in either part." He flipped open the top of a small cooler. "Want a beer?"

"No."

"Well, I'm fresh out of champagne." Watching her, he twisted off the top, tossed it toward a plastic bucket, then drank deeply. "You know, if you think about it, you'd see it's a little tough to swallow. The lady of the manor, well-bred, well-off, and the struggling artist. Doesn't play, babe. You'd be better off dropping the whole thing and concentrating on planting your flowers. Isn't that what you're doing these days?"

He could make her angry, she thought, but he wasn't going to shake her from her purpose. "My sisters' lives were threatened, my home has been broken into. Idiots are sneaking around in my garden and digging up my rosebushes." She stood, tall and slim and furious. "I have no intention of dropping the whole thing."

"Your business." He flicked the cigarette away before

jumping effortlessly onto the pier. It shook and swayed beneath them. He was taller than she remembered, and she had to angle her chin to keep her eyes level. "Just don't expect to suck me into it."

"All right then. I'll just stop wasting my time and yours."

He waited until she'd stepped off the pier. "Suzanna." He liked the way it sounded when he said it. Soft and feminine and old-fashioned. "You ever learn to drive?"

Eyes stormy, she took a step back toward him. "Is that what this is all about?" she demanded. "You're still steaming because you fell off that stupid motorcycle and bruised your inflated male ego?"

"That wasn't the only thing that got bruised—or scraped, or lacerated." He remembered the way she'd looked. God, she couldn't have been more than sixteen. Rushing out of her car, her hair windblown, her face pale, her eyes dark and drenched with concern and fear.

And he'd been sprawled on the side of the road, his twenty-year-old pride as raw as the skin the asphalt had abraded.

"I don't believe it," she was saying. "You're still mad, after what, twelve years, for something that was clearly your own fault."

"My fault?" He tipped the bottle toward her. "You're the one who ran into me."

"I never ran into you or anyone. You fell."

"If I hadn't ditched the bike, you would have run into me. You weren't looking where you were going."

"I had the right of way. And you were going entirely too fast."

"Bull." He was starting to enjoy himself. "You were

checking that pretty face of yours in the rearview mirror."

"I certainly was not. I never took my eyes off the road."

"If you'd had your eyes on the road, you wouldn't have run into me."

"I didn't—" She broke off, swore under her breath. "I'm not going to stand here and argue with you about something that happened twelve years ago."

"You came here to try to drag me into something that happened eighty years ago."

"That was an obvious mistake." She would have left it at that, but a very big, very wet dog came bounding across the lawn. With two happy barks, the animal leaped, planting both muddy feet on Suzanna's shirt and sending her staggering back.

"Sadie, down!" As Holt issued the terse command, he caught Suzanna before she hit the ground. "Stupid bitch."

"I beg your pardon?"

"Not you, the dog." Sadie was already sitting, thumping her dripping tail. "Are you all right?" He still had his arms around her, bracing her against his chest.

"Yes, fine." He had muscles like rock. It was impossible not to notice. Just as it was impossible not to notice that his breath fluttered along her temple, that he smelled very male. It had been a very long time since she had been held by a man.

Slowly he turned her around. For a moment, a moment too long, she was face-to-face with him, caught in the circle of his arms. His gaze flicked down to her mouth, lingered. A gull wheeled overhead, banked, then soared out over the water. He felt her heart thud against his. Once, twice, three times.

"Sorry," he said as he released her. "Sadie still sees herself as a cute little puppy. She got your shirt dirty."

"Dirt's my business." Needing time to recover, she crouched down to rub the dog's head. "Hi, there, Sadie."

Holt pushed his hands into his pockets as Suzanna acquainted herself with his dog. The bottle lay where he'd tossed it, spilling its contents onto the lawn. He wished to God she didn't look so beautiful, that her laugh as the dog lapped at her face didn't play so perfectly on his nerves.

In that one moment he'd held her, she'd fit into his arms as he'd once imagined she would. His hands fisted inside his pockets because he wanted to touch her. No, that wasn't even close. He wanted to pull her inside the cottage, toss her onto the bed and do incredible things to her.

"Maybe a man who owns such a nice dog isn't all bad." She tossed a glance over her shoulder and the cautious smile died on her lips. The way he was looking at her, his eyes so dark and fierce, his bony face so set had the breath backing up in her lungs. There was violence trembling around him. She'd had a taste of violence from a man, and the memory of it made her limbs weak.

Slowly he relaxed his shoulders, his arms, his hands. "Maybe he isn't," he said easily. "But it's more a matter of her owning me at this point."

Suzanna found it more comfortable to look at the dog than the master. "We have a puppy. Well, he's growing by leaps and bounds so he'll be as big as Sadie soon.

In fact, he looks a great deal like her. Did she have a litter a few months ago?"

"No."

"Hmm. He's got the same coloring, the same shaped face. My brother-in-law found him half-starved. Someone had dumped him, I suppose, and he'd managed to get up to the cliffs."

"Even I draw the line at abandoning helpless puppies."

"I didn't mean to imply—" She broke off because a new thought had jumped into her mind. It was no crazier than looking for missing emeralds. "Did your grandfather have a dog?"

"He always had a dog, used to take it with him wherever he went. Sadie's one of the descendants."

Carefully she got to her feet again. "Did he have a dog named Fred?"

Holt's brows drew together. "Why?"

"Did he?"

Holt was already sure he didn't like where this was leading. "The first dog he had was called Fred. That was before the First World War. He did a painting of him. And when Fred exercised the right *de seigneur* around the neighborhood, my grandfather took a couple of the puppies."

Suzanna rubbed suddenly damp hands on her jeans. It took all of her control to keep her voice low and steady. "The day before Bianca died, she brought a puppy home to her children. A little black puppy she called Fred." She saw his eyes change and knew she had his attention, and his interest. "She'd found him out on the cliffs—the cliffs where she went to meet Christian." She moistened her lips as Holt continued to stare at her and say nothing. "My great-grandfather wouldn't allow the dog to stay. They argued about it, quite seriously. We were able to locate a maid who'd worked there, and she'd heard the whole thing. No one was sure what happened to that dog. Until now."

"Even if that's true," Holt said slowly, "it doesn't change the bottom line. There's nothing I can do for you."

"You can think about it, you can try to remember if he ever said anything, if he left anything behind that could help."

"I've got enough to think about." He paced a few feet away. He didn't want to be involved with anything that would bring him into contact with her again and again.

Suzanna didn't argue. She could only stare at the long, jagged scar that ran from his shoulder to nearly his waist. He turned, met her horrified eyes and stiffened.

"Sorry, if I'd known you were coming to call, I'd have put on a shirt."

"What—" She had to swallow the block of emotion in her throat. "What happened to you?"

"I was a cop one night too long." His eyes stayed steady on hers. "I can't help you, Suzanna."

She shook away the pity he obviously would detest. "You won't."

"Whatever. If I'd wanted to dig around in other people's problems, I'd still be on the force."

"I'm only asking you to do a little thinking, to let us know if you remember anything that might help."

He was running out of patience. Holt figured he'd already given her more than her share for one day. "I was a kid when he died. Do you really think he'd have told me if he'd had an affair with a married woman?"

"You make it sound sordid."

"Some people don't figure adultery's romantic." Then he shrugged. It was nothing to him either way. "Then again, if one of the partners turns out to be a washout, I guess it's tough to come down on the other for looking someplace else."

She looked away at that, closing in on a private pain. "I'm not interested in your views on morality, Holt. Just your memory. And I've taken up enough of your time."

He didn't know what he'd said to put that sad, injured look in her eyes. But he couldn't let her leave with that haunting him. "Look, I think you're reaching at straws here, but if anything comes to mind, I'll let you know. For Sadie's ancestor's sake."

"I'd appreciate it."

"But don't expect anything."

With a half laugh she turned to walk to her truck. "Believe me, I won't." It surprised her when he crossed the lawn with her.

"I heard you started a business."

"That's right." She glanced around the yard. "You could use me."

The faint sneer came again. "I ain't the rosebush type."

"The cottage is." Unoffended, she fished her keys out of her pocket. "It wouldn't take much to make it charming."

"I'm not in the market for posies, babe. I'll leave the puttering around the rose garden to you."

She thought of the aching muscles she took home

with her every night and climbed into the truck to slam the door. "Yes, puttering around the garden is something we women do best. By the way, Holt, your grass needs fertilizer. I'm sure you have plenty to spread around."

She gunned the engine, set the shift in reverse and pulled out.

Chapter 2

The children came rushing out of the house, followed by a big-footed black dog. The boy and the girl skimmed down the worn stone steps with the easy balance and grace of youth. The dog tripped over his own feet and somersaulted. Poor Fred, Suzanna thought as she climbed out of the truck. It didn't look as though he would ever outgrow his puppy clumsiness.

"Mom!" Each child attached to one of Suzanna's jean-clad legs. At six, Alex was already tall for his age and dark as a gypsy. His sturdy tanned legs were scabbed at the knees and his bony elbows were scraped. Not from clumsiness, Suzanna thought, but from derring-do. Jenny, a year younger and blond as a fairy princess, carried the same badges of honor. Suzanna forgot her irritation and fatigue the moment she bent to kiss them.

"What have you two been up to?"

"We're building a fort," Alex told her. "It's going to be impregnant."

"Impregnable," Suzanna corrected, tweaking his nose.

"Yeah, and Sloan said he could help us with it on Saturday."

"Can you?" Jenny asked.

"After work." She bent to pet Fred, who was trying to push his way through the children for his rightful share of affection. "Hello, boy. I think I met one of your relatives today."

"Does Fred have relatives?" Jenny wanted to know.

"It certainly looked that way." She walked over to sit with the children on the steps. It was a luxury to sit, to smell the sea and flowers, to have a child under each arm. "I think I met his cousin Sadie."

"Where? Can she come to visit? Is she nice?"

"In the village," Suzanna said, answering Alex's rapid-fire questions in turn. "I don't know, and yes, she's very nice. Big, like Fred's going to be when he grows into his feet. What else did you do today?"

"Loren and Lisa came over," Jenny told her. "We killed hundreds of marauders."

"Well, we can all sleep easy tonight."

"And Max told us a story about storming the beach at Normally."

Chuckling, Suzanna kissed the top of Jenny's head. "I think that was Normandy."

"Lisa and Jenny played dolls, too." Alex gave his sister a brotherly smirk.

"She wanted to. She got the brand-new Barbie and her car for her birthday."

"It was a Ferrari," Alex said importantly, but didn't

want to admit that he and Loren had played with it when the girls were out of the room. He inched closer to toy with his mother's ponytail. "Loren and Lisa are going to Disney World next week."

Suzanna bit back a sigh. She knew her children dreamed of going to that enchanted kingdom in central Florida. "We'll go someday."

"Soon?" Alex prompted.

She wanted to promise, but couldn't. "Someday," she repeated. The weariness was back when she rose to take each child by the hand. "You guys run and tell Aunt Coco I'm home. I need to shower and change. Okay?"

"Can we go to work with you tomorrow?"

She gave Jenny's hand a quick squeeze. "Carolanne's watching the shop tomorrow. I have site work." She felt their disappointment as keenly as her own. "Next week. Go ahead now," she said as she opened the massive front door. "And I'll look at your fort after dinner."

Satisfied with that, they barreled down the hall with the dog at their heels.

They didn't ask for much, Suzanna thought as she climbed the curving stairs to the second floor. And there was so much more she wanted to give them. She knew they were happy and safe and secure. They had a huge family who loved them. With one of her sisters married, and two others engaged, her children had men in their lives. Maybe uncles didn't replace a father, but it was the best she could do.

They hadn't heard from Baxter Dumont for months. Alex hadn't even rated a card on his birthday. The child support check was late again—as it was every month. Bax was too sharp a lawyer to neglect the payment completely, but he made certain it arrived weeks after its due date. To test her, she knew. To see if she would beg for it. Thank God she hadn't needed to yet.

The divorce had been final for a year and a half, but he continued to take out his feelings for her on the children—the only truly worthwhile thing they had made together.

Perhaps that was why she had yet to get over the nagging disillusionment, the sense of betrayal and loss and inadequacy. She no longer loved him. That love had died before Jenny had been born. But the hurt... Suzanna shook her head. She was working on it.

She stepped into her room. Like most of the rooms in The Towers, Suzanna's bedroom was huge. The house had been built in the early 1900s by her great-grandfather. It had been a showpiece, a testament to his vanity, his taste for the opulent and his need for status. It was five stories of somber granite with fanciful peaks and parapets, two spiraling towers and layering terraces. The interior was lofty ceilings, fancy woodwork, mazelike hallways. Part castle, part manor house, it had served first as summer home, then as permanent residence.

Through the years and financial reversals, the house had fallen on hard times. Suzanna's room, like the others, showed cracks in the plaster. The floor was scarred, the roof leaked and the plumbing had a mind of its own. As one, the Calhouns loved their family home. Now that the west wing was under renovation, they hoped it would be able to pay its own way.

She went to the closet for a robe, thinking that she'd been one of the lucky ones. She'd been able to bring her children here, into a real home, when their own had crumbled. She hadn't had to interview strangers to care for them while she made a living. Her father's sister, who had raised Suzanna and her sisters after their parents had died, was now caring for Suzanna's children. Though Suzanna was aware that Alex and Jenny were a handful, she knew there was no one better suited for the task than Aunt Coco.

And one day soon they would find Bianca's emeralds, and everything would settle back to what passed for normal in the Calhoun household.

"Suze." Lilah gave the door a quick knock then poked her head in. "Did you see him?"

"Yes, I saw him."

"Terrific." Lilah, her red hair curling to her waist, strolled in. She stretched out diagonally on the bed, plumping a pillow against the tiered headboard. Easily she settled into her favorite position. Horizontal. "So tell me."

"He hasn't changed much."

"Uh-oh."

"He was abrupt and rude." Suzanna pulled the T-shirt over her head. "I think he considered shooting me for trespassing. When I tried to explain what was going on, he sneered." Remembering that look, she tugged down the zipper of her jeans. "Basically, he was obnoxious, arrogant and insulting."

"Mmm. Sounds like a prince."

"He thinks we made the whole thing up to get publicity for The Towers when we open the retreat next year."

"What a crock." That stirred Lilah enough to have her sitting up. "Max was nearly killed. Does he think we're crazy?"

"Exactly." With a nod, Suzanna dragged on her robe.

"I couldn't begin to guess why, but he seems to have a grudge against the Calhouns in general."

Lilah gave a sleepy smile. "Still stewing because you knocked him off his motorcycle."

"I did not—" On an oath, Suzanna gave up. "Never mind, the point is I don't think we're going to get any help from him." After pulling the band out of her hair, she ran her hands through it. "Though after the business with the dog, he did say he'd think about it."

"What dog?"

"Fred's cousin," she said over her shoulder as she walked into the bath to turn on the shower.

Lilah came to the doorway just as Suzanna was pulling the curtain closed. "Fred has a cousin?"

Over the drum of the water, Suzanna told her about Sadie, and her ancestors.

"But that's fabulous. It's just one more link in the chain. I'll have to tell Max."

With her eyes closed, Suzanna stuck her head under the shower. "Tell him he's on his own. Christian's grandson isn't interested."

He didn't want to be. Holt sat on the back porch, the dog at his feet, and watched the water turn to indigo in twilight.

There was music here, the symphony of insects in the grass, the rustle of wind, the countermelody of water against wood. Across the bay, Bar Island began to fade and merge into dusk. Nearby someone was playing a radio, a lonely alto sax solo that suited Holt's mood.

This was what he wanted. Quiet, solitude, no responsibilities. He'd earned it, hadn't he? he thought as he tipped the beer to his lips. He'd given ten years of his life to other people's problems, their tragedies, their miseries.

He was burned out, bone-dry and tired as hell.

He wasn't even sure he'd been a good cop. Oh, he had citations and medals that claimed he had been. But he also had a twelve-inch scar on his back that reminded him he'd nearly been a dead one.

Now he just wanted to enjoy his retirement, repair a few motors, scrape some barnacles, maybe do a little boating. He'd always been good with his hands and knew he could make a decent living repairing boats. Running his own business, at his own pace, in his own way. No reports to type, no leads to follow up, no dark alleys to search.

No knife-wielding junkies springing out of the shadows to rip you open and leave you bleeding on the littered concrete.

Holt closed his eyes and took another pull of beer. He'd made up his mind during the long, painful hospital stay. There would be no more commitment in his life, no more trying to save the world from itself. From that point on, he would start looking out for himself. Just himself.

He'd taken the money he'd inherited and had come home, to do as little as possible with the rest of his life. Sun and sea in the summer, roaring fires and howling winds in the winter. It wasn't so damn much to ask.

He'd been settling in, feeling pretty good about himself. Then she'd come along.

Hadn't it been bad enough that he'd looked at her and felt—Lord, the way he'd felt when he'd been twenty years old. Churned up and hungry. He was still hung up on her.

The lovely, and unattainable, Suzanna Calhoun of the Bar Harbor Calhouns. The princess in the tower. She'd lived high up in her castle on the cliffs. And he had lived in a cottage on the edge of the village. His father had been a lobsterman, and Holt had often delivered a catch to the Calhouns' back door—never going beyond the kitchen. But he'd sometimes heard voices or laughter or music. And he had wondered and wanted.

Now she had come to him. But he wasn't a love-struck boy any longer. He was a realist. Suzanna was out of his league, just as she had always been. Even if it had been different, he wasn't interested in a woman who had home and hearth written all over her.

As far as the emeralds went, there was nothing he could do to help her. Nothing he wanted to do.

He'd known about the emeralds, of course. That particular story had made national press. But the idea that his grandfather had been involved, had loved and been loved by a Calhoun woman. That was fascinating.

Even with the coincidence about the dogs, he wasn't sure he believed it. Holt hadn't known his grandmother, but his grandfather had been the hero of his childhood. He'd been the dashing and mysterious figure who had gone off to foreign places, come back with fabulous stories. He'd been the man who had been able to perform magic with a canvas and brush.

He could remember climbing up the stairs to the studio as a child to watch the tall man with the snow-white hair at work. Yet it had seemed more like combat than work. An elegant and passionate duel between his grandfather and the canvas.

They would take long walks, the young boy and the old man, along the shore, across the rocks. Up on the cliffs. With a sigh, Holt sat back. Very often they had walked to the cliffs just below The Towers. Even as a child he'd understood that as his grandfather had looked out to sea, he had gone someplace else.

Once, they had sat on the rocks there and his grandfather had told him a story about the castle on the cliffs, and the princess who'd lived there.

Had he been talking about The Towers, and Bianca?

Restless, Holt rose to go inside. Sadie glanced up, then settled her head on her front paws again as the screen door slammed.

The cottage suited him more than the home he'd grown up in. That had been a neat and soulless place with worn linoleum and dark paneled walls. Holt had sold it after his mother's death three years before. Recently he'd used the profits for some repairs and modernization of the cottage, but preferred keeping the old place much as it had been in his grandfather's day.

It was a boxy house, with plaster walls and wood floors. The original stone fireplace had been pointed up, and Holt looked forward to the first cool night when he could try it out.

The bedroom was tiny, almost an afterthought that jutted out from the main structure. He liked lying in bed at night and listening to rain drumming on the tin roof. The stairs to his grandfather's studio had been reinforced, as well as the railing that skirted along the open balcony. He climbed up now, to look at the wide, airy space, dim with twilight.

Now and then he thought about putting skylights in the angled roof, but he never considered refinishing the floor. The dark old wood was splattered with paint that had dripped from brush or palette. There were streaks of carmine and turquoise, drops of emerald green and canary yellow. His grandfather had preferred the vivid, the passionate, even the violent in his work.

Against one wall, canvases were stacked, Holt's legacy from a man who had only begun to find critical and financial success in his last years. They would, he knew, be worth a hefty sum. Yet as he never considered sanding the paint from the floors, he had never considered selling this part of his inheritance.

Crouching down, he began to look through the paintings. He knew them all, had studied them countless times, wondering how he could have come from a man with such vision and talent. Holt turned over the portrait, knowing that was why he had come up here.

The woman was as beautiful as a dream—the fine-featured oval face, the alabaster skin. Rich red-gold hair was swept up off a graceful neck. Full, soft lips were curved, just a little. But it was the eyes that drew Holt, as they always had. They were green, like a misty sea. It wasn't their color that pulled at him, but the expression in them, the look, the emotion that had been captured by his grandfather's brush and skill.

Such quiet sadness. Such inner grief. It was almost too painful to look at, because to look too long was to feel. He had seen that expression today, in Suzanna's eyes.

Could this be Bianca? he wondered. The resemblance was there, in the shape of the face, the curve of the mouth. The coloring was certainly wrong and the similarities slight. Except the eyes, he thought. When he looked at them, he thought of Suzanna.

Because he was thinking of her too much, he told himself. He rose, but he didn't turn the portrait back to the wall. He stood staring at it for a long time, wondering if his grandfather had loved the woman he'd painted.

It was going to be another hot one, Suzanna thought. Though it was barely seven, the air was already sticky. They needed rain, but the moisture hung in the air and stubbornly refused to fall.

Inside her shop, she checked on the refrigerated blooms and left a note for Carolanne to push the carnations by selling them at half price. She checked the soil in the hanging pots of impatiens and geraniums, then moved on to the display of gloxinia and begonias.

Satisfied, she took her sprayer out to drench the flats of annuals and perennials. The rosebushes and peonies were moving well, she noted. As were the yews and junipers.

By seven-thirty, she was checking on the greenhouse plants, grateful that her inventory was dwindling. What didn't sell, she would winter over. She would also take cuttings for next year's plants. But winter, and that quiet work, was months away.

By eight her pickup was loaded, and she was on her way to Seal Harbor. She would put in a full day's work there on the grounds of a newly constructed home. The buyers were from Boston, and wanted their summer home to have an established yard, complete with shrubs, trees and flower beds.

It would be hot, sweaty work, Suzanna mused. But it would also be quiet. The Andersons were in Boston this week, so she would have the yard to herself. She liked nothing better than working with the soil and living things, tending something she had planted and watching it grow and thrive.

Like her children, she thought with a smile. Her babies. Every time she put them to bed at night or watched them run in the sunlight, she knew that nothing that had happened to her before, nothing that would happen to her in the future would dim that glow of knowing they were hers.

The failed marriage had left her shaken and uncertain, and there were times she still had terrible doubts about herself as a woman. But not as a mother. Her children had the very best she could give them. The bond nourished her, as well as them.

Over the past two years, she'd begun to believe that she could be a success in business. Her flair for gardening had been her only useful skill and had been a kind of salvation during the last months of her dying marriage. In desperation she had sold her jewelry, taken out a loan and had plunged into Island Gardens.

It had made her feel good to use her maiden name. She hadn't wanted any frivolous or clever name for the business, but something straightforward. The first year had been rough—particularly when she'd been pouring every cent she could spare into legal fees to fight a custody suit.

The thought of that, the memory of it, still made her blood run cold. She couldn't have lost them.

Bax hadn't wanted the children, but he'd wanted to make things difficult for her. When it had been over, she'd lost fifteen pounds, countless hours of sleep and had been up to her neck in debt. But she had her children. The ugly battle had been won, and the price meant nothing.

Gradually she was pulling out. She'd gained back a few of the pounds, had caught up a bit on her sleep and was slowly, meticulously hacking away at the debt. In the two years since she'd opened the business, she'd earned a reputation as dependable, reasonable and imaginative. Two of the resorts had tried her out, and it looked as though they'd be negotiating long-term contracts.

That would mean buying another truck, hiring on full-time labor. And maybe, just maybe, that trip to Disney World.

She pulled up in the driveway of the pretty Cape Cod house. Now, she reminded herself, it meant getting to work.

The grounds took up about a half acre and were gently sloped. She had had three in-depth meetings with the owners to determine the plan. Mrs. Anderson wanted plenty of spring flowering trees and shrubs, and the long-term privacy factor of evergreens. She wanted to enjoy a perennial bed that was carefree and full of summer color. Mr. Anderson didn't want to spend his summers maintaining the yard, particularly the side portion, which fell in a more dramatic grade. There, Suzanna would use ground covers and rockeries to prevent erosion.

By noon, she had measured off each area with stakes and strings. The hardy azaleas were planted. Two long-blooming fairy roses flanked the flagstone walk and were already sweetening the air. Because Mrs. Anderson had expressed a fondness for lilacs, Suzanna placed a trio of compact shrubs near the master bedroom window, where the next spring's breezes would carry the scent indoors.

The yard was coming alive for her. It helped her ignore the aching muscles in her arms as she drenched the new plants with water. Birds were chirping, and somewhere in the near distance, a lawn mower was putting away.

One day, she would drive by and see that the fast-growing hedge roses she had planted along the fence had spread and bloomed until they covered the chain link. She would see the azaleas bloom in the spring and the maple leaves go red in the fall, and know that she'd been part of that.

It was important, more important than she could admit to anyone, that she leave a mark. She needed that to remind herself that she wasn't the weak and useless woman who had been so callously tossed aside.

Dripping with sweat, she picked up her water bottle and shovel and headed around to the front of the house again. She'd put in the first of the flowering almonds and was digging the hole for the second when a car pulled into the driveway behind her truck. Resting on her shovel, Suzanna watched Holt climb out.

She let out a little huff of breath, annoyed that her solitude had been invaded, and went back to digging.

"Out for a drive?" she asked when his shadow fell over her.

"No, the girl at the shop told me where to find you. What the hell are you doing?"

"Playing canasta." She shoveled some more dirt. "What do you want?"

"Put that shovel down before you hurt yourself. You've got no business digging ditches."

"Digging ditches is my business—more or less. Now, what do you want?"

He watched her dig for another ten seconds before

he snatched the shovel away from her. "Give me that damn thing and sit down."

Patience had always been her strong point, but she was hard-pressed to find it now. Working at it, she adjusted the brim of the fielder's cap she wore. "I'm on a schedule, and I have six more trees, two rosebushes and twenty square feet of ground cover to plant. If you've got something to say, fine. Talk while I work."

He jerked the shovel out of her reach. "How deep do you want it?" She only lifted a brow. "How deep do you want the hole?"

She skimmed her gaze down, then up again. "I'd say a little more than six feet would be enough to bury you in."

He grinned, surprising her. "And you used to be so sweet." Plunging the shovel in, he began to dig. "Just tell me when to stop."

Normally she repaid kindness with kindness. But she was going to make an exception. "You can stop right now; I don't need any help. And I don't want the company."

"I didn't know you had a stubborn streak." He glanced up as he tossed dirt aside. "I guess I had a hard time getting past that pretty face." That pretty face, he noted, was flushed and damp and had shadows of fatigue under the eyes. It annoyed the hell out of him. "I thought you sold flowers."

"I do. I also plant them."

"Even I know that thing there is a tree."

"I plant those, too." Giving up, she took out a bandanna and wiped at her neck. "The hole needs to be wider, not deeper."

He shifted to accommodate her. Maybe he needed

to do a little reevaluating. "How come you don't have anybody doing the heavy work for you?"

"Because I can do it myself."

Yes, there was stubbornness in the tone, and just a touch of nastiness. He liked her better for it. "Looks like a two-man job to me."

"It is a two-man job—the other man quit yesterday to be a rock star. His band got a gig down in Brighton Beach."

"Big time."

"Hmm. That's fine," she said, and turned to heft the three-foot tree by its balled roots. As Holt frowned at her, she lifted it, then set it carefully in the hole.

"Now I guess I fill it back in."

"You've got the shovel," she pointed out. As he worked, she dragged a bag of peat moss closer and began to mix it with the soil.

Her nails were short and rounded, he noted as she dug her already grimed fingers into the soil. There was no wedding ring on her finger. In fact, she wore no jewelry at all, though she had hands that were meant to wear beautiful things.

She worked patiently, her head down, her cap shielding her eyes. He could see the nape of her neck and wondered what it would be like to press his lips there. Her skin would be hot now, and damp. Then she rose, switching on the garden hose to drench the dirt.

"You do this every day?"

"I try to take a day or two in the shop. I can bring the kids in with me." With her feet, she tamped down the damp earth. When the tree was secure, she spread a thick lawyer of mulch, her moves competent and practiced. "Next spring, this will be covered with blooms."

She wiped the back of her wrist over her brow. The little tank top she wore had a line of sweat down the front and back that only emphasized her fragile build. "I really am on a schedule, Holt. I've got some aspens and white pine to plant out in back, so if you need to talk to me, you're going to have to come along."

He glanced around the yard. "Did you do all this today?"

"Yes. What do you think?"

"I think you're courting sunstroke."

A compliment, she supposed, would have been too much to ask. "I appreciate the medical evaluation." She put a hand on the shovel, but he held on. "I need this."

"I'll carry it."

"Fine." She loaded the bags of peat and mulch into a wheelbarrow. He swore at her, tossed the shovel on top then nudged her away to push the wheelbarrow himself.

"Where out back?"

"By the stakes near the rear fence."

She frowned after him when he started off, then followed him. He began digging without consulting her so she emptied the wheelbarrow and headed back to her truck. When he glanced up, she was pushing out two more trees. They planted the first one together, in silence.

He hadn't realized that putting a tree in the ground could be soothing, even rewarding work. But when it stood, young and straight in the dazzling sunlight, he felt soothed. And rewarded.

"I was thinking about what you said yesterday," he began when they set the second tree in its new home.

"And?"

He wanted to swear. There was such patience in the single word, as if she'd known all along he would bring it up. "And I still don't think there's anything I can do, or want to do, but you may be right about the connection."

"I know I'm right about the connection." She brushed mulch from her hands to her jeans. "If you came out here just to tell me that, you've wasted a trip."

She rolled the empty wheelbarrow to the truck. She was about to muscle the next two trees out of the bed when he jumped up beside her.

"I'll get the damn things out." Muttering, he filled the wheelbarrow and rolled it back to the rear of the yard. "He never mentioned her to me. Maybe he knew her, maybe they had an affair, but I don't see how that helps you."

"He loved her," Suzanna said quietly as she picked up the shovel to dig. "That means he knew how she felt, how she thought. He might have had an idea where she would have hidden the emeralds."

"He's dead."

"I know." She was silent a moment as she worked. "Bianca kept a journal—at least we're nearly certain she did, and that she hid it away with the necklace. Christian might have kept one, too."

Annoyed, he grabbed the shovel again. "I never saw it."

She suppressed the urge to snap at him. However much it might grate, he could be a link. "I suppose most people keep a private journal in a private place. Or he might have kept some letters from her. We found one Bianca wrote him and was never able to send."

"You're chasing windmills, Suzanna."

"This is important to my family." She set the white pine carefully in the hole. "It's not the monetary value of the emeralds. It's what they meant to her."

He watched her work, the competent and gentle hands, the surprisingly strong shoulders. The delicate curve of her neck. "How could you know what they meant to her?"

She kept her eyes down. "I can't explain that to you in any way you'd understand or accept."

"Try me."

"We all seem to have some kind of bond with her—especially Lilah." She didn't look up when she heard him digging the next hole. "We'd never seen the emeralds, not even a photograph. After Bianca died, Fergus, my great-grandfather, destroyed all pictures of her. But Lilah…she drew a sketch of them one night. It was after we'd had a séance."

She did look up then and caught his look of amused disbelief. "I know how it sounds," she said, her voice stiff and defensive. "But my aunt believes in that sort of thing. And after that night, I think she may be right to. My youngest sister, C.C. had an…experience during the séance. She saw them—the emeralds. That's when Lilah drew the sketch. Weeks later, Lilah's fiancé found a picture of the emeralds in a library book. They were exactly as Lilah had drawn them, exactly as C.C. had seen them."

He said nothing for a moment as he set the next tree in place. "I'm not much on mysticism. Maybe one of your sisters saw the picture before, and had forgotten about it."

"If any of us had seen a picture, we wouldn't have

forgotten. Still, the point is that all of us feel that finding the emeralds is important."

"They might have been sold eighty years ago."

"No. There was no record. Fergus was a maniac about keeping his finances." Unconsciously she arched her back, rolled her shoulders to relieve the ache. "Believe me, we've been through every scrap of paper we could find."

He let it drop, mulling it over as they planted the last of the trees.

"You know the bit about the needle in the haystack?" he asked as he helped her spread mulch. "People don't really find it."

"They would if they kept looking." Curious, she sat back on her heels to study him. "Don't you believe in hope?"

He was close enough to touch her, to rub the smudge of dirt from her cheek or run a hand down the ponytail. He did neither. "No, only in what is."

"Then I'm sorry for you." They rose together, their bodies nearly brushing. She felt something rush along her skin, something race through her blood, and automatically stepped back. "If you don't believe in what could be, there isn't any use in planting trees, or having children or even watching the sun set."

He'd felt it, too. And resented and feared it every bit as much as she. "If you don't keep your eye on what's real, right now, you end up dreaming your life away. I don't believe in the necklace, Suzanna, or in ghosts, or in eternal love. But if and when I'm certain that my grandfather was involved with Bianca Calhoun, I'll do what I can to help you."

She gave a half laugh. "You don't believe in hope

or love, or anything else apparently. Why would you agree to help us?"

"Because if he did love her, he would have wanted me to." Bending, he picked up the shovel and handed it back to her. "I've got things to do."

Chapter 3

Suzanna pulled up to the shop, pleased that she had to squeeze between a station wagon and a hatchback in the graveled parking area. There were a few people wandering around the flats of annuals, and a young couple deliberating over the climbing roses. A woman, hugely pregnant, strolled about, carrying a tray of mixed pots. The toddler by her side held a single geranium like a flag.

Inside, Carolanne was ringing up a sale and flirting with the young man who held a ceramic urn of pink double begonias. "Your mother will love them," she said, and swept her long lashes over doe-colored eyes. "There's nothing like flowers for a birthday. Or any-time. We're having a special on carnations." She smiled and tossed her long, curling brown hair. "If you have a girlfriend."

"Well, no…" He cleared his throat. "Not really. Right now."

"Oh." Her smile warmed several degrees. "That's too bad." She gave him his change and a long look. "Come back anytime. I'm usually here."

"Sure. Thanks." He shot a glance over his shoulder, trying to keep her in sight, and nearly ran over Suzanna. "Oh. Sorry."

"That's all right. I hope your mother enjoys them." Chuckling, she joined the pert brunette at the cash register. "You're amazing."

"Wasn't he cute? I love it when they blush. Well." She turned her smile on Suzanna. "You're back early."

"It didn't take as long as I thought." She didn't feel it was necessary to add she'd had unexpected and unwanted help. Carolanne was a hard worker, a skilled salesperson, and an inveterate gossip. "How are things here?"

"Moving along. All this sunshine must be inspiring people to beef up their gardens. Oh, Mrs. Russ was back. She liked the primroses so much, she made her husband build her another window box so she could buy more. Since she was in the mood, I sold her two hibiscus—and two of those terra-cotta pots to put them in."

"I love you. Mrs. Russ loves you, and Mr. Russ is going to learn to hate you." At Carolanne's laugh, Suzanna looked out through the glass. "I'll go and see if I can help those people decide which roses they want."

"The new Mr. and Mrs. Halley. They both wait tables over at Captain Jack's, and just bought a cottage. He's studying to be an engineer, and she's going to start teaching at the elementary school in September."

Shaking her head, Suzanna laughed. "Like I said, you're amazing."

"No, just nosy." Carolanne grinned. "Besides, people buy more if you talk to them. And boy, do I love to talk."

"If you didn't, I'd have to close up shop."

"You'd just work twice as hard, if that's possible." She waved a hand before Suzanna could protest. "Before you go, I asked around to see if anyone needed any part-time work." Carolanne lifted her hands. "No luck yet."

It wasn't any use moaning, Suzanna thought. "This late in the season, everyone's already working."

"If Tommy the creep Parotti hadn't jumped ship—"

"Honey, he had a chance to make a break and do something he's always wanted to do. We can't blame him for that."

"You can't," Carolanne muttered. "Suzanna, you can't keep doing all the site work yourself. It's too hard."

"We're getting by," she said absently, thinking of the help she'd had that day. "Listen, Carolanne, after we deal with these customers, I have another delivery to make. Can you handle things until closing?"

"Sure." Carolanne let out a sigh. "I'm the one with a stool and a fan, you're the one with the pick and the shovel."

"Just keep pushing the carnations."

An hour later, Suzanna pulled up at Holt's cottage. It wasn't just impulse, she told herself. And it wasn't because she wanted to pressure him. Lecturing herself, she climbed out of the truck. It certainly wasn't because she wanted his company. But she was a Calhoun, and Calhouns always paid their debts.

She walked up the steps to the porch, again thinking it was a charming place. A few touches—morning glories climbing up the railing, a bed of columbine and larkspur, with some snapdragons and lavender.

Day lilies along that slope, she thought as she knocked. A border of impatiens. Miniature roses under the windows. And there, where the ground was rocky and uneven, a little herb bed, set off with spring bulbs.

It could be a fairy-tale place—but the man who lived there didn't believe in fairy tales.

She knocked again, noting that his car was there. As she had before, she walked around the side, but he wasn't in the boat this time. With a shrug, she decided she would do what she'd come to do.

She'd already picked the spot, between the water and the house, where the shrub could be seen and enjoyed through what she'd determined was the kitchen window. It wasn't much, but it would add some color to the empty backyard. She wheeled around what she needed, then began to dig.

Inside his work shed, Holt had the boat engine broken down. Rebuilding it would require concentration and time. Which was just what he needed. He didn't want to think about the Calhouns, or tragic love affairs, or responsibilities.

He didn't even glance up when Sadie rose from her nap on the cool cement and trotted outside. He and the dog had an understanding. She did as she chose, and he fed her.

When she barked, he kept on working. As a watchdog, Sadie was a bust. She barked at squirrels, at the wind in the grass, and in her sleep. A year before there'd been an attempted burglary in his house in Portland.

Holt had relieved the would-be thief of his stereo equipment while Sadie had napped peacefully on the living room rug.

But he did look up, he did stop working when he heard the low, feminine laughter. It skimmed along his skin, light and warm. When he pushed away from the workbench, his stomach was already in knots. When he stood in the doorway and looked at her, the knots yanked tight.

Why wouldn't she leave him alone? he wondered, and shoved his hands into his pockets. He'd told her he'd think about it, hadn't he? She had no business coming here again.

They didn't even like each other. Whatever she did to him physically was his problem, and so far he'd managed quite nicely to keep his hands off her.

Now here she was, standing in his yard, talking to his dog. And digging a hole.

His brows drew together as he stepped out of the shed. "What the hell are you doing?"

Her head shot up. He saw her eyes, big and blue and alarmed. Her face, flushed from the heat and her work, went very pale. He'd seen that kind of look before—the quick, instinctive fear of a cornered victim. Then it was gone, fading so swiftly he nearly convinced himself he'd imagined it. Color seeped slowly into her cheeks again as she managed to smile.

"I didn't think you were here."

He stayed where he was and continued to scowl. "So, you decided to dig a hole in my yard."

"I guess you could say that." Steady now, annoyed with herself for the instinctive jolt, she plunged the shovel in again, braced her foot on it and deepened the hole. "I brought you a bush."

Damned if he was going to take the shovel from her this time and dig the hole himself. But he did cross to her. "Why?"

"To thank you for helping me out today. You saved me a good hour."

"So you use it to dig another hole."

"Uh-huh. There's a breeze off the water today." She lifted her face to it for a moment. "It's nice."

Because looking at her made his palms sweat, he scowled down at the tidy shrub pregnant with sassy yellow blooms. "I don't know how to take care of a bush. You put it there, you're condemning it to death row."

With a laugh, she scooped out the last of the dirt. "You don't have to do much. This one's very hardy, even when it's dry, and it'll bloom for you into the fall. Can I use your hose?"

"What?"

"Your hose?"

"Yeah." He raked a hand through his hair. He hadn't a clue how he was supposed to react. It was certainly the first time anyone had given him flowers—unless you counted the batch the guys at the precinct had brought in when he'd been in the hospital. "Sure."

At ease with her task, she continued to talk as she went to the outside wall to turn on the water. "It'll stay neat. It's a very well behaved little bush and won't get over three feet." She petted Sadie, who was circling the bush and sniffing. "If you'd like something else instead…"

He wasn't going to let himself be touched by some

idiotic plant or her misplaced gratitude. "It doesn't matter to me. I don't know one from the other."

"Well, this is a *hypericum kalmianum*."

His lips quirked into what might have been a smile. "That tells me a lot."

Chuckling, she set it in place. "A sunshine shrub in layman's terms." Still smiling, she tilted her head back to look at him. If she didn't know better, she'd have thought he was embarrassed. Fat chance. "I thought you could use some sunshine. Why don't you help me plant it? It'll mean more to you then."

He'd said he wasn't going to get sucked in, and damn it, he'd meant it. "Are you sure this isn't your idea of a bribe? To get me to help you out?"

Sighing a little, she sat back on her heels. "I wonder what makes someone so cynical and unfriendly. I'm sure you have your reasons, but they don't apply here. You did me a favor today, and I'm paying you back. Very simple. Now if you don't want the bush, just say so. I'll give it to someone else."

He lifted a brow at the tone. "Is that how you keep your kids in line?"

"When necessary. Well, what's it to be?"

Maybe he was being too hard on her. She'd made a gesture and he was slapping it back in her face. If she could be casually friendly, so could he. "I've already got a hole in my yard," he pointed out then knelt beside her. The dog lay down in the sunlight to watch. "We might as well put something in it."

And that, she supposed, was his idea of a thank-you. "Fine."

"So how old are your kids?" Not that he cared, he told himself. He was just making conversation.

"Five and six. Alex is the oldest, then Jenny." Her eyes softened as they always did when she thought of them. "They're growing up so fast, I can hardly keep up."

"What made you come back here after the divorce?"

Her hands tensed in the soil, then began to work again. It was a small and quickly concealed gesture, but he had very sharp eyes. "Because it's home."

There was a tender spot, he thought and eased around it. "I heard you're going to turn The Towers into a hotel."

"Just the west wing. That's C.C.'s husband's business."

"It's hard to picture C.C. married. The last time I saw her she was about twelve."

"She's grown up now, and beautiful."

"Looks run in the family."

She glanced up, surprised, then back down again. "I think you've just said something nice."

"Just stating a fact. The Calhoun sisters were always worth a second look." To please himself, he reached out to toy with the tip of her ponytail. "Whenever guys got together, the four of you were definitely topics of conversation."

She laughed a little, thinking how easy life had been back then. "I'm sure we'd have been flattered."

"I used to look at you," Holt said slowly. "A lot."

Wary, she lifted her head. "Really? I never noticed."

"You wouldn't have." His hand dropped away again. "Princesses don't notice peasants."

Now she frowned, not only at the words but at the clipped tone. "What a ridiculous thing to say."

"It was easy to think of you that way, the princess in the castle."

"A castle that's been crumbling for years," she said dryly. "And as I recall, you were too busy swaggering around and juggling girls to notice me."

He had to grin. "Oh, between the swaggering and juggling, I noticed you all right."

Something in his eyes set off a little warning bell. It might have been some time since she'd heard that particular sound, but she recognized it and heeded it. She looked down again to firm the dirt around the bush.

"That was a long time ago. I imagine we've both changed quite a bit."

"Can't argue with that." He pushed at the dirt.

"No, don't shove at it, press it down—firm, but gentle." Scooting closer, she put her hands over his to show him. "All it needs is a good start, and then—"

She broke off when he turned his hands over to grip hers.

They were close, knees brushing, bodies bent toward each other. He noted that her hands were hard, callused, a direct and fascinating contrast to the soft eyes and tea rose complexion. There was a strength in her fingers that would have surprised him if he hadn't seen for himself how hard she worked. For reasons he couldn't fathom, he found it incredibly erotic.

"You've got strong hands, Suzanna."

"A gardener's hands," she said, trying to keep her voice light. "And I need them to finish planting this bush."

He only tightened his grip when she tried to draw away. "We'll get to it. You know, I've thought about kissing you for fifteen years." He watched the faint smile fade away from her face and the alarm shoot into her eyes. He didn't mind it. It might be best for both of them if she was afraid of him. "That's a long time to think about anything."

He released one hand, but before she could let out a sigh of relief, he had cupped the back of her neck. His fingers were firm, his grip determined. "I'm just going to get it out of my system."

She didn't have time to refuse. He was quick. Before she could deny or protest, his mouth was on hers, covering and conquering. There was nothing soft about him. His mouth, his hands, his body when he pulled her against him, were hard and demanding. The swift frisson of fear had her lifting a hand to push against his shoulder. She might as well have tried to move a boulder.

Then the fear turned to an ache. She fisted her hand against him, forced to fight herself now rather than him.

She was taut as a wire. He could feel her nerves sizzle and snap as he clamped her against him. He knew it was wrong, unfair, even despicable, but damn it, he needed to wipe out this fever that continued to burn in him. He needed to convince himself that she was just another woman, that his fantasies of her were only remnants of a boy's foolish dreams.

Then she shuddered. A soft, yielding sound followed. And her lips parted beneath his in irresistible and avid invitation. Swearing, he plunged, dragging her head back by the hair so that he could take more of what she so mindlessly offered.

Her mouth was a banquet, and he too racked with hunger to stem the greed. He could smell her hair, fresh as rainwater, her skin, seductively musky with heat and labor, and the rich and primitive fragrance of earth newly turned. Each separate scent slammed into his system, pumping through his blood, roaring through his head to churn a need he'd hoped to dispel.

She couldn't breathe, or think. All of the weighty and worrisome cares she carried in her vanished. In their place, rioting sensations sprinted. The tensed ripple of muscle under her fingers, the hot and desperate taste of his mouth, the thunder of her heartbeat that raced with dizzying speed. She was wrapped around him now, her fingers digging in, her body straining, her mouth as urgent and impatient as his.

It had been so long since she had been touched. So long since she had tasted a man's desire on her lips. So long since she had wanted any man. But she wanted now—to feel his hands on her, rough and demanding, to have his body cover hers on the soft, sunny grass. To be wild and willful and wanton until this clawing ache was soothed.

The sheer power of that want ripped through her, tearing through her lips in a sobbing moan.

His fingers were curled into her shirt, had nearly ripped it aside before he caught himself, cursed himself. And released her. Her shallow ragged breaths were both condemnation and seduction as he forced himself to pull away. Her eyes had gone to cobalt and were wide with shock.

Small wonder, he thought in livid self-disgust. The woman had nearly been shoved to the ground and ravished in broad daylight.

Her lashes lowered before he could see the shame.

"I hope you feel better now."

"No." His hands were far from steady, so he curled them into fists. "I don't."

She didn't look at him, couldn't. Nor could she afford to think, just at this moment, of what she had done. To comfort herself she began to spread mulch around the newly planted bush. "If it stays dry, you'll have to water this regularly until it's established."

For a second time, he gripped her hands. This time she jolted. "Aren't you going to belt me?"

Using well-honed control, she relaxed and looked up. There was something in her eyes, something dark and passionate, but her voice was very calm. "There doesn't seem to be much point in that. I'm sure you're of the opinion that a woman like me would be…needy."

"I wasn't thinking about your needs when I kissed you. It was a purely selfish act, Suzanna. I'm good at being selfish."

Because his grip was light, she slipped her hands from under his. "I'm sure you are." She brushed her palms on her thighs before she rose. The only thought in her head was of getting away, but she made herself load the wheelbarrow calmly. Until he gripped her arm and whirled her around.

"What the hell is this?" His eyes were stormy, his voice as rough as his hands. He wanted her to rage at him—needed it to soothe his conscience. "I all but took you on the ground, without giving a hell of a lot of consideration to whether you'd have liked it or not, and now you're going to load up your cart and go away?"

She was very much afraid she would have liked it. That was why it was imperative that she stay very calm and very controlled. "If you want to pick a fight or a casual lover, Holt, you've come to the wrong person. My children are expecting me home, and I'm very tired of being grabbed."

Yes, her voice was calm, he thought, even firm, but

her arm was trembling lightly under his hold. There was something here, he realized, some secrets she held behind those sad and beautiful eyes. The same stubbornness that had had him pursuing his gold shield made it essential that he discover them.

"Grabbed in general, or just by me?"

"You're the one doing the grabbing." Her patience was wearing thin. The Calhoun temper was always difficult to control. "I don't like it."

"That's too bad, because I have a feeling I'm going to be doing a lot more of it before we're through."

"Maybe I haven't made myself clear. We are through." She shook loose and grabbed the handles of the wheelbarrow.

He simply put his weight on it to stop her. He wasn't sure if she realized she'd just issued an irresistible challenge. His grin came slowly. "Now you're getting mad."

"Yes. Does that make you feel better?"

"Quite a bit. I'd rather have you claw at me than crawl off like a wounded bird."

"I'm not crawling anywhere," she said between her teeth. "I'm going home."

"You forgot your shovel," he told her, still grinning.

She snatched it up and tossed it into the wheelbarrow with a clatter. "Thanks."

"You're welcome."

He waited until she'd gone about ten feet. "Suzanna."

She slowed but didn't stop, and tossed a look over her shoulder. "What?"

"I'm sorry."

Her temper eased a bit as she shrugged. "Forget it."

"No." He dipped his hands into his pockets and

rocked back on his heels. "I'm sorry I didn't kiss you like that fifteen years ago."

Swearing under her breath, she quickened her pace. When she was out of sight, he glanced back at the bush. Yeah, he thought, he was sorry as hell, but planned to make up for lost time.

She needed some time to herself. That wasn't a commodity Suzanna found very often in a house as filled with people as The Towers. But just now, with the moon on the rise and the children in bed, she took a few precious moments alone.

It was a clear night, and the heat of the day had been replaced by a soft breeze that was scented with the sea and roses. From her terrace she could see the dark shadow of the cliffs that always drew her. The distant murmur of water was a lullaby, as sweet as the call of a night bird from the garden.

Tonight it wouldn't ease her into sleep. No matter how tired her body was, her mind was too restless. It didn't seem to matter how often she told herself she had nothing to worry about. Her children were safely tucked into bed, dreaming about the day's adventures. Her sisters were happy. Each one of them had found her place in the world, just as each one of them had found a mate who loved her for who and what she was. Aunt Coco was happy and healthy and looking forward to the day when she would become head chef of The Towers Retreat.

Her family, always Suzanna's chief concern, was content and settled. The Towers, the only real home she'd ever known, was no longer in danger of being sold, but would remain the Calhoun home. It was pointless to worry about the emeralds. The family was doing all that could be done to find the necklace.

If they hadn't been exploring every avenue, she would never have gone to Holt Bradford. Her fingers curled on the stone wall. That, she thought, had been a useless exercise. He was Christian Bradford's grandson, but he didn't feel the connection. It was obvious that the past held no interest for him. He thought only about the moment, about himself, about his own comfort and pleasures.

Catching herself, Suzanna sighed and forced herself to relax her hands. If only he hadn't made her so angry. She despised losing her temper, and it had come dangerously close to breaking loose that day. It was her own fault, and her own problem that something else had broken loose.

Needs. She didn't want to need anyone but her family—the family she could love and depend on and worry about. She'd already learned a painful lesson about needing a man, one man. She didn't intend to repeat it.

He'd kissed her on impulse, she reminded herself. It had been a kind of dare to himself. There had certainly been no affection in it, no softness, no romance. The fact that it had stirred her was strictly chemical. She'd cut herself off from men for more than two years. And the last year or so of her marriage—well, there had been no affection, softness or romance there, either. She'd learned to do without those things when it came to men. She could continue to do without them.

If only she hadn't responded to him so…blatantly. He might as well have knocked her over the head with a club and dragged her into a cave by the hair for all the finesse he'd shown. Yet she had thrown herself into the moment, clinging to him, answering those hard and demanding lips with a fervor she'd never been able to show her own husband.

By doing so, she'd humiliated herself and amused Holt. Oh, the way he had grinned at her at the end had had her steaming for hours afterward. That was her problem, too, she thought now. Just as it was her problem that she could still taste him.

Perhaps she shouldn't be so hard on herself. As embarrassing as the moment had been, it had proved something. She was still alive. She wasn't the cold shell of a woman that Bax had tossed so carelessly aside. She could feel, and want.

Closing her eyes, she pressed a hand to her stomach. Want too much, it seemed. It was like a hunger, and the kiss, like a crust of bread after a long fast, had stirred the juices. She could be glad of that—to feel something again besides remorse and disillusionment. And feeling it, she could control it. Pride would prevent her from avoiding Holt. Just as pride would save her from any new humiliation.

She was a Calhoun, she reminded herself. Calhoun women went down fighting. If she had to deal with Holt again in order to widen the trail to the emeralds, then she would deal with him. She would never, never let herself be dismissed and destroyed by a man again. He hadn't seen the last of her.

"Suzanna, there you are."

Her thoughts scattered as she turned to see her aunt striding through the terrace doors. "Aunt Coco."

"I'm sorry, dear, but I knocked and knocked. Your light was on so I just peeked in."

"That's all right." Suzanna slipped an arm around

Coco's sturdy waist. This was a woman she'd loved for most of her life. A woman who had been mother and father to her for more than fifteen years. "I was lost in the night, I guess. It's so beautiful."

Coco murmured an agreement and said nothing for a moment. Of all of her girls, she worried most about Suzanna. She had watched her ride away, a young bride radiant with hope. She had been there when Suzanna had come back, barely four years later, a pale, devastated woman with two small children. In the years since, she'd been proud to see Suzanna gain her feet, devoting herself to the difficult task of single parenthood, working hard, much too hard, to establish her own business.

And she had waited, painfully, for the sad and haunted look that clouded her niece's eyes, to finally fade forever.

"Couldn't you sleep?" Suzanna asked her.

"I haven't even thought about sleep yet." Coco let out a huff of breath. "That woman is driving me out of my mind."

Suzanna managed not to smile. She knew *that woman* was her great-aunt Colleen, the eldest of Bianca's children, and the sister of Coco's father. The rude, demanding and perpetually cranky woman had descended on them a week before. Coco was certain the move had been made with the sole purpose of making her life a misery.

"Did you hear her at dinner?" Tall and stately in her draping caftan, Coco began to pace. Her complaints were issued in an indignant whisper. Colleen might have been well past eighty, her bedroom may have been two dozen feet away, but she had ears like a cat. "The sauce was too rich, the asparagus too soft. The idea of her telling *me* how to prepare coq au vin. I wanted to take that cane and wrap it around her—"

"Dinner was superb, as always," Suzanna soothed. "She has to complain about something, Aunt Coco, otherwise her day wouldn't be complete. And as I recall, there wasn't a crumb left on her plate."

"Quite right." Coco drew in a deep breath, releasing it slowly. "I know I shouldn't let the woman get on my nerves. The fact is, she's always frightened me half to death. And she knows it. If it wasn't for yoga and meditation, I'm sure I'd have already lost my sanity. As long as she was living on one of those cruise ships, all I had to do was send her an occasional duty letter. But actually living under the same roof." Coco couldn't help it—she shuddered.

"She'll get tired of us soon, and sail off down the Nile or the Amazon or whatever."

"It can't be too soon for me. I'm afraid she's made up her mind to stay until we find the emeralds. Which is what this is all about anyway." Coco calmed herself enough to stand at the wall again. "I was using my crystal to meditate. So soothing, and after an evening with Aunt Colleen—" She broke off because she was clenching her teeth. "In any case, I was just drifting along, when thoughts and images of Bianca filled my head."

"That's not surprising," Suzanna put in. "She's on all of our minds."

"But this was very strong, dear. Very clear. There was such melancholy. I tell you, it brought tears to my eyes." Coco pulled a handkerchief out of her caftan. "Then suddenly, I was thinking of you, and that was just as strong and clear. The connection between you and Bianca was unmistakable. I realized there had to be a reason, and thinking it through, I believe it's because of Holt Bradford." Coco's eyes were shining now with discovery and enthusiasm. "You see, you've spoken to him, you've bridged the gap between Christian and Bianca."

"I don't think you can call my conversations with Holt a bridge to anything."

"No, he's the key, Suzanna. I doubt he understands what information he might have, but without him, we can't take the next step. I'm sure of it."

With a restless move of her shoulders, Suzanna leaned against the wall. "Whatever he understands, he isn't interested."

"Then you have to convince him otherwise." She put a hand on Suzanna's and squeezed. "We need him. Until we find the emeralds, none of us will feel completely safe. The police haven't been able to find that miserable thief, and we don't know what he may try next time. Holt is our only link with the man Bianca loved."

"I know."

"Then you'll see him again. You'll talk to him."

Suzanna looked toward the cliffs, toward the shadows. "Yes, I'll see him again."

I knew she would come back. However unwise, however wrong it might have been, I looked for her every afternoon. On the days she did not come to the cliffs, I would find myself staring up at the peaks of The Towers, aching for her in a way I had no right to ache for another man's wife. On the days she walked toward me, her hair like melted flame, that small, shy smile on her lips, I knew a joy like no other.

In the beginning, our conversations were polite and

distant. The weather, unimportant village gossip, art and literature. As time passed, she became more at ease with me. She would speak of her children, and I came to know them through her. The little girl, Colleen, who liked pretty dresses and yearned for a pony. Young Ethan who only wanted to run and find adventure. And little Sean, who was just learning to crawl.

It took no special insight to see that her children were her life. Rarely did she speak of the parties, the musicals, the social gatherings I knew she attended almost nightly. Not at all did she speak of the man she had married.

I admit I wondered about him. Of course, it was common knowledge that Fergus Calhoun was an ambitious and wealthy man, one who had turned a few dollars into an empire during the course of his life. He commanded both respect and fear in the business world. For that I cared nothing.

It was the private man who obsessed me. The man who had the right to call her wife. The man who lay beside her at night, who touched her. The man who knew the texture of her skin, the taste of her mouth. The man who knew how it felt to have her move beneath him in the dark.

I was already in love with her. Perhaps I had been from the moment I had seen her walking with the child through the wild roses.

It would have been best for my sanity if I had chosen another place to paint. I could not. Already knowing I would have no more of her, could have no more than a few hours of conversation, I went back. Again and again.

She agreed to let me paint her. I began to see, as an

artist must see, the inner woman. Beyond her beauty, beyond her composure and breeding was a desperately unhappy woman. I wanted to take her in my arms, to demand that she tell me what had put that sad and haunted look in her eyes. But I only painted her. I had no right to do more.

I have never been a patient or a noble man. Yet with her, I found I could be both. Without ever touching me, she changed me. Nothing would be the same for me after that summer—that all too brief summer when she would come, to sit on the rocks and look out to sea.

Even now, a lifetime later, I can walk to those cliffs and see her. I can smell the sea that never changes, and catch the drift of her perfume. I have only to pick a wild rose to remember the fiery lights of her hair. Closing my eyes, I hear the murmur of the water on the rocks below and her voice comes back as clear and as sweet as yesterday.

I am reminded of the last afternoon that first summer, when she stood beside me, close enough to touch, as distant as the moon.

"We leave in the morning," she said, but didn't look at me. "The children are sorry to go."

"And you?"

A faint smile touched her lips but not her eyes. "Sometimes I wonder if I've lived before. If my home was an island like this. The first time I came here, it was as if I had been waiting to see it again. I'll miss the sea."

Perhaps it was only my own needs that made me think, when she glanced at me, that she would miss me, as well. Then she looked away again and sighed.

"New York is so different, so full of noise and ur-

gency. It's hard to believe such a place exists when I stand here. Will you stay on the island through the winter?"

I thought of the cold and desolate months ahead and cursed fate for taunting me with what I could never have. *"My plans change with my mood."* I said it lightly, fighting to keep the bitterness out of my voice.

"I envy you your freedom." She turned away then to walk back to where her nearly completed portrait rested on my easel. *"And your talent. You've made me more than what I am."*

"Less." I had to curl my hands into fists to keep from touching her. *"Some things can never be captured with paint and canvas."*

"What will you call it?"

"Bianca. Your name is enough."

She must have sensed my feelings, though I tried desperately to hold them in myself. Something came into her eyes as she looked at me, and the look held longer than it should. Then she stepped back, cautiously, like a woman who had wandered too close to the edge of a cliff.

"One day you'll be famous, and people will beg for your work."

I couldn't take my eyes off her, knowing I might never see her again. *"I don't paint for fame."*

"No, and that's why you'll have it. When you do, I'll remember this summer. Goodbye, Christian."

She walked away from me—for what I thought was the last time—away from the rocks, through the wild grass and the flowers that fight through both for the sun.

Chapter 4

Coco Calhoun McPike didn't believe in leaving things up to chance—particularly when her horoscope that day had advised her to take a more active part in a family matter and to visit an old acquaintance. She felt she could do both by paying an informal call on Holt Bradford.

She remembered him as a dark, hot-eyed boy who had delivered lobster and loitered around the village, waiting for trouble to happen. She also remembered that he had once stopped to change a flat for her while she'd been struggling on the side of the road trying to figure out which end of the jack to put under the bumper. He'd refused—stiffly, she recalled—her offer of payment and had hopped back on his motorcycle and ridden off before she'd properly thanked him.

Proud, defiant, rebellious, she mused as she maneuvered her car into his driveway. Yet, in a grudging sort of way, chivalrous. Perhaps if she was clever—and Coco thought that she was—she could play on all of those traits to get what she wanted.

So this had been Christian Bradford's cottage, she mused. She'd seen it before, of course, but not since she'd known of the connection between the families. She paused for a moment. With her eyes closed she tried to *feel* something. Surely there was some remnant of energy here, something that time and wind hadn't washed away.

Coco liked to consider herself a mystic. Whether it was a true evaluation, or her imagination was ripe, she was certain she did feel some snap of passion in the air. Pleased with it, and herself, she trooped to the house.

She'd dressed very carefully. She wanted to look attractive, of course. Her vanity wouldn't permit otherwise. But she'd also wanted to look distinguished and just the tiniest bit matronly. She felt the old and classic Chanel suit in powder blue worked very well.

She knocked, putting what she hoped was a wise and comforting smile on her face. The wild barking and the steady stream of curses from within had her placing a hand on her breast.

Five minutes out of the shower, his hair dripping and his temper curdled, Holt yanked open the door. Sadie bounded out. Coco squeaked. Good reflexes had Holt snatching the amorous dog by the collar before she could send Coco over the porch railing.

"Oh my." Coco looked from dog to man, juggling the plate of double-fudge brownies. "Oh, goodness. What a very *large* dog. She certainly does look like our Fred, and I'd so hoped he'd stop growing soon. Why you

could practically *ride* her if you liked, couldn't you?"
She beamed a smile at Holt. "I'm so sorry, have I interrupted you?"

He continued to struggle with the dog, who'd gotten a good whiff of the brownies and wanted her share.
Now. "Excuse me?"

"I've interrupted," Coco repeated. "I know it's early,
but on days like this I just can't stay in bed. All this sun
and twittering birds. Not to mention the sawing and
hammering. Do you suppose she'd like one of these?"
Without waiting for an answer, Coco took one of the
brownies off the plate. "Now you sit and behave."

With what was certainly a grin, Sadie stopped straining, sat and eyed Coco adoringly.

"Good dog." Sadie took the treat politely then pad-
ded back into the house to enjoy it. "Well, now." Pleased
with the situation, Coco smiled at Holt. "You probably
don't remember me. Goodness, it's been years."

"Mrs. McPike." He remembered her, all right, though
the last time he'd seen her, her hair had been a dusky
blond. It had been ten years, he thought, but she looked
younger. She'd either had a first-class face-lift or had
discovered the fountain of youth.

"Why, yes. It's so flattering to be remembered by an
attractive man. But you were hardly more than a boy
the last time. Welcome home." She offered the plate of
brownies.

And left him no choice but to accept it and ask her in.

"Thanks." He studied the plate as she breezed inside. Between plants and brownies, the Calhouns were
making a habit of bearing gifts. "Is there something I
can do for you?"

"To tell you the truth, I've just been dying to see the

place. To think this is where Christian Bradford lived
and worked." She sighed. "And dreamed of Bianca."

"Well, he lived and worked here, anyway."

"Suzanna tells me you're not quite convinced they
loved each other. I can appreciate your reluctance to fall
right in with the story, but you see, it's a part of my family history. And yours. Oh, what a glorious painting!"

She crossed the room to a misty seascape hung above
the stone fireplace. Even through the haze of fog, the
colors were ripe and vivid, as though the vitality and
passion were fighting to free themselves from the thin
graying curtain. Turbulent whitecaps, the black and
toothy edge of rock, the gloom-crowned shadows of
islands marooned in a cold, dark sea.

"It's powerful," she murmured. "And, oh, lonely. It's
his, isn't it?"

"Yes."

She let out a shaky sigh. "If you'd like to see that
view, you've only to walk on the cliffs beneath The
Towers. Suzanna walks there, sometimes with the children, sometimes alone. Too often alone." Shaking off
the mood, Coco turned back. "My niece seems to feel
that you're not particularly interested in confirming
Christian and Bianca's relationship, and helping to find
the emeralds. I find that difficult to believe."

Holt set the plate aside. "It shouldn't be, Mrs. McPike.
But what I told your niece was that if and when I was
convinced there had been a connection of any impor-
tance, I'd do what I could to help. Which, as I see it, is
next to nothing."

"You were a police officer, weren't you?"

Holt hooked his thumbs in his pockets, not trusting
the change of subject. "Yeah."

"I have to admit I was surprised when I heard you'd chosen that profession, but I'm sure you were well suited to the job."

The scar on his back seemed to twinge. "I used to be."

"And you'd have solved cases, I suppose."

His lips curved a little. "A few."

"So you'd have looked for clues and followed them up until you found the right answer." She smiled at him. "I always admire the police on television who solve the mystery and tidy everything up before the end of the show."

"Life's not tidy."

On certain men, she thought, a sneer was not at all unattractive. "No, indeed not, but we could certainly use someone on our side who has your experience." She walked back toward him, and she was no longer smiling. "I'll be frank. If I had known what trouble it would cause my family, I might have let the legend of the emeralds die with me. When my brother and his wife were killed, and left their girls in my care, I was also left the responsibility of passing along the story of the Calhoun emeralds—when the time was right. By doing what I consider my duty, I've put my family in danger. I'll do anything in my power, and use anyone I can, to keep them from being hurt. Until those emeralds are found, I can't be sure my family is safe."

"You need the police," he began.

"They're doing what they can. It isn't enough." Reaching out, she put a hand on his. "They aren't personally involved, and can't possibly understand. You can."

Her faith and her obstinate logic made him uneasy. "You're overestimating me."

"I don't think so." Coco held his hand another moment, then gave it a brief squeeze before releasing it. "But I don't mean to nag. I only came so I could add my input to Suzanna's. She has such a difficult time pushing for what she wants."

"She does well enough."

"Well, I'm glad to hear it. But with her work and Mandy's wedding, and everything else that's been going on, I know she hasn't had time to speak with you again for the last couple of days. I tell you, our lives have been turned upside down for the last few months. First C.C.'s wedding, and the renovations, now Amanda and Sloan—and Lilah already setting a date to marry Max." She paused and hoped to look wistful. "If I could only find some nice man for Suzanna, I'd have all my girls settled."

Holt didn't miss the speculative look. "I'm sure she'll take care of that herself when she's ready."

"Not when she doesn't give herself a moment to look. And after what that excuse for a man did to her." She cut herself off there. If she started on Baxter Dumont, it would be difficult to stop. And it would hardly be proper conversation. "Well, in any case, she keeps herself too busy with her business and her children, so I like to keep my eye out for her. You're not married, are you?"

At least no one could accuse her of being subtle, Holt thought, amused. "Yeah. I've got a wife and six kids in Portland."

Coco blinked, then laughed. "It was a rude question," she admitted. "And before I ask another, I'll leave you alone." She started for the door, pleased that he had enough manners to accompany her and open it for her. "Oh, by the way, Amanda's wedding is Saturday, at six. We're holding the reception at the ballroom in The Towers. I'd like for you to come."

The unexpected curve had him hesitating. "I really don't think it's appropriate."

"It's more than appropriate," she corrected. "Our families go back quite a long way, Holt. We'd very much like to have you there." She started toward her car then turned, smiling again. "And Suzanna doesn't have an escort. It seems a pity."

The thief called himself by many names. When he had first come to Bar Harbor in search of the emeralds, he had used the name Livingston and had posed as a successful British businessman. He had only been partially successful and had returned under the guise of Ellis Caufield, a wealthy eccentric. Due to bad luck and his partner's fumbling, he'd had to abandon that particular cover.

His partner was dead, which was only a small inconvenience. The thief now went under the name of Robert Marshall and was developing a certain fondness for this alter ego.

Marshall was lean and tanned and had a hint of a Boston accent. He wore his dark hair nearly shoulder length and sported a drooping mustache. His eyes were brown, thanks to contact lenses. His teeth were slightly bucked. The oral device had cost him a pretty penny, but it had also changed the shape of his jaw.

He was very comfortable with Marshall, and delighted to have signed on as a laborer on The Towers renovation. His references had been forged and had added to his overhead. But the emeralds would be worth it. He intended to have them, whatever the price.

Over the past months they had gone from being a job to an obsession. He didn't just want them. He needed them. He found the risk of working so close to the Calhouns only added spice to the game. He had, in fact, passed within three feet of Amanda when she had come into the west wing to talk to Sloan O'Riley. Neither of them, who had known him only as Livingston, had given him a second glance.

He did his job well, hauling equipment, cleaning up debris. And he worked without complaint. He was friendly with his co-workers, even joining them occasionally for a beer after work.

Then he would go back to his rented house across the bay and plan.

The security at The Towers posed no problem—not when it would be so easy for him to disengage it from the inside. By working for the Calhouns, he could stay close, he could be certain he would hear about any new developments in their search for the necklace. And with care and skill, he could do some searching on his own.

The papers he had stolen from them had offered no real clue as yet. Unless it came from the letter he'd discovered. One that had been written to Bianca and signed only "Christian." A love letter, Marshall mused as he stacked lumber. It was something he had to look into.

"Hey, Bob. Got a minute?"

Marshall looked up and gave his foreman an affable smile. "Sure, nothing but minutes."

"Well, they need some tables moved into the ballroom for that wedding tomorrow. You and Rick give the ladies a hand."

"Right."

Marshall strolled along, fighting back a trembling excitement at being free to walk through the house. He took his instructions from a flustered Coco, then hefted his end of the heavy hunt table to move it up to the next floor.

"Do you think he'll come?" C.C. asked Suzanna as they finished washing down the glass on the mirrored walls.

"I doubt it."

C.C. brushed back her short cap of black hair as she stood aside to search for streaks. "I don't see why he wouldn't. And maybe if we all gang up on him, he'll break down and join ranks."

"I don't think he's a joiner." Suzanna glanced around and saw the two men struggling in with the table. "Oh, it goes against that wall. Thanks."

"No problem," Rick managed through gritted teeth. Marshall merely smiled and said nothing.

"Maybe if he sees the picture of Bianca and hears the tape from the interview Max and Lilah had with the maid who used to work here back then, he'll pitch in. He's Christian's only surviving family."

"Hey!" Rick muffled a curse when Marshall bobbled the table.

"I don't think he's big on family feeling," Suzanna put in. "One thing that hasn't changed about Holt Bradford is that he's still a loner."

Holt Bradford. Marshall committed the name to memory before he called across the room. "Is there anything else we can do for you ladies?"

Suzanna glanced over her shoulder with an absent smile. "No, not right now. Thanks a lot."

Marshall grinned. "Don't mention it."

"Some lookers, huh?" Rick muttered as they walked back out.

"Oh, yeah." But Marshall was thinking of the emeralds.

"I tell you, bud, I'd like to—" Rick broke off when two other women and a young boy came to the top of the stairs. He gave them both a big, toothy smile. Lilah gave him a lazy one in return and kept walking.

"Man, oh, man," Rick said with a hand to his heart. "This place is just full of babes."

"Pardon the leers," Lilah said mildly. "Most of them don't bite."

The slim strawberry blonde gave a weak smile. At the moment a couple of leering carpenters were the least of her worries. "I really don't want to get in the way," she began in a soft Southwestern drawl. "I know what Sloan said, but I really think it would be best if Kevin and I checked into a hotel for the night."

"This late in the season, you couldn't check into a tent. And we want you here. All of us. Sloan's family is our family now." Lilah smiled down at the dark-haired boy who was gawking at everything in sight. "It's a wild place, isn't it? Your uncle's making sure it doesn't come crashing down on our heads." She walked into the ballroom.

Suzanna was standing on a ladder, polishing glass, while C.C. sat on the floor, hitting the low spots. Lilah bent to the boy. "I was supposed to be in on this," she whispered. "But I played hooky."

The idea made him laugh, and the laughter, so much like Alex's, had Suzanna glancing over.

She was expecting them. Their arrival had been anticipated for weeks. But seeing them here, knowing who they were, had her nerves jolting.

The woman wasn't just Sloan's sister, nor was the boy just his nephew. A short time before, Suzanna had learned that Megan O'Riley had been her husband's lover, and the boy his child. The woman who was staring at her now, the boy's hand gripped in hers, had been only seventeen when Baxter had charmed her into bed and seduced her with vows of love and promises of marriage. And all the while, he had been planning to marry Suzanna.

Which one of us, Suzanna wondered, had been the other woman?

It didn't matter now, she thought, and she climbed down. Not when she could see the nerves so clearly in Megan O'Riley's eyes, the tension in the set of her body, and the courage in the angle of her chin.

Lilah made introductions so smoothly that an outsider might have thought there was nothing but pleasantries in the ballroom. As Suzanna offered a hand, all Megan could think was that she had overdressed. She felt stiff and foolish in the trim bronze-colored suit, while Suzanna seemed so relaxed and lovely in faded jeans.

This was the woman she had hated for years, for taking away the man she'd loved and stealing the father of her child. Even after Sloan had explained Suzanna's innocence, even knowing the hate had been wasted, Megan couldn't relax.

"I'm so glad to meet you." Suzanna put both hands over Megan's stiff one.

"Thank you." Feeling awkward, Megan drew her hand away. "We're looking forward to the wedding."

"So are we all." After a bracing breath, Suzanna let herself look down at Kevin, the half brother to her children. Her heart melted a little. He was taller than her son, and a full year older. But they had both inherited their father's dark good looks. Unconsciously Suzanna reached out to brush back the lock of hair that fell, the twin of Alex's, over Kevin's brow.

Megan's arm came around his shoulders in an instinctive move of defense. Suzanna let her hand drop to her side.

"It's nice to meet you, Kevin. Alex and Jenny could hardly sleep last night knowing you'd be here today."

Kevin gave her a fleeting smile, then glanced up at his mother. She'd told him he was going to meet his half brother and sister, and he wasn't too sure he was happy about it. He didn't think his mother was, either.

"Why don't we go down and find them?" C.C. put a hand on Suzanna's shoulder, gently rubbing. Megan noted that Lilah had already flanked her sister's other side. She didn't blame them for sticking together against an outsider, and her chin came up to prove it.

"It might be best if we—"

She never got to finish. Alex and Jenny came clattering down the hall to burst into the room, breathless and flushed. "Is he here?" Alex demanded. "Aunt Coco said he was, and we want to see—" He cut himself off, skidding to a halt on the freshly polished floor.

The two boys eyed each other, interested and cautious, like two terriers. Alex wasn't sure he was pleased that his new brother was bigger than he was, but he'd already decided it would be neat to have something besides a sister.

"I'm Alex and this is Jenny," Alex said, taking over introductions. "She's only five."

"Five and a half," Jenny put in, and marched up to Kevin. "And I can beat you up if I have to."

"Jenny, I don't think that'll be necessary." Suzanna spoke mildly, but the lifted brows said it all.

"Well, I could," Jenny muttered, still sizing him up. "But Mom says we have to be nice 'cause we're family."

"Do you know any Indians?" Alex demanded.

"Yeah." Kevin was no longer gripping his mother's hand for dear life. "Lots of them."

"Want to see our fort?" Alex asked.

"Yeah." He sent a pleading glance at his mother. "Can I?"

"Well, I—"

"Lilah and I'll take them out." C.C. gave Suzanna's shoulder a final squeeze.

"They'll be fine," Suzanna assured Megan as her sisters hustled the children along. "Sloan designed the fort, so it's sturdy." She picked up her rag again to run it through her hands. "Does Kevin know?"

"Yes." Megan turned her purse over and over in restless hands. "I didn't want him to meet your children without understanding." She took a deep breath and prepared to launch into the speech she'd prepared. "Mrs. Dumont—"

"Suzanna. This is hard for you."

"I don't imagine it's easy, or comfortable for either of us. I wouldn't have come," she continued, "if it hadn't been so important to Sloan. I love my brother, and I won't do anything to spoil his wedding, but you must see that this is an impossible situation."

"I can see it's a painful one for you. I'm sorry." Her

hands lifted then fell. "I wish I had known sooner, about you, about Kevin. It's unlikely that I could have made any difference as far as Bax is concerned, but I wish I had known." She glanced down at the rag she was gripping too tightly, then put it aside. "Megan, I realize that while you were giving birth to Kevin, alone, I was in Europe, honeymooning with Kevin's father. You're entitled to hate me for that."

Megan could only stare and shake her head. "You're nothing like I expected. You were supposed to be cool and remote and resentful."

"It would be hard to resent a seventeen-year-old girl who was betrayed and left alone to raise a child. I wasn't much older than that when I married Bax. I understand how charming he could be, how persuasive. And how cruel."

"I thought we'd live happily ever after," Megan said with a sigh. "Well, I grew up quickly, and I learned fast." She let out another long breath as she studied Suzanna. "I hated you, for having everything I thought I wanted. Even when I'd stopped loving him, it helped get me through to hate you. And I was terrified of meeting you."

"That's something else we have in common."

"I can't believe I'm here, talking to you like this." To relieve her nerves she wandered around the ballroom. "I imagined it so many times all those years ago. I'd face you down, demand my rights." She gave a soft laugh. "Even today, I had a whole speech planned out. It was very sophisticated, very mature—maybe just a little vicious. I didn't want to believe that you hadn't known about Kevin, that you'd been a victim, too. Because it was so much easier to think of myself as the only one who'd been betrayed. Then your children came in." She closed her eyes. "How do you deal with the hurt, Suzanna?"

"I'll let you know when I figure it out."

Smiling a little, Megan glanced out of the window. "It hasn't affected them. Look."

Suzanna walked over. Down in the yard she could see her children, and Megan's son, climbing into the plywood fort.

Holt gave it a lot of thought. Up until the moment when he dragged the suit out of his closet, he'd been certain he wasn't going. What the devil was he supposed to do at a society wedding? He didn't like socializing or making small talk or picking at those tiny little canapés. You never knew what the hell was in them anyway.

He didn't like strangling himself with a tie or having to iron a shirt.

So why was he doing it?

He loosened the hated knot of the tie and frowned at himself in the dusty mirror over the bureau. Because he was an idiot and couldn't resist an invitation to the castle on the cliffs. Because he was twice an idiot and wanted to see Suzanna again.

It had been over a week since they had planted the yellow bush. A week since he'd kissed her. And a week since he'd admitted that one kiss, however turbulent, wasn't going to be enough.

He wanted to get a handle on her and thought the best way was to observe her in the midst of the family she seemed to love so much. He wasn't quite sure if she was the cool and remote princess of his youth, the hot-blooded woman he'd held in his arms or the vulnerable one whose eyes were haunting his dreams.

Holt was a man who liked to know exactly what he was up against, whether it was a suspect, a dinky motor or a woman. Once he had Suzanna pegged, he'd move at his own pace.

He didn't want to admit that she'd gotten to him with her fervent belief in the connection between his grandfather and her ancestor. More, he hated to admit that the visit by Coco McPike had made him feel guilty and responsible.

He wasn't going to the wedding to help anyone, he reminded himself. He wasn't making any commitments. He was going to please himself. This time he didn't have to stop at the kitchen door.

It wasn't a long drive, but he took his time, drawing it out. His first glimpse of The Towers bounced him back a dozen years. It was, as it had always been, a fanciful place, a maze of contrasts. It was built of somber stone, yet it was flanked with romantic towers. From one angle, it seemed formidable, from another graceful. At the moment, there was scaffolding on the west side, but instead of looking unsightly, it simply looked productive.

The sloped lawn was emerald green and guarded by gnarled and dignified trees, dashed with fragile and fragrant flowers. There was already a crowd of cars, and Holt felt foolish handing over the keys to his rusted Chevy to the uniformed valet.

The wedding was to take place on the terrace. Since it was about to begin, Holt kept well to the back of the crowd of people. There was organ music, very stately. He had to force himself not to drag at his tie and light a cigarette. There were a few murmured comments and sighs as the bridesmaids started down a long white runner spread over the lawn.

He barely recognized C.C. as the stunning goddess in the long rose-colored dress. Yeah, the Calhoun girls had always been lookers, he thought, and skimmed his gaze over the woman who walked behind her. Her dress was the color of sea foam, but he hardly noticed. It was the face—the face in the portrait in his grandfather's loft. Holt let out the breath between his teeth. Lilah Calhoun was a dead ringer for her great-grandmother. And Holt wasn't going to be able to deny the connection any longer.

He stuffed his hands into his pockets, wishing he hadn't come after all.

Then he saw Suzanna.

This was the princess of his youthful imagination. Her pale gold hair fell in soft curls to her shoulders under a fingertip veil of misty blue. The dress of the same color flowed around her, skirts billowing in the breeze as she walked. She carried flowers in her hands; more were scattered in her hair. When she passed him, her eyes as soft and dreamy as the dress, he felt a longing so deep, so intense, he could barely keep from speaking her name.

He remembered nothing about the brief and lovely ceremony except how her face had looked when the first tear slipped down her cheek.

As it had been so many years ago, the ballroom was filled with light and music and flowers. As for the food, Coco had outdone herself. The guests were treated to lobster croquettes, steamship round, salmon mousse and champagne by the bucket. Dozens of chairs had been set up in corners and along the mirrored walls, and the terrace doors had been thrown open to allow the guests to spill outside.

Holt held himself apart, sipping the cold, frothy wine and using the time to observe. As his first visit to The Towers, it was quite a show, he decided. Mirrors tossed back the reflection of women in pastel dresses as they stood or sat or were lured out to dance. Music and the scent of gardenias filled the air.

The bride was stunning, tall and regal in white lace, her face luminous as she danced with the big, bronzed man who was now her husband. They looked good together, Holt thought idly. The way people were meant to, he supposed, when they were in love. He saw Coco dancing with a tall, fair man who looked as if he'd been born in a tuxedo.

Then he looked back, as he already had several times, at Suzanna. She was leaning over now, saying something to a dark-haired little boy. Her son? Holt wondered. It was obvious the kid was on the verge of some kind of rebellion. He was shuffling his feet and tugging at the bow tie. He had Holt's sympathy. There couldn't be anything much worse for a kid on a summer evening than being stuck in a mini tuxedo and having to hang around with adults. Suzanna whispered something in his ear, then tugged on it. The boy's mutinous expression turned into a grin.

"Still brooding in corners, I see."

Holt turned and was once again struck by Lilah Calhoun's resemblance to the woman his grandfather had painted. "Just watching the show."

"It is worth the price of a ticket. Max." Lilah laid a

hand on the arm of the tall, lanky man at her side. "This is Holt Bradford, whom I was madly in love with for about twenty-four hours some fifteen years ago."

Holt's brow lifted. "You never told me."

"Of course not. At the end of the day I decided I didn't want to be in love with the surly, dangerous sort after all. This is Max Quartermain, the man I'm going to love for the rest of my life."

"Congratulations." Holt took Max's offered hand. Firm grip, Holt mused, steady eyes and a slightly embarrassed smile. "You're the teacher, right?"

"I was. And you're Christian Bradford's grandson."

"That's right," Holt agreed, and his voice had cooled.

"Don't worry, we're not going to hound you as long as you're a guest." Studying him, Lilah ran a fingertip around the rim of her glass. "We'll do that later. I'll have Max show you the scar he got while we were having our little publicity stunt."

"Lilah." Max's voice was soft with an underlying command.

Lilah merely shrugged and sipped champagne. "You remember C.C." She gestured as her sister joined them.

"I remember a gangly kid with engine grease on her face." He relaxed enough to smile. "You look good."

"Thanks. My husband, Trent. Holt Bradford."

It was Coco's dance partner, Holt noted as the two men summed each other up during the polite introductions.

"And the bride and groom," Lilah announced, toasting the couple before she drank again.

"Hello, Holt." Though she was still glowing, Amanda's eyes were steady and watchful. "I'm glad you could come." As she introduced Sloan, Holt realized he'd been surrounded quite neatly. They didn't press. No, the emeralds were never mentioned. But they'd joined ranks, he thought, in a solid wall of determination he had to admire, even as he resented it.

"What is this, a family meeting?" Suzanna hurried up. "You're supposed to be mingling, not huddling in a corner. Oh. Holt." Her smile wavered a bit. "I didn't know you were here."

"Your aunt invited me."

"Yes, I know, but—" She broke off and put her hostess's smile back in place. "I'm glad you could make it."

Like hell, he thought and lifted his glass. "It's been... interesting so far."

At some unspoken signal, her family drifted away, leaving them alone in the corner beside a tub of gardenias. "I hope they didn't make you uncomfortable."

"I can handle it."

"That may be, but I wouldn't want you badgered at my sister's wedding."

"But it doesn't bother you if it's someplace else."

Before she could retort, small impatient hands were tugging at her skirt. "Mom, when can we have the cake?"

"When Amanda and Sloan are ready to cut it." She skimmed a finger down Alex's nose.

"But we're hungry."

"Then go over to the buffet table and stuff your little face."

He giggled at that but didn't relent. "The cake—"

"Is for later. Alex, this is Mr. Bradford."

Not particularly interested in meeting another adult who would pat his head and tell him what a big boy he was, Alex pouted up at Holt. When he was offered a very manly handshake, he perked up a bit.

"Are you the policeman?"

"I used to be."

"Did you ever get shot in the head?"

Holt muffled a chuckle. "No, sorry." For some reason he felt as though he'd lost face. "I did catch one in the leg once."

"Yeah?" Alex brightened. "Did it bleed and bleed?"

He had to grin. "Buckets."

"Wow. Did you shoot lots of bad guys?"

"Dozens of them."

"Okay! Wait a minute." He raced off.

"I'm sorry," Suzanna began. "He's going through a murder-and-mayhem stage."

"I'm sorry I didn't get shot in the head."

She laughed. "Oh, that's all right, you made up for it by telling him you shot lots of bad guys." She wondered, but didn't ask, if he'd been telling the truth.

"Suzanna, would—"

"Hey." Alex skidded to a halt, with two other children in tow. "I told them how you got shot in the leg."

"Did it hurt?" Jenny wanted to know.

"Some."

"It bled and bled," Alex said with relish. "This is Jenny, she's my sister. And this is my brother, Kevin."

Suzanna wanted to kiss him. She wanted to pull Alex up in her arms and smother him with kisses for accepting so easily what adults had made so complicated. Instead, she brushed a hand over his hair.

The three of them bombarded Holt with questions until Suzanna called a halt. "I think that's enough gore for now."

"But, Mom—"

"But, Alex," she mimicked. "Why don't you go get some punch?"

Since it seemed like a pretty good idea, they trooped off.

"Quite a brood," Holt murmured, then looked back at Suzanna. "I thought you had two kids."

"I do."

"Seems to me I just saw three."

"Kevin is my ex-husband's son," she said coolly. "Now, if you'll excuse me."

He put a hand on her arm. Another secret, he thought, and decided he would dig up that answer, as well. Not now. Now he was going to do something he'd thought about doing since he'd seen her walk down the white satin runner in the floaty blue dress.

"Would you like to dance?"

Chapter 5

She couldn't quite relax in his arms. She told herself it was foolish, that the dance was just a casual social gesture. But his body was so close, so firm, the hand at her back so possessive. It reminded her too clearly of the moment he had pulled her against him to send her soaring into a kiss.

"It's quite a house," he said, and gave himself the pleasure of feeling her hair against his cheek. "I always wondered what it was like inside."

"I'll have to give you a tour sometime."

He could feel her heart thud against his. Experimenting, he skimmed his hand up her spine. The rhythm quickened. "I'm surprised you haven't been back to nag me."

There was annoyance in her eyes as she drew her head back. "I have no intention of nagging you."

"Good." He brushed his thumb over her knuckles and felt her tremble. "But you will come back."

"Only because I promised Aunt Coco."

"No." He increased the pressure on her spine and brought her an inch closer. "Not only because of that. You wonder what it would be like, the same way I've wondered half my life."

A little line of panic followed his fingers up her spine. "This isn't the place."

"I choose my own ground." His lips hovered bare inches from hers. He watched her eyes darken and cloud. "I want you, Suzanna."

Her heart had leaped up to throb in her throat so that her voice was husky and uneven. "Am I supposed to be flattered?"

"No. You'd be smart to be scared. I won't make things easy on you."

"What I am," she said with more control, "is uninterested."

His lips curved. "I could kiss you now and prove you wrong."

"I won't have a scene at my sister's wedding."

"Fine, then come to my place tomorrow morning."

"No."

"All right then." He lowered his head. She turned hers away so that his lips brushed her temple, then nibbled on her ear.

"Stop it. My children—"

"Should hardly be shocked to see a man kiss their mother." But he did stop, because his knees were going weak. "Tomorrow morning, Suzanna. There's something I need to show you. Something of my grandfather's."

She looked up again, struggling to steady her pulse. "If this is some sort of game, I don't want to play."

"No game. I want you, and this time I'll have you. But there is something of my grandfather's you have the right to see. Unless you're afraid to be alone with me."

Her spine stiffened. "I'll be there."

The next morning, Suzanna stood on the terrace with Megan. They watched their children race across the lawn with Fred.

"I wish you could stay longer."

With a half laugh, Megan shook her head. "I'm surprised to say I wish I could, too. I have to be back at work tomorrow."

"You and Kevin are welcome here anytime. I want you to know that."

"I do." Megan shifted her gaze to meet Suzanna's. There was a sadness there she understood, though she rarely allowed herself to feel it. "If you and the kids decide to visit Oklahoma, you've got a home with us. I don't want to lose touch. Kevin needs to know this part of his family."

"Then we won't." She stooped to pick up a rose petal that had drifted from a bouquet to float to the terrace. "It was a beautiful wedding. Sloan and Mandy are going to be happy—and we'll have nieces and nephews in common."

"God, the world's a strange place." Megan took Suzanna's hand. "I'd like to think we can be friends, not only for our children's sakes or for Sloan and Amanda."

Suzanna smiled. "I think we already are."

"Suzanna!" Coco signaled from the kitchen door.

"A phone call for you." She was chewing her lip when Suzanna reached her. "It's Baxter."

"Oh." Suzanna felt the simple pleasure of the morning drain. "I'll take it in the other room."

She braced herself as she walked down the hallway. He couldn't hurt her any longer, she reminded herself. Not physically, not emotionally. She slipped into the library, took a long, steadying breath, then picked up the phone.

"Hello, Bax."

"I suppose you considered it sly to keep me waiting on the phone."

And there it was again, she thought, that clipped, critical tone that had once made her shiver. Now she only sighed. "I'm sorry. I was outside."

"Digging in the garden, I suppose. Are you still pretending to make a living pruning rosebushes?"

"I'm sure you didn't call to see how my business is going."

"Your business, as you call it, is nothing to me but a slight embarrassment. Having my ex-wife selling flowers on the street corner—"

"Clouds your image, I know." She passed a hand over her hair. "We're not going to go through that again, are we?"

"Quite the little shrew these days." She heard him murmur something to someone else, then laugh. "No, I didn't call to remind you you're making a fool of yourself. I want the children."

Her blood turned to ice. "What?"

The shaky whisper pleased him enormously. "I believe it states quite clearly in the custody agreement that I'm entitled to two weeks during the summer. I'll pick them up on Friday."

"You…but you haven't—"

"Don't stammer, Suzanna. It's one of your more annoying traits. If you didn't comprehend, I'll repeat. I'm exercising my parental rights. I'll pick the children up on Friday, at noon."

"You haven't seen them in nearly a year. You can't just pick them up and—"

"I most certainly can. If you don't choose to honor the agreement, I'll simply take you back to court. It isn't legal or wise for you to try to keep the children from me."

"I've never tried to keep them from you. You haven't bothered with them."

"I have no intention of rearranging my schedule to suit you. Yvette and I are going to Martha's Vineyard for two weeks, and have decided to take the children. It's time they saw something of the world besides the little corner you hide in."

Her hands were shaking. She gripped the receiver more tightly. "You didn't even send Alex a card on his birthday."

"I don't believe there's anything in the agreement about birthday cards," he said shortly. "But it is very specific on visitation rights. Feel free to check with your lawyer, Suzanna."

"And if they don't want to go?"

"The choice isn't theirs—or yours." But his, he thought, which was exactly as he preferred it. "I wouldn't try to poison them against me."

"I don't have to," she murmured.

"See that they're packed and ready. Oh, and Suzanna,

I've been reading quite a bit about your family lately. Isn't it odd that there wasn't any mention of an emerald necklace in our settlement agreement?"

"I didn't know it existed."

"I wonder if the courts would believe that."

She felt tears of frustration and rage fill her eyes. "For God's sake, didn't you take enough?"

"It's never enough, Suzanna, when you consider how very much you disappointed me. Friday," he said. "Noon." And hung up.

She was trembling. Even when she lowered carefully into a chair, she couldn't stop. She felt as though she'd been jerked back five years, into that terrible helplessness. She couldn't stop him. She'd read the custody agreement word for word before signing it, and he was within his rights. Oh, technically she could have demanded more notice, but that would only postpone the inevitable. If Bax had made up his mind, she couldn't change it. The more she fought, the more she argued, the harder he would twist the knife.

And the more difficult he would make it on the children.

Her babies. Rocking, she covered her face with her hands. It was only for a short time—she could survive it. But how would they feel when she shipped them off, giving them no choice?

She would have to make it sound like an adventure. With the right tone, the right words, she could convince them this was something they wanted to do. Pressing her lips together, she rose. But not now. She would never be able to convince them of anything but her own turmoil if she spoke with them now.

"Damn place is like Grand Central Station." The familiar thump of a cane nearly had Suzanna sinking back into the chair again. "People coming and going, phone ringing. You'd think nobody ever got married before." Suzanna's great-aunt Colleen, her magnificent white hair swept back and diamonds glittering at her ears, stopped in the doorway. "I'll have you know those little monsters of yours tracked dirt up the stairs."

"I'm sorry."

Colleen only huffed. She enjoyed complaining about the children, because she had grown so fond of them. "Hooligans. The one blessed day of the week there's not hammering and sawing every minute, and there's packs of children shrieking through the house. Why the hell aren't they in school?"

"Because it's July, Aunt Colleen."

"Don't see what difference that makes." Her frown deepened as she studied Suzanna. "What's the matter with you, girl?"

"Nothing. I'm just a little tired."

"Tired my foot." She recognized the look. She'd seen it before—the weary desperation and helplessness—in her own mother's eyes. "Who was that on the phone?"

Suzanna's chin came up. "That, Aunt Colleen, is none of your business."

"Well, you've climbed on your high horse." And it pleased her. She preferred that her grandniece bite back rather than take a slap. Besides, she'd just badger Coco until she learned what was going on.

"I have an appointment," Suzanna said as steadily as possible. "Would you mind telling Aunt Coco that I've gone out?"

"So now I'm a messenger boy. I'll tell her, I'll tell

her," Colleen muttered, waving her cane. "It's high time she fixed me some tea."

"Thank you. I won't be long."

"Go out and clear your head," Colleen said as Suzanna started by. "There's nothing a Calhoun can't handle."

Suzanna sighed and kissed Colleen's thin cheek. "I hope you're right."

She didn't allow herself to think. She left the house and climbed into her pickup, telling herself she would handle whatever needed to be handled—but she would calm herself first.

She had become very skilled at pulling in her emotions. A woman couldn't sit in a courtroom with her children's futures hanging in the balance and not learn control.

It was possible to feel panic or rage or misery and function normally. When she was certain she could, she would speak with the children.

There was an appointment to be kept. Whatever Holt had to show her might distract her enough to help her keep control of her emotions until they leveled.

She thought she was calm when she pulled up at his house. As she got out of the truck, she combed a hand through her windblown hair. When she realized she was gripping her keys too hard she deliberately relaxed her fingers. She slid the keys into her pocket and knocked.

The dog sent up a din. Holt had one hand on Sadie's collar as he opened the door. "You made it. I thought I might have to come after you."

"I told you I'd be here." She stepped inside. "What do you have to show me?"

When he was sure Sadie would do no more than sniff

and whine for attention, he released her. "Your aunt showed a lot more interest in the cottage."

"I'm a little pressed for time." After giving the dog an absent pat, she stuck her hands into the pockets of her baggy cotton slacks. "It's very nice." She glanced around, took in nothing. "You must be comfortable here."

"I get by," he said slowly, his eyes keen on her face. There wasn't a trace of color in her cheeks. Her eyes were too dark. He'd wanted to make her aware of him, maybe uncomfortably aware, but he hadn't wanted to make her sick with fear at the thought of seeing him again.

"You can relax, Suzanna." His voice was curt and dismissive. "I'm not going to jump you."

Her nerves stretched taut on the thin wire of control. "Can we just get on with this?"

"Yeah, we can get on with it, as soon as you stop standing there as if you're about to be chained and beaten. I haven't done anything—yet—to make you look at me that way."

"I'm not looking at you in any way."

"The hell you're not. Damn it, your hands are shaking." Furious, he grabbed them. "Stop it," he demanded. "I'm not going to hurt you."

"It has nothing to do with you." She yanked her hands away, hating the fact that she couldn't stop them from trembling. "Why should you think that anything I feel, any way I look depends on you? I have my own life, my own feelings. I'm not some weak, terrified woman who falls apart because a man raises his voice. Do you really think I'm afraid of you? Do you really think you could hurt me after—"

She broke off, appalled. She'd been shouting, and the furious tears were still burning her eyes. Her stomach was clenched so tight she could hardly breathe. Sadie had retreated to a corner and sat quivering. Holt stood a foot away, staring at her, eyes narrowed in speculation.

"I have to go," she managed, and bolted for the door. His hand slapped the wood and held it shut. "Let me go." When her voice broke, she bit down on her lip. She struggled with the door then whirled on him, eyes blazing. "I said let me go."

"Go ahead," he said with surprising calm, "take a punch at me. But you're not going anywhere while you're churned up like this."

"If I'm churned up, it's my own business. I told you, this has nothing to do with you."

"Okay, so you're not going to hit me. Let's try another release valve." He put his hands firmly on either side of her face and covered her mouth with his.

It wasn't a kiss meant to soothe or comfort. It did neither. This was raw and turbulent emotion and matched her own feelings completely.

Her arms were caught between them, her hands still fisted. Her body trembled; her skin heated. At the first flicker of response, he dived into the rough, desperate kiss until he was certain the only thing she was thinking about was him.

Then he took a moment longer, to please himself. She was a volcano waiting to erupt, a storm ready to blow. Her pent-up passion packed a punch more stunning than her fist could have. He intended to be around for the explosion, but he could wait.

When he released her, she leaned back against the

door, her eyes closed, breath hitching. Watching her, he realized he'd never seen anyone fight so hard for control.

"Sit down." She shook her head. "All right, stand." With a dismissive shrug, he moved away to light a cigarette. "Either way you're going to tell me what set you off."

"I don't want to talk to you."

He sat on the arm of a chair and blew out a stream of smoke. "Lots of people haven't wanted to talk to me. But I usually find out what I want to know."

She opened her eyes. They were dry now, which relieved him considerably. "Is this an interrogation?"

With another shrug, he brought the cigarette to his lips again. It wouldn't do her any good if he caved in and offered soft words. He wasn't even sure he had them. "It can be."

She thought about pulling the door open and leaving. But he would only stop her. She'd learned the hard way that there were some battles a woman couldn't win.

"It isn't worth it," she said wearily. "I shouldn't have come while I was upset, but I thought I had gotten myself under control."

"Upset about what?"

"It isn't important."

"Then it shouldn't be a problem to tell me."

"Bax called. My ex-husband." To comfort herself she began to roam the room.

Holt studied the tip of his cigarette, reminding himself that jealousy was out of place. "Looks like he can still stir you up."

"One phone call. One, and I'm back under his thumb." There was a bitterness in her voice he hadn't expected from her. He said nothing. "There's nothing I can do.

Nothing. He's going to take the children for two weeks. I can't stop him."

Holt let out an impatient breath. "For God's sake, is that what all this hysteria's about? So the kids go off with Daddy for a couple of weeks." Disgusted, he crushed out his cigarette. And to think he'd been worried about her. "Save the vindictive-wife routine, babe. He's got a right."

"Oh yes, he's got the right." Her voice shook with an emotion so deep that Holt's head snapped up again. "Because it says so on a piece of paper. And he was there when they were conceived, so that makes him their father. Of course, that doesn't mean he has to love them, or worry about them or struggle to raise them without malice. It doesn't mean he has to remember Christmas or birthdays. It's just as Bax told me on the phone. There's nothing in the custody agreement that obligates him to send birthday cards. But it does obligate me to turn the children over to him when he has the whim."

There were tears threatening again, but she refused them. Tears in front of a man never brought anything but humiliation. "Do you think this is about me? He can't hurt me anymore. But my children don't deserve to be used so that he can try to pay me back for being so much less than he wanted."

Holt felt something hot and lethal spread in his gut. "He did a good job on you, didn't he?"

"That isn't the point. Alex and Jenny are the point. Somehow I have to convince them that the father who hasn't bothered to contact them in months, who could barely tolerate them when they lived under the same roof, is going to take them on a wonderful two-week vacation." Suddenly tired, she pushed her hands through her hair. "I didn't come here to talk about this."

"Yes, you did." Calmer, Holt lit another cigarette. If he didn't do something with his hands, he was going to touch her again, and he wasn't sure either of them could handle it. "I'm not family, so I'm safe. You can dump on me and figure I won't lose any sleep over it."

She smiled a little. "Maybe you're right. Sorry."

"I didn't ask for an apology. How do the kids feel about him?"

"He's a stranger."

"Then they probably don't have any preset expectations. Seems to me they might think of the whole thing as an adventure—and that you're letting him push your buttons. If he is using them to get to you, he hit a bull's-eye."

"I'd already come to those same conclusions myself. I needed to vent some excess frustration." She tried a smile again. "Usually I just pull some weeds."

"I think kissing me worked better."

"It was different, anyway."

He tapped out his cigarette and rose. The hell with what they could handle. "Is that the best description you can come up with?"

"Off the top of my head. Holt," she began when he slid his arms around her.

"Yeah?" He nipped at her chin, then her mouth.

"I don't want to be held." But she did, too much.

"That's too bad." His arms tightened, bringing her closer.

"You asked me to come here so you could..." She made a little sound of distress when he closed his teeth over her earlobe. "You could show me something of your grandfather's."

"That's right." Her skin smelled like the air high on the cliffs—laced with the sea and wildflowers and hot summer sunlight. "I also asked you here so I could get my hands on you again. We'll just take one thing at a time."

"I don't want to get involved." But even as she said it, her mouth was moving to meet his.

"Me, either." He changed the angle and sucked on her bottom lip.

"This is just—oh—chemistry." Her fingers tangled in his hair.

"You bet." His rough-palmed hands slipped under her shirt to explore.

"It can't go anywhere."

"It already has."

He was right about that, as well. For one brief moment she let herself fall into the kiss, into the heat. She needed something, someone. If she couldn't have comfort or compassion, she would take desire. But the more she took, the more her body strained for something just out of reach. Something she couldn't afford to want or need again.

"This is too fast," she said breathlessly, and struggled away. "I'm sorry, I realize it must seem as though I'm sending you mixed signals."

He was watching her eyes, just her eyes, as his body pulsed. "I think I can sort them out."

"I don't want to start something I won't be able to finish." She moistened her lips still warm from his. "And I have too many responsibilities, too much to worry about right now to even think about having…"

"An affair?" he finished. "You're going to have to think about it." With his eyes still on hers, he gathered her hair in his hand. "Go ahead, take a few days. I can afford to be patient as long as I get what I want. And I want you."

Nerves skittered along her spine. "Just because I find you attractive, physically, doesn't mean I'm going to jump into bed with you."

"I don't much care whether you jump, crawl or have to be dragged. We can decide on the method later." Before she could think of a name to call him, he grinned, kissed her then stepped back. "Now that that's settled, I'll take you up and show you the portrait."

"If you think it's settled because you— What portrait?"

"You take a look, then tell me."

He led the way up into the loft. Torn between curiosity and fury, Suzanna followed him. The only thing she was certain of at the moment was that since she'd met Holt Bradford again, her emotions had been on a roller coaster. All she wanted out of life was a nice smooth, uneventful ride.

"He worked up here."

The simple statement captured her attention and her interest. "Did you know him well?"

"I don't think anyone did." Holt moved over to open a tilt-out window. "He came and went pretty much as he pleased. He'd come back here for a few days, or a few months. I'd sit up here sometimes and watch him work. If he got tired of me hanging around, he'd send me out with the dog, or into the village for ice cream."

"There's still paint on the floor." Unable to resist, Suzanna bent down to touch. She glanced up, met Holt's eyes and understood.

He'd loved his grandfather. These splotches of paint, more than the cabin itself, were memories. She reached a hand out for his, rising when their fingers linked. Then she saw the portrait.

The canvas was tilted against the wall, its frame old and ornate. The woman looked back at her, with eyes full of secrets and sadness and love.

"Bianca," Suzanna said, and let her own tears come. "I knew he must have painted her. He'd have had to."

"I wasn't certain until I saw Lilah yesterday."

"He never sold it," Suzanna murmured. "He kept it, because it was all he had left of her."

"Maybe." He wasn't entirely comfortable that the exact thought had occurred to him. "I've got to figure there was something between them. I don't see how that helps you get any closer to the emeralds."

"But you'll help."

"I said I would."

"Thank you." She turned to face him. Yes, he would help, she thought. He wouldn't break his word no matter how much it annoyed him to keep it.

"The first thing I have to ask you, is if you'll bring the portrait to The Towers so my family can see it. It would mean a great deal to them."

At Suzanna's insistence, they took Sadie as well. She rode in the back of the pickup, grinning into the wind. When they arrived at The Towers, they saw Lilah and Max sitting out on the lawn. Fred, spotting the truck, tore across the yard, then came to a stumbling halt when Sadie leaped nimbly out of the back.

Body aquiver, he approached her. The dogs gave each other a thorough sniffing over. With a flick of her tail, Sadie pranced across the yard. She sent Fred one come-hither look over her shoulder that had him scrambling after her.

"Looks like love at first sight for old Fred," Lilah commented as she walked with Max to the truck. "We wondered where you'd gone." She ran a hand down Suzanna's arm, letting her know without words that she knew about the call from Bax.

"Are the kids around?"

"No, they went into the village with Megan and her parents to help Kevin pick out some souvenirs before they leave."

With a nod, Suzanna took her hand. "There's something you have to see." Stepping back, she gestured. Through the open door of the truck, Lilah saw the painting. Her fingers tightened on her sister's.

"Oh, Suze."

"I know."

"Max, can you see?"

"Yes." Gently he kissed the top of her head and looked at the portrait of a woman who was the double for the one he loved. "She was beautiful. This is a Bradford." He glanced at Holt with a shrug. "I've been studying your grandfather's work for the past couple of weeks."

"You've had this all along," Lilah began.

Holt let the accusation in the tone roll off him. "I didn't know it was Bianca until I saw you yesterday."

She subsided, studying his face. "You're not as nasty as you'd like people to think. Your aura's much too clear."

"Leave Holt's aura alone, Lilah," Suzanna said with a laugh. "I want Aunt Coco to see this. Oh, I wish Sloan and Mandy hadn't left on their honeymoon."

"They'll only be gone two weeks," Lilah reminded her.

Two weeks. Suzanna struggled to keep the smile in place as Holt carried the portrait inside.

The moment she saw it, Coco wept. But that was only to be expected. Holt had propped the painting on the love seat in the parlor, and Coco sat in the wing chair, drenching her handkerchief.

"After all this time. To have part of her back in this house."

Lilah touched her aunt's shoulder. "Part of her has always been in the house."

"Oh, I know, but to be able to look at her." She sniffled. "And see you."

"He must have loved her so much." Damp eyed, C.C. rested her head on Trent's shoulder. "She looks just as I imagined her, just as I knew she looked that night when I felt her."

Holt kept his hands in his pockets. "Look, sentiment and séances aside, it's the emeralds you need. If you want my help, then I need to know everything."

"Séance." Coco dried her eyes. "We should hold another one. We'll hang the portrait in the dining room. With that to focus on we're bound to be successful. I've got to check the astrological charts." She got up and hurried out of the room.

"And she's off and running," Suzanna murmured.

Trent nodded. "Not to discredit Coco, but it might be best if I filled in Holt in a more conventional way."

"I'll make some coffee." Suzanna sent one last glance at the portrait before heading for the kitchen.

There wasn't so very much Trent could tell him, she thought as she ground beans. Holt already knew about the legend, the research they'd done, the danger her sisters had faced. It was possible that he might make more of it, with his training, than they had. But would he care, even a fraction of the amount her family did?

She understood that emotional motivation could change lives. And that without it, nothing worthwhile could be accomplished.

He had passion. But could his passions run deeper than a physical need? Not for her, she assured herself, measuring the coffee carefully. She'd meant what she'd said about not wanting to become involved. She couldn't afford to love again.

She was afraid he was right about an affair. If she couldn't be strong enough to resist him, she hoped she could be strong enough to hold her heart and her body separate. It couldn't be wrong to need to be touched and wanted. Perhaps by giving herself to him, in a physical way, she could prove to herself that she wasn't a failure as a woman.

God, she wanted to feel like a woman again, to experience that rush of pleasure and release. She was nearly thirty, she thought, and the only man with whom she'd been intimate had found her wanting. How much longer could she go on wondering if he was right?

She jolted when hands came down on her shoulders.

Slowly, aware of how easily she paled, Holt turned her to face him. "Where were you?"

"Oh. Up to my ears weeding pachysandra."

"That's a pretty good lie if you'd put more flair into

it." But he let it go. "I'm going to run down and talk with Lieutenant Koogar. Rain check the coffee."

"All right, I'll drive you down."

"I'm hitching a ride with Max and Trent."

Her brow lifted. "Men only, I take it."

"Sometimes it works better that way." He rubbed a thumb over the line between her brows in a gentle gesture that surprised them both. Catching himself, he dropped his hand again. "You worry too much. I'll be in touch."

"Thank you. I won't forget what you're doing for us."

"Forget it." He hauled her against him and kissed her until she went limp. "I'd rather you remember that."

He strode out, and she sank weakly into a chair. She wouldn't have any choice but to remember it.

Chapter 6

He wasn't playing Good Samaritan, Holt assured himself. After getting a clearer handle on the situation, he was doing what he felt was best. Somebody had to keep an eye on her until Livingston was under wraps. The best way to keep an eye on her was to stick close.

Swinging into the graveled lot, he pulled up next to her pickup. He saw that she was outside the shop with customers, so amused himself by roaming around.

He'd driven by Island Gardens before but had never stopped in. There hadn't been any reason to. There were a lot of thriving blossoms crowded on wooden tables or sitting in ornamental pots. Though he couldn't tell one from the other, he could appreciate their appeal. Or maybe it was the fact that the air smelled like Suzanna.

It was obvious she knew what she was doing here, he reflected. There was a tidiness to the place, enhanced by a breezy informality that invited browsers to browse even as it tempted them to buy.

Colorful pictures were set up here and there, describing certain flowers, their planting instructions and maintenance. Along the side of the main building were stacks of fifty- and hundred-pound bags of planting medium and mulch.

He was looking over a tray of snapdragons when he heard a rustle in the bush behind him. He tensed automatically, and his fingers jerked once toward the weapon he no longer wore. Letting out a quiet breath, he cursed himself. He had to get over this reaction. He wasn't a cop anymore, and no one was likely to spring at his back with an eight-inch buck knife.

He turned his head slightly and spotted the young boy crouched behind a display of peonies. Alex grinned and popped up. "I got you!" He danced gleefully around the peonies. "I was a pygmy and I zapped you with my poison blow dart."

"Lucky for me I'm immune to pygmy poison. If it'd been Ubangi poison, I would've been a goner. Where's your sister?"

"In the greenhouse. Mom gave us seeds and stuff, but I got bored. It's okay for me to come out here," he said quickly, knowing how fast adults could make things tough for you. "As long as I don't go near the street or knock over anything."

He wasn't about to give the kid a hard time. "Have you killed many customers today?"

"It's pretty slow. 'Cause it's Monday, Mom says. That's why we can come to work with her and Carolanne can have the day off."

"You like coming here?"

Holt wasn't sure how it had happened, but he and the boy were walking among the flats of flowers, and Alex's hand was in his.

"Sure, it's neat. We get to plant things. Like, see those?" He pointed at an edging of multicolored flowers that sprang up beside the gravel. "Those are zinnias, and I planted them myself, so I get to water them and stuff. Sometimes we get to carry things to the car for people, and they give you quarters."

"Sounds like a good deal."

"And Mom closes up at lunchtime and we walk down the street and get pizza and play the video games. We get to come almost every Monday. Except—" He broke off and kicked at the gravel.

"Except what?"

"Next week we'll have to be on vacation, and Mom won't come."

Holt looked down at the boy's bent head and wondered what the hell to do. "I, ah, guess she's pretty busy here."

"Carolanne or somebody could work, and she could come. But she won't."

"Don't you figure she'd go with you if she could?"

"I guess." Alex kicked at the gravel again and, when Holt didn't scold, kicked a third time. "We have to go to somebody named Martha's yard, with my father and his new wife. Mom says it'll be fun, and we'll go to the beach and have ice cream."

"Sounds pretty good."

"I don't want to go. I don't see how come I have to. I want to go to Disney World with Mom."

When the little voice broke, Holt let out a deep breath and crouched down. "It's tough having to do things you don't want to. I guess you'll have to look after Jenny while you're gone."

Alex shrugged and sniffled. "I guess. She's scared to go. But she's only five."

"She'll be okay with you. Tell you what, I'll look after your mom while you're gone."

"Okay." Feeling better, Alex wiped his nose with the back of his hand. "Can I see on your leg where they shot you?"

"Sure." Holt pointed to a scar about six inches above his kneecap on his left leg.

"Wow." Since Holt didn't seem to mind, Alex ran a fingertip over it. "I guess since you were a policeman and all, you'll take good care of Mom."

"Sure I will."

Suzanna wasn't sure what she felt when she saw Holt and her son, dark heads bent close. But she knew something warm stirred when Holt lifted a hand and brushed it through Alex's hair.

"Well, what's all this?"

Both males looked over then back at each other to exchange a quick and private look before Holt rose. "Man talk," he said, and gave Alex's hand a squeeze.

"Yeah." Alex pushed out his chest. "Man talk."

"I see. Well, I hate to interrupt, but if you want pizza, you'd better go wash your hands."

"Can he come?" Alex asked.

"His name," Suzanna said, "is Mr. Bradford."

"His name is Holt." Holt sent Alex a wink and got a grin in return.

"Can he?"

"We'll see."

"She says that a lot," Alex confided, then raced off to find his sister.

"I suppose I do." Suzanna sighed then turned back to Holt. "What can I do for you?"

She was wearing her hair loose, with a little blue cap over it that made her look about sixteen. Holt suddenly felt as foolish and awkward as a boy asking for his first date.

"Do you still need part-time help?"

"Yes, without any luck." She began to pinch off begonias. "All the high school and college kids are set for the summer."

"I can give you about four hours a day."

"What?"

"Maybe five," he continued as she stared at him. "I've got a couple of repair jobs, but I call my own hours."

"You want to work for me?"

"As long as I only have to haul and plant the things. I ain't selling flowers."

"You can't be serious."

"I mean it. I won't sell them."

"No, I mean about working for me at all. You've already started up your own business, and I can't afford to pay more than minimum wage."

His eyes went very dark, very fast. "I don't want your money."

Suzanna blew the hair out of her eyes. "Now, I am confused."

"Look, I figured we could trade off. I'll do some of the heavy work for you, and you can fix up my yard some."

Her smile bloomed slowly. "You'd like me to fix up your yard?"

Women always made things complicated, he thought and stuffed his hands into his pockets. "I don't want you to go crazy or anything. A couple more bushes maybe. Now do you want to make a deal or don't you?"

Her smile turned to a laugh. "One of the Andersons' neighbors admired our team effort. I'm scheduled to start tomorrow." She held out a hand. "Be here at six."

He winced. "A.M.?"

"Exactly. Now, how about lunch?"

He put his hand in hers. "Fine. You're buying."

Good God, the woman worked like an elephant. She worked like two elephants, Holt corrected as the sweat poured down his back. He had a pick or shovel in his hand so often, he might as well be on a chain gang.

It should've been cooler up here on the cliffs. But the lawn they were landscaping—attacking, he thought as he brought the pick down again—was nothing but rock.

In the three days he'd worked with her, he'd given up trying to stop her from doing any of the heavy work. She only ignored him and did as she pleased. When he went home in the midafternoon, every muscle twinging, he wondered how in holy hell she kept it up.

He couldn't put in more than four or five hours and juggle his own jobs. But he knew she worked eight to ten every day. It wasn't difficult to see that she was throwing herself into her work to keep from thinking about the fact that the kids were leaving the next day.

He brought the pick down again, hit rock. The shock sang up his arms. At the low, steady swearing, Suzanna glanced up from her own work. "Why don't you take a break. I can finish that."

"Did you bring the dynamite?"

The smile touched her lips for only a moment. "No, really. Go get a drink out of the cooler. We're nearly ready to plant."

"Fine." He hated to admit that the whole business was wearing him out. There were blisters on top of his blisters, his muscles felt as though he'd gone ten rounds with the champ—and lost. Wiping his face and neck dry, he walked over to the cooler they'd set in the shade of a beech tree. As he pulled out a ginger ale, he heard the pick ring against the rocky soil. It was no use telling her she was crazy, he thought as he guzzled down the cold liquid. But he couldn't help it.

"You're a lunatic, Suzanna. This is the kind of work they give to people with numbers across their chest."

"What we have here," she said in a thick Southern drawl, "is a failure to communicate."

Her quote of the line from *Cool Hand Luke* made him grin, but only for an instant. "Stark, raving mad," he continued, watching her swing the pick. "What the hell do you think's going to grow in that rock?"

"You'd be surprised." She took a moment to wipe at the sweat that was dripping in her eyes. "See those lilies on the bank there?" She gave a little grunt as she dislodged a rock. "I planted them two years ago in September."

He glanced at the profusion of tall, colorful flowers with grudging admiration. He had to admit that they were an improvement over the rough, rocky soil, but was it worth it?

"The Snyders gave me my first real job." She hefted

a rock and tossed it into the wheelbarrow. Stretching her back, she listened to the fat bees buzzing in the gaillardia. "A sympathy job, seeing as they were friends of the family and poor Suzanna needed a break." Her breath whooshed out as she struck soil, and she blinked away the little red dots in front of her eyes. "Surprised them that I knew what I was doing, and I've been working here on and off ever since."

"Great. Would you put that damn thing down a minute?"

"Almost done."

"You won't be done until you keel over. Who's going to see a few posies wilting all the way up here?"

"The Snyders will see them, their guests will see them." She shook her head to clear a haze brought on by the heat. "The photographer from *New England Gardens* will see them." Lord, the bees were loud, she thought as the buzzing filled her head. "And nothing's going to wilt. I'm putting in pinks and campanula and some coreopsis, some lavender for scent and monarda for the hummingbirds." She pressed a hand to her head, ran it over her eyes. "In September we'll plant some bulbs. Dwarf irises and windflowers. Some tuberoses and…" She staggered under a hot wave of dizziness. Holt made the dash from shade to sun as the pick slid out of her hands. When he grabbed her she seemed to melt into his arms.

Cursing her helped relieve the fright as he carried her over and laid her down under the tree. Her body was like hot wax he could all but pour onto the cool grass. "That's it." He plunged his hand into the cooler then rubbed icy water over her face. "You're finished, do you understand? If I see a pick in your hands again, I'll murder you."

"I'm all right." Her voice was weak, but the irritation was clear enough. "Just a little too much sun." The water on her face felt heavenly, even if his hands were a bit rough. She took the ginger ale from him and drank carefully.

"Too much sun," he was ranting, "too much work. And not enough food or sleep from the look of you. You're a mess, Suzanna, and I'm tired of it."

"Thank you very much." She pushed his hands away and leaned back against the tree. She needed a minute, she'd admit. But she didn't need a lecture. "I should have taken a break," she said in disgust. "I know better, but I've got things on my mind."

"I don't care what you've got on your mind." God, she was white as a sheet. He wanted to hold her until the color came back into her cheeks, to stroke her hair until she was strong and rested again. But the concern came out in fury. "I'm taking you home and you're going to bed."

Steadier, she set the bottle aside. "I think you're forgetting who works for whom."

"When you pass out on me, I take over."

"I didn't pass out," she said irritably. "I got dizzy. And nobody takes over for me, not now, not ever again. Stop splashing water in my face, you're going to drown me."

She was recovering fast enough, he thought, but it didn't cool his temper. "You're stubborn, hardheaded and just plain stupid."

"Fine. If you've finished yelling at me, I'm going to take my lunch break." She knew she had to eat. She didn't mind being stubborn or hardheaded, but she did mind being stupid. Which, she thought as she snatched a sandwich out of the cooler, was exactly what she had been to skip breakfast.

"Maybe I haven't finished yelling."

She shrugged as she unwrapped the sandwich. "Then you can yell while I eat. Or you can stop wasting time and have some lunch."

He considered dragging her to the truck. He liked the idea, but the benefits would only be short-term. Short of tying her up and locking her in a room, he couldn't stop her from working herself into the ground.

At least she was eating, he reflected. And the color had seeped back into her cheeks. Maybe there was another tack to getting his way. Casually he took out a sandwich.

"I've been thinking about the emeralds."

The change in topic and attitude surprised her. "Oh?"

"I read the transcript Max put together from the interview with Mrs. Tobias, the maid. And I listened to the tape."

"What do you think?"

"I think she's got a good memory, and that she was impressed by Bianca. From her viewpoint, the setup was that Bianca was unhappy in her marriage, devoted to her children and in love with my grandfather. She and Fergus were already on shaky ground when they had the blowout over the dog. We'll figure that was the straw that broke it. She decided to leave him, but she didn't go that night. Why?"

"Even if she'd finally made the decision," Suzanna said slowly, "there would have been arrangements to make. She'd have had to consider the children." This she understood all too well. "Where could she take them? How could she be certain she could provide for them? Even if the marriage was a disaster, she would have to plan carefully how to tell them she was taking them away from their father."

"So when Fergus left for Boston after they fought, she started to work it out. We have to figure she went to my grandfather, because he ended up with the dog."

"She loved him," Suzanna murmured. "She would have gone to him first. And he loved her, so he would have wanted to go away with her and the children."

"If we go with that, we take it to the next step. She went back to The Towers to pack, to get the kids together. But instead of meeting my grandfather and riding off into the sunset, she takes a jump out of the tower window. Why?"

"She was in turmoil." With her eyes half-closed, Suzanna stared into the sunlight. "She was about to take a step that would end her marriage, separate her children from their father. Break her vows. It's so difficult, so frightening. Like dying. Maybe she thought she was a failure, and when her husband came home, and she had to face him and herself, she couldn't."

Holt ran a hand over her hair. "Is that what it was like for you?"

Her shoulders stiffened. "We're talking about Bianca. And I don't see what her reasons for killing herself have to do with the emeralds."

Holt took his hand away. "First we decide why she hid them, then we go for where."

Slowly she relaxed again. "Fergus gave them to her when their first son was born. Not their first child. A girl didn't rate." She took another sip of her ginger ale and washed away some of her own bitterness. "She would have resented that, I think. To be rewarded—like a prize mare—for producing an heir. But, they were hers because the child was hers."

Because her eyes were heavy, she let them drift closed. "Bax gave me diamonds when Alex was born. I didn't feel guilty about selling them to start the business. Because they were mine. She might have felt the same way. The emeralds would have bought a new life for her, for the children."

"Why did she hide them?"

"To make certain he didn't find them if he stopped her from leaving. So that she knew she'd have something of her own."

"Did you hide your diamonds, Suzanna?"

"I put them in Jenny's diaper bag. The last place Baxter would look." With a half laugh, she plucked at the grass. "That sounds so melodramatic."

But he wasn't smiling or sneering, she noted. He was frowning out at the dianthiums where the bees hovered and hummed. "It sounds damn smart to me. She spent a lot of time in the tower, right?"

"We've looked there."

"We'll look again, and take her bedroom apart."

"Lilah will love that." Suzanna closed her eyes again. The food and the shade were making her sleepy. "It's her bedroom now. And we've looked there, too."

"I haven't."

"No." She decided it wouldn't hurt to stretch out while they finished talking it through. The grass was blissfully cool and soft. "If we found her journal, we'd know the answers. Mandy went through every book

in the library, just in case it got mixed in like the pur-
loined letter."

He began to stroke her hair again. "We'll take another look."

"Mandy wouldn't have missed anything. She's too
organized."

"I'd rather check over old ground than depend on
a séance."

She made a sound that was half laugh and half sigh.
"Aunt Coco'll talk you into it." Her voice grew heavy
with fatigue. "We need to plant the pinks first."

"Okay." He'd moved his hands down and was gently
massaging her shoulders.

"It'll trail right over the rocks and down the bank. It
doesn't give up," she murmured, and was asleep.

"You're telling me."

He left her there in the shade and walked back into
the sunlight.

The grass was tickling her cheek when she woke.
She'd rolled over onto her stomach and had slept like a
stone. Groggy, she opened her eyes. She saw Holt sitting
back against the tree, his legs crossed at the ankles. He
was watching her as he brought a cigarette to his lips.

"I must have dozed off."

"You could say that."

"Sorry." She pushed herself up on her elbow. "We
were talking about the emeralds."

He flicked the cigarette away. "We've talked enough
for now." In one swift move, he hooked his hands under
her arms and pulled her against him. Before she was fully
awake, she was in his lap and his mouth was on hers.

He'd watched her sleep. And as he had watched her

sleep, the need to touch her had boiled inside him until his blood was like lava. She'd looked so perfect, the sleeping princess, creamy skin dappled by hazy shade, her cheek resting on her hand, her hand on the grass.

He'd wanted those soft, warm lips under his, to feel that long, fragile body molded to him, to hear that quick little catch in her breathing. So he took, feverishly.

Disarmed, disoriented, she struggled back. Her blood had gone from slow and cool to rapid and hot. Her body, relaxed by sleep, was now taut as a bow. She dragged in a single ragged breath. All she could see was his face, his eyes dark and dangerous, his mouth hard and hungry. Then all was a blur as his lips brushed down on hers again.

She let him take what he seemed to need to take so desperately. Under the shade of the beech she pressed against him, answering each demand. When the dizziness came again, she reveled in it. This was not a weakness she had to fight. It was one she had wanted to feel as long as she could remember.

On an oath, he buried his face at her throat where her pulse jackhammered. Nothing and no one had ever made him feel like this. Frantic and shaky. Each time his mouth came back to hers it was with a new edge of desperation, each keener than the last. Dozens of sensations knifed into him, all sharp and deadly. He wanted to shove her aside, walk away before they cut him to ribbons. He wanted to roll with her on the cool, soft grass and drive out all the aches and jagged needs.

But her arms were around him, her hands moving restlessly through his hair while her body trembled. Then her cheek was against his, nuzzling there in a gesture that was almost unbearably sweet.

"What are we going to do?" she murmured. Wanting comfort, she turned her lips to his skin and sighed.

"I think we both know the answer to that."

Suzanna closed her eyes. It was so simple for him. She rested against him a moment, listening to the bees buzz in the flowers. "I need time."

He put his hands on her shoulders, pushing her back until they were face-to-face. "I may not be able to give it to you. We're not children anymore, and I'm tired of wondering what it would be like."

She let out a shaky breath. The turmoil wasn't only hers, she realized. She could feel it, shimmering out of him. "If you ask for more than I can give, we'll both be disappointed. I want you." She bit back a gasp when his fingers tightened. "But I can't make another mistake."

His eyes darkened and narrowed. "Do you want promises?"

"No," she said quickly. "No, I don't. But I have to keep the ones I made to myself. If I come to you, I have to be sure it's not just something I want, but something I can live with." Reaching out, she laid a hand on his cheek. "The one thing I can promise you is that if we're lovers, I won't regret it."

He couldn't argue, not when she looked at him that way. "When," he corrected.

"When," she said with a nod, then rose. Her legs weren't as shaky as she'd thought they would be. She felt stronger. *When,* she thought again. Yes, she'd already accepted that it was only a matter of time. "But for now, we'll have to take things as they come. We've got a job to finish."

"It's finished." He pulled himself to his feet as she turned.

The plants were in place, the ground smoothed and mulched. Where there had only been rocks and thin, thirsty soil were bright hopeful young flowers and tender green leaves.

"How?" she began, already hurrying over to study his work.

"You slept three hours."

"Three—" Appalled, she looked back at him. "You should have woken me up."

"I didn't," he said simply. "Now I've got to get back, I'm running late."

"But you shouldn't have—"

"It's done." Impatience shimmered around him. "Do you want to rip the damn things out and do it yourself?"

"No." As she studied him she realized he wasn't just angry, he was embarrassed. Not only had he done something sweet and considerate, but he'd spent three hours planting what he still sneeringly called posies.

So he stood there, she thought, looking very male and ruffled in the streaming sun, the charming rockery at his feet and his rough, clever hands stuffed in his pockets. Thank me and I'll snarl, he seemed to say.

It was then, facing him on the rocky slope, that she realized what she had refused to admit in his arms. What she had insisted was only passion and need. She loved him. Not just for the hot-blooded kisses or the demanding hands. But for the man beneath. The man who would run a careless hand over her son's hair or answer her little girl's incessant questions. The man who would leave paint splattered on the floor in memory of his grandfather.

The one who would plant flowers for her while she slept.

As she continued to stare, Holt shifted uncomfortably. "Look, if you're going to faint again, I'm going to leave you where you fall. I haven't got time to play nursemaid."

A smile moved slowly, beautifully over her face, confusing him. She loved him for that, too—that snapping impatience that covered the compassion. She would need time to think, of course. Time to adjust. But for now, for this moment, she could simply hold tight to this rush of feeling and be content.

"You did a good job."

He glanced back at the flowers, certain he'd rather cut out his tongue than admit how much he'd enjoyed the work. "You stick them in and cover them up." He moved his shoulders in dismissal. "I put the tools and stuff in the truck. I've got to go."

"I put the Bryce job off until Monday. Tomorrow—I have to be home tomorrow."

"All right. See you later."

As he walked off to his car, Suzanna knelt down to touch the fragile new blooms.

In the cottage near the water, the man who called himself Marshall completed a thorough search. He found a few things of minor interest. The ex-cop liked to read and didn't cook. There were shelves of well-worn books in the bedroom, and only a few scattered supplies in the kitchen. He kept his medals in a box tossed in the bottom of a drawer, and a loaded .32 at the ready in the nightstand.

After rifling through a desk, Marshall discovered that Christian's grandson had made a few shrewd investments. He found it amusing that a former Vice cop had had the sense to create a tidy nest egg. He also found it interesting that training had caused Holt to write up a detailed report on everything he knew about the Calhoun emeralds.

His temper threatened as he read of the interview with the former servant—the servant that Maxwell Quartermain had located. That grated. Quartermain should have been working for him. Or he should have been dead. Marshall was tempted to wreck the place, to toss furniture, break lamps. To give in to an orgy of destruction.

But he forced himself to stay calm. He didn't want to tip his hand. Not yet. Perhaps he hadn't found anything particularly enlightening, but he knew as much as the Calhouns did.

Very carefully, he put the papers back in place, shut the drawers. The dog was beginning to bark out in the yard. He detested dogs. Sneering at the sound, he rubbed at the scar on his leg where the little Calhoun mutt had bitten him. They would have to pay for that. They would all have to pay.

And so they would, he thought. When he had the emeralds.

He left the cottage precisely as he had found it.

I will not write of the winter. That is not a memory I wish to relive. But I did not leave the island. Could not leave it. She was never out of my mind in those months. In the spring, she remained with me. In my dreams.

And then, it was summer.

It isn't possible for me to write how I felt when I saw her running to me. I could paint it, but I could never find the words. I haunted those cliffs, waiting for her,

*hoping for her. It had become easy to convince myself
that it would be enough just to see her, just to speak
with her again. If she would only walk down the slope,
through the wildflowers and sit on the rocks with me.*

*Then all at once, she was calling my name, running,
her eyes so filled with joy. She was in my arms, her
mouth on mine. And I knew she had suffered as I had
suffered. She loved as I loved.*

*We both knew it was madness. Perhaps I could have
been stronger, could have convinced her to go and leave
me. But something had changed in her over the winter.
No longer would she be content with only emptiness,
as I learned her marriage was for her. Her children,
so dear to her, could not forge a bond between her and
the husband who wanted only obedience and duty. Yet
I could not allow her to give herself to me, to take the
step that could cause her guilt or shame or regret.*

*So we met, day after day on the cliffs, in all inno-
cence. To talk and laugh, to pretend the summer was
endless. Sometimes she brought the children, and it was
almost as if we were a family. It was reckless, but somehow we didn't believe anything could touch us while we
stood, cupped between sky and sea, with the peaks of
the house far up at our backs.*

*We were happy with what we had. There have been
no happier days in my life before or since. Love like that
has no beginning or end. It has no right or wrong. In
those bright summer days, she was not another man's
wife. She was mine.*

*A lifetime later, I sit here in this aging body and look
out at the water. Her face, her voice, come so clearly
to me.*

She smiled. "I used to dream of being in love."

I had taken the pins from her hair so that my hands could lose themselves in it. A small, precious pleasure. "Do you still?"

"Now I don't have to." She bent toward me, to touch her lips to mine. "I'll never have to dream again. Only wish."

I took her hand to kiss it, and we watched an eagle soar. "There's a ball tonight. I'll wish you were there, to waltz with me."

I got to my feet, drew her to hers and began to dance with her through the wild roses. "Tell me what you'll wear, so I can see you."

Laughing, she lifted her face to mine. "I shall wear ivory silk with a low bodice that bares my shoulders and a draped beaded skirt that catches the light. And my emeralds."

"A woman shouldn't look sad when she speaks of emeralds."

"No." She smiled again. "These are very special. I've had them since Ethan was born, and I wear them to remind me."

"Of what?"

"That no matter what happens, I've left something behind. The children are my real jewels." As a cloud came over the sun she pressed her head to my shoulder. "Hold me closer, Christian."

Neither of us spoke of the summer that was so quickly coming to an end, but I know we both thought of it at that moment when my arms held her tight and our hearts beat together in the dance. The fury of what I was soon to lose again rushed through me.

"I would give you emeralds, and diamonds, sap-

phires." I crushed my mouth to hers. "All that and more, Bianca, if I could."

"No." She brought her hands to my face, and I saw the tears sparkling in her eyes. "Only love me," she said.

Only love me.

Chapter 7

Holt was home for less than three minutes when he knew someone had broken in. He might have turned in his shield, but he still had cop's eyes. There was nothing obviously out of place—but an ashtray was closer to the edge of the table, a chair was pulled at a slightly different angle to the fireplace, a corner of the rug was turned up.

Braced and at alert, he moved from the living room into the bedroom. There were signs here, as well. He noted them—the fractional rearrangement of the pillows, the different alignment of the books on the shelves—as he crossed to get his gun from the drawer. After checking the clip, he took his weapon with him as he searched the house.

Thirty minutes later, he replaced the gun. His face was set, his eyes flat and hard. His grandfather's can-

vases had been moved, not much, but enough to tell Holt
that someone had touched them, studied them. And that
was a violation he couldn't tolerate.

Whoever had tossed the place had been a pro. Nothing had been taken, little had been disturbed, but Holt
was certain every inch of the cottage had been combed.

He was also certain who had done the combing. That
meant that Livingston, by whatever guise he was using,
was still close. Close enough, Holt thought, that he had
discovered the Bradford connection to the Calhouns.
And the emeralds.

Now, he decided as he dropped a hand on the head of
the dog who whined at his feet, it was personal.

He went through the kitchen door to sit on the porch
with his dog and a beer and watch the water. He would
let his temper cool and his mind drift, sorting through
all the pieces of the puzzle, arranging and rearranging
until a picture began to form.

Bianca was the key. It was her mind, her emotions,
her motivations he had to tap into. He lit a cigarette,
resting his crossed ankles on the porch rail as the light
began to soften and pearl toward twilight.

A beautiful woman, unhappily married. If the current crop of Calhoun women were anything to go by,
Bianca would also have been strong willed, passionate and loyal. And vulnerable, he added. That came
through strongly in the eyes of the portrait, just as it
came through strongly in Suzanna's eyes.

She'd also been on the upper rungs of society's ladder, one of the privileged. A young Irishwoman of good
family who had married extremely well.

Again, like Suzanna.

He drew on the cigarette, absently stroking Sadie's

ears when she nuzzled her head into his lap. His gaze was drawn toward the little yellow bush, the slice of sunshine Suzanna had given him. According to the interview with the former maid, Bianca had also had a fondness for flowers.

She had had children, and by all accounts had been a good and devoted mother, while Fergus had been a strict and disinterested father. Then Christian Bradford had come into the picture.

If Bianca had indeed taken him as a lover, she had also taken an enormous social risk. Like Caesar's wife, a woman in her position was expected to be unblemished. Even a hint of an affair—particularly with a man beneath her station—and her reputation would have been in tatters.

Yet she had become involved.

Had it all grown to be too much for her? Holt wondered. Had she been eaten up by guilt and panic, hidden the emeralds away as some kind of last-ditch show of defiance, only to despair at the thought of the disgrace and scandal of divorce? Unable to face her life, she had chosen death.

He didn't like it. Shaking his head, Holt blew out a slow stream of smoke. He just didn't like the rhythm of it. Maybe he was losing his objectivity, but he couldn't see Suzanna giving up and hurling herself onto the cliffs. And there were too many similarities between Bianca and her great-granddaughter.

Maybe he should try to get inside Suzanna's head. If he understood her, maybe he could understand her star-crossed ancestor. Maybe, he admitted with a pull on the beer, he could understand himself. His feelings for her seemed to undergo radical changes every day, until he no longer knew exactly what he felt.

Oh, there was desire, that was clear enough. But it wasn't simple. He'd always counted on it being simple.

What made Suzanna Calhoun Dumont tick? Her kids, Holt thought immediately. No contest there, though the rest of her family ran a dead heat. Her business. She would work herself ragged making it run. But Holt suspected that her thirst to succeed in business doubled right back around to her children and family.

Restless, he rose to pace the length of the porch. A whippoorwill came to roost in the old wind-bent maple and lifted its voice in its three-note call. Roused, the insects began to whisper in the grass. The first firefly, a lone sentinel, flickered near the water that lapped the bank.

This, too, was something he wanted. The simple quiet of solitude. But as he stood, looking out into the night, he thought of Suzanna. Not just the way she had felt in his arms, the way she made his blood swim. But what it would be like to have her beside him now, waiting for moonrise.

He needed to get inside her head, to make her trust him enough to tell him what she felt, how she thought. If he could make the link with her, he would be one step closer to making it with Bianca.

But he was afraid he was already in too deep. His own thoughts and feelings were clouding his judgment. He wanted to be her lover more than he had ever wanted anything. To sink into her, to watch her eyes darken with passion until that sad, injured look was completely banished. To have her give herself to him the way she had never given herself to anyone—not even the man she had married.

Holt pressed his hands to the rail, leaned out into the growing dark. Alone, with night to cloak him, he admitted that he was following the same pattern as his grandfather.

He was falling in love with a Calhoun woman.

It was late before he went back inside. Later still before he slept.

Suzanna hadn't slept at all. She had lain awake all night trying not to think about the two small suitcases she had packed. When she managed to get her mind off that, it had veered toward Holt. Thoughts of him only made her more restless.

She'd been up at dawn, rearranging the clothes she'd already packed, adding a few more things, checking yet again to be sure she had included a few of their favorite toys so that they wouldn't feel homesick.

She'd been cheerful at breakfast, grateful that her family had been there to add support and encouragement. Both children had been whiny, but she'd nearly joked them out of it by noon.

By one, her nerves had been frayed and the children were cranky again. By two she was afraid Bax had forgotten the entire thing, then was torn between fury and hope.

At three the car had come, a shiny black Lincoln. Fifteen horrible minutes later, her children were gone.

She couldn't stay home. Coco had been so kind, so understanding, and Suzanna had been afraid they would both dissolve into puddles of tears. For her aunt's sake as much as her own, she decided to go to work.

She would keep herself busy, Suzanna vowed. So busy that when the children got back, she hardly would have noticed they'd been gone.

She stopped by the shop, but Carolanne's sympathy and curiosity nearly drove her over the edge.

"I don't mean to badger you," Carolanne apologized when Suzanna's responses became clipped. "I'm just worried about you."

"I'm fine." Suzanna was selecting plants with almost obsessive care. "And I'm sorry for being short with you. I'm feeling a little rough today."

"And I'm being too nosy." Always good-natured, Carolanne shrugged. "I like the salmon-colored ones," she said as Suzanna debated over the group of New Guinea impatiens. "Listen, if you want to blow off some steam, just call me. We can have a girls' night out."

"I appreciate that."

"Anytime," Carolanne insisted. "It'll be fine. That's a really nice grouping," she added as Suzanna began to load her choices into the truck. "Are you putting in another bed?"

"Paying off a debt." Suzanna climbed into the truck, gave a wave then drove off. On the way to Holt's, she busied her mind by designing and redesigning the arrangement for the flower bed. She'd already scouted out the spot, bordering the front porch so he could enjoy it whenever he came or went from the cottage. Whether he wanted to or not.

The job would take her the rest of the day, then she would unwind by walking along the cliffs. Tomorrow she would put in a full day at the shop, then spend the cool of the evening working the gardens at The Towers.

One by one, the days would pass.

She didn't bother to announce herself after she'd parked the truck, but set right to work staking out the bed. The result was not what she'd hoped for. As she dug and hoed and worked the soil there was no soothing response. Her mind didn't empty of worries and fill with the pleasure of planting. Instead a headache began to work nastily behind her eyes. Ignoring it, she wheeled over a load of planting medium and dumped it. She was raking it smooth when Holt stepped out.

He'd watched her from the window for nearly ten minutes, hating the fact that the strong shoulders were slumped and her eyes dull with sadness.

"I thought you were taking the day off."

"I changed my mind." Without glancing up, she rolled the wheelbarrow back to the truck and loaded it with flats of plants.

"What the hell are all of those?"

"Your paycheck." She started with snapdragons, delphiniums and bright shasta daisies. "This was the deal."

Frowning, he came down a couple of steps. "I said maybe you could put in a couple of bushes."

"I'm putting in flowers." She packed down the soil. "Anyone with an ounce of imagination can see that this place is crying for flowers."

So she wanted to fight, he noted, rocking back on his heels. Well, he could oblige her. "You could have asked before you dug up the yard."

"Why? You'd just sneer and make some nasty macho remark."

He came down another step. "It's my yard, babe."

"And I'm planting flowers in it. *Babe*." She tossed her head up. Yeah, she was mad enough to spit nails, he noted. And she was also miserable. "If you don't want to bother to give them any water or care, then I will. Why don't you go back inside and leave me to it?"

Without waiting for a response, she went back to work. Holt took a seat while she added lavender and larkspur, dahlias and violas. He smoked lazily, noting that her hands were as sure and graceful as usual.

"Planting posies doesn't seem to be improving your mood today."

"My mood is just fine. In fact, it's dandy." She snapped a sprig off some freesia and swore. "Why shouldn't it be, just because I had to watch Jenny get in that damn car with tears running down her cheeks? Just because I had to stand there and smile when Alex looked back at me, his little mouth quivering and his eyes begging me not to make him go."

When her eyes filled, she shook the tears away. "And I had to stand there and take it when Bax accused me of being an overprotective, smothering mother who was turning his children, *his* children into timid weaklings."

She hacked her spade into the dirt. "They're not timid or weak," she said viciously. "They're just children. Why shouldn't they be afraid to go with him, when they hardly know him? And with his wife who stood there in her silk suit and Italian heels looking distressed and helpless. She won't have a clue what to do if Jenny has a bad dream or Alex gets a stomachache. And I just let them go. I just stood there and let them get in that awful car with two strangers. So I'm feeling just fine. I'm feeling terrific."

She sprang up to shove the wheelbarrow back to the truck. When she came back to do the mulching, he was gone. She forced herself to do the work carefully, reminding herself that at least here, over this one thing, she had control.

Holt came back, dragging the hose from around the other side of the house and holding two beers. "I'll water them. Have a beer."

Swiping a hand over her brow, she frowned at the bottles. "I don't drink beer."

"That's all I've got." He shoved one into her hand, then pushed the lever for the sprayer. "I think I can handle this part by now," he said dryly. "Why don't you have a seat?"

Suzanna walked to the steps and sat. Because she was thirsty she took one long sip, then rested her chin on her hand and watched him. He'd learned not to drown the plants, or pound them with a heavy spray. She let out a little sigh, then sipped again.

No words of sympathy, she thought. No comforting pats or claims to understand just how she felt. Instead, he'd given her exactly what she'd needed, a silent wall to hurl her misery and anger against. Did he know he'd helped her? She couldn't be sure. But she knew she had come here, to him, not only to plant flowers, not only to get out of the house, but because she loved him.

She hadn't given herself time to think about that, not since the feeling had opened and bloomed inside of her. Nor had she given herself a chance to wonder what it would mean to either of them.

It wasn't something she wanted. She wanted never to love again, never to risk hurt and humiliation at a man's hands again. But it had happened.

She hadn't looked for it. She had looked only for peace of mind, for security for her children, for simple contentment for herself. Yet she had found it.

And what would his reaction be if she told him. Would it please his ego? Would it shock or appall or amuse? It didn't matter, Suzanna told herself as she slipped an arm around the dog who had come to join her. For now, perhaps for always, the love was hers. She no longer expected emotions to be shared.

Holt shut off the spray. The colorful bed added charm to the simple wooden cottage. It even pleased him that he recognized some of the blooms by name. He wasn't going to ask her about the ones that were unfamiliar. But he'd look them up.

"It looks pretty good."

"They're mostly perennials," she said in the same casual tone. "I thought you might find it rewarding to see them come back year after year."

He might, but he also thought he would remember, much too vividly, how hurt and unhappy she'd looked when she'd planted them. He didn't dare dwell on how much it upset him to picture Alex and Jenny climbing tearfully into a car and driving away.

"They smell okay."

"That's the lavender." She took a deep breath of it herself before rising. "I'll go around and turn off the hose." She'd nearly turned the corner when he called her name.

"Suzanna. They'll be all right."

Not trusting her voice, she nodded and continued around back. She was crouched down, the dog's face in hers when he joined her.

"You know, if you put some day lilies and some sedum on that bank, you'd solve most of the erosion problem."

He cupped a hand under her elbow to pull her to her

feet. "Is working the only thing you use to take your mind off things?"

"It does the job."

"I've got a better idea."

Her heart gave a quick jolt. "I really don't—"

"Let's go for a ride."

She blinked. "A ride?"

"In the boat. We've got a couple of hours before dark."

"A ride in the boat," she said, unaware that she amused him with her long, relieved sigh. "I'd like that."

"Good." He took her hand and pulled her to the pier. "You cast off." When the dog jumped in beside him, Suzanna realized this was an old routine. For a man who didn't want to appear to have any sentiment, it was a telling thing that he took a dog along for company when he set out to sea.

The engine roared to life. Holt waited only until Suzanna had climbed on board before he headed into the bay.

The wind slapped against her face. Laughing, she clapped a hand to her cap to keep it from flying off. After she'd pulled it on more securely, she joined him at the wheel.

"I haven't been out on the water in months," she shouted over the engine.

"What's the use of living on an island if you never go out on the water?"

"I like to watch it."

She turned her head and caught the bright glint of window glass from the secluded houses on Bar Island. Overhead gulls wheeled and screamed. Sadie barked at them, then settled on the boat cushions with her head on the side so that the wind could send her ears flying.

"Has she ever jumped out?" Suzanna asked him.

He glanced back at the dog. "No. She just looks stupid."

"You'll have to bring her by the house again. Fred hasn't been the same since he met her."

"Some women do that to a man." The salt breeze was carrying her scent to him, wrapping it around his senses so that he drew her in with every breath. She was standing close, braced against the boat's motion. The expression in her eyes was still far off and troubled, and he knew she wasn't thinking of him. But he thought of her.

He moved expertly through the bay traffic, keeping the speed slow and steady as he maneuvered around other boats, passed a hotel terrace where guests sat under striped umbrellas drinking cocktails or eating an early dinner. Far to starboard, the island's three-masted schooner streamed into port with its crowd of waving tourists.

Then the bay gave way to the sea and the water became less serene. The cliffs roared up into the sky. Arrogantly, defiantly, The Towers sat on its ridge overlooking village and bay and sea. Its somber gray stone mirrored the tone of the rain clouds out to the west. Its old, wavy glass glinted with fanciful rainbows. Like a mirage, there were streaks and blurs of color that were Suzanna's garden.

"Sometimes when I went lobstering with my father, I'd look up at it." And think of you. "Castle Calhoun," Holt murmured. "That's what he called it."

Suzanna smiled, shading her eyes with the flat of her

hand as she studied the imposing house on the cliffs. "It's just home. It's always been home. When I look up at it I think of Aunt Coco trying out some new recipe in the kitchen and Lilah napping in the parlor. The children playing in the yard or racing down the stairs. Amanda sitting at her desk and working her meticulous way through the mounds of bills it takes to hold a home together. C.C. diving under the hood of the old station wagon to see if she could make a miracle happen and get one more year out of the engine. Sometimes I see my parents laughing at the kitchen table, so young, so alive, so full of plans." She turned around to keep the house in sight. "So many things have changed, and will change. But the house is still there. It's comforting. You understand that or you wouldn't have chosen to live in Christian's cottage, with all his memories."

He understood exactly, and it made him uneasy. "Maybe I just like having a place on the water."

Suzanna watched Bianca's tower disappear before she shifted to face him. "Sentiment doesn't make you weak, Holt."

He frowned out over the water. "I could never get close to my father. We came at everything from different directions. I never had to explain or justify anything I felt or wanted to my grandfather. He just accepted. I guess I figured there was a reason he left me the place when he died, even though I was only a kid."

It moved her in a very soft, very lovely way that he had shared even that much with her. "So you came back to it. We always come back to what we love." She wanted to ask him more, what his life had been like during the span of years he'd been away. Why he had turned his back on police work to repair boat motors and props. Had he been in love, or had his heart broken? But he hit the throttle and sent the boat streaking out over the wide expanse of water.

He hadn't come out to think deep thoughts, to worry or to wonder. He had come to give her, and himself, an hour of relaxation, a respite from reality. Wind and speed worked that particular miracle for him. It always had. When he heard her laugh, when she tossed her face up into the sun, he knew he'd chosen well.

"Here, take the wheel."

It was a challenge. She could hear the dare in his voice, see it in his eyes when he grinned at her. Suzanna didn't hesitate, but took his place at the helm.

She gloried in the control, in the power vibrating under her fingertips. The boat sliced through the water like a blade, racing to nowhere. There was only sea and sky and unlimited freedom. The Atlantic roughened, adding a dash of danger. The air took on a bite that shivered along the skin and made each breath a drink of icy wine.

Her hands were firm and competent on the wheel, her body braced and ready. The wistful look in her eyes had been replaced by a bright fearlessness that quickened his blood. Her face was flushed with excitement, dampened by the spray. She didn't look like a princess now, but like a queen who knew her own power and was ready to wield it.

He let her race where she chose, knowing that she would end where he had wanted her for most of his life. He wouldn't wait another day. Not even another hour.

She was breathless and laughing when she gave him the wheel again. "I'd forgotten what it was like. I haven't handled a boat in five years."

"You did all right." He kept the speed high as he turned the boat in a wide half circle.

Still laughing, she rubbed her hands over her arms. "Lord, it's freezing."

He glanced toward her and felt the punch low in his gut. She was glowing—her eyes as blue as the sky and only more vital, the thin cotton pants and blouse plastered against her slender body, her hair streaming out from under the cap.

When his palms grew damp and unsteady on the wheel, he looked away. Not falling in love, he realized. He'd stopped falling and had hit the ground with a fatal smack. "There's a jacket in the cabin."

"No, it feels wonderful." She closed her eyes and let the sensations hammer her. The wild wind, the golden evening sun, the smell of salt and sea and the man beside her, the roar of the motor and the churning wake. They might have been alone, completely, with nothing but excitement and speed, with either of them free to take the wheel and spear off into that fabulous aloneness.

She didn't want to go back. Suzanna drank deeply of the tangy air and thought how liberating it would be to race and race in no direction at all, then to drift wherever the current took her.

But the air was already warming. They were no longer alone. She heard the long, droning horn of a tourist boat as Holt cut the speed and glided toward the harbor.

This too was lovely, she thought. Coming home. Knowing your place, certain of your welcome. She let out a little sigh at the simple familiarity. The blue water of Frenchman Bay deepening now with evening, the buildings crowded with people, the clang of buoys. It was all the more comforting after the frantic race to nowhere.

They said nothing as he navigated across the bay and circled around to drift to his pier. But she was relaxed when she jumped out to secure the lines, when she ran her hands over the dog who leaned against her legs, begging for attention.

"You're quite the sailor, aren't you, girl?" She crouched down to give the dog a good rub. "I think she wants to go again."

Holt stepped nimbly to the dock and stood a foot apart. "There's a storm coming in."

Suzanna glanced up and saw that the clouds were blowing slowly but determinedly inland. "You're right. We can certainly use the rain." Foolish, she thought, to feel awkward now and start talking of the weather. She rose, uncertain of her moves now that he was standing here, tension in every line of his body, his eyes dark and intent on hers. "Thanks for the ride. I really enjoyed it."

"Good." The pier swayed when he started forward. Suzanna took two steps back and felt better when her feet hit solid ground.

"If you get a chance, maybe you can bring Sadie to visit Fred this weekend. He'll be lonely without the kids around."

"All right."

She was halfway across the yard, and he was still a foot away. If it hadn't seemed so paranoid, she would have said he was stalking her. "The bush is doing well." She ran her fingers over it as she passed. "But you really need to feed this lawn. I could recommend a simple and inexpensive program."

His lips curved slightly, but his eyes stayed on hers. "You do that."

"Well, I...it's getting late. Aunt Coco—"

"Knows you're a big girl." He took her arm to hold her still. "You're not going anywhere tonight, Suzanna."

Perhaps if she'd been wiser or more experienced, she would have gauged his mood before he touched her. There was no mistaking it now, not when his fingers had closed over her with taut possession, not when his needs, and his intention of satisfying them, were so clear in those deep gray eyes.

She wished she could have been so certain of her own mood and her own needs.

"Holt, I told you I needed time."

"Time's up," he said simply, with an underlying edge that had her pulse jerking.

"This isn't something I intend to take casually."

Heat flashed into his eyes. From miles away came the violent rumble of thunder. "There's nothing casual about it. We both know that."

She did know it, and the knowledge was terrifying. "I think—"

He swore and swept her into his arms. "You think too much."

The moment the shock wore off she began to struggle. By then he had already carried her onto the back porch. "Holt. I won't be pressured." The screen door slammed behind them. Didn't he know she was afraid? That she was so afraid if she took this step he would find her dull, shrug her off and leave her shattered? "I'm not going to be rushed into this."

"If you had your way, it would take another fifteen years." He kicked open the door to the bedroom then dropped her onto the bed. It wasn't what he had planned, but he was too knotted up with terror and longings to struggle with soft words.

She was off the bed in a shot to stand beside it, slim and straight as an arrow. The lowering light, already gathering gloom, crept through the window at her back. "If you think you can cart me in here and throw me on the bed—"

"That's exactly what I've done." His eyes stayed hard on hers as he pulled his shirt over his head. "I'm tired of waiting, Suzanna, and I'm damn tired of wanting you. We're going to do this my way."

It had been like this for her before, she thought as her heart sank to her stomach like a stone. Only then it had been Bax, ordering her into bed, peeling off his clothes before he climbed on top of her to take his marital rights, quick and hard and without affection. And after, there would come his derision and disgust for her.

"Your way's hardly new," she said tightly. "And it doesn't interest me. I'm not obligated to go to bed with you, Holt. To let you demand and take and tell me I'm not good enough to satisfy. I'm not going to be used again, by anyone."

He caught her arms before she could storm from the room, dragged her struggling and swearing against him to crush his heated mouth to hers. The force of it sent her reeling. She would have stumbled away if his arms hadn't banded her so tightly.

Over the fear and the anger her own needs swelled. She wanted to scream at him for pulling them from her, for leaving her raw and naked and defenseless. But she could only hold on.

He yanked her away, arm's length, his breath already

ragged and shallow. Her eyes were dark as midnight and held as many secrets. He would uncover them, that he promised himself. One by one he would learn them all. And tonight, he would begin.

"No one is going to be used here, and I'm only going to take what you give." His tensed fingers flexed on her arms. "Look at me, Suzanna. Look at me and tell me you don't want me, and I'll let you go."

Her lips parted on a shaky breath. She loved him, and she was no longer a girl who could hold love to herself like a comforting pillow in the night. If she was not as strong as she hoped and able to hold her heart and body separate, then she had no choice but to unite them. If that heart was broken, she would survive.

Hadn't she promised them both there would be no regrets?

She lifted a hand to his gently though she expected no gentleness in return. The choice was one she made freely.

"I can't tell you I don't want you. There's no need to wait any longer."

Chapter 8

If his nerves hadn't been so tangled, if the need hadn't been so acute, he might have been able to show her tenderness. If his blood hadn't been so hot, desire so greedy, he would have tried to give her some romance. But he was certain if he didn't possess now, possess quickly, he would shatter into hundreds of jagged shards of desperation.

So his mouth was fevered with impatience, his hands rough with urgency. At the first potent taste he understood she was already his. But it wasn't enough. Maybe it could never be enough.

She didn't tremble or hesitate. The vulnerability was cloaked inside a generosity that urged him to take his fill. As her hands roamed restlessly over his back he felt only her hunger, and none of her doubt.

He pushed the cap from her hair, then yanked the

band from it so that his hands could take fistfuls of
honey-colored silk. And the hands that gripped were
unsteady, even as his mouth ruthlessly devoured hers.

She opened for him, releasing a soft and sultry moan
of pleasure as his tongue plunged to duel with hers.
He wanted so badly, and that want vibrating from him
aroused her own. She had risen on her toes, unaware
that she was fighting to meet him flare for flare. Her
body was quaking with passions long suppressed.

And there was fear in that, fear in not knowing what
would become of her if she lost that last toehold on control. She had to show him that she could give pleasure,
make him enjoy and continue to want. If she fumbled
now, lessened her grip on proving herself a woman,
might he not find her less than his fantasy?

Yet she had never been wanted like this. Not like
this with the violence of desire pulsing in the air so
that every breath was like breathing temptation. She
strained against him, hoping what she had to give would
be enough while her system jolted along the battering
tide of sensations.

His mouth raced over her face, down her throat
where his teeth and the rough stubble of beard scraped.
And his hands—Lord, his hands were fast and lethal.

She had to keep her head, but her knees were watery
and her mind was spinning from the onslaught. Desperately she dug her nails into his back as she struggled away from the edge and tried to remember what
a man would like.

She was quivering like a plucked bow, so tensed and
wired he thought she might snap in two in his hands.
She was holding back. The knowledge that she could
do so when he was half-crazed brought on a kind of

virulent fury. He tore the blouse aside as he pushed her onto the bed.

"Damn you, I want it all." Breath heaving, he encircled her wrists and dragged her arms over her head. "I'll have it all." When his mouth swooped down to capture hers, her hands strained under his grip, her pulse jittering in quick, rabbit jumps under his fingers.

His body was like a furnace, hot damp flesh fusing with hers in a way that made her shudder from the sheer wonder of it. Like iron, his fingers clamped hers still while his free hand raked over her in a merciless assault. She could feel the anger, taste the frustrated and furious desire. Desperate, she tried to pull in a breath to beg him to wait, to give her a moment, but all she could manage were jagged moans.

The wind kicked the curtains aside, letting dusk pour through. The first drops of rain hit the roof, sounding to her sensitized ears like gunshots that echoed the war he was waging on her. Again thunder rumbled, closer now, warning of a reckless power.

When his mouth found her breast, he let out a hot groan of pleasure. Here she was as soft as a summer breeze and as potent as whiskey. As she writhed beneath him, he dampened and tugged on the taut nipple, losing himself in the taste and texture while her heartbeat hammered against his mouth.

And she wanted as he wanted. He could feel the urgent excitement raging through her, hear it in her quick, sobbing breaths. Her hips arched and plunged against his until he was senseless. He ranged lower, his teeth nipping at her rib cage, his tongue laying a line of wet heat over her belly.

Her hands were free now and her fingers gripped his

hair, then tore at the bedspread. She couldn't breathe. She needed to tell him. Her body was too full of aches and heat. She needed…

She needed.

Someone cried out. Suzanna heard the quick desperate sound, felt it tear from her own throat as her body arched up. Whole worlds exploded inside of her with a roar more huge than the thunder that stalked just overhead. Stunned, she lay shuddering under him as he lifted his head to stare at her.

Her eyes were dark, her face flushed with fresh fever. Beneath his, her body shook with aftershocks even as her hands slipped limply from his back to the ravaged bed. He hadn't guessed what it would do to him to see that kind of dazed pleasure on her face.

But he knew he wanted more.

He was driving her up again before she could recover. Now she could only embrace the speed and the thrill of danger. As the rain began to pound, she rolled with him, too giddy to be shocked by her own greed. Her hands were as rough and ready as his now, her mouth as merciless. When he dragged the slacks down her legs, her quick gasp was one of triumph. Her fingers were equally impatient as they yanked the denim over his hips, as they streaked and pressed over slick, heated flesh.

She wanted to touch as urgently as she needed to be touched. To possess even as she was possessed. She craved the madness, the turbulent hunger she hadn't known she could feel, and this tempestuous desire that reared up like a wild wolf to consume.

There was no thought of control now, not from either of them. When he sent her racing up again, then again, she rode each slashing crest only frantic for more. More was what he wanted to give her, and what he wanted to take. As the blood fired through his veins he drove himself into her, claiming possession in a frenzy of speed and heat. She matched him, beat for wild beat, the long, nurturing fingers digging into his hips.

They were alone again, but this time the sea was violently churning and the air was flaming hot. Here, at last, was the power and the freedom. The speed was reckless, the journey a glorious risk. She felt him shudder, bury his face in her hair as he reached the end. Suzanna locked tight around him, and followed.

He'd wondered what it would be like for fifteen years. From boy to man he had dreamed about her, imagined her, wanted her. None of his fantasies had come close. She had been like a volcano, smoldering and shuddering, then erupting hot. Now she lay like warm wax beneath him, her body meltingly soft with passions spent. Her hair smelled of sun and sea. He thought he could stay just so for eternity, molded against her with the rain drumming on the roof and the wind blowing the curtains.

But he wanted to see her.

When he shifted, she made a small sound of protest and reached out. He said nothing, only kissed her until she relaxed again. Her eyes were drifting shut when he turned the lamp beside the bed on low.

Lord, she was beautiful, with her hair fanned out on the pillows, her skin glowing, her mouth soft and full. She tensed, but he ignored her discomfort as he took a long, silent study of the rest of her.

"Like I said," he murmured when his eyes came back to hers. "The Calhoun women are all lookers."

She didn't know what she was supposed to say or how she was expected to act. She knew that he had taken her to a new place, an extraordinary place, but she had no idea if he had experienced the same mind-spinning ride. Then he frowned and her stomach twisted. With his eyes narrowed, he traced a finger down her throat, over the swell of her breasts.

"I should have shaved," he said abruptly, hating the fact that he'd scraped and reddened her skin. "You could have told me I was hurting you."

"I guess I didn't notice."

"Sorry." He touched his lips gently to her throat. Her look of dazed surprise made him feel like an idiot. When he rolled away, she reached out tentatively for his hand.

"You didn't hurt me," she said softly. "It was wonderful." And she waited, hopeful that he would tell her the same.

"I've got to let the dog in." His voice was rough, but he gave her fingers a quick squeeze before he left the room.

Suzanna heard it now, the whining howls, the scratching at the screen. She told herself it wasn't a rejection. It only meant that he could go from passion to practicality more quickly than she. They had shared something, something vital. She could cling to that. She sat up, more than a little amazed to see the state of the bed. The spread was a heap on the floor, the sheets a tangled knot at the foot. Her clothes—what was left of them—were scattered with his.

She rose and, uncomfortable naked, tugged on his

shirt before she lifted her own. One button out of five remained, hanging by a thread. Laughing, she hugged it to herself. To have been wanted like that. With a little sigh, she bent down to search for her buttons. Maybe now he could be cool and collected, maybe his life hadn't been changed as hers had, but she had been wanted, desperately. She would never forget it.

"What are you doing?"

She looked up to see him standing in the doorway. Obviously walking around buck naked didn't concern him in the least, she thought and felt her steady pulse jerk and dance again. He looked angry. She wished she understood what she had done, or hadn't done, to put that scowl on his face.

"My blouse," she said. "I found the buttons." She gripped them in one hand, the thin cotton in the other. "Do you have a needle and thread?"

"No." Didn't she know what she did to him, standing there in nothing but his shirt, her hair tousled, her eyes heavy? Did she want him to get down on his knees and beg?

"Oh." She swallowed and tried to smile. "Well, I can fix it at home. If I could just borrow your shirt. I'd better get back."

He closed the door behind him. "No," he said again, and crossed the room to take her.

The rain stopped at dawn, leaving the air washed clean. Suzanna awoke to the lazy music of water dripping from the gutters. Before her mind had adjusted to where she was, her mouth was captured in a hot, hungry kiss. Her body catapulted from sleep to desire in one breathless leap.

He'd awakened wanting her. That burning need wouldn't ease no matter how much he took, how willingly she gave. There were no words, none he knew, that could express what she had come to mean to him. From a boy's fantasy to a man's salvation.

He could only show her.

He covered her. He filled her. Watching her face in the watery morning sunlight, he knew he would never be content unless she was with him.

"You're mine." He threw the words out like a curse as her body shuddered beneath his. "Say it." His hands fisted on the sheets and he buried his face against her throat. "Damn it, Suzanna, say it."

She could say nothing but his name as he dragged her over the edge.

When her hands slid limply from his back, he rolled over, locking her close so that she lay over him. He could be content with her head resting on his heart. He told himself that he'd already pushed her hard and fast enough. But he'd wanted badly to hear the words.

His hands were fisted in her hair. As if, she thought dizzily, he would yank her back if she tried to move. Her body felt achy and bruised and glorious. She smiled, listening to the rapid thud of his heart and the liquid beauty of morning birdsong.

Her eyes flew open, her head up. He did pull her hair, but more from reflex than intent. "It's morning," Suzanna said.

"That usually happens when the sun comes up."

"No, I—ouch."

"Sorry," he muttered, and reluctantly released her hair.

"I must have fallen asleep."

"Yeah." He ran his hands up and down her back. He liked the long, smooth feel of it. "You dozed off before I could interest you in another round."

Her color fluctuated, but when she tried to scramble up, he held her firmly in place.

"Going somewhere?"

"I have to get home. Aunt Coco must be frantic."

"She knows where you are." Because it was easier to keep her in place, he reversed positions again and began to nibble at her throat. Nothing could have pleased him more than feeling the instant quickening of her pulse under his lips. "And in all likelihood, she's got a pretty good idea what you've been up to."

Without much hope of dislodging him, she pushed at his shoulder. "I didn't tell her where I was going."

"I called her last night when I let Sadie in. Scratch my back, will you? Base of the spine."

She obliged automatically, even while her thoughts spun. "You—you told my aunt that I..."

"I told her you were with me. I figure she could put the rest together. That's good. Thanks."

Suzanna let out a long breath. Oh yes, Aunt Coco wouldn't have any trouble adding two and two. And there was absolutely no reason to feel uncomfortable or embarrassed. But she was both. Not only relating to her aunt but to the man whose naked body was spread over hers.

It had been one thing to face him at night. But the morning...

He lifted his head to study her. "What's the problem?"

"Nothing." When he lifted a brow she shifted in what

passed for a shrug. "It's just that I'm not sure what to do now. I've never done this before."

He grinned at her. "How'd you get two kids?"

"I don't mean that I've never... I mean I've never..."

His grin only widened. "Well, get used to it, babe." Considering, he trailed a finger over her jawline. "Want me to help you out with morning-after etiquette?"

"I want you to stop leering at me."

"No, you see that's part of the form." He replaced his trailing finger with a light nip of his teeth. "I'm supposed to leer at you in the morning so you don't start feeling that you look like a hag."

"A—" The word caught in her throat. "A hag?"

"And you're supposed to tell me I was incredible."

Her brow lifted. "I am?"

"That, and any other superlatives you can come up with. Then—" he rolled her over again "—you're supposed to go fix me breakfast, to show me your talents are versatile."

"I can't tell you how grateful I am that you're filling me in on the procedure."

"No problem. And after you fix me breakfast, you should seduce me back into bed."

She laughed and pressed her cheek to his in a move that disarmed and delighted him. "I'll have to practice up on that, but I could probably handle a couple of scrambled eggs."

"Let me know if you find any."

"Have you got a robe?"

"What for?"

She looked up again. He was still leering. "Never mind." Sliding away, she instinctively turned her back as she groped on the floor for his shirt. "And what do you do while I'm fixing breakfast?"

He caught the ends of her hair, let them shift through his fingers. "I watch you."

And he enjoyed it, seeing her move around his kitchen, his shirt skimming her thighs with the scent of coffee ripening the air and her voice low and amused as she spoke to the dog.

She felt more at ease here, with familiar chores. The bush they had planted was a cloud of sunlight outside the window, and the breeze still smelled of rain.

"You know," she said as she grated cheese into the eggs, "you could use more than a toaster, one pot and a skillet."

"Why?" He kicked back in the chair and took a comfortable drag on his cigarette.

"Well, some people actually use this room to prepare entire meals."

"Only if they haven't heard of take-out." He saw that the coffee had dripped through and rose to pour them both a cup. "What do you take in this?"

"Just black. I need the kick."

"If you ask me, what you need is more sleep."

"I have to be at work in an hour or so." With the bowl of eggs in her hands, she stopped to stare out of the window. He recognized the look in her eyes and rubbed a hand over her shoulder.

"Don't."

"I'm sorry." She turned to the stove to pour the beaten eggs into the skillet. "I can't help but wonder what they're doing, if they're having a good time. They've never been away before."

"Hasn't he taken them for a weekend?"

"No, just a couple of afternoons that weren't terribly successful." She made an effort to shake the mood as she stirred the eggs. "Well, there's only thirteen days left to go."

"You're not helping them or yourself by getting worked up." His impotence grated as he fought to massage the tension from her shoulders.

"I'm fine. I will be fine," she corrected. "I've got more than enough to keep me busy for the next couple of weeks. And with the kids gone, I can put in more time trying to find the emeralds."

"You leave that to me."

She glanced over her shoulder. "This is a team effort, Holt. It always has been."

"I'm involved now, and I'll handle it."

She dished the eggs up as carefully as she chose her words. "I appreciate your help. All of us do. But they're called the Calhoun emeralds for a reason. Two of my sisters have been threatened because of them."

"Exactly my point. You're out of your league with Livingston, Suzanna. He's smart and he's brutal. He won't ask you nicely to get out of his way."

Turning, she handed him his plate. "I'm accustomed to smart, brutal men, and I've already spent enough of my life being afraid."

"What's that supposed to mean?"

"Just what I said." She lifted her plate, and the mug of coffee. "I won't let some thief intimidate me or make me afraid to do what's best for myself and my family."

But Holt was shaking his head. That wasn't the answer he'd wanted. "Are you afraid of Dumont? Physically?"

Her gaze wavered then leveled. "We're talking

about the emeralds." She tried to move by him, but Holt blocked her path. His eyes had gone dark, but when he spoke his voice was softer, more controlled than she had ever heard it.

"Did he hit you?"

Her color deepened, then raced away from her cheeks. "What?"

"I want to know if Dumont ever hit you."

Nerves were tightening her throat. No matter how quiet his voice, there was a terrible gleam of violence in his eyes. "The eggs are getting cold, Holt, and I'm hungry."

He fought back the urge to hurl the plate against the wall. He sat, waited for her to take the seat across from him. She looked very frail and very composed in the stream of sunlight. "I want an answer, Suzanna." He picked up his coffee and sipped as she toyed with her food. He knew how to wait and how to push.

"No." Her voice was flat as she took the first bite. "He never hit me."

"Just knocked you around?" He kept his voice casual and ate without tasting. Her gaze flicked up to his, then away.

"There are a lot of ways to intimidate and demoralize, Holt. After that, humiliation is a snap." Picking up a slice of toast, she buttered it carefully. "You're nearly out of bread."

"What did he do to you?"

"Let it go."

"What," he repeated slowly, "did he do to you?"

"He made me face facts."

"Such as?"

"That I was pitifully inadequate as a wife of a corporate lawyer with social and political ambitions."

"Why?"

She slammed down the knife. "Is this how you interrogate suspects?"

Anger, he thought. That was better. "It's a simple question."

"And you want a simple answer? Fine. He married me because of my name. He thought there was a bit more money as well as prestige attached to it, but the Calhoun name was more than adequate. Unfortunately it became quickly apparent that I wasn't the social boon he'd imagined. My dinner party conversation was pedestrian at best. I could be dressed up to look the part of the prominent wife of a politically ambitious attorney, but I could never quite pull it off. It was, as he told me often, a huge disappointment that I couldn't get it through my head what was expected of me. That I was boring, in the drawing room, the dining room and the bedroom."

She sprang up to scrape the rest of her meal into Sadie's bowl. "Does that answer your question?"

"No." Holt pushed his plate away and pulled out a cigarette. "I'd like to know how he convinced you that you were at fault."

Keeping her back to him, she straightened. "Because I loved him. Or I loved the man I thought I'd married, and I wanted, very badly, to be the woman he'd be proud of. But the harder I tried, the more I failed. Then I had Alex, and it seemed… I had done something so incredible. I'd brought that beautiful baby into the world. And it was so easy, so natural for me to be a mother. I never had any doubts, any missteps. I was so happy, so focused on the child and the family we'd begun, that I didn't realize that Bax was discreetly finding more exciting companionship. Not until I found out I was going to have Jenny."

"So he cheated on you." His voice was deceptively mild. "What did you do about it?"

She didn't turn around, but began to run water in the sink to wash the dishes. "You can't understand what it's like to be betrayed that way. To already feel as though you're inadequate. To be carrying a man's child and find out that you've already been replaced."

"No, I can't. But it seems to me I'd be ticked off."

"Was I angry?" She nearly laughed. "Yes, I was angry, but I was also…wounded. I don't like to remember how easy it was for him to shatter me. Alex was only a few months old, and Jenny hadn't been planned. But I was so happy to be pregnant. He didn't want her. Nothing he'd done to me before had hurt or shocked me the way his reaction did when I told him I was pregnant again. He wasn't angry so much as…irked." She decided on a half laugh and plunged her hands into the soapy water.

"He had a son," she continued, "so the Dumont name would continue. He didn't intend to clutter up his life with children, and he certainly didn't want to have to drag me around the social wheel a second time while I was fat and tired and unattractive. The most practical solution was to terminate the pregnancy. We fought horribly about that. It was the first time I'd had the nerve to stand up to him—which only made it worse. Bax was used to getting his own way, he always had. Since he couldn't force me to do what he wanted, he paid me back, expertly."

Calmer now, she set the dish aside to drain and began to wash out the skillet. "He was still discreet publicly with his affairs, but he made sure I knew about them, and how sadly I compared to the women he slept with. He took my name off the checking and charge accounts so that I had to ask him whenever I needed money. That was one of his more subtle humiliations. The night Jenny was born, he was with another woman. He made certain I knew about that when he came to the hospital so the press could snap his picture while he played the proud father."

Holt hadn't moved. He didn't trust himself to move. "Why did you stay with him?"

"At first, because I kept hoping I would wake up beside the man I'd fallen in love with. Then, when I started to consider that my marriage was a failure, I had one child and was pregnant with another." She picked up a cloth and began to dry the dishes. "And I stayed because for a long time, a very long time I was convinced he was right about me. I wasn't clever and witty and sharp. I wasn't sexy or seductive. So the least I could be was loyal. When I realized I couldn't even be that, I had to consider the effect on the children. They weren't to be hurt. I couldn't have stood it if dissolving my marriage to Bax had hurt them. One day, I suddenly understood that it was all for nothing, that I was not only wasting my life but probably doing more harm to Alex and Jenny by pretending there was a marriage. Bax paid little attention to his son, and none at all to his daughter. He spent a great deal more time with his lover than he did with his family."

She sighed, set the dishes down. "So I hid my diamonds in Jenny's diaper bag and asked for a divorce."

When she turned, the weariness was back on her face. "Does that answer your question?"

Very slowly, his eyes on hers, he rose. "Did it ever occur to you, did it ever once cross your mind that he was inadequate, that he was a failure? That he was a spoiled, selfish bastard?"

Her lips curved a little. "Well, the last part certainly occurred to me. It also occurs to me that my little story is one-sided. I imagine Bax's view of our relationship would differ from mine, and not without some merit."

"He's still pushing your buttons," Holt said with barely suppressed fury. "So you're not clever? I guess anyone could manage to raise two kids and run a business. Dull, too?" He took a step toward her, only more furious when he saw her instinctive move to brace. "Yeah, I don't know when I've been so bored by anyone, but then most men are bored with women with brains and guts, especially when they're softhearted and hardheaded. Nothing puts me to sleep faster than a woman who'll sweat all day to make sure her kids are provided for. God knows you're not sexy. I just didn't have anything better to do last night than to spend it going crazy over you."

He'd trapped her against the sink with his body and with an anger so ripe she could almost taste it. "You asked and I answered. I don't know what you want me to say now."

"I want you to say you don't give a damn about him." He grabbed her by the shoulders, his face close to hers. "I want you to tell me what I told you to tell me when I was inside you, when I was so full of you I couldn't breathe. You're mine, Suzanna. Nothing that happened before counts because you're mine now. That's what I want to hear."

His hands slipped down to clamp over her wrists. Even as she opened her mouth to speak he saw the quick wince of pain. Swearing, he looked down and saw the bruises he'd already put on her. He jerked back as if she'd slapped him.

"Holt—"

He raised a hand to silence her, turning away until he could clear the red haze of fury from his mind. He'd put marks on her skin. It had been done in passion and without intention, but that didn't erase them. By putting them there, he was no better than the man who had bruised her soul.

He jammed his hands into his pockets before he turned. "I've got things to do."

"But—"

"We got off the track, Suzanna. My fault. I know you have to get to work, and so do I."

So that was that, she thought. She'd bared her soul, now he would walk away. "All right. I'll see you on Monday."

With a nod, he headed for the back door, then swore, stopping with his hand on the screen. "Last night meant something to me. Do you understand that?"

She let out a quiet breath. "No."

His hand curled into a fist on the screen. "You're important to me. I care about you, and having you here, this way, is… I need you. Is that clear enough?"

She studied him—a fist on the door, impatience in his eyes, his body rigid with passions she couldn't quite understand. It was enough, she realized. For now it was more than enough.

"Yes, I think it's clear."

"I don't want it to end there." He turned his head, and his eyes were dark and fierce again. "It's not going to end there."

She continued to study his face, keeping her voice calm. "Are you asking me to come back?"

"You know damn well—" He cut himself off and closed his eyes. "Yes, I'm asking you to come back. And I'm asking you to think about spending time with me that isn't at work or in bed. If that doesn't spell it out for you, then—"

"Would you like to come to dinner?"

He gave her a blank stare. "What?"

"Would you like to come to dinner, tonight? Maybe we could take a drive after."

"Yeah." He dragged a hand through his hair, not sure if he was relieved or uneasy that it had been so simple. "That would be good."

Yes, it would be good, she thought and smiled. "I'll see you about seven then. Bring Sadie if you like."

Chapter 9

It wasn't candlelight and moonbeams, Suzanna thought, but it was a romance. She hadn't believed she would find it again, or want it. Flexing her back as she drove up the curving road to The Towers, she smiled.

Of course, a relationship with Holt Bradford was lined with rough edges, but it had its softer moments. She'd had a lovely time discovering them over the past few days. And nights.

There was the way he'd shown up at the shop once or twice, just before lunchtime. He hadn't said anything about the children, or her missing the routine—just that he'd come into the village for some parts and felt like eating.

Or how he'd come up behind her at odd moments to rub the tension out of her shoulders. The evening he'd surprised her after a particularly grueling day by dragging her and a wicker basket filled with cold chicken into the boat.

He was still demanding, often abrupt, but he never made her feel less than what she wanted to be. When he loved her, he loved her with an urgency and ferocity that left no doubt as to his desire.

No, she hadn't been looking for romance, she thought as she parked the truck behind Holt's car. But she was terribly glad she'd found it.

The moment she opened the door, Lilah pounced. "I've been waiting for you."

"So I see." Suzanna lifted a brow. Lilah was still in her park service uniform. Knowing her schedule, Suzanna was sure her sister had been home nearly an hour. As a matter of routine, Lilah should have been in her most comfortable clothes and spread out dozing on the handiest flat surface. "What's up?"

"Can you do anything with that surly hulk you've gotten tangled up with?"

"If you mean Holt, not a great deal." Suzanna pulled off her cap to run her hands through her hair. "Why?"

"Right now, he's upstairs, taking my room apart inch by inch. I couldn't even change my clothes." She aimed a narrowed glance up the steps. "I told him we'd already looked there, and that if I'd been sleeping in the same room as the emeralds all these years, I'd know it."

"And he ignored you."

"He not only ignored me, he kicked me out of my own bedroom. And Max." She let out a hiss of breath and sat on the stairs. "Max grinned and said it was a damn good idea."

"Want to gang up on them?"

A wicked gleam came into Lilah's eyes. "Yeah." She

rose then swung an arm over Suzanna's shoulders as they started up. "You're really serious about him, aren't you?"

"I'm taking it one step at a time."

"Sometimes when you love someone it's better to take it by leaps and bounds." Then she yawned and swore. "I missed my nap. It'd be satisfying if I could say I disliked that pushy jerk, but I can't. There's something too solid and steady under the bad manners."

"You've been looking at his aura again."

Lilah laughed and stopped at the top of the stairs. "He's a good guy, as much as I'd like to belt him right now. It's good to see you happy again, Suze."

"I haven't been unhappy."

"No, just not happy. There's a difference."

"I suppose there is. Speaking of happy, how are the wedding plans coming?"

"Actually, Aunt Coco and the relative from hell are in the kitchen arguing over them right now." She turned laughing eyes to her sister. "And having a delightful time. Our great-aunt Colleen is pretending she simply wants to make certain the event will live up to the Calhoun reputation, but the fact is, she's getting a big kick out of making guest lists and shooting down Aunt Coco's menus."

"As long as she's entertained."

"Wait until she gets hold of you," Lilah warned. "She has some very creative ideas for floral arrangements."

"Terrific." Suzanna stopped in Lilah's doorway. Holt was definitely hard at work. Never particularly ordered, Lilah's room looked as though someone had scooped up every piece of furniture and dropped it down again like pick-up sticks. At the moment, he had his head in the fireplace, and Max was crawling on the floor.

"Having fun, boys?" Lilah said lazily.

Max looked up and grinned. She was mad, all right, he thought. He'd learned to handle and enjoy her temper. "I found that other sandal you've been looking for. It was under the cushion of the chair."

"There's good news." She lifted a brow, noting that Holt was now sitting on Lilah's hearth, looking at Suzanna. And Suzanna was looking at him. "You need a break, Max."

"No, I'm fine."

"You definitely need a break." She walked in to take his hand and pull him to his feet. "You can come back and help Holt invade my privacy later."

"I told you she wouldn't like it," Suzanna said when Lilah dragged Max from the room.

"That's too bad."

With her hands on her hips she surveyed the damage. "Did you find anything?"

"Not unless you count the two odd earrings and one of those lacy things we found behind the dresser." He tilted his head. "You got any of those lacy things?"

"Not really." She looked down at her sweaty T-shirt. "Up until a few days ago, I didn't think I'd need any."

"You've got a real nice way of wearing denim, babe." He rose, and since she wasn't coming any closer, moved to her. "And..." He ran his hands over her shoulders, down her back to her hips. "I get a real charge out of taking it off you." He kissed her hard, in the deep and urgent way she'd come to expect. Then he nipped her bottom lip and grinned. "But anytime you want to borrow one of those lacy things from Lilah..."

She laughed and gave him a quick, affectionate hug, the kind she gave so freely that never failed to warm him from the inside out. "Maybe I'll surprise you. How long have you been here?"

"I came straight from the site. Did you get the rest of those whatdoyoucallits in?"

"Russian olives, yes." And her back was still aching. "You were a lot of help on the retaining wall."

"You were out of your mind to think you could build that thing on your own."

"I had a part-time laborer when I contracted."

He shook his head and went back to searching the fireplace. "You may be tough, Suzanna, but you're not equipped to haul around lumber and swing a sledge-hammer."

"I'd have done it—"

"Yeah." He glanced around. "I know." He tested another brick. "It did look pretty good."

"It looked terrific. And since you didn't swear at me more than half a dozen times when you were hefting landscape timbers, why don't I reward you?"

"Oh, yeah?" He lost his interest in the bricks.

"I'll go get you a beer."

"I'd rather have—"

"I know." She laughed as she walked out. "But you'll have to settle for a beer. For now."

It felt good, she thought, to be able to joke like that. Not to be embarrassed or edgy. There was no need to feel anything but content, knowing he cared for her. In time, they might have something deeper.

Full of energy and hope, she rounded the last step and turned into the hall. All at once, there was chaos. She heard the dogs first, Fred and Sadie, barking fiendishly, then the clatter of feet on the porch and two high bellowing shouts.

"Mom!" Both Jenny and Alex yelled the single syllable as they burst into the house.

The rich and fast joy came first as she bent to scoop them up in her arms. Laughing, she smothered them both with kisses as the dogs dashed in mad circles.

"Oh, I missed you. I missed you both so much. Let me look at you." When she drew them back arm's length, her smile faltered. They were both on the edge of tears. "Baby?"

"We wanted to come home." Jenny's voice trembled as she buried her face against her mother's shoulder. "We hate vacation."

"Shh." She stroked Jenny's hair as Alex rubbed a fist under his eyes.

"We were unmanageable and bad," he said in a trembly voice. "And we don't care, either."

"Just the attitude I've come to expect," Bax said as he walked through the open front door. Jenny's arms tightened around Suzanna's neck, but Alex turned and threw out his Calhoun chin.

"We didn't like the dumb party, and we don't like you, either."

"Alex!" Her tone sharp, she dropped a hand on his shoulder. "That's enough. Apologize."

His lips quivered, but the stubborn gleam remained in his eyes. "We're sorry we don't like you."

"Take your sister upstairs," Bax said tightly. "I want to speak with your mother in private."

"You and Jenny go in the kitchen." Suzanna brushed a hand over Alex's cheek. "Aunt Coco's there."

Bax took a careless swipe at Fred with his foot. "And take these damn mutts with you."

"Chéri?" This from the svelte brunette who continued to hover in the doorway.

"Yvette." Keeping her arms around the children, Suzanna rose. "I'm sorry, I didn't see you."

The Frenchwoman waved distracted hands. "I beg your pardon, it's so confusing, I see. I just wondered— Bax, the children's bags?"

"Have the driver bring them in," he snapped. "Can't you see I'm busy?"

Suzanna sent the frazzled woman a look of sympathy. "He can just leave them here in the hall. If you'd like to come into the parlor…go see Aunt Coco," she told the children. "She'll be so happy you're back."

They went, holding each other's hand, with the dogs prancing at their heels.

"If you could spare a moment of your time," Bax said, then cast a glance up and down her work clothes, "out of your obviously fascinating day."

"The parlor," she repeated and turned. She struggled for calm, knowing it was essential. Whatever had caused him to change his plans and bring the children home a full week early was undoubtedly going to fall on her head. That she could handle. But the fact that the children had been upset was a different matter.

"Yvette—" Suzanna gestured to a chair "—can I get you something?"

"Oh, if you would be so kind. A brandy?"

"Of course. Bax?"

"Whiskey, a double."

She went to the liquor cabinet and poured, grateful her hands were steady. As she served Yvette, she thought she caught a glance of apology and embarrassment.

"Well, Bax, would you like to tell me what happened?"

"What happened began years ago when you had the mistaken idea you could be a mother."

"Bax," Yvette began, and was rounded on.

"Get out on the terrace. I prefer to do this privately."

So that hadn't changed, Suzanna thought. She gripped her hands together as Yvette crossed the room and exited through the glass doors.

"At least this little experiment should have rid her of the notion of having a child."

"Experiment?" Suzanna repeated. "Your visit with the children was an experiment?"

He sipped at the whiskey and watched her. He was still a striking man with a charmingly boyish face and fair hair. But temper, as it always had, added an edge to his looks that was anything but appealing.

"My reasons for taking the children are my concern. Their unforgivable behavior is yours. They haven't any conception of how to act in public and in private. They have the manners and dispositions of heathens and as little control. You've done a poor job, Suzanna, unless it was your intention to raise two miserable brats."

"Don't think you can stand here and speak about them that way in my house." Eyes dangerously bright, she walked toward him. "I don't give a damn if they fit your standards or not. I want to know why you've brought them back this way."

"Then listen," he suggested, and shoved her into a chair. "Your precious children don't have a clue what's expected of a Dumont. They were loud and unmanageable in restaurants, whiny and fidgety on the drive. When corrected they became defiant or sulky. At the resort, among several of my acquaintances, their behaviour was an embarrassment."

Too incensed for fear, Suzanna pulled herself out of the chair. "In other words, they were children. I'm sorry your plans were upset, Baxter, but it's difficult to expect a five- and six-year-old to present themselves as socially correct on all occasions. Even more difficult when they're thrust into a situation that wasn't any of their doing. They don't know you."

He swirled whiskey, swallowed. "They're perfectly aware that I'm their father, but you've seen to it that they have no respect for that relationship."

"No, you've seen to it."

Deliberately he set the whiskey aside. "Do you think I don't know what you tell them? Sweet, harmless little Suzanna." She stepped back automatically, pleasing him.

"I don't tell them anything about you," she said, furious with herself for retreating.

"Oh, no? Then you didn't mention the fact that they had a bastard brother out in Oklahoma?"

So that was it, she realized, struggling to settle. "Megan O'Riley's brother married my sister. There was no way to keep the situation a secret, even if I had wanted to."

"And you just couldn't wait to sling my name around." He gave her another shove that sent her stumbling back.

"The boy's their half brother. They accept that, and they're too young to understand what a despicable thing you did."

"My affairs are mine. Don't you forget it." Gripping her shoulders, he pushed her up against the wall. "I have no intention of letting you get away with your pitiful plots for revenge."

"Take your hands off me." She twisted, but he forced her back again.

"When I'm damn good and ready. Let me warn you, Suzanna. I won't have you spreading my private business around. If even a hint of this gets out, I'll know where it started, and you know who'll pay for it."

She kept herself rigid, kept her eyes steady. "You can't hurt me anymore."

"Don't count on it. You make sure your children keep this business of half brothers to themselves. If it's mentioned again—" he tightened his grip and jerked her up on her toes "—ever, you'll be very sorry."

"Take your threats and get out of my house."

"Yours?" He closed a hand around her throat. "Remember, it's only yours because I didn't want this crumbling anachronism. Push me, and I'll have you back in court in a heartbeat. And I'll have it all this time. Those children might benefit from a nice, Swiss boarding school, which is exactly where they'll be if you don't watch your step."

He saw her eyes change, but it wasn't the fear he'd expected. It was fury. She lifted a hand, but before she could strike out, he was jerked away and tumbling to the floor. She watched Holt drag him up again by the collar, then send him crashing into a Louis Quinze table.

She'd never seen murder in a man's eyes before, but she recognized it in Holt's as he pounded a fist into Baxter's face.

"Holt, don't—"

She started forward only to have her arm gripped with surprising strength. "Let him alone," Colleen said, her mouth grim, her eyes bright.

He wanted to kill him, and might have, if the man had fought back. But Bax slumped in his hold, nose and mouth seeping blood. "You listen to me, you bastard." Holt slammed him against the wall. "Put your hands on her again, and you're dead."

Shaken, hurting, Bax fumbled for a handkerchief. "I can have you arrested for assault." Holding the cloth to his nose, he looked around and saw his wife standing inside the terrace doors. "I have a witness. You assaulted me and threatened my life." It was his first taste of humiliation, and he detested it. His glance veered toward Suzanna. "You'll regret this."

"No, she won't," Colleen put in before Holt could give in to the satisfaction of smashing his fist into the sneering mouth. "But you will, you miserable, quivering, spineless swine." She leaned heavily on her cane as she walked toward him. "You'll regret it for what's left of your worthless life if you ever lay hands on any member of my family again. Whatever you think you can do to us, I can do only more viciously to you. If you're unclear about my abilities, my name is Colleen Theresa Calhoun, and I can buy and sell you twice over."

She studied him, a pitiful man in a rumpled suit, bleeding into a silk handkerchief. "I wonder what the governor of your state—who happens to be my godchild—will have to say if I mention this scene to him." She gave a slow, satisfied nod when she saw she was understood. "Now get your miserable hide out of my house. Young man—" she inclined her head to Holt "—you'll be so kind as to show our guest to the door."

"My pleasure." Holt dragged him into the hall. The last thing Suzanna saw when she ran from the house was Yvette's fluttering hands.

"Where did she go?" Holt demanded when he found Colleen alone in the parlor.

"To lick her wounds, I suppose. Get me a brandy. Damn it, she'll keep a minute," she muttered when he hesitated. Colleen eased herself into a chair and waited for her heart rate to settle. "I knew she'd had a difficult time, but I wasn't fully aware of the extent of it. I've had this Dumont looked into since the divorce." She took the brandy and drank deeply. "Pitiful excuse for a man. I still wasn't aware he had abused her. I should have been, the first time I saw that look in her eyes. My mother had the same look." She closed her own and leaned back. "Well, if he doesn't want to see his political ambitions go up in smoke, he'll leave her be." Slowly she opened her eyes and gave Holt a steely look. "You did well for yourself—I admire a man who uses his fists. I only regret I didn't use my cane on him."

"I think you did better. I just broke his nose, you scared the—"

"I certainly did." She smiled and drank again. "Damn good feeling, too." She noted that Holt was staring at the open terrace doors, his hands still fisted. Suzanna could do worse, she thought and swirled the remaining brandy. "My mother used to go to the cliffs. You might find Suzanna there. Tell her the children are having cookies and spoiling their dinner."

She had gone to the cliffs. She didn't know why when she'd needed to run, that she had run there. Only for a moment, she promised herself. She would only need a moment alone.

She sat on a rock, covered her face and wept out the bitterness and shame.

He found her like that, alone and sobbing, the wind carrying off the sounds of her grief, the sea pounding restlessly below. He didn't know where to begin. His mother had always been a sturdy woman, and whatever tears she had shed, had been shed in private.

Worse, he could still see Suzanna pushed against the wall, Dumont's hand on her throat. She'd looked so fragile, and so brave.

He stepped closer, laid a hesitant hand on her hair. "Suzanna."

She was up like a shot, choking back tears, wiping them from her damp face. "I have to get back in. The children—"

"Are in the kitchen stuffing themselves with cookies. Sit down."

"No, I—"

"Please." He sat, easing her down beside him. "I haven't been here in a long time. My grandfather used to bring me. He used to sit right here and look out to sea. Once he told me a story about a princess in the castle up on the ridge. He must have been talking about Bianca, but later, when I remembered it, I always thought of you."

"Holt, I'm so sorry."

"If you apologize, you're only going to make me mad."

She swallowed another hot ball of tears. "I can't stand that you saw, that anyone saw."

"What I saw was you standing up to a bully." He

turned her face to his. When he saw the fading red marks on her throat, he had to force back an oath. "He's never going to hurt you again."

"It was his reputation. The children must have talked about Kevin."

"Are you going to tell me?"

She did, as clearly as she was able. "When Sloan told me," she finished, "I knew it was important that the children understand they had a brother. What Bax doesn't realize is that I never thought about him, never cared. It was the children who mattered, all of them. The family."

"No, he wouldn't understand that. Or you." He brought her hand to his lips to kiss it gently. The stunned look on her face had him scowling out to sea. "I haven't been Mr. Sensitivity myself."

"You've been wonderful."

"If I had you wouldn't look like I hit you with a rock when I kiss your hand."

"It just isn't your style."

"No." He shrugged and dug out a cigarette. "I guess it's not." Then he changed his mind and slipped an arm around her shoulders instead. "Nice view."

"It's wonderful. I've always come here, to this spot. Sometimes…"

"Go ahead."

"You'll just laugh at me, but sometimes it's as if I can almost see her. Bianca. I can feel her, and I know she's here, waiting." She rested her head on his shoulder and shut her eyes. "Like right now. It's so warm and real. Up in the tower, her tower, it's bittersweet, more of a longing. But here, it's anticipation. Hope. I know you think I'm crazy."

"No." When she started to shift, he pulled her closer so that her head nestled back on his shoulder. "No, I can't. Not when I feel it, too."

From the west tower, the man who called himself Marshall watched them through field glasses. He didn't worry about being disturbed. The family no longer came above the second floor in the west wing, and the crew had knocked off thirty minutes before. He'd hoped to take advantage of the time that Sloan O'Riley was away with his new bride on his honeymoon to move more freely around the house. The Calhouns were so accustomed to seeing men in tool belts that they rarely gave him a second glance.

And he was interested, very interested in Holt Bradford, finding it fascinating that he was being drawn into this generation of Calhouns. It pleased him that he could continue his work right under the nose of an ex-cop. Such irony added to his vanity.

He would continue to keep tabs, he thought, while the cop completed his search. And he would be there to take what was his the moment the treasure was found. Whoever was in the way would simply be eliminated.

Suzanna spent all evening with her children, soothing ruffled feathers and trying to turn their unhappy experience into a silly misadventure. By the time she got them tucked into bed, Jenny was no longer clinging and Alex had rebounded like a rubber ball.

"We had to ride in the car for hours and hours." He bounced on his sister's bed while Suzanna smoothed Jenny's sheets. "And they had dumb music on the radio the *whole* time. People were singing like this."

He opened his mouth wide and let out what he thought passed for an operatic aria. "And you couldn't understand a word."

"Not like that, like this." Jenny let out a screech that could have shattered crystal. "And we had to be quiet and appreciate."

Suzanna held her temper and tweaked her daughter's nose. "Well, you appreciated that it was awful, didn't you?"

That made Jenny giggle and reach up for another kiss. "Yvette said we could play a word game, but he said it gave him a headache, so she went to sleep."

"And that's what you should do, right now."

"I liked the hotel," Alex continued, hoping to postpone the inevitable. "We got to jump on the beds when nobody was looking."

"You mean like you do in your room?"

He grinned. "They had little bars of soap in the bathroom, and they put candy on your pillow at night."

Suzanna cocked her head. "You can forget that idea, toadface."

After Jenny was settled with her night-light and army of stuffed animals, Suzanna carried Alex to his room. He didn't let her pick him up and cuddle often anymore, but tonight, he seemed to need it as much as she did.

"You've been eating bricks again," she murmured, and nuzzled his neck.

"I had five bricks for lunch." He flew out of her arms and onto the bed. She wrestled with him until he was breathless. He flopped back, laughing, then leaped out of bed again.

"Alex—"

"I forgot."

"You've already stretched it tonight, kid. In the bed or I'll have you cooked over a slow fire."

He pulled something out of the jeans he'd been wearing when he'd come home. "I saved it for you."

Suzanna took the flattened, broken chocolate wrapped in gold paper. It was more than a little melted, certainly inedible and more precious than diamonds.

"Oh, Alex."

"Jenny had one, too, but she lost it."

"That's all right." She brought him close for a fierce hug. "Thanks. I love you, you little worm."

"I love you, too." It didn't embarrass him to say it as it sometimes did, and he cuddled against her a moment longer. When his mother tucked him into bed, he didn't complain when she stroked his hair. "Night," he said, ready to sleep.

"Good night." She left him alone, weeping a little over the smashed mint. In her room, she opened the little case that had once held her diamonds, and tucked her son's gift inside.

She undressed then slipped into a thin white nightgown. There was paperwork waiting on her desk in the corner, but she knew her mind and nerves were still too rattled. To soothe herself, she opened the terrace doors and, taking her brush, walked outside to feel the night.

There was an owl hooting, crickets singing, the quiet whoosh of the sea. Tonight the moon was gilded and its light clear as glass. Smiling to herself, she lifted her face to it and skimmed the brush lazily through her hair.

Holt had never seen anything more beautiful than Suzanna brushing her hair in the moonlight. He knew he made a poor Romeo and was deathly afraid he'd make a fool of himself trying, but he had to give her something, to somehow show her what it meant to have her in his life.

He came out of the garden and started up the stone steps. He moved quietly, and she was dreaming. She didn't know he was there until he said her name.

"Suzanna."

She opened her eyes and saw him standing only a foot away, his hair ruffled by the breeze, his eyes dark in the shimmering light. "I was thinking about you. What are you doing here?"

"I went home, but… I came back." He wanted her to go on brushing her hair, but was certain the request would sound ridiculous. "Are you all right?"

"I'm fine, really."

"The kids?"

"They're fine, too. Sleeping. I didn't even thank you before. Maybe it's petty, but now that I've had a chance to settle, I can admit I really enjoyed seeing Bax's nose bleed."

"Anytime," Holt said, and meant it.

"I don't think it'll be necessary again, but I appreciate it." She reached out to touch his hand, and pricked her finger on a thorn. "Ow."

"That's a hell of a start," he mumbled, and thrust the rose at her. "I brought you this."

"You did?" Absurdly touched, she brushed the petals to her cheek.

"I stole it out of your garden." He stuck his hands into his pockets and wished for a cigarette. "I don't guess it counts."

"It certainly does." She had had two gifts that night, she thought, from the two men she loved. "Thank you."

He shrugged and wondered what to do next. "You look nice."

She smiled and glanced down at the simple white gown. "Well, it's not lacy."

"I watched you brushing your hair." His hand came out of his pocket of its own volition to touch. "I just stood there, down at the edge of the garden and watched you. I could hardly breathe. You're so beautiful, Suzanna."

Now it was she who couldn't breathe. He'd never looked at her just this way. His voice had never sounded so quiet. There was a reverence in it, as in the hand that stroked over her hair.

"Don't look at me like that." His fingers tightened in her hair and he had to force them to relax again. "I know I've been rough with you."

"No, you haven't."

"Damn it, I have." He fought against a welling impatience as she only stared at him. "I've pushed you around and grabbed on. I ripped your blouse."

A smile touched her lips. "When I sewed the buttons back on I remembered that night, and what it felt like to be needed that way." More than a little baffled, she shook her head. "I'm not fragile, Holt."

Couldn't she see how wrong she was? Didn't she know how she looked right now, her hair smooth and shining in the moonlight, the thin white gown flowing down?

"I want to be with you tonight." He slid his hand down to touch her cheek. "Let me love you tonight."

She couldn't have denied him anything. When he lifted her to carry her in, she pressed her lips to his throat. But his mouth didn't turn hot and ready to hers.

He laid her down carefully, took the brush and rose from her to set it on the nightstand. Then he turned the lights low.

When his mouth came to hers at last, it was soft as a whisper. His hands didn't race to excite, but moved with exquisite patience to seduce.

He felt her confusion, heard it in the unsteady murmur of his name, but he only rubbed his lips over hers, tracing the shape with his tongue. His strong hands moved with an artist's grace over the tensed slope of her shoulders.

"Trust me." He took his mouth on a slow, quiet journey over her face. "Let go and trust me, Suzanna. There's more than one way." Over her jaw, down the line of her throat, back to her trembling lips his mouth whispered. "I should have showed you before."

"I can't..." Then his kiss had her sinking, deep, deeper still into some thick velvet haze. She couldn't right herself. Didn't want to. Surely this endless, echoing tunnel was paradise.

He touched, hardly touching at all, and left her weak. His mouth, gliding like a cool breeze over her flesh, was rapture. She could hear him murmur to her, incredible promises, soft, lovely words. There was passion in them, in the fingertips that seemed designed only to bring her pleasure, yet this was a passion to give she had never expected.

He stroked her through the thin cotton, delighting in the liquid movements of her body beneath his hands. He could watch her face in the lamplight, feed on that alone, knowing she was steeped in him, in what he offered her. There was no need to strap down greed, desire was no less, but it had taken a different hue.

When she sighed, he brought his lips back to hers to swallow the flavor of his name.

He undressed her slowly, bringing the gown down inch by inch, wallowing in the delight of warming newly bared skin. Fascinated with each tremor he brought her, he lingered. Then took her gently over the first crest.

Unbearably sweet. Each movement, each sigh. Exquisitely tender. Every touch, every murmur. He had imprisoned her in a world of silk, gently bringing dozens of pulses to a throbbing ache that was like music. Never had she been more aware of her body than now as he explored it so thoroughly, so patiently.

At last she felt his flesh against hers, the warm, hard body she had come to crave. Opening heavy eyes, she looked. Lifting weighted limbs, she touched.

He hadn't known a need could be so strong yet so quiet. She enfolded him. He slipped into her. For both, it was like coming home.

I could not have foreseen that the day would be my last with her. Would I have looked more closely, held more tightly? The love could have been no greater, but could it have been treasured more completely?

There is no answer.

We found the little dog, cowering and half-starved in the rocks by our cliffs. Bianca found such pleasure in him. It was foolish, I suppose, but I think we both felt this was something we could share, since we had found him together.

We called him Fred, and I must admit I was sad to see him go when it was time for her to return to The Towers. Of course, it was right that she take the orphaned pup to her children so that they could make him a family. I went home alone, to think of her, to try to work.

When she came to me, I was stunned that she should have taken such a risk. Only once before had she been to the cottage, and we had not dared chance that again. She was frantic and overwrought. Under her cloak, she carried the puppy. Because she was pale as a ghost, I made her sit and poured her brandy.

She told me, as I sat, hardly daring to speak, of the events that had taken place since we'd parted.

The children had fallen in love with the dog. There had been laughter and light hearts until Fergus had returned. He refused to have the dog, a stray mutt, in his home. Perhaps I could have forgiven him for that, thought of him only as a rigid fool. Bianca told me that he had ordered the dog destroyed, holding firm even on the tears and pleas of his children.

On the girl, young Colleen, he had been the hardest. Fearing a harsher, perhaps a physical reprisal, Bianca had sent the children and the dog up to their nanny.

The argument that had followed was bitter. She did not tell me all, but her tremors and the flash of fear in her eyes said enough. In his fury, he had threatened and abused her. It was then I saw in the light of my lamp, the marks on her throat where his hands had squeezed.

I would have gone then. I would have killed him. But her terror stopped me. Never before and never again in my life have I felt a rage such as that. To love as I loved, to know that she had been hurt and frightened. There are times I wish to God I had gone, and had killed. Perhaps things would have been different. But I'll never be sure.

I didn't leave her, but stayed while she wept and

told me that he had gone to Boston, and that when he returned he intended to bring a new governess of his choosing. He had accused her of being a poor mother, and would take the care and control of the children from her.

If he had threatened to cut out her heart, he could not have done more damage. She would not see her children raised by a paid servant, overseen by a cold, ambitious father. She feared most for her daughter, knowing if nothing was done, Colleen would one day be bartered off into marriage—even as her mother had been.

It was this great fear that forced her decision to leave him.

She knew the risks, the scandal, the position she would be giving up. Nothing could sway her. She would take her children away where she knew they would be safe. Her wish was for me to go with them, but she did not beg or call upon my love.

She did not need to.

I would make the arrangements the next day, and she would prepare the children. Then she asked me to make her mine.

For so long I had wanted her. Yet I had promised myself I would not take her. That night I broke one promise, and I made another. I would love her eternally.

I still remember how she looked, her hair unbound, her eyes so dark. Before I touched her I knew how she would feel. Before I laid her in my bed, I knew how she would look there. Now it is only a dream, the sweetest memory of my life. The sound of the water and the crickets, the smell of wildflowers.

In that timeless hour, I had everything a man could want. She was beauty and love and promise. Seductive *and innocent, shy and wanton. Even now, I can taste her mouth, smell her skin. And ache for her.*

Then she was gone. What I had thought was a beginning was an end.

I took what money I had, sold paints and canvases for more and bought four tickets on the evening train. She did not come. There was a storm brewing. Hot lightning, vicious thunder, heavy wind. I told myself it was the weather that turned my blood so cold. But God help me, I think I knew. There was such a sharp, terrifying pain, such unreasonable fear. It consumed me.

For the first time, and the last, I went to The Towers. The rain began to slash as I beat on the door. The woman who answered was hysterical. I would have pushed past her, run through the house calling for Bianca, but at that moment, the police arrived.

She had jumped from the tower, thrown herself through the window onto the rocks. This is unclear now, as it was even then. I remember running, shouting for her over the howling wind. The lights of the house were blinding, slashing through the gloom. Men were already scrambling on the ridge and below with lanterns. I stood, looking down at her. My love. Taken from me. Not by her own hand. I could never accept that. But gone. Lost.

I would have leaped off that ridge myself. But she stopped me. I will swear it was her voice that stopped me. Instead, I sat on the ground, the rain pouring over me.

I could not join her then. Somehow I would have to live out my life without her. I have done so, and perhaps some good has come from the time I have spent here. The boy, my grandson. How Bianca would have loved him. There are times I take him to our cliffs and I'm sure she's there with us.

There are still Calhouns in The Towers. Bianca would have wanted that. Her children's children, and theirs. Perhaps one day another lonely young woman will walk those cliffs. I hope her fate is a kinder one.

I know, in my heart, that it is not ended yet. She waits for me. When my time comes at last, I will talk with Bianca again. I will love her as I once promised. Eternally.

Chapter 10

Holt waited for Trent in the pergola along the seawall. Lighting a cigarette, he looked over the wide lawn to The Towers. One of the gargoyles along the center peak had lost its head while the other sat grinning down, more charming than ferocious. There were clematis—he recognized it now—and roses climbing up to the first terrace. The old stone glowered in the hazy sunlight. There was really no other word for it, but the flowers gave it a kind of magical, Sleeping Beauty aura. Towers and turrets speared up, arrogant of form, dignified with age.

Scaffolding bracketed the west end, and the high whine of a power saw cut the air. A lift truck was parked under the balcony, its mechanism groaning as it hefted its load of equipment to a trio of bare-backed men. A radio jolted out hard rock.

Maybe it was right and just that the house held so tenaciously to the past even while it accepted the present, Holt mused. If it was possible for stone and mortar to absorb emotion and memory, The Towers had done so. Already he felt as though it harbored some of his.

The windows of the room where he had spent most of the night with Suzanna winked back at him. He remembered every second of those hours, every sigh, every movement. He also remembered that he had confused her. No, tenderness wasn't his style, he thought, but it had been easy with her.

She hadn't asked him for softness. She hadn't asked him for anything. Was that why he felt compelled to give? Without trying, she had tapped into something inside him he hadn't known was there—and was still more than a little uncomfortable with. Finding it, feeling it, left him as vulnerable as she. He'd yet to work out the right way to tell her.

She deserved the music, the candlelight, the flowers. She deserved the soft poetic words. He was going to try to give them to her, no matter how big a fool it made him feel.

In the meantime, he had a job to do. He was going to find those damn emeralds for her. And he was going to put Livingston behind bars.

Holt tossed the cigarette away as he saw Trent come out of the house. In the pergola, they would have relative privacy. The clatter of construction echoed in countertime to the beat and drum of waves. Whatever they said wouldn't carry above ten feet. Anyone looking out of the house would see two men sharing a late-afternoon beer, away from the women.

Trent stepped inside and offered a bottle.

"Thanks." Holt leaned negligently against a post and lifted the beer. "Did you get the list?"

"Yeah." Trent took a seat on one of the stone benches so that he could watch the house as he drank. "We've only signed on four new men in the last month."

"References?"

"Of course." The faint annoyance in his tone was instinctive. "Sloan and I are well aware of security."

Holt merely shrugged. "A man like Livingston wouldn't have any problem getting references. They'd cost him." Holt drank deeply. "But he'd get them."

"You'd know more about that sort of thing than I." Trent's eyes narrowed as he watched two of the men replacing shingles on the roof of the west wing. "But I have a hard time buying that he could be here, working right under our noses."

"Oh, he's here." Holt took out another cigarette, lighted it, then took a thoughtful drag. "Whoever tossed my place knew about the connection almost as soon as you did. Since none of you go around talking about the situation at cocktail parties, he'd have heard something here, in the house. He didn't sign on at the start of the job, because he was busy elsewhere. But the last few weeks…" He paused as the children ran out, dogs in tow, to race to their fort. "He wouldn't just sit and wait, not as long as there's a possibility you could knock out a wall and have the emeralds fall into your hand. And where better to keep an eye on things than inside?"

"It fits," Trent admitted. "But I don't like the idea of my wife, or any of the others, being that close." He thought of C.C., the baby she carried, and his eyes darkened. "If there's a chance you're right, I want to move on it."

"Give me the list, and I'll check it out. I've still got

connections." Holt's gaze remained on the children. "He's not going to hurt any of them. That's a fact."

Trent nodded. He was a businessman and had never done anything more violent than a little boxing in college. But he would do whatever it took to protect his wife and unborn child. "I filled Max in, and Sloan and Amanda decided to break off their honeymoon. They should be here in a couple of hours."

That was good, Holt thought. It was best having the family all in one place. "What did Sloan tell her?"

"That there was some problem with the job." More comfortable now that wheels were in motion, Trent grinned a little. "If she finds out he's stringing her along, there'll be hell to pay."

"The less the women know, the better."

This time Trent laughed. "If any of them heard you say that, you'd lose three layers of skin. They're a tough bunch."

Holt thought of Suzanna. "They think they are."

"No, they are. It took me quite a while to accept it. Individually they're strong—velvet-coated steel. Not to mention stubborn, impulsive and feverishly loyal. Together..." Trent smiled again. "Well, I'll admit I'd rather face a pair of sumo wrestlers than the Calhoun women on a roll."

"When it's over, they can be as mad as they want."

"As long as they're safe," Trent finished, and noted that Holt was watching the children. "Great kids," he commented.

"Yeah. They're okay."

"They've got a hell of a mother." Trent drank contemplatively. "Too bad they don't have a real father."

Even the thought of Baxter Dumont made Holt's blood boil. "How much do you know about him?"

"More than I like. I know he put Suzanna through hell. He nearly broke her with the custody suit."

"Custody suit?" Stunned, Holt looked back. "He went after the kids?"

"He went after her," Trent corrected. "What better way? She doesn't talk about it. I got the story from C.C. Apparently he was annoyed that she filed for the divorce. Not good for his image, particularly since he's got his eye on a senate seat. He dragged her through a long, ugly court battle, trying to prove she was unstable and unfit."

"Bastard." Choking on rage, Holt turned away to flick the cigarette onto the rocks.

"He didn't want them. The idea was to ship them off to a boarding school. Or that was the threat. He backed off when Suzanna made the settlement."

His hands were on the stone rail now, fingers digging in. "What settlement?"

"She gave him damn near everything. He dropped the case so the arrangements could be made privately. He got the house, all the property, along with a chunk of her inheritance. She could have fought it, but she and the kids were already an emotional mess. She didn't want to take any chances with them, or put them through any more stress."

"No, she wouldn't." Holt drank in a futile attempt to wash the bitterness from his throat. "He's not going to hurt her or the kids anymore. I'll see to it."

"I thought you would." Trent rose, satisfied. He pulled a list out of his pocket and exchanged it for Holt's empty bottle. "Let me know what you find out."

"Yeah."

"The séance tonight." Trent saw Holt grimace and laughed again. "It may surprise you."

"The only thing that surprises me is that Coco talked me into it."

"If you plan on sticking around, you'll have to get used to being talked into all manner of things."

He was going to stick around, all right, Holt thought as Trent walked away. He just needed to find the right way to tell Suzanna. After glancing at the names on the list, Holt tucked it away. He'd make a couple of calls and see what he could dig up.

As he started across the lawn, the dogs galloped up to him, Fred devotedly pressing to Sadie's side. When they stopped jumping long enough to be petted, Fred lapped frantically at her face. Sadie tolerated it, then turned away and ignored him.

"They've got a name for women like you," Holt told her.

"Remember the Alamo!" Alex shouted. He stood spread-legged on the roof of his fort, a plastic sword in his hand. Because he counted on his challenge being answered, his eyes gleamed as they met Holt's. "You'll never take us alive."

"Oh yeah?" Unable to resist, Holt moved closer. "What makes you think I want you, monkey brain?"

"'Cause we're the patriots and you're the evil invaders."

Jenny popped her head through an opening that served as a window. Before Holt could evade it, he was hit dead center of the chest with a splat of water from her pistol. Alex let out a triumphant hoot as Holt scowled down at his shirt.

"I suppose you know," Holt said slowly, "this means war."

As Jenny shrieked, he grabbed her and pulled her through the window. To her delight, he held her upside down so that her two blond ponytails brushed the grass.

"He's taken a hostage!" Alex bellowed. "Death to the last man." He scrambled inside then burst out of the doorway, brandishing his sword. Holt barely had time to right Jenny before the little missile plowed into him. "Off with his head," Alex chanted, echoed by his sister. Holt let his body go lax and took them both to the ground with him.

There were screams and giggles as he wrestled with them. It wasn't as easy as he'd supposed. They were both agile and slick, wriggling out of his hold to attack. He found himself at a disadvantage as Alex sat on his chest and Jenny found a spot on his ribs to tickle.

"I'm going to have to get rough," he warned them. When he took a spray of water in the face, he swore, making them both howl with laughter. A quick roll and he dislodged the pistol, then snatched it up to drench them both. With shrieks and giggles, they fell on him.

It was a wet and messy battle, and when he finally managed to pin them, they were all out of breath.

"I massacred you both," Holt managed. "Say uncle." Jenny poked a finger in his ribs, making him twitch. In defense he lowered his cheek to her neck and rubbed a day's worth of stubble over her skin.

"Uncle, uncle, uncle!" She screamed, gurgling with laughter. Satisfied, he used the same weapon on Alex until, victorious, he rolled over and lay stomach down on the grass.

"You killed us," Alex admitted, not displeased. "But you're morally wounded."

"Yeah, but I think you mean mortally."

"Are you going to take a nap?" Jenny climbed onto his back to bounce. "Lilah sleeps in the grass sometimes."

"Lilah sleeps anywhere," Holt muttered.

"You can take a nap in my bed if you want," she invited, then pressed a curious finger on the edge of the scar she saw beneath his hitched-up T-shirt. "You have a hurt on your back."

"Uh-huh."

Alex was already scrambling to look. "Can I see?"

Holt tensed automatically, then forced himself to relax. "Sure."

As Alex pushed up the shirt, both children's eyes widened. It wasn't like the neat little scar they had both admired on his leg. This was long and jagged and mean, slashing from the waist so high up on his back they couldn't push the shirt up enough to see the end of it.

"Gee," was all Alex could think to say. He swallowed, then gamely touched a finger to the scar. "Did you get in a big fight?"

"Not exactly." He remembered the pain, the incredible flash of white heat. "One of the bad guys got me," he said, and hoped it would satisfy. When he felt Jenny's little mouth lower to his back, he went very still.

"Does it feel better now?" she asked.

"Yeah." He had to let out a long breath to steady his voice. "Thanks." Turning over, he sat up to brush a hand through her hair.

Suzanna stood a few feet away, watching them with her heart in her throat. She'd seen the battle from the kitchen doorway. It had touched her to see how easily Holt had joined in the game with her children. She'd been smiling when she'd started out to join them—then she had watched Jenny and Alex examining the scar on Holt's back, and Jenny's kiss to make it better. She had seen the look of ragged emotion on Holt's face when he'd turned to sweep his hand over her little girl's hair.

Now the three of them were on the grass, Jenny cuddled on his lap, Alex's arm slung affectionately around his shoulder. She took a moment to make certain her eyes were dry before she continued toward them.

"Is the war over?" she asked, and three pair of eyes lifted.

"He won," Alex told her.

"It doesn't look as though it was an easy victory." She scooped Jenny up when the girl lifted her arms. "You're all wet."

"He blasted us—but I got him first."

"That's my girl."

"And he's ticklish," Jenny confided. "*Real* ticklish."

"Is that so?" Suzanna sent Holt a slow smile. "I'll keep that in mind. Now you two scat. I noticed nobody put away the game you were playing."

"But, Mom—" Alex had his excuses ready, but she stopped them with a look.

"If you don't clean it up, I will," she said mildly. "But then I'll have your share of strawberry shortcake tonight."

That was a tough one. Alex agonized over it for a minute, then caved in. "I'll do it. Then I get Jenny's share."

"Do not." Jenny sprinted toward the house with her brother giving chase.

"Very smooth, Mom," Holt commented as he rose.

"I know their weaknesses." She put her arms around him, surprising and pleasing him. It was very rare for her to make the first move. "You're all wet, too."

"Sniper fire, but I picked them off like flies." Bringing her closer, he rested his cheek on her hair. "They're terrific kids, Suzanna. I'm, ah…" He didn't know how to tell her he'd fallen in love with them, any more than he knew how to tell her he'd fallen in love with their mother. "I'm getting you wet." Feeling awkward, he drew away.

Smiling, she touched a hand to his cheek. "Want to take a walk?"

He thought of the list in his pocket. It could wait an hour, he decided, and took her hand.

He'd known she would head to the cliffs. It seemed right that they would walk there as the shadows lengthened and the air cooled toward evening. She talked a little of the job she'd finished that day, he of the hull he'd repaired. But their minds weren't on work.

"Holt." She looked out to sea, her hand in his. "Will you tell me why you resigned from the force?" She felt his fingers stiffen, but didn't turn.

"It's done," he said flatly. "There's nothing to tell."

"The scar on your back—"

"I said it's done." He withdrew and pulled out a cigarette.

"I see." She absorbed the rejection. "Your past and your personal feelings about it are none of my business."

He took an impatient drag. "I didn't say that."

"You certainly did. You have the right to know all there is to know about me. I'm supposed to trust you with everything, unquestioningly. But I'm not to pry into what's yours."

He turned angry eyes on her. "What is this, some kind of test?"

"Call it what you like," she tossed back. "I'd hoped you trusted me by now, that you cared enough to let me in."

"I do care, damn it. Don't you know it still rips me up to remember it? Ten years of my life, Suzanna. Ten years." He whirled away to flick the cigarette over the edge.

"I'm sorry." Instinctively she put her hands on his shoulders to soothe. "If anyone knows how painful it is to dredge up old wounds, it's me. Why don't we go back? I'll see if I can find you a clean shirt."

"No." His jaw was clenched, his body tight as a spring. "You want to know, you've got a right. I tossed it in because I couldn't handle it. I spent ten years telling myself I could make a difference, that none of the crap I had to wade through would affect me. I could rub shoulders with dealers and pimps and victims all day and not lose any sleep at night. If I had to kill somebody, it was line of duty. Not something you want to think about too much, but something you live with. I saw a few cops burn out along the way, but it wasn't going to happen to me."

She said nothing, just continued to rub at the knotted muscles of his shoulders while she waited for him to go on. He kept looking out to sea, smelling her, and the dusky scent of the wild roses that were at their peak.

"Vice takes you into the pits, Suzanna. You get so you understand the people you're trying to wipe out.

You think like them. You have to when you go under, or you don't come out again. There are things I'm never going to tell you, because I do care. Ugly things, and I just…" He closed his eyes, and jammed his hands into his pockets. "I just didn't want to see it anymore. I was already thinking about coming back here—just sort of kicking it around."

Suddenly weary, he lifted his hands to rub the heels over his eyes. "I was tired, Suzanna, and I wanted to live like a normal person again. The kind who doesn't strap on a gun every day or make deals with slime in back rooms. We were on a routine investigation, looking for a small-time dealer who we thought we could pressure information out of. Doesn't matter why," he said impatiently. "Anyway, we got a tip where to find him, and when we cornered him in this little dive, he snapped. Turned out the jerk had about twenty thousand in coke strapped under his clothes, and more than a couple lines in his system. He panicked. He dragged some half-stoned woman with him and bolted."

His palms were beginning to sweat, so he wiped them against his jeans. "My partner and I separated to cut him off. He pulled the woman out in the alley. With us on either end, he didn't have any hope of getting away. I had my weapon out. It was dark. The garbage had turned."

He could still smell it, rank and fetid, as the sweat began to run down his back. "I could hear my partner coming up the other side, and hear the woman crying. He'd sliced her up a little and she was balled up on the concrete. I couldn't be sure how bad she was hurt. I remember thinking the creep was going to be up for more than distribution. Then he jumped me. He had the knife in before I could get off a shot."

He could still feel it ripping through his flesh, still smell his own blood. "I knew I was dead, and I kept thinking that I wouldn't be able to come home. That I was going to die in that damn alley with the stink of that garbage. I killed him as I went down. That's what they told me. I don't remember. The thing I remember next was waking up in the hospital feeling like I'd been sliced in half and sewn back together. I told myself that if I made it, I was coming back here. Because I knew if I had to walk down another alley, I wouldn't come back out."

Suzanna had her arms tight around him now, her cheek pressed against his back. "Do you think because you came home instead of facing another alley, you failed?"

"I don't know."

"I did, for a long time. No one had put a knife in my back, but I came to understand that if I stayed with Bax, if I'd kept that promise, part of me would die. I chose survival, do you think I should be ashamed of that?"

"No." He turned, taking her shoulder. "No."

She lifted her hands to cup his face. In her eyes was understanding, and the sympathy he couldn't have accepted even a week before. "Neither do I. I hate what happened to you, but I'm glad it brought you here." Offering comfort, she touched her lips to his. Slowly, with a sweetness that was unbearably moving, she felt him let go.

His body relaxed against hers even as he pulled her closer. His mouth softened even as it heated. Here, at last, was the next level. There was not only passion, not only tenderness, but trust. As the wind whispered through the wild grass and the bright, brave flowers, she thought she heard something else, something so quiet and lovely that it brought tears to her eyes. When he lifted his head, when she saw his face, she knew he'd heard it, too. She smiled.

"We're not alone here," she murmured. "They must have stood in this same spot, holding each other like this. Wanting each other like this." Filled with the moment, she pressed his hand to her lips. "Holt, do you believe that fate and time can run in a circle?"

"I'm beginning to."

"They still come here, to wait. I wonder if they ever find each other. I think they will, if we can make things right." She kissed him again, then slipped an arm around his waist. "Let's go home. I have a feeling it's going to be an interesting evening."

"Suzanna," he began as they started back. "After the séance…" He trailed off, looking pained, and made her laugh.

"Don't worry, at The Towers we only have friendly ghosts."

"Right. Just don't expect me to put much stock in chanting and trances, but anyway, I was wondering if after—look, I know you don't like to leave the kids, but I thought you could come back to my place for a little while. There's some stuff I want to talk to you about."

"What stuff?"

"Just—stuff," he said lamely. If he was going to ask her to marry him, he wanted to do it right. "I'd appreciate it if you could get away for an hour or two."

"All right, if it's important. Is it about the emeralds?"

"No. It's... I'd rather wait, okay? Listen, I've got a couple of things to do before we start calling up spirits."

"Aren't you going to stay for dinner?"

"I can't. I'll be back." As they came up the slope and passed the stone wall, he pulled her against him for a brief hard kiss. "See you later."

She frowned after him and might have pursued, but her name was called from the second-level terrace. Shading her eyes, she saw her sister.

"Amanda!" With a laugh, she raced across the lawn and up the stone steps. "What are you doing back?" She gathered the new bride into her arms and squeezed. "You look wonderful—but you were supposed to be gone nearly another week. Is anything wrong?"

"No, nothing." She kissed both of Suzanna's cheeks. "Come on, I'll fill you in."

"Where are we going?"

"Bianca's tower. Family meeting."

They climbed up, then went inside to ascend the narrow circular stairs that led to the tower. C.C. and Lilah were already waiting.

"Aunt Coco?" Suzanna asked.

"We'll let her know what we discuss," Amanda answered. "But it would look too suspicious if we pulled her up here now."

With a nod, Suzanna took a seat on the floor at Lilah's feet. "So I take it this is women only?"

"No more than they deserve," C.C. said, and crossed her arms. "They've been skulking off to have their boy's club meetings for days now. It's time we set things straight."

"Max has definitely got something up his sleeve," Lilah put in. "He's acting much too innocent. And, he's been hanging around the construction crew for the last couple of days."

"I don't suppose he wants to learn how to set tile," Suzanna murmured.

"If he did, he'd have twenty books on it by now." Lilah rolled her shoulders and leaned back. "And this afternoon when I got home from work, I saw Trent and Holt powwowing in the pergola. Somebody who didn't know better might have thought they were just hanging out and having a beer, but something was going on."

"So they know something they're not telling us." Thoughtful, Suzanna drummed her fingers on her knees. She'd had a feeling something was going on, but Holt had done such a good job of distracting her, she hadn't acted on it.

"Sloan had a long, mumbling conversation with Trent on the phone two days ago. He claimed there was some problem with materials that he had to see to personally." Tossing her hair, Amanda gave a sniff. "And he thought I was stupid enough to buy it. He wanted to get back because they're on to something—and they want to keep the little women out of the way."

"Fat chance," C.C. muttered. "I'm for marching downstairs right now and demanding they tell us whatever they know. If Trent thinks I'm going to sit around twiddling my thumbs while he handles Calhoun business, he's got another think coming."

"Bamboo shoots and brass knuckles," Lilah mused, not terribly displeased with the image. "That'll just make them more stubborn. Male egos on the line, ladies. Get out your hard hats and flak jackets."

Suzanna laughed and patted her leg. "You've got a point. Let's see what we know… Sloan gets called back so they must think they're getting close. I can't see them being secretive if they thought they'd hit on the location of the emeralds."

"Neither can I." Because she thought best on her feet, Amanda paced. "Remember how stiff-necked they got when we decided to look for the yacht Max had jumped off? Sloan threatened to...what was it? Hog-tie," she said viciously. "Yes, that was it. He threatened to hog-tie me if I so much as thought about trying to find Livingston on my own."

"Trent won't even discuss Livingston with me," C.C. added, then wrinkled her nose. "It isn't good for me to be upset in my delicate condition."

From her sprawled perch on the window seat, Lilah gave a hoot. "I'd like to see any man go through child-birth then have the nerve to call a woman delicate."

"Holt says that Livingston is out of our league. *Ours*," Suzanna explained, making a circular motion with her finger. "Not his."

"Jerk." C.C. plopped down on the window seat beside Lilah. "So are we agreed? They've got a line on Livingston and they're keeping it to themselves."

The vote was unanimous.

"Now, we need to find out what they know." Amanda stopped pacing and tapped her foot. "Suggestions?"

"Well..." Suzanna looked down at her nails and smiled. "I say divide and conquer. The four of us should be able to dig information out of them—each in our own way. Then we rendezvous here, tomorrow, same time, and put the pieces together."

"I like it." Lilah sat up to put a hand on Suzanna's shoulder. "The poor guys haven't got a chance."

Suzanna reached up to lay her hand on Lilah's as Amanda and C.C. added theirs. "And when it's over," she said, "maybe they'll realize the Calhoun women take care of their own."

Chapter 11

Holt had never felt more ridiculous in his life. He was about to take part in a séance. If that wasn't bad enough, before the night was over, he was going to ask the woman who was currently laughing at him, to be his wife.

"It isn't a firing squad." Chuckling, Suzanna patted his cheek. "Relax."

"Damn foolishness is what it is." From the foot of the table, Colleen scowled at everyone in general. "The idea of talking to spirits. Hogwash. And you—" She stabbed a finger toward Coco. "Not that you ever kept an ounce of sense in that flighty head of yours, but I'd have thought even you would know better than to raise these girls on such bilge."

"It isn't bilge." As always, the steely gaze made Coco tremble, but she felt fairly safe with the length of the table between them. "You'll see after we begin."

"What I see is a table full of dolts." Though her face remained in stern lines, Colleen's heart melted as she looked up at the portrait of her mother, which had been hung over the fireplace. "I'll give you ten thousand for it."

Holt shrugged. She'd been dogging him for days about buying the painting. "It isn't for sale."

"If you think you're going to hose me, young man, you're mistaken. I know a hustle."

He grinned at her. He would have bet his last nickel she'd hustled plenty herself. "I'm not selling it."

"It's worth more, anyway," Lilah put in, unable to resist. "Isn't that right, Professor?"

"Well, actually, yes." Max cleared his throat. "Christian Bradford's early work is increasing in value. At Sotheby's two years ago, one of his seascapes went for thirty-five thousand."

"What are you," Colleen snapped, "his agent?"

Max swallowed a grin. "No, ma'am."

"Then hush. Fifteen thousand, and not a penny more."

Holt ran his tongue around his teeth. "Not interested."

"Maybe if we got on with the matter at hand." Coco held her breath, waiting for her aunt's wrath to fall. When Colleen only muttered and scowled, she relaxed. "Amanda, dear, light the candles. Now we must all try to empty our minds of all worries, all doubts. Concentrate on Bianca." When the candles were glowing, and the chandelier extinguished, she gave a last glance around the table. "Join hands."

Holt grumbled under his breath but took Suzanna's hand in his right, Lilah's in his left.

"Focus on the picture," Coco whispered, closing her eyes to bring it into her mind since it was behind her on the wall. Tingles of anticipation raced up and down her spine. "She's close to us, very close to us. She wants to help."

Holt let his mind drift because it helped him forget what he was doing. He tried to imagine what it would be like when he and Suzanna were alone in the cottage. He'd bought candles. Not the sturdy type he kept in the kitchen drawer for power outages, but slender white tapers that smelled of jasmine.

There was champagne chilling beside the six-pack in his refrigerator, and two new clear flutes beside his coffee mugs. Even now the jeweler's box was burning a hole in his hip pocket.

Tonight, he thought, he'd take the step. The words would come exactly as he planned. The music would be playing. She would open the box, look inside…

Her hands were draped with emeralds. He frowned, giving himself a little shake. That wasn't right. He hadn't bought her emeralds. But the image focused so clearly. Suzanna on her knees holding emeralds. Three glittering tiers flanked by icy diamonds and centered by a glowing teardrop stone of dreamy green.

The Calhoun necklace. He felt the chill on his neck and ignored it. He'd seen the picture Max had found in the old library book. He knew what the emeralds looked like. It was the atmosphere, the humming silence and the flickering candles that made him think of them. That made him see them.

He didn't believe in visions. But when he closed his eyes to clear it from his mind, it seemed imprinted there.

Suzanna kneeling on the floor with emeralds dripping from her fingers.

He felt a hand on his shoulder and looked around. There was no one there, only shadows and light thrown by the candles. But the feeling remained, with an urgency that had his hackles rising.

It was crazy, he told himself. And it was time to put an end to the whole insane business.

"Listen," he began. And the portrait of Bianca crashed to the floor.

Coco gave a piping squeak and jolted out of the chair. "Oh, my. Oh, my goodness," she murmured, patting her speeding heart.

Amanda was already racing forward. "Oh, I hope it isn't damaged."

"I don't think it will be." Lilah released Holt's hand. "Do you?"

The clear and steady gaze made him uncomfortable. Ignoring her, he turned to Suzanna. Her hand was like ice in his. "What is it? What's wrong?"

"Nothing." But she gave a quick shudder. "I think you'd better check the portrait."

He rose to go over where the others were crouched. As he did, Suzanna looked down the length of the table at her great-aunt. Colleen's white skin had paled like glass. Her eyes were dark and damp. Without a word, Suzanna rose and poured her a brandy. "It's going to be all right," she murmured, laying a hand on the thin shoulder.

"The frame cracked." Sloan ran a finger along it before he rose. "Funny that it would fall that way. Those nails are sturdy."

Holt started to shrug it off, but when he bent closer

to where the frame had separated from the backing, he went very still. "There's something between the canvas and the back." Hefting the portrait, he laid it facedown on the table. "I need a knife."

Sloan pulled out his pocketknife and offered it. Holt made a long thin slit just beneath the cracked frame and slid out several sheets of paper.

"What is it?" The question was muffled as Coco had her hands pressed to her mouth.

"It's my grandfather's writing." The emotion sprang up strong and fast. It churned in Holt's eyes as he lifted them to Suzanna's. "It looks like a kind of diary. It's dated 1965."

"Sit down, dear." Coco put a comforting hand on his shoulder. "Trent, would you pour the brandy? I'll brew some tea for C.C."

He did need to sit, and he hoped the drink would steady him. For now, he could only stare at the papers and see his grandfather. Sitting on the back porch of the cottage, watching the water. Standing in his loft, slashing paint on canvas. Walking on the cliffs, telling a young boy stories.

When Suzanna came back to lay a hand on his, he turned his palm up and gripped her fingers. "It's been there all this time, and I didn't know."

"You weren't meant to know," she said quietly. "Until tonight." When he looked at her again, she curled her fingers tight around his. "Some things we just have to take on faith."

"Something happened tonight. Something upset you."

"I'll tell you. Not yet."

Composed, Coco brought in the tea, then took her

seat. "Holt, whatever your grandfather wrote belongs to you. No one here will ask you to share it. If after you read it, you feel you prefer to keep it to yourself, we'll understand."

He glanced down at the papers again, then lifted the first sheet. "We'll read it together." He took a long breath, kept Suzanna's hand tight in his. "'The moment I saw her, my life changed.'"

No one spoke as Holt read through his grandfather's memories. But around the table, hands linked again. There was no sound but his voice and the wind breathing through the trees outside the windows. When he was finished, the room remained silent.

Lilah spoke first, her voice thick with tears while others slid down her cheeks. "He never stopped loving her. Always, even though he made a life for himself, he loved her."

"How he must have felt, to come here that night and find out she was gone." Amanda leaned her head on Sloan's shoulder.

"But he was right." Suzanna watched one of her tears drop on the back of Holt's hand. "She didn't take her own life. She couldn't have. Not only did she love him too much, but she would have tolerated anything to protect her children."

"No, she didn't jump." Colleen whispered the words. She lifted her snifter with a trembling hand, then set it down again. "I've never spoken of that night, not to anyone. Through the years I've sometimes thought what I saw was a dream. A terrible, terrible nightmare."

Determined, she cleared her blurred vision and strengthened her voice. "He understood her, her Christian. He couldn't have written about her that way and not have known her heart. She was beautiful, but she was also kind and generous. I have never been loved as I was loved by my mother. And I have never hated as I hated my father."

She straightened her shoulders. Already the burden had lessened. "I was too young to understand her unhappiness or her desperation. In those days a man ruled his home, his family, as he chose. No one dared to question my father. But I remember the day she brought the puppy home, the little puppy my father would not have in his home. She did send us upstairs, but I hid at the top and listened. I had never heard her raise her voice to him before. Oh, she was valiant. And he was cruel. I didn't understand the names he called her. Then."

She paused to drink again, for her throat was dry and the memory bitter. "She defended me against him, knowing as even I knew he barely tolerated me, a female. When he left the house after the argument, I was glad. I prayed that night he would never come back. The next day, my mother told me we were going to take a trip. She hadn't told my brothers yet, but I was the eldest. She wanted me to understand that she would take care of us, that nothing bad would happen.

"Then, he came back. I knew she was upset, even frightened. I was to stay in my room until she came for me. But she didn't come. It grew late, and there was a storm. I wanted my mother." Colleen pressed her lips together. "She wasn't in her room, so I went up to the tower where she often spent her time. I heard them as I crept up the stairs. The door was open and I heard them. The terrible argument. He was raging, crazed with fury. She told him that she would no longer live with him, that she wanted nothing from him but her children and her freedom."

Because Colleen was shaking, Coco rose and walked down to take her hand.

"He struck her. I heard the slap and raced to the door. But I was afraid, too afraid to go in. She had a hand to her cheek, and her eyes were blazing. Not with fear, with fury. I will always remember that there was no fear in her at the end. He threatened her with scandal. He screamed at her that if she left his house, she would never lay eyes on any of his children again. She would never ruin his reputation. She would never throw an obstacle in the path of his ambitions."

Though her lips trembled, Colleen lifted her chin. "She did not beg. She did not weep. She hurled words back at him like thunderbolts." Fisting a hand, she pressed it to her mouth to smother her own tears. "She was magnificent. Her children would never be taken from her, and scandal be damned. Did he think she cared what people thought of her? Did he think she feared his power to have society shun her? She would take her children and she would make a life where both she and they could be loved. And I think it was that which drove him mad. The idea that she would choose another man over him. Over him. Fergus Calhoun. That she would toss his money and power and position back at him, rather than bow to his wishes. He grabbed her, lifting her from her feet, shaking her, screaming into her face while his own purpled with rage. I think I screamed then, and hearing me, she began to fight. When she struck him, he threw her aside. I heard the crash of the glass. He ran to it, roaring for her, but she was gone. How long he stood there while the wind and rain poured in, I don't know. When he turned his face was white, his eyes glazed. He walked past me without even seeing me. I went inside, over to the broken window and looked down until Nanny came and carried me away."

Coco pressed a kiss to the white hair, then gently stroked. "Come with me, dear. I'll take you upstairs. Lilah will bring you a nice cup of tea."

"Yes, I'll be right there." Lilah wiped her cheeks dry. "Max?"

"I'll come with you." He slipped an arm around her waist as Coco led Bianca's daughter from the room.

"Poor little girl," Suzanna murmured, and let her head rest on Holt's shoulder as he drove away from The Towers. "To have seen something so horrible, to have had to live with it all of her life. I think of Jenny—"

"Don't." He put a firm hand over hers. "You got out. Bianca didn't." He waited a moment. "You knew, didn't you? Before Colleen told us the story."

"I knew she hadn't committed suicide. I can't explain how, but tonight, I knew. It was as if she was standing right behind me."

He thought of the sensation of having a hand on his shoulder. "Maybe she was. After a night like this, it's hard for me to convince myself the picture falling off the wall was a coincidence."

Suzanna closed her eyes. "It was beautiful, what your grandfather wrote about her. If we never find the emeralds, we have that—we'll know she had that. To love that way," she said on a sigh. "It hardly seems possible. I don't want to think of the tragedy or sadness, but of the time they had together. Dancing in the wild roses."

He'd never danced with her in the sunlight, Holt thought. Or read her poetry or promised her eternal love.

When they reached the cottage, Sadie leaped out the back window of the car to race around the yard and sniff at the flower bed she'd planted for him. When Holt leaned across her, Suzanna looked down in surprise.

"What are you doing?"

"I'm opening the door for you." He shoved it open. "If I'd gotten out to do it, you wouldn't have waited."

Amused, Suzanna stepped out. "Thank you."

"You're welcome." When he reached the house, he unlocked the front door, then held that open. Keeping her face sober, Suzanna inclined her head as she slipped past him.

"Thank you."

Holt just let the screen slam shut. Brow lifted, Suzanna scanned the room.

"You've done something different."

"I cleaned it up," he muttered.

"Oh. It looks nice. You know, Holt, I've been meaning to ask you if you think Livingston is still on the island."

"Why? Did something happen?"

His response was much too abrupt, Suzanna noted and moved casually around the room. "No, I've just been wondering where he may be staying, what his next move might be." She ran a fingertip down one of the candles he'd bought. "Any ideas?"

"How should I know?"

"You're the expert on crime."

"And I told you to leave Livingston to me."

"And I told you I couldn't do that. Maybe I'll start poking around on my own."

"Try it and I'll handcuff you and lock you in a closet."

"The urban counterpart to hog-tying," she murmured. "I wouldn't have to try it if you'd tell me what you know. Or what you think."

"What brought this up now?"

She moved her shoulder. "Since we have a little time to ourselves, I thought we could talk about it."

"Look, why don't you just sit down?" He pulled out his lighter.

"What are you doing?"

"I'm lighting candles." His nerves were stretching like taffy. "What does it look like I'm doing?"

She did sit, and steepled her hands. "Since you're so cranky, I have to assume that you do know something."

"You don't have to assume anything except that you're ticking me off." He stalked to the stereo.

"How close are you?" she asked as a bluesy sax filled the air.

"I'm nowhere." Since that was a lie, he decided to temper it with part of the truth. "I think he's in the area because he broke in here and took a look around a couple of weeks ago."

"What?" She catapulted out of the chair. "A couple of weeks ago, and you didn't tell me?"

"What were you going to do about it?" he countered. "Pull out a magnifying glass and deer-hunter's hat?"

"I had a right to know."

"Now you know. Just sit down, will you? I'll be back in a minute."

He stalked out and she began to pace. Holt knew more than he was saying, but at least she'd annoyed a piece from him. Livingston was close, close enough that he'd known Holt might have something of interest. The fact that Holt was wound like a top at the moment made her think something more was working on him. It shouldn't be difficult, she thought, now that she already had him irritated, to push a little more out of him.

The candles were scented, she noted, and smiled to herself. She couldn't imagine that he'd bought jasmine candles on purpose. Especially a half a dozen of them. She traced a finger over the calla lilies he'd stuck—not very artistically—in a vase. Maybe working with flowers was getting to him, she thought. He wasn't pretending so hard not to like them.

When he came back in, she smiled then looked puzzled. "Is that champagne?"

"Yeah." And he was thoroughly disgusted. He'd imagined she'd be charmed. Instead she questioned everything. "Do you want some or not?"

"Sure." The curt invitation was so typical she didn't take offense. After he'd poured, she tapped her glass absently against his. "Now, if you're sure it was Livingston who broke in, I think—"

"One more word," he said with dangerous calm. "One more word about Livingston and I'll pour the rest of the bottle over your hard head."

She sipped, knowing she'd have to be careful if she didn't want to waste a bottle of champagne and end up with sticky hair. "I'm only trying to get a clear picture."

He let out what was close to a roar of frustration and spun away. Champagne sloshed over his glass as he paced. "She wants a clear picture, and she's blind as a bat. I shoveled two months' worth of dust out of this place. I bought candles and flowers. I had to listen to some jerk try to teach me about wine. That's the picture, damn it."

She'd wanted to irritate information from him, not infuriate him. "Holt—"

"Just sit down and shut up. I should have known this would get screwed up. God knows why I tried to do it this way."

A light dawned, and she smiled. He'd set the stage, but she'd been too focused on her own scheme to take note. "Holt, it's very sweet of you to do all of this. I'm sorry if I didn't seem to appreciate it. If you wanted me to come here tonight so we could make love—"

"I don't want to make love with you." He swore, viciously. "Of course I want to make love with you, but that's not it. I'm trying to ask you to marry me, damn it, so will you sit *down!*"

Since her legs had dissolved from knees to toe, she slid into a chair.

"This is perfect." He gulped down champagne and started pacing again. "Just perfect. I'm trying to tell you that I'm crazy about you, that I don't think I can live without you, and all you can do is ask me what I'm doing and nag me about some obsessed jewel thief."

Cautiously she brought the glass to her lips. "Sorry."

"You should be sorry," he said bitterly. "I was ready to make a fool of myself tonight for you, and you won't even let me do that. I've been in love with you nearly half my life. Even when I moved away, I couldn't get you out of my mind. You spoiled every other woman for me. I'd start to get close to someone, and then…they weren't you. They just weren't you, and I'd never even gotten past your back door."

In love. The two words reeled in her head. *In love.*
"I thought you didn't even like me."

"I couldn't stand you." He raked his free hand
through his hair. "Every time I looked at you I wanted
you so much I couldn't breathe. My mouth would go
dry and my stomach would knot, and you'd just smile
and keep walking." His dark and turbulent eyes locked
on hers. "I wanted to strangle you. Then you ran into
me and knocked me off my bike and I was lying there
bleeding and—and mortified. You were leaning over
me, smelling like heaven and running your hands over
me to see if anything was broken. One more minute
of that and I'd have dragged you onto the asphalt with
me." He rubbed his hand over his face. "Lord, you were
only sixteen."

"You swore at me."

His face was a picture of anger and disgust. "Damn
right, I swore at you. You were better off with that than
with what I wanted to do to you." He was calming, little by little. He sipped again but kept pacing. "I talked
myself into believing it was just an adolescent fantasy.
Even a crush, and that was tough to swallow. Then you
came walking across my yard. I looked at you and my
throat went dry, my stomach knotted up. We were both
past being adolescents."

He set his glass down, noting that she was gripping
hers with both hands. Her eyes were huge and fixed on
his. Cursing both of them, he fumbled for a cigarette
then tossed it aside.

"I'm not good at this, Suzanna. I thought I could
pull it off. Set the mood, you know? And after you'd
had enough champagne, I'd convince you I could make
you happy."

She couldn't relax her grip. She tried but couldn't. "I don't need champagne and candlelight, Holt."

He smiled a little. "Babe, you were born for it. I could lie to you and tell you I'll remember to give it to you every night. But I won't."

She looked down at her glass and wondered if she was ready to take this sort of chance again. Loving him was one thing. Being loved by him was incredible. But marriage... "Why don't you just tell me the truth then?"

He walked over to sit on the arm of the couch and face her. "I love you. I've never felt about anyone the way I feel about you. Whatever happens, I'll never feel like this about anyone else again. There's no taking back what's happened to either of us in the last few years, but maybe we can make things better for both of us. For the kids."

Her eyes changed, darkened. "It may never be easy. Bax would always be their legal father."

"He wouldn't be the one who loved them." When her eyes filled, he shook his head. No, she hadn't needed candlelight and champagne to make her vulnerable and open to his needs. Only a mention of her children. "I won't use them to get to you. I know I could, but first it has to be between you and me. Maybe I'm stuck on them, and I want to—I think I could be pretty good at being their father, but I don't want you to marry me for them."

She took a deep breath. Odd, her fingers had relaxed on the stem of the glass without her being aware. "I never wanted to love anyone again. And I certainly never wanted to get married." Her lips curved. "Until you." Setting the glass aside, she reached for his hand.

"I can't claim to have loved you as long, but you couldn't love me more than I love you."

He didn't settle for her hand, but pulled her into his arms. When he at last managed to tear his mouth from hers, he buried his face in her hair. "Don't tell me you need to think about it, Suzanna."

"I don't need to think about it." She couldn't remember the last time her heart and mind had been so at peace. "I'll marry you."

Before the words were out of her mouth, she was tumbling with him onto the couch. She was laughing as they tugged at each other's clothes, laughing still when the frantic movements sent them rolling onto the floor.

"I knew it." She nipped his bare shoulder. "You did bring me here to make love."

"Can I help it if you can't keep your hands off me?" He trailed a necklace of quick kisses around her throat.

She smiled, tilting her head to give him easy access. "Holt, did you really think about pulling me down on the street after you'd fallen off your bike?"

"After you'd run into me," he corrected, nuzzling her ear. "Yeah. Let me show you what I had in mind."

Later they lay like rag dolls on the floor, a tangle of limbs. When she could manage it, she lifted her head from his chest. "It was much better that we didn't try that twelve years ago."

Lazily he opened his eyes. She was smiling down at him, her hair brushing his shoulders, the candlelight glowing in her eyes. "Much better. I wouldn't have had any skin left on my back."

She chuckled then shifted to trace the shape of his face. "You always scared me a little. Looking so dark and dangerous. And, of course, the girls used to talk about you."

"Oh, yeah? What did they say?"

"I'll tell you when you're sixty. You could probably use it then." He pinched her, but she only laughed then rested her cheek on his. "When you're sixty, we'll be an old married couple with grandchildren."

He liked the thought of it. "And you still won't be able to keep your hands off me."

"And I'll remind you of the night you asked me to marry you, when you gave me flowers and candlelight, then shouted at me and raged up and down the room, making me love you even more."

"If that's all it takes, you'll be delirious about me by the time I'm sixty."

"I already am." She lowered her mouth to his.

"Suzanna." He drew her closer, started to roll her under him, then swore. "It's your own fault," he said as he nudged her aside.

"What?"

"You were supposed to be sitting over there, dazed by my romantic abilities." He fought to untangle his jeans and pull the jeweler's box from the pocket. "Then I was going to get down on one knee."

Eyes wide, she stared at the box, then at him. "You were not."

"Yes, I was. I was going to feel like an idiot, but I was going to do it. You've got no one to blame but yourself that we're lying naked on the floor. Here."

"You bought me a ring," she whispered.

"There could be a frog in there for all you know." Impatient with her, he flipped up the top himself. "I didn't want to give you diamonds." He shrugged when she said nothing, only stared into the box. "I figured you'd already had those. I thought about emeralds, but those are something you will have. And this is more like your eyes."

When the tears blurred her vision, the light refracted. There were diamonds, tiny, lovely stones in a heart shape about the deep and brilliant sapphire. They weren't cold, as the ones she had sold, but warmed by the rich blue fire they encircled.

Holt watched the first tear fall with a great deal of discomfort. "If you don't like it, we can take it back. You can pick out what you want."

"It's beautiful." She dashed a tear away with the back of her hand. "I'm sorry. I hate to cry. It's just so beautiful, and you bought it for me because you love me. And when I put it on—" she lifted drenched eyes to his "—I'm yours."

He dropped his brow to hers. Those were the words he'd wanted. The ones he'd needed. Taking the ring from the box, he slipped it onto her finger. "You're mine." He kissed her fingers, then her lips. "I'm yours." Bringing her close again, he remembered his grandfather's words. "Eternally."

Chapter 12

Suzanna took the children to the shop with her in the morning. She couldn't tell the rest of her family the news until she'd gauged Alex's and Jenny's feelings. The day was bright and hot. Knowing it would be a busy one, she arrived a full hour before opening. Because they wanted to check the herbs they had planted, she took them into the greenhouse to look at the tender shoots.

She let them argue for a while over whose plants would be the biggest or the best, supervising as they gave the shoots their morning drink.

"Do you guys like Holt?" she asked casually, nerves drumming.

"He's neat." Alex was tempted to turn the sprayer on his sister, but he'd gotten in trouble the last time he'd indulged himself.

"He plays with us sometimes." Jenny danced from foot to foot, waiting her turn. "I like when he throws me up in the air."

"I like him, too." Suzanna relaxed a little.

"Does he throw you up in the air?" Jenny wanted to know.

"No." With a laugh, Suzanna ruffled her hair.

"He could. He's got big muscles." Reluctantly Alex passed the sprayer to his sister. "He let me feel them." Screwing up his face, Alex flexed his own. Obliging, Suzanna pinched the tiny biceps.

"Wow. You're pretty tough."

"That's what he said."

"I was wondering…" Suzanna wiped nervous hands on her jeans. "How would you feel if he lived with us, all the time?"

"That'd be good," Jenny decided. "He plays with us even when we don't ask."

One down, Suzanna thought and turned to her son. "Alex?"

He shuffled his feet, frowning a little. "Are you going to get married like C.C. and Amanda?"

Sharp little devil, she thought, and crouched down. "I was thinking about it. What do you think?"

"Do I have to wear a dumb tuxedo again?"

She smiled and stroked his cheek. "Probably."

"Is he going to be our uncle, like Trent and Sloan and Max?" Jenny asked.

Suzanna got up to turn off the spray before answering her daughter. "No. He'd be your stepfather."

Brother and sister exchanged looks. "Would he still like us?"

"Of course he would, Jenny."

"Would we have to go away and live someplace else?"

She sighed and combed a hand through Alex's hair. "No. He would come to live with us at The Towers, or maybe we'd go and live with him at his cottage. We'd be a family."

Alex thought it over. "Would he be Kevin's stepfather, too?"

"No." She had to kiss him. "Megan's Kevin's mom, and maybe one day she'll fall in love and get married. Then Kevin will have a father."

"Did you fall in love with Holt?" Jenny asked.

"Yes, I did." She felt Alex shift uncomfortably and smiled. "I'd like to marry him so we could all live together. But Holt and I both wanted to see how you felt about it."

"I like him," Jenny announced. "He lets me ride on his shoulders."

Alex shrugged, a bit more cautious. "Maybe it's okay."

Concerned, Suzanna rose. "We can talk about it some more. Let's go set up."

They stepped out of the greenhouse just as Holt pulled up in the graveled lot. He knew he'd told her he'd wait until lunchtime, but he hadn't been able to. He'd awakened realizing he'd rather face another alley than those two kids who could so easily reject him. He stuffed his hands into his pockets and tried to look casual.

"Hi."

"Hi." Suzanna wanted to reach out to him, but her children held her hands.

"I thought I'd drop by and...how's it going?"

Jenny gave him a shy smile and huddled closer to her mother. "Mom says you're going to get married and be our stepfather and live with us."

Holt had to knock back an urge to shuffle his feet. "That's the plan."

Alex tightened his fingers around Suzanna's as he stared up at Holt. "Are you going to yell at us?"

After a quick glance at Suzanna, Holt stooped down until he was eye to eye with the boy. "Maybe. If you need it."

Alex trusted that answer more than he would have an unqualified no. "Do you hit?" He remembered the swats he'd received during his vacation. They'd insulted more than hurt, but he still resented it.

Holt put a hand under the boy's chin and held it firm. "No," he said, and the look in his eyes made Alex believe. "But I might hang you up by your thumbs, or boil you in oil. If I get really mad, I'll stake you to an anthill."

Alex's lips twitched, but he wasn't finished with the interrogation. "Are you going to make Mom cry like he did?"

"Alex," Suzanna began, but Holt cut her off.

"I might sometimes, if I'm stupid. But not on purpose. I love her a lot, so I want to make her happy. Sometimes I might screw up."

Alex frowned and considered. "Are you going to do all that kissing stuff? Since Trent and Sloan and Max came, there's always kissing."

"Yeah." Holt's face relaxed into a smile. "I'm going to do all that kissing stuff."

"But you won't like it," Alex said, hopeful. "You'll just do it 'cause Mom likes it."

"Sorry, I like it, too."

"Jeez," Alex muttered, deflated.

"Do it now." Jenny danced and giggled. "Do it now so I can see."

Willing to oblige, Holt straightened and pulled Suzanna close. When he took his lips from Suzanna's, Alex was red faced and Jenny was clapping. "I hate to tell you," Holt said soberly. "but one day you'll like it, too."

"Uh-uh. I'd rather eat dirt."

With a laugh, Holt hoisted him up, relieved and delighted when Alex slung a friendly arm around his neck. "Tell me that in ten years."

"I like it," Jenny insisted, and tugged on his leg. "I like it now. Kiss me." He hauled her in his other arm and kissed her tiny, waiting lips. She smiled, big blue eyes beaming. "You kissed Mom different."

"That's 'cause she's the mom and you're the kid."

She liked the way he smelled, the way his arm supported her. When she rubbed a hand over his cheek, she was a little disappointed that it was smooth today. "Can I call you Daddy?" she asked, and Holt felt his heart lurch in his chest.

"I—ah—sure. If you want."

"Daddy's for babies," Alex said in disgust. "But you can be Dad."

"Okay." He looked over at Suzanna. "Okay."

Holt wished he could have spent the day with them, but there were things that had to be done. He had a family now—it still dazed him—and he meant to protect them. He'd already put in calls to his contacts in Portland and was awaiting the rundowns on the four names from Trent's list. While he waited, he put in calls to the Department of Motor Vehicles, the credit bureau and the Internal Revenue, stretching it a bit by giving his old badge number and rank.

Between information and instinct, he whittled the four names down to two. While he waited for another call back, he read over his grandfather's diary.

He understood the feelings beneath the words, the longing, the devotion. He understood the rage his grandfather had felt when he'd learned the woman he loved had suffered abuse by the hands of the man she'd married. Was it coincidence or fate that his relationship with Suzanna had so many similarities to that of their ancestors? At least this time, the tale would have a happy ending.

Suzanna's diamonds, he thought, drumming his fingers on the pages. Bianca's emeralds. Suzanna had hidden her jewels, the one material thing she felt belonged to her from the marriage, as security for her children. He had to believe Bianca had done the same.

So, where was the equivalent of Jenny's diaper bag? he wondered.

When the phone rang, he snatched it up on the first ring. Before he hung up again, Holt had little doubt he had his man. Going into the bedroom, he checked his weapon, balancing the familiar weight in his hand. He strapped it to his calf.

Fifteen minutes later, he was walking through the chaos of construction in the west wing. He found Sloan in what was a nearly completed two-level suite. There was a smell of new lumber and male sweat. Sloan, in a tool belt and jeans, was supervising the construction of a new staircase.

"I didn't know architects swung hammers," Holt commented.

Sloan grinned. "I got a personal interest in this job."

Nodding, Holt scanned the crew. "Which one's Marshall?"

Alerted, Sloan unbuckled the tool belt. "He's up on the next level."

"I'd like to have a little talk with him."

Sloan's eyes flashed, but he merely nodded again. "I'll go with you." He waited until they were out of range of the crew. "You think he's the one?"

"Robert Marshall didn't apply for a Maine driver's license until six weeks ago. He's never paid taxes under the name and social security number he's using. Employers don't usually check with the DMV or IRS when they hire a laborer."

Sloan swore and flexed his fingers. He could still see Amanda racing along the terrace pursued by a man holding a gun. "I get first crack at him."

"I appreciate the sentiment, but you'll have to strap it in."

The hell he would, Sloan thought, and signaled the foreman. "Marshall," he said briefly.

"Bob?" The foreman pulled out a bandanna to wipe his neck. "You just missed him. I had him drive Rick into Emergency. Rick took a pretty good slice out of his thumb, figured he needed stitches."

"How long ago?" Holt demanded.

"'Bout twenty minutes, I guess. Told them to take the rest of the day, since we're knocking off at four." He stuffed the bandanna back into his pocket. "Problem?"

"No." Sloan bit down on temper. "Let me know if Rick's okay."

"Sure thing." He shouted at one of the carpenters, then lumbered off.

"I need an address," Holt said.

"Trent's got the paperwork." They started out. "Are you going to turn it over to Lieutenant Koogar?"

"No," Holt said simply.

"Good."

They found Trent in the office he'd thrown together on the first floor, a stack of files at his fingertips, a phone at his ear. He took one look at the two men. "I'll get back to you," he said into the phone and hung up. "Who is it?"

"He's using the name Robert Marshall." Holt pulled out a cigarette. "Foreman let him go early. I want an address."

Saying nothing, Trent crossed to a file cabinet to pull out a folder. "Max is upstairs. He has a stake in this, too."

Holt skimmed the information in Marshall's file. "Then get him. We'll do this together."

The apartment Marshall had listed was on the edge of the village. The woman who opened the door after Holt's third booming knock was bent and withered and out of sorts.

"What? What?" she demanded. "I'm not buying any encyclopedias or vacuum cleaners."

"We're looking for Robert Marshall," Holt told her.

"Who? Who?" She peered through the thick lenses of her glasses.

"Robert Marshall," he repeated.

"I don't know any Marshalls," she grumbled. "There's a McNeilly next door and a Mitchell down below, but no Marshalls. I don't want to buy any insurance, either."

"We're not selling anything," Trent said in his most patient voice. "We're looking for a man named Robert Marshall who lives at this address."

"I told you there's no Marshalls here. I live here. Lived here for fifteen years, since that worthless clot I married passed on and left me with nothing but bills. I know you," she said abruptly, pointing a gnarled finger at Sloan. "Saw your picture in the paper." Reaching to the table beside the door, she hefted an iron bookend. "You robbed a bank."

"No, ma'am." Later, Sloan thought, much later, he might find the whole business amusing. "I married Amanda Calhoun."

The woman held on to the bookend while she considered. "One of the Calhoun girls. That's right. The youngest one—no, not the youngest one, the next one." Satisfied, she set the bookend down again. "Well, what do you want?"

"Robert Marshall," Holt said again. "He gave this building and this apartment as his address."

"Then he's a liar or a fool, because I've lived here for fifteen years ever since that no-account husband of mine caught pneumonia and died. Here one day, gone the next." She snapped her bent fingers. "And good riddance."

Thinking it was a dead end, Holt glanced at Sloan. "Give her a description."

"He's about thirty, six feet tall, trim, black hair, shoulder length, big droopy moustache."

"Don't know him. The boy downstairs, the Pierson boy's got hair past his shoulders. A disgrace if you ask me. Bleaches it, too, just like a girl. He's no more'n six-teen. You'd think his mother would make him cut that hair, but no. Plays the music so loud I have to bang on the floor."

"Excuse me," Max put in and described the man he had known as Ellis Caufield.

"Sounds like my nephew. Lives in Rochester with his second wife. Sells used cars."

"Thanks." Holt wasn't surprised the thief had given a phony address, but he was annoyed. As they came out of the building, he dug a quarter from his pocket.

"I guess we wait until morning," Max was saying. "He doesn't know we're on to him, so he'll show up for work."

"I'm finished waiting." Holt headed for a phone booth. After dropping in the coin, he punched in numbers. "This is Detective Sergeant Bradford, Portland P.D., badge number 7375. I need a cross-check." He reeled off the phone number from Marshall's file. Then he held on with a cop's patience while the operator set her computer to work. "Thanks." He hung up and turned to the three men. "Bar Island," he said. "We'll take my boat."

While their men prepared to sail across the bay, the Calhoun women met in Bianca's tower. "So," Amanda began, pad and pencil at the ready. "What do we know?"

"Trent's been cross-checking the personnel files," C.C. supplied. "He claimed there was some hitch in withholding taxes, but that's bull."

"Interesting," Lilah mused. "Max stopped me from going over to the west wing this morning. I'd wanted to see how things were going, and he made all kinds of lame excuses why I shouldn't distract the men while they were working."

"And Sloan shoved a couple of files into a drawer, and locked it when I came into the room last night." Amanda tapped her pencil on the pad. "Why wouldn't they want us to know if they're checking up on the crews?"

"I think I have an idea," Suzanna said slowly. She'd been chewing it over most of the day. "Last night I found out that Holt's cottage had been broken into and searched."

Her three sisters pounced on that, hammering her with questions.

"Just wait." She lifted a hand. "He was irritated with me, which is why it came out. He was even more irritated that it had. But he did tell me, because he wanted to scare me into backing off, that he was certain it was Livingston."

"Which means," Amanda concluded, "that our old friend knows Holt's connected. Who else knows besides us?" In her organized way, she began to list names.

"Oh, stop fussing," Lilah said with a negligent wave of her hand. "No one knows except the family. None of us have mentioned it outside of this house."

"Maybe he found out the same way Max did," C.C. suggested. "From the library."

"Max checked out the books." Lilah shook her head. "Maybe he found the information in the papers he stole from us."

"It's possible." Amanda noted it down. "But he's had the papers for weeks. When did he break into the cottage?"

"A couple weeks ago, but I don't think he made the connection that way. I think he got it from us."

There was an instant argument. Suzanna stood, throwing up both hands to cut it off. "Listen, we're agreed that none of us have discussed this outside of the house. And we're agreed that the men are trying to keep us from finding out they're checking out the crews. Which means—"

"Which means," Amanda interrupted and shut her eyes, "the bastard's working for us. Like a fly on the wall, so he can pick up little pieces of information, poke around the house. We're so used to seeing guys hauling lumber, we wouldn't give him a second look."

"I think Holt already came to that conclusion." Suzanna lifted her hands again. "The question is, what do we do about it?"

"We give the construction boys a thrill tomorrow, and visit the west wing." Lilah straightened from the window seat. "I don't care what he's made himself look like this time, I'll know him if I get close enough." With that settled, she sat back. "Now, Suzanna, why don't you tell us when bad boy Bradford asked you to marry him?"

Suzanna grinned. "How did you know?"

"For an ex-cop, he's got great taste in jewelry." She took Suzanna's hand to show off the ring to her other sisters.

"Last night," she said as she was hugged and kissed and wept over. "We told the kids this morning."

"Aunt Coco's going to go through the roof." C.C. gave Suzanna another squeeze. "All four of us in a matter of months. She'll be in matchmaker heaven."

"All we need now is to get that creep behind bars and

find the emeralds." Amanda dashed a tear away. "Oh, no! Do you realize what this means?"

"It means you have to organize another wedding," Suzanna answered.

"Not just that. It means we're going to be stuck with Aunt Colleen at least until the last handful of rice gets tossed."

Holt returned to The Towers in a foul mood. They'd found the house. Empty. They had no doubt that Livingston was living there. Bending the law more than a little, he had broken in and given the place as meticulous a search as Livingston had given his cottage. They'd found the stolen Calhoun papers, the lists the thief had made and a copy of the original blueprints of The Towers.

They'd also found a typed copy of each woman's weekly schedule, along with handwritten comments that left no doubt as to the fact that Livingston had followed and observed each one of them. There was a well-ordered inventory of the rooms he had searched and the items he'd felt valuable enough to steal.

They had waited an hour for his return, then uneasy about leaving the women alone, had phoned in the information to Koogar. While the police staked out the rented house on Bar Island, Holt and his companions returned to The Towers.

It was only a matter of waiting now. That was something he had learned to do well in his years on the force. But now it wasn't a job, and every moment grated.

"Oh, my dear, dear boy." Coco flew at him the moment he stepped into the house. He caught her by her sturdy hips as she covered his face with kisses.

"Hey," was all he could manage as she wept against his shoulder. Her hair, he noted, was no longer gleaming black but fire-engine red. "What'd you do to your hair?"

"Oh, it was time for a change." She drew back to blow her nose into her hankie, then fell into his arms again. Helpless, he patted her back and looked at the grinning men around him for assistance.

"It looks okay," he assured her, wondering if that was what she was weeping about. "Really."

"You like it?" She pulled back again, fluffing at it. "I thought I needed a bit of dash, and red's so cheerful." She buried her face in the soggy hankie. "I'm so happy," she sobbed. "So very happy. I had hoped, you see. And the tea leaves indicated that it would all work out, but I couldn't help but worry. She's had such a dreadful time, and her sweet little babies, too. Now everything's going to be all right. I'd thought it might be Trent, but he and C.C. were so perfect. Then Sloan and Amanda. Then almost before I could blink, our dear Max and Lilah. Is it any wonder I'm overwhelmed?"

"I guess not."

"To think, all those years ago when you'd bring lobsters to the back door. And that time you changed a tire for me and were too proud to even let me thank you. And now, now, you're going to marry my baby."

"Congratulations." Trent grinned and slapped Holt on the back while Max dug out a fresh handkerchief for Coco.

"Welcome to the family." Sloan offered a hand. "I guess you know what you're getting into."

Holt studied the weeping Coco. "I'm getting the picture."

"Stop all that caterwauling." Colleen clumped down

the stairs. "I could hear you wailing all the way up in my room. For heaven's sake, take that mess into the kitchen." She gestured with her cane. "Pour some tea into her until she pulls herself together. Out, all of you," she added. "I want to talk to this boy here."

Like rats deserting a sinking ship, Holt thought as they left him alone. Gesturing for him to follow, Colleen strode into the parlor.

"So, you think you're going to marry my grand-niece."

"No. I am going to marry her."

She sniffed. Damned if she didn't like the boy. "I'll tell you this, if you don't do better by her than that scum she had before, you'll answer to me." She settled into a chair. "What are your prospects?"

"My what?"

"Your prospects," she said impatiently. "Don't think you're going to latch on to my money when you latch on to her."

His eyes narrowed, pleasing her. "You can take your money and—"

"Very good," she said with an approving nod. "How do you intend to keep her?"

"She doesn't need to be kept." He whirled around the room. "And she doesn't need you or anyone else poking into her business. She's managed just fine on her own, better than fine. She came out of hell and managed to put her life together, take care of the kids and start a business. The only thing that's going to change is that she's going to stop working herself into the ground, and the kids'll have someone who wants to be their father. Maybe I won't be able to give her diamonds and take her to fancy dinner parties, but I'll make her happy."

Colleen tapped her fingers on the head of her cane. "You'll do. If your grandfather was anything like you, it's no wonder my mother loved him. So..." She started to rise, then saw the portrait over the mantel. Where her father's stern face had been was her mother's lovely one. "What's that doing there?"

Holt dipped his hands into his pockets. "It seemed to me that was where it belonged. That's where my grandfather would have wanted it."

Colleen eased herself back into the chair. "Thank you." Her voice was strained, but her eyes remained fierce. "Now go away. I want to be alone."

He left her, amazed that he was growing fond of her. Though he didn't look forward to another scene, he started toward the kitchen to ask Coco where he could find Suzanna.

But he found her himself, following the music that drifted down the hall. She was sitting at a piano, playing some rich, haunting melody he didn't recognize. Though the music was sad, there was a smile on her lips and one in her eyes. When she looked up, her fingers stilled, but the smile remained.

"I didn't know you played."

"We all had lessons. I was the only one they stuck with." She reached out a hand for his. "I was hoping we'd have a minute alone, so I could tell you how wonderful you were with the kids this morning."

With his fingers meshed with hers, he studied the ring he'd given her. "I was nervous." He laughed a little. "I didn't know how they'd take it. When Jenny asked if she could call me Daddy...it's funny how fast you can fall in love. Suzanna." He kept toying with her hands, studying the ring. "I think I understand now what a parent would feel, what he'd go through to make sure his kids were safe. I'd like to have more. I know you'd need to think about it, and I don't want you to feel that I would care less about Alex and Jenny."

"I don't have to think about it." She pressed a kiss to his cheek. "I've always wanted a big family."

He drew her close so her head rested on his shoulder. "Suzanna, do you know where the nursery was when Bianca lived here?"

"On the third floor of the east wing. It's been used as a storeroom as long as I can remember." She straightened. "You think she hid the necklace there?"

"I think she hid them somewhere Fergus wouldn't look, and I can't see him spending a lot of time in the nursery."

"No, but you'd think someone would have come across them. I don't know why I say that," she corrected. "The place is filled with boxes and old furniture. The Tower's version of a garage sale."

"Show me."

It was worse than he'd imagined. Even overlooking the cobwebs and dust, it was a mess. Boxes, crates, rolled-up rugs, broken tables, shadeless lamps stood, sat or reclined over every inch of space. Speechless, he turned to Suzanna who offered a sheepish grin.

"A lot of stuff collects in eighty-odd years," she told him. "Most of what's valuable's been culled out, and a lot of that was sold when we were—well, when things were difficult. This floor's been closed off for a long time, since we couldn't afford to heat it. We had to concentrate on keeping up the living space. Once we got everything under some kind of control, we were going to kind of attack the other sections a room at a time."

"You need a bulldozer."

"No, just time and elbow grease. We had plenty of the latter, but not nearly enough of the former. Over the last couple of months, we've gone through a lot of the old rooms, inch by inch, but it's a slow process."

"Then we might as well get started."

They worked for two grueling and dirty hours. They found a tattered parasol, an amazing collection of nineteenth-century erotica, a trunk full of musty clothes from the twenties and a box of warped phonograph records. There was also a crate filled with toys, a miniature locomotive, a sad, faded rag doll, assorted yo-yos and tops. Among them was a set of lovely old fairy-tale prints that Suzanna set aside.

"For our nursery," she told him. "Look." She held up a yellow christening gown. "It might have been my grandfather's."

"You'd have thought this stuff would have been packed up with more care."

"I don't think Fergus ran a very tidy household after Bianca died. If any of this stuff belonged to his children, I'd wager the nanny bundled it away. He wouldn't have cared enough."

"No." He pulled a cobweb out of her hair. "Listen, why don't you take a break?"

"I'm fine."

It was useless to remind her that she'd been working all day, so he used another tactic. "I could use a drink. You think Coco's got anything cold in the refrigerator—maybe a sandwich to go with it?"

"Sure. I'll go check."

He knew that her aunt would insist on putting the quick meal together, and Suzanna would get that much time to sit and do nothing. "Two sandwiches," he added, and kissed her.

"Right." She rose, stretching her back. "It's sad to think about those three children, lying in here at night knowing their mother wasn't going to come and tuck them in again. Speaking of which, I'd better tuck in my own before I come back."

"Take your time." He was already headfirst in another crate.

She started out, thinking wistfully of Bianca's babies. Little Sean, who'd barely have been toddling, Ethan, who would grow up to father her father, Colleen, who was even now downstairs surely finding fault with something Coco had done. How the woman had ever been a sweet little girl…

A little girl, Suzanna thought, stopping on the second-floor landing. The oldest girl who would have been five or six when her mother died. Suzanna detoured and knocked on her great-aunt's door.

"Come in, damn it. I'm not getting up."

"Aunt Colleen." She stepped in, amused to see the old woman was engrossed in a romance novel. "I'm sorry to disturb you."

"Why? No one else is."

Suzanna bit the tip of her tongue. "I was just wondering, the summer…that last summer, were you still in the nursery with your brothers?"

"I wasn't a baby, no need for a nursery."

"So you had your own room," Suzanna prompted, struggling to contain the excitement. "Near the nursery?"

"At the other end of the east wing. There was the nursery, then Nanny's room, the children's bath, and the three rooms kept for children of guests. I had the corner room at the top of the stairs." She frowned down at her book. "The next summer, I moved into one of the guest rooms. I didn't want to sleep in the room my mother had decorated for me, knowing she wouldn't come back to it."

"I'm sorry. When Bianca told you that you were going away, did she come to your room?"

"Yes. She let me pick out a few of my favorite dresses, then she packed them herself."

"Then after—I suppose they were unpacked again."

"I never wore those dresses again. I never wanted to. Shoved the trunk under my bed."

"I see." So there was hope. "Thank you."

"Moth-eaten by now," Colleen grumbled as Suzanna went out again. She thought of her favorite white muslin with its blue satin sash and with a sigh got up to walk to the terrace.

Dusk was coming early, she thought. Storm brewing. She could smell it in the wind, see it in the bad-tempered clouds already blocking the sun.

Suzanna raced up the stairs again. The sandwiches would have to wait. She pushed open the door of Colleen's old room. It too had been consigned to storage, but being smaller than the nursery wasn't as cramped. The wallpaper, perhaps the same that Bianca had picked for her daughter, was faded and spotted, but Suzanna could still see the delicate pattern of rosebuds and violets.

She didn't bother with the cases or boxes, but dragged or pushed them aside. She was looking for a traveling trunk, suitable for a young girl. What better place? she thought as she pushed aside a crate marked

Winter Draperies. Fergus hadn't cared for his daughter. He would hardly have bothered to look through a trunk of dresses, particularly when that trunk had been shoved out of sight by a traumatized young girl.

It had no doubt been opened in later years. Perhaps someone—Suzanna's own mother?—had shaken out a dress or two, then finding them quaint but useless, had designated them to storage.

It could be anywhere, of course, she mused. But what better place to start than the source?

Her heart pounded dully as she stumbled across an old leather-strapped trunk. Pulling it open, she found bolts of material carefully folded in tissue. But no little girl's dresses. And no emeralds.

Because the light was growing dim, she rose and started toward the door. She would get Holt, and a flashlight, before continuing. In the gloom, she rapped her shin sharply. Swearing, she looked down and saw the small trunk.

It had once been a glistening white, but now it was dull with age and dust. It had been shoved to the side, piled with other boxes and nearly hidden by them and a faded tapestry. Kneeling in the half-light, Suzanna uncovered it. She flexed her unsteady fingers then opened the lid.

There was a smell of lavender, sealed inside perhaps for decades. She lifted the first dress, a frilly white muslin, going ivory with time and banded by a faded blue satin sash. Suzanna set it carefully aside and drew out another. There were leggings and ribbons, pretty bows and a lacy nightie. And there, at the bottom, beside a small stuffed bear, a box and a book.

Suzanna put a trembling hand to her lips, then slowly reached down to lift the book.

Her journal, she thought as tears misted her eyes. Bianca's journal. Hardly daring to breathe, she turned the first page.

Bar Harbor, June 12, 1912
I saw him on the cliffs, overlooking Frenchman Bay

Suzanna let out an unsteady breath and laid the book in her lap. This was not for her to read alone. It would wait for her family. Heart pounding, she reached down to take the box from the trunk. She knew before she opened it. She could feel the change in the room, the trembling of the air. As the first tear slid down her cheek, she opened the lid and uncovered Bianca's emeralds.

They pulsed like green suns, throbbing with life and passion. She lifted the necklace, the glorious three tiers, and felt the heat on her hands. Hidden eighty years before, in hope and desperation, they were now free. The gloom that filled the room was no match for them.

As she knelt, the necklace dripping from her fingers, she reached into the box and took out the matching earrings. Strange, she thought. She'd all but forgotten them. They were lovely, exquisite, but the necklace dominated. It was made to dominate.

Stunned, she stared down at the power in her hands. They weren't just gems, she realized. They were far from being simply beautiful stones. They were Bianca's passions and hopes and dreams. From the time she had placed them in the box until now, when they had been lifted out by her descendant, they had waited to see the light again.

"Oh, Bianca."

"A charming sight."

Her head jerked up at the voice. He stood in the doorway, hardly more than a shadow. When he stepped into the room, she saw the glint of the gun in his hand.

"Patience pays off," Livingston said. "I watched you and the cop go into the room down the hall. I've been losing quite a bit of sleep wandering these rooms at night."

As he came closer, she stared at him. He didn't look like the man she remembered. His coloring was wrong, even the shape of his face. She rose very slowly, clutching the book and earrings in one hand, the necklace in the other.

"You don't recognize me. But I know you. I know all of you. You're Suzanna, just one of the Calhouns who owes me quite a bit."

"I don't know what you're talking about."

"Three months of my time, and not a little trouble. Then there was the loss of Hawkins, of course. He wasn't much of a partner, but he was mine. Just as those are mine." He looked down at the necklace and his mouth watered. They dazzled him. More than he had dreamed, more than he had imagined. Everything he wanted. His fingers trembled lightly on the gun as he reached out. Suzanna jerked away. He lifted a brow. "Do you really think you can keep them from me? They're meant to be mine. And when they are, everything they are will be mine."

He stepped closer, and as she looked around for the best route of escape, his hand closed over her hair.

"Some stones have power," he told her softly. "Tragedy seeps into them, making them stronger. Death and grief. It hones them. Hawkins didn't understand that, but he was a simple man."

And the one she was facing was a mad one. "The necklace belongs to the Calhouns. It always has. It always will."

He jerked her hair hard and fast. She would have yelped, but the gun was now pressed against the racing pulse in her throat. "It belongs to me. Because I've been clever enough, I've been determined enough to wait for it. The moment I read about it, I knew. Now tonight, it's done."

She wasn't certain what she would have done—given it to him, tried to reason. But at the moment, her little girl moved into the doorway. "Mom." Her voice trembled as she rubbed her eyes. "It's thundering. You're supposed to come get me when it thunders."

It happened fast. He turned, swinging the gun. With all her strength, Suzanna hurled herself at him, blocking his aim. "Run!" she screamed to Jenny. "Run down the hall to Holt." She shoved, and raced after her daughter. The decision had to be made the minute she hit the doorway. As she watched Jenny streak toward the right and—she hoped—safety, Suzanna plunged in the opposite direction.

He would follow her, not the child, she told herself. Because she still had the necklace. The next decision had to be made at the steps. To go down to her family and risk them. Or to go up, alone.

She was halfway up the stairs when she heard him pounding behind her. She jerked in shock as a bullet plowed into the plaster an inch from her shoulder.

Breathless, she streaked up, only now hearing the boom of thunder that had frightened Jenny and made her look for her mother. Her single thought was to put as much distance between the madman behind her and her child. Her feet clattered on the winding metal staircase that led to Bianca's tower.

His fingers darted through the open treads and snatched at her ankle. With a sound of terror and fury, she kicked out, dislodging them, then stumbled up the rest of the way. The door was shut. She nearly wept as she threw her weight against the thick wood. It gave, with painful slowness, then allowed her to fall inside. But before she could slam it closed, he was hurtling in.

She braced, certain it would be only seconds before she felt the bullet. He was panting, sweating, his eyes glazed. At the corner of his mouth, a muscle ticked and jerked. "Give it to me." The gun shook as he advanced on her. A flash of lightning had him looking wildly around the shadowy room. "Give it to me now."

He's afraid, she realized. Of this room. "You've been in here before."

He had, only once, and had run out again, terrified. There was something here, something that hated him. It crawled cold as ice along his skin. "Give me the necklace, or I'll just kill you and take it."

"This was her room," Suzanna murmured, keeping her eyes on his. "Bianca's room. She died when her husband threw her from that window."

Unable to resist, he looked at the glass, dark with gloom, then away again.

"She still comes here, to wait, and to watch the cliffs." She heard, as she had known she would, the sound of Holt racing up the steps. "She's here now.

Take them." She held the emeralds out. "But she won't let you leave with them."

His face was bone white and sheened with sweat as he reached for the necklace. He gripped it, but rather than the heat Suzanna had felt, he felt only cold. And a terror.

"They're mine now." He shivered and stumbled.

"Suzanna," Holt said quietly from the doorway. "Move away from him." His weapon was drawn, gripped in both hands. "Move away," he repeated. "Slow."

She took one step back, then two, but Livingston paid no attention to her. He was wiping his gun hand over his dry lips.

"It's over," Holt told him. "Drop the gun, kick it aside." But Livingston continued to stare at the necklace, breathing raggedly. "Drop it." Braced, Holt moved closer. "Get out, Suzanna."

"No, I'm not leaving you."

He didn't have time to swear at her. Though he was prepared to kill, he could see that the man was no longer concerned with his weapon, or with escape. Instead, Livingston merely stared down at the emeralds and trembled.

With his eyes trained on Livingston, Holt reached up to grasp the wrist of his gun hand. "It's over," he said again.

"It's mine." Wild with rage and fear, Livingston lunged. He fired once into the ceiling before Holt disarmed him. Even then he struggled, but the struggle was brief. With the next crash of thunder, he howled, striking out wildly even as the others raced into the room. Disoriented or terrified, stunned by Holt's blow to his jaw or no longer sane, he whirled.

There was the crash of breaking glass. Then a sound Suzanna would never forget. A man's horrified scream. Even as Holt leaped forward to try to save him, Livingston pinwheeled through the broken window and tumbled to the rain-swept rock below.

"My God." Suzanna pressed back against the wall, her hands over her mouth to stop her own screams. There were arms around her, a babble of voices.

Her family poured into the tower room. She bent to her children, pressing kisses on their cheeks. "It's all right," she soothed. "It's all right now. There's nothing to be afraid of." She looked up at Holt. He stood facing her, the black space at his back, the glitter of emeralds at his feet. "Everything's all right now. I'm going to take you downstairs."

Holt pushed the gun back in its holster. "We'll take them down."

An hour later, when the children were soothed and sleeping, he took her by the arm and pulled her out on the terrace. All the fear and rage he'd felt since Jenny had run crying down the hallway came pouring out.

"What the hell did you think you were doing?"

"I had to keep him away from Jenny." She thought she was calm, but her hands began to shake. "I suddenly had an idea about the emeralds. It was so simple, really. And I found them. Then he was there—and Jenny. He had a gun, and God, oh God, I thought he would kill her."

"All right, all right," Holt said. Suzanna didn't choke back the tears this time, but clung to him as they shuddered out of her. "The kids are fine, Suzanna. Nobody's going to hurt them. Or you."

"I didn't know what else to do. I wasn't trying to be brave or stupid."

"You were both. I love you." He framed her face in his hands and kissed her. "Did he hurt you?"

"No." She sniffled a little and wiped her eyes. "He chased me up there, and then…he snapped. You saw how he was when you came in."

"Yeah." Two feet away from her, with a gun in his hand. Holt's fingers tightened on her shoulders. "Don't you ever scare me like that again."

"It's a deal." She rubbed her cheek against his, for comfort and for love. "It's really over now, isn't it?"

He kissed the top of her head. "It's just beginning."

Epilogue

It was late when the family gathered together in the parlor. The police had finally finished and left them alone. They were drawn together, a solid, united front beneath the portrait of Bianca.

Colleen sat, a dog at her feet, the emeralds in her lap. She had shed no tears when Suzanna had explained how and where she had found them, but took comfort in having that small, precious memory of her mother.

There was no talk of death.

Holt kept Suzanna close, his arm firm around her. The storm had passed, and the moon had risen. The parlor was washed with light. The only sound was Suzanna's soft, clear voice as she read from Bianca's journal.

She turned the last page and spoke of Bianca's thoughts as she'd prepared to hide the emeralds.

"'I didn't think of their monetary value as I took

them out, held them in my hands and watched them gleam in the light of the lamp. They would be a legacy for my children, and their children, a symbol of freedom, and of hope. And with Christian, of love.

"'As dawn broke, I decided to put them, together with this journal, in a safe place until I joined Christian again.'"

Slowly, quietly, Suzanna closed the book. "I think she's with him now. That they're with each other."

She smiled when Holt's fingers gripped hers. Looking around the room, she saw her sisters, the men they loved, her aunt smiling through tears, and Bianca's daughter, gazing up at the portrait that had been painted with unconquerable love.

"It was Bianca, more than the emeralds, who brought us all together. I like to think that by finding them, by bringing them back, we've helped them find each other."

Beyond the house, the moon glimmered on the cliffs far above where the sea churned and fought with the rocks. The wind whispered through the wild roses and warmed the lovers who walked there.

* * * * *